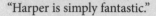

"Molly Harper is the queen of side-splitting quips. . . . Hilariously original with imaginative adventures and one-of-a-kind characters."

—*Single Titles*

THE ART OF SEDUCING A NAKED WEREWOLF

"Harper's gift for character building and crafting a smart, exciting story is showcased well."

—*RT Book Reviews* (4 stars)

"The characters are appealing and the plot is intriguingly original."

—*Single Titles*

HOW TO FLIRT WITH A NAKED WEREWOLF
RT Book Reviews TOP PICK!

"A rollicking, sweet novel that made me laugh aloud. . . . Mo's wisecracking, hilarious voice makes this novel such a pleasure to read."

—*New York Times* bestselling author Eloisa James

"A page-turning delight . . . fraught with sexual tension."

—*RT Book Reviews* (4½ stars)

"A light, fun, easy read, perfect for lazy days."

—*New York Journal of B*

NICE GIRLS DON'T LIVE FOREVER
RT Book Reviews TOP PICK and
Reviewers' Choice Award winner!

"Hilariously fun."

—*RT Book Reviews* (4

"A wonderful mix of humor, romance, mystery, and small-town flair."

—*Bitten by Books*

"If you aren't reading Molly Harper, you should be. The Jane Jameson books are sheer fun and giggle. No, make that chortling, laugh-out-loud till you gasp for breath fun."

—*Night Owl Reviews*

NICE GIRLS DON'T DATE DEAD MEN

"Fast-paced, mysterious, passionate, and hilarious."

—*RT Book Reviews* (4½ stars)

"With its quirky characters and the funny situations they get into, whether they be normal or paranormal, *Nice Girls Don't Date Dead Men* is an amazing novel."

—*Romance Reviews Today*

NICE GIRLS DON'T HAVE FANGS
RT Book Reviews TOP PICK!

"Harper's take on vampire lore will intrigue and entertain. . . . Jane's snarky first-person narrative is as charming as it is hilarious."

—*Publishers Weekly* (starred review)

"Jane is an everygirl with a wonderful sense of humor and quick sarcasm. Add in the mystery and romance and you have your next must-read novel!"

—*RT Book Reviews* (4½ stars)

"So many funny lines and scenes that I dog-eared my copy just to go back and re-read them."

—*All About Romance*

ALSO BY MOLLY HARPER

A

Witch's
Handbook of
Kisses and Curses

MOLLY HARPER

Pocket Books

New York   London   Toronto   Sydney   New Delhi

Pocket Books
A Division of Simon & Schuster, Inc.
1230 Avenue of the Americas
New York, NY 10020

This book is a work of fiction. Names, characters, places, and incidents either are products of the author's imagination or are used fictitiously. Any resemblance to actual events or locales or persons, living or dead, is entirely coincidental.

First Pocket Books paperback edition June 2013

POCKET and colophon are registered trademarks of Simon & Schuster, Inc.

For information about special discounts for bulk purchases, please contact Simon & Schuster Special Sales at 1-866-506-1949 or business@simonandschuster.com.

The Simon & Schuster Speakers Bureau can bring authors to your live event. For more information or to book an event, contact the Simon & Schuster Speakers Bureau at 1-866-248-3049 or visit our website at www.simonspeakers.com.

Manufactured in the United States of America

10 9 8 7 6 5 4 3 2 1

ISBN 978-1-4516-4185-1
ISBN 978-1-4516-4188-2 (ebook)

For the teachers who help "flighty, imaginative children" everywhere find direction

Acknowledgments

Thank you, as always, to the people who always support me through my ridiculously self-complicated writing process. Thank you to the readers who love the characters of Half-Moon Hollow as much as I do. To my husband and kids, for putting up with unfolded laundry and Mommy's talking to imaginary people. To my agent, Stephany, who is always patient. And to my editor, Abby, who is to blame for the possum-related content of this book.

A
Witch's
Handbook of
Kisses and Curses

**If you are fortunate enough to receive a message
from the other side, pay attention to it.**
—*A Witch's Compendium of Curses*

My week started with spectral portents of doom
floating over my bed while I was trying to have anniversary sex with my boyfriend. It was all downhill from
there.

Stephen had not been pleased when I'd pushed him
off of me, rolled out of bed, and yelled, "That's it! I'm
going!" at the image of a half-moon burning against
my ceiling. I mean, I guess there are limits to what men
are willing to put up with, and one's girlfriend interacting with invisible omens is a bit out of a perfectly nice
investment broker's scope. He seemed to think I was
huffing off after taking offense to that counterclockwise
tickle he'd improvised near the end.

Of course, telling him about the increasingly forceful
hints I'd received from my noncorporeal grandmother
for the last two weeks would have made the situation
worse. Stephen tended to clam up when we discussed
my family and our "nonsense." He refused to discuss

Nana Fee or the promise I'd made to her that I'd travel all the way from our tiny village to the wilds of America. So I'd tried ignoring the dreams, the omens, the way my alphabet soup spelled out "HlfMunHollw."

I tried to rationalize that a deathbed promise to a woman who called herself a witch wasn't exactly a binding contract. But my grandma interrupting the big O to make her point was the final straw.

And so I was moving to Half-Moon Hollow, Kentucky, indefinitely, so I could locate four magical objects that would prevent a giant witch-clan war and maintain peace in my little corner of northwestern Ireland.

Yes, I was aware that statement sounded absolutely ridiculous.

Sometimes it paid to have a large, tech-savvy family at your disposal. When you tell them, "I have a few days to rearrange my life so I can fly halfway across the world and secure the family's magical potency for the next generation," they hop to do whatever it takes to smooth the way. Aunt Penny had not only booked my airline tickets but also located and rented a house for me. Uncle Seamus had arranged quick shipping of the supplies and equipment I would need to my new address. And my beloved, and somewhat terrifying, teenage cousin Ralph may have broken a few international laws while online "arranging" a temporary work visa so I wouldn't starve while I was there. Not everybody in our family could work magic, but each had his or her own particular brand of hocus-pocus.

Although my mother was an only child, my nana was

one of nine. So I had great-aunts and uncles coming out of my ears, and their children were the right age to serve as proper aunts and uncles. I had more third and fourth cousins than I could count. Literally—I tried once at Christmas, got dizzy, and had to sit down. They never treated me as if there were any sort of line dividing me from the rest of the McGavocks. So when my mother walked out and I was shipped off to my nana, it was as if the whole town was one very large, very loud family. When Aunt Penny permed my hair, to disastrous results, it was my schoolteacher who undid the damage in her kitchen sink. When my uncles were too traumatized by incidents that shall remain undisclosed to let me get behind the wheel of a car again, it was the postman, Tom Warren, who taught me to drive. They gave me a home I could depend on for the first time in my life. They gave me a family. They gave me back chunks of my childhood I'd missed until then. I would do whatever it took to make sure they were healthy and protected.

Given how Stephen felt about my family, I'd decided it was more prudent to tell him I'd accepted an offer for a special nursing fellowship in Boston. The spot came open when another nurse left the program unexpectedly, I told him, so I had to make a quick decision. He argued that it was too sudden, that we had too many plans hanging in the balance for me to run off to the States for half a year, no matter how much I loved my job.

I didn't want to leave Stephen. For months, he had been a bright spot in a life desperately needing sunshine, with the loss of Nana and my struggles to keep the family buoyed. And yet, somehow, here I was, sprawled in the back of a run-down cab as it bumped down a sunlit gravel road in Half-Moon Hollow, Kentucky. The term "cab" could be applied only loosely to the faded blue Ford station wagon—the only working taxi in the entire town, the driver informed me proudly. We had a fleet of two working in Kilcairy, and we had only about four hundred people living inside the town limits. Clearly, living in Boston until my early teens hadn't prepared me for life in the semirural South.

Yawning loudly, I decided to worry about cultural adjustments later. I was down-to-the-bone tired. My skirt and blouse were a grubby shambles. I smelled like airplane sweats and the manky Asian candy my seatmate insisted on munching for most of the flight from Dublin to New York. It took an additional two-hour hop to Chicago and another hour ride on a tiny baby plane-let before I finally arrived in the Hollow. I just wanted to go inside, take a shower, and sleep. While I was prepared to sleep on the floor if necessary, I prayed the house was indeed furnished as Aunt Penny had promised.

While the McGavock clan had collectively bankrolled my flight, I needed to save the extra cash they'd provided as "buy money" for my targets. Living expenses were left to me to figure out. I would have to start looking for some acceptable part-time work as soon as my brain was functional again. I squinted against the golden spring afternoon light pouring through the cab windows, interrupted only by the occasional patch of shade from tree branches arching over the little lane. The sky was so clear and crystal blue that it almost hurt to look out at the odd little clusters of houses along the road. It was so tempting just to lay my head back, close my eyes, and let the warm sunshine beat hot and red through my eyelids.

"You know you're rentin' half of the old Wainwright place?" the cabdriver, Dwayne-Lee, asked as he pulled a sharp turn onto yet another gravel road. I started awake just in time to keep my face from colliding with the spotty cab window. Dwayne-Lee continued on, blithe as a newborn babe, completely oblivious. "That place always creeped me out when I was a kid. We used to dare each other to run up to the front door and ring the bell."

I lifted a brow at his reflection in the rearview. "And what happened?"

"Nothin'," he said, shrugging. "No one lived there."

I blew out a breath and tried to find the patience not to snap at the man. Dwayne-Lee had, after all, been nice enough to make a special trip to the Half-Moon Hollow Municipal Airport to pick me up. Dwayne-Lee had been sent by Iris Scanlon, who handled various business dealings for my new landlord. Dwayne-Lee's skinny frame was puffed up with pride at being tasked with welcoming a "newcomer" as he'd handed me an envelope from Iris containing a key to my new house, a copy of my lease, her phone number, and a gift certificate for a free pizza delivered by Pete's Pies.

Anyone who tried to make my life easier was aces in my book. So from that moment on, I was a little in love with Iris Scanlon. Less so with Dwayne-Lee, who was currently nattering on about the Wainwright place and its conversion to a rental duplex after Gilbert Wainwright had moved closer to town years before. I closed my eyes against the sunlight, and the next thing I knew, the cab was pulling to a stop.

Wiping furiously at the wet drool on my chin, I opened my door while Dwayne-Lee unloaded my luggage from the trunk. Separated from the other houses on the street by a thicket of dense trees, the rambling old Victorian was painted a faded robin's-egg blue with sun-bleached white trim. The house was two stories, with a turret off to the left and a small central garden separating the two front doors. Given that the opposite side of the front porch seemed occupied with lawn chairs and a disheveled garden gnome, I assumed that the "tower side" of the house was mine. I grinned, despite my bone-aching fatigue. I'd always been fascinated by the idea of having a tower as a kid, although I'd long since cut my hair from climbing length.

The grass grew scrabbled in patches across the lawn. A section of brick had fallen loose from the foundation on the west corner. Knowing my luck, there was a colony of bats living in the attic, to complete that *Addams Family* look.

"I'll have bats in my belfry." I giggled, scrubbing at my tired eyes.

"You feelin' all right, ma'am?" Dwayne-Lee asked.

"Hmm?" I said, blinking blearily at him. "Oh, sorry, just a little out of sorts."

I pulled a wad of cash from my pocket and handed him enough for my fare and a generous tip.

Dwayne-Lee cleared his throat. "Um, ma'am, I can't take Monopoly money."

I glanced down at the bills in my hand. I was trying to pay Dwayne-Lee in euros. "Sorry."

With Dwayne-Lee compensated in locally legal tender, I took my key out of Iris's envelope, unlocked the door, and hauled my stuff inside. My half of the old Wainwright place consisted of two bedrooms and a bath upstairs, plus a parlor and a kitchen downstairs. It was a bit shocking to have this much room to myself. I was used to living in Nana Fee's tiny cottage, where I still whacked my elbows on the corner of the kitchen counter if I wasn't careful.

The house appeared to have been decorated by a fussy old lady fond of dark floral wallpaper and feathered wall sconces. The house was old, but someone had paid some attention to its upkeep recently. The hardwood floors gleamed amber in the afternoon light. The stairs were recently refurbished and didn't creak once while I climbed them. The turret room turned out to be a little sitting area off my bedroom, lined with bookshelves. I ran my fingers along the dusty shelves. I loved a good book. If I stayed long enough, I could put a little reading chair there . . . if I had a reading chair. I'd need to do something about getting some more furniture.

Despite Aunt Penny's assurances, the rooms were furnished in only the meanest sense. There were a table and chairs in the kitchen, a beaten sofa in the parlor, plus a dresser and a bare mattress in the front bedroom. Sighing deeply and promising myself I wouldn't mention this to my aunt, I drew the travel sack—a thin, portable sleeping bag for people phobic about touching hotel sheets—over the bare mattress. The travel sack was a Christmas gift from Stephen. I smiled at the thought of my dear, slightly anal-retentive boyfriend and resolved to call him as soon as it was a decent hour overseas.

I found blankets in the bottom drawer of the dresser. I wasn't too keen on using them as covers, given their musty state, but they would make a good shade for the window so the sun wouldn't keep me awake. I boosted myself against the dresser to hang one . . . only to observe that some sort of Greek statue had come to life in my back garden.

He was built like a boxer, barrel-chested and broad-shouldered, with narrow hips encased in ripped jeans. Thick sandy hair fell forward over his face while he worked. His sculpted chest was bare, golden, and apparently quite sweaty, given the way it glistened while he planted paving stones near a pristine concrete patio.

I wavered slightly and grabbed the window frame, my weakening knees caused by more than jet lag. Was this my next-door neighbor? I wasn't sure if I was comfortable living with a he-man who could lift giant stones as if they were dominoes. And when had it gotten so bloody hot in here? I hadn't noticed that I was warm in the cab . . . Oh, wait, it was time for the he-man to take a water break. He took a few long pulls off a bottle from his cooler and dumped the rest over his head.

My jaw dropped, nearly knocking against my chest. "You've got to be kidding me."

Just then, he looked up and spotted me ogling him from above. Our eyes connected . . .

And he winked at me like some Lothario gardener out of a particularly dirty soap opera! I spluttered indignant nonsense before tucking the blanket over the window with a decisive shove.

I pressed my hands over my eyes, trying to coax some moisture around my dry, tacky contact lenses. I didn't have the mental reserves for this. I needed to sleep, eat, and bathe, most likely in that order. I would deal with the man reenacting scenes from *A Streetcar Named Desire* in my back garden at a later date. My shoulders tense and heavy, I crawled onto the mattress, bundled my shirt under my head, and plummeted into sweet unconsciousness.

I woke up bleary and disoriented, unable to figure out where the hell I was. Why was it so dark? Was I too late? Were *they* here already? Where was my family? Why couldn't I hear anyone talking? I lurched up from the mattress and snagged the blanket from the window, letting in the weak twilight.

As soon as I saw the paving stones, I remembered the flight, the mad taxi ride, and the Adonis in the back garden.

"Oh." I sighed, scrubbing my hand over my face. "Right."

I stumbled into the bathroom and splashed cool water on my face. The grimy mirror reflected seven kinds of hell. My face was pale and drawn. My thick coffee-colored hair was styled somewhere near "crazy cat lady," and my normally bright, deep-set brown eyes were marked with dark smudges that weren't entirely composed of mascara. I had my grandfather's features, straight lines, delicate bones, and a particularly full bottom lip. Of course, that meant I looked like my mother, too, which was not something I liked to dwell on. I swiped my hand across the fly-specked glass, smearing the haggard image.

I stripped out of my clothes, standing under the lukewarm spray and letting it wash away the grime. The heavy claw-footed tub actually wobbled a little when I moved, and I worried that it was going to fall through the floor. Long after the water cooled, I climbed out of the tub, only to remember that I hadn't thought to bring any towels into the bathroom with me. Aunt Penny had stuffed a few into my suitcase because she knew the house wouldn't have them. But my suitcase was downstairs, next to the door. And I was stark naked.

"Moron." I cursed myself as I made a shivering dash across the bedroom to retrieve my jacket. I took the stairs carefully—because I wasn't about to die in a household accident wearing only an outdated rain jacket—and carefully avoided windows as I made my way to my luggage. The towels, somehow, still smelled line-fresh, like the lavender and rosemary in Nana Fee's back garden. I pressed one to my face before wrapping it around myself toga-style.

I mentally blessed Penny for packing some ginger tea in my bag, which was good for postflight stomachs. I retrieved the tea bags and cast a longing glance at the kitchen. Did the "furnished" bit include dishes and cups? I could function—I might even be able to dress myself properly—if I just had some decent tea in me. Even if it meant boiling the water in a microwave.

I shuddered. Blasphemy.

If I set the water to boil now, it would be ready by the time I picked out clothes. Multitasking would be the key to surviving here. There would be no loving aunties to make my afternoon tea, no uncles to pop into town if I needed something. I was alone here with my thoughts, for the first time in a long time. And considering my thoughts of late, that could be a dangerous thing.

"Staring into space isn't going to brew the tea," I chided myself. Securing my towel, I made my way to the stove, careful to avoid the windows. I didn't know if my neighbor was doing his sweaty work out in the yard, and I didn't fancy being winked at while wearing this getup.

After setting the tea bags on the counter, I began rummaging through the cupboards, finding dirty, abandoned cookware but no kettle. I sighed and thunked my head against the cupboard. I just wanted some tea. Just a little tea, and I'd be right as rain . . . as right as rain could be.

I was starting to sound like one of the less sane characters in *Alice in Wonderland*.

I could take the risk of heating it by less conventional means. Honestly, I'd been on a plane for hours. It had been days since I'd used any proper magic—or improper magic, for that matter. Maybe the hiatus and the change in environment would help with my little . . . problem.

Maybe, for the first time in months, I would have a handle on it.

I took a deep, cleansing breath and filled a ceramic mug with tap water. After glancing around, as if some random stranger might be pressing his face to the window to catch me using illicit, magical tea-brewing techniques, I wrapped my fingers around the mug and imagined energy flowing from my hands, into the ceramic, into the water. I closed my eyes and pictured heat growing between my hands into a glowing ball of energy that slipped between all of the tiny molecules in the water and got them moving, got them hot, got them boiling. I pictured how good it would feel to get dressed, put my feet up, and have a nice cuppa. I felt the smooth material grow hot beneath my fingertips and the steam rising from the cup, curling around my face. But too quickly, the pleasant, soothing heat turned volcanic. I hissed, yanking my hands away from the burning-hot mug, watching with resigned frustration as it cracked down the middle and spilled boiled water all over the counter.

Dodging out of range, I scrubbed a hand over my face in defeat. Clearly, my self-imposed ban on nonessential magic was for my own good, in addition to that of the general populace.

I tossed the remains of the destroyed cup into the sink and tried to mop up the water with the corner of my towel. I grabbed another mug, opened the top cupboard nearest the refrigerator, and—

"ACCCK!" I shrieked at the sight of beady black eyes glaring out at me from the cupboard shelf. The furry gray creature's mouth opened, revealing rows of sharp white fangs. It swiped its paws at me, claws spread, and hissed like a brassed-off cobra.

I let loose a bloodcurdling scream and ran stumbling out of the kitchen, through a screen door, and into the moonless purple light of early evening. With my eyes trained behind me to make sure it, whatever it was, didn't follow me, I slammed into a solid, warm object. The force of my momentum had me wrapping my arms and legs around it as I struggled away from the fanged menace.

"Oof!" the object huffed.

The object was a person. To be specific, the shirtless, sweaty person who'd been standing in my back garden earlier. Dropping a couple of yard tools with a *clank,* he caught my weight with his hands, stumbling under the impact of struggling, panicked woman. Certainly as surprised to find me in his arms as I was to be there.

Slashing dark eyebrows shot skyward. The full lips parted to offer, "Hello?"

Oh, saints and angels, I was doomed. He was even better-looking up close. Tawny, whiskey-colored eyes. A classic straight nose with a clear break on the bridge. Wide, generous lips currently curved into a naughty, tilted line as he stared up at me.

Completely. Doomed.

Focus, I told myself. *There's a mutant rodent in your cupboard, waiting to devour your very soul, then terrorize the townsfolk.*

"In my kitchen!" I shouted in his face.

"What?" The man seemed puzzled, and not just by

the fact that I seemed to be wrapped around him like some sort of cracked-up spider monkey.

"In. My. KITCHEN!" I yelled, scrabbling to keep my grip on his shoulders while leaning back far enough to make eye contact. Despite my all-out terror, I couldn't help but notice the smooth, warm skin or the tingles traveling down my arms, straight to my heart. He smelled . . . wild. Of leather and hay and deep, green pockets of forest. As my weight shifted backward, his large, warm hands slid around my bottom, cupping my cheeks to keep me balanced against him. "Th-there's a creature!" I cried. "In my kitchen! Some demon rat sent from hell! It tried to bite my face off!"

The fact that his hand was ever so subtly squeezing my unclothed ass managed to subdue my mind-numbing terror and replace it with indignant irritation. I didn't know this man. I certainly hadn't invited him to grope me, spider-monkey climbing or no. And I had a perfectly lovely boyfriend waiting for me at home, who would not appreciate some workman's callused hands on my ass.

"You can move your hand now," I told him, trying to dismount gracefully, but his hands remained cupped under my left cheek.

"Hey, you tackled me!" he protested in a smoky, deeply accented tenor.

I narrowed my eyes. "Move your hand, or I'll mail it back to you by a very slow post."

"Fine." He sighed, gently lowering me to my feet. "Let's get a look at this creature in your kitchen."

Struggling to keep my towel in place, I led him into

my kitchen and tentatively pointed toward the home of the Rodent of Unusual Size. I could hear the beast hissing and growling inside, batting at the closed door with its claws. I was surprised it hadn't managed to eat its way through yet. But somehow my would-be rescuer seemed far more interested in looking around, noting the pile of luggage by the door.

"Haven't had much time to unpack yet, huh?" he asked. I glared at him. He shrugged. "Fine, fine, critter crisis. I'm on it."

He opened the cupboard door, let out a horrified gasp, and slammed it shut. He grabbed a grimy old spatula I'd left on the counter during my rummaging and slid it through the cupboard handles, trapping the monster inside. He turned on me, his face grave while his amber eyes twinkled. "You're right. I'm going to have to call in the big guns."

He disappeared out the door on quick, quiet feet. I stared after him, wondering if I'd just invited help from a complete lunatic, when the early-evening breeze filtering in through the back door reminded me that I was standing there in just a towel. I scrambled over to my suitcase and threw on a loose peasant skirt and a blue tank top. I wondered what he meant by "big guns." Was he calling the police? The National Guard? MI5?

I was slipping on a pair of knickers under my skirt just as my bare-chested hero came bounding back into the kitchen with a large, lidded pot and a spoon.

"Are you going to cook it?" I gasped, ignoring the

bald-faced grin he gave my lower quadrants as the floaty blue skirt fell back into place.

"Well, my uncle Ray favors a good roast possum. He says it tastes like chicken," he drawled, holding the lid over his thick forearm like a shield as he tapped the spatula out of place. "Personally, I have to wonder if he's eaten chicken that tastes like ass, but that's neither here nor there."

I darted away as he opened the cupboard door. A feral growl echoed through the empty house as he maneuvered the pot over the front of the cupboard. He used the wooden spoon to reach over the grumpy animal and nudge the possum into the pot. Slapping the lid over it, he turned and gave me a proud grin.

"Thank you." I sighed. "Really, I don't know what I would have done—"

The giant rat began thrashing around inside the pot and making the lid dance.

"I want that thing tested for steroids!" I yelped.

"It's just a baby," he said, placing one of his ham-sized hands on the lid. "These things burrow in pretty much wherever they want to, doors and walls be damned."

"This is a baby?" I peered down at the dancing pot. "How big do the mothers get?"

He shrugged. "Better question: where is his mama?"

"Oh," I groaned as he opened the back door, crossed the yard, and gently shook the possum out of the pot and into the tall grass near the trees. I called after him, "Why did you have to say that? I have to sleep here!"

Climbing my back steps, he looked far more relaxed than he should have been after evicting a vicious furred fiend from my kitchen. Shirtless. "I have to sleep here, too. And if it makes you feel better, there's a good chance that the mama could be sleepin' under my side of the house," he told me. "I'm Jed, by the way."

I giggled, a hysterical edge glinting under the laughter, as he extended his hand toward me. "You're kidding."

He arched a sleek sandy eyebrow. "I'm sorry?"

I cleared my throat, barely concealing a giggle. "No, I'm sorry. I've never met a Jed before."

He chuckled. "I'd imagine not, with that accent and all."

Now it was my turn to raise the bitch-brow, a super-extension of the eyebrow combined with one's best frosty expression. He of the sultry backwoods drawl was mocking my accent? That was disappointing. Since landing in New York, I'd worked hard to control whatever lilt I'd picked up in the fifteen years I'd lived with Nana Fee. It wouldn't do for the locals to know where I was from.

"Your accent," he said, his forehead creasing. "Boston, right? 'Pahk the cah in the yahd'?"

I blushed a little and regretted the bitch-brow. I'd forgotten how muddled my manner of speaking was, compared with my new neighbor's Southern twang. My accent was vaguely Boston, vaguely Irish. Nana Fee had tried to correct my lack of Rs in general and attempted to teach me Gaelic, but the most I picked up were some of the more interesting expressions my aunts and uncles used. Mostly the dirty ones. So I spoke in a bizarre mish-mash of dialects and colloquialisms, which led to awkward conversations over what to call chips, elevators, and bathrooms.

"Oh, right," I said, laughing lightly. "Boston—born and raised."

Technically, it wasn't a lie.

Jed looked at me expectantly. I looked down to make sure I hadn't forgotten some important article of clothing. "If you don't give me your name, I'm just gonna make one up," he said, leaning against the counter. "And fair warnin', you look like a Judith."

"I do not!" I exclaimed.

"Half-dressed girls who climb me like a tree are usually named Judith," he told me solemnly.

"This happens to you often?" I deadpanned.

He shrugged. "You'd be surprised."

"It's Nola," I told him. "Nola Leary."

"Jed Trudeau," he said, shaking my outstretched hand. "If you don't mind me sayin', you look beat. Must've been a long flight."

"It was," I said, nodding. "If you don't mind, I think I'll just go back to bed."

There was a spark of mischief in his eyes, but I think he picked up on the fact that I was in no mood for saucy talk. His full lips twitched, but he clamped them together. He held up one large, work-roughened hand. "Hold on."

He disappeared out the back door, and I could hear

his boot steps on the other side of my kitchen wall. He returned a few moments later, having donned a light cotton work shirt, still unbuttoned. He placed a large, cold, foil-wrapped package in my hands. "Chicken and rice casserole. One of the ladies down at the Baptist church made it for me. Well, several of the church ladies made casseroles for me, so I have more than I can eat. Just pop a plateful in the microwave for three minutes."

I stared at the dish for a long while before he took it out of my hands and placed it in my icebox. "Do local church ladies often cater your meals?"

"I don't go to Sunday services, so they're very concerned about my soul. I can't cook to save my life. They're afraid I'm just wasting away to nothing," he said, shaking his head in shame, but there was that glint of trouble in his eyes again. He gave me a long, speculative look. "Well, I'll let you get back to sleep. Welcome to the neighborhood."

"Thanks," I said as he moved toward the door. I locked it behind him, then turned and sagged against the dusty sheers covering the window in the door. "If there are any greater powers up there—stop laughing."

I massaged my temples and set about making my tea. Jed seemed nice, if unfortunately named. And it was very kind of him to give a complete stranger a meal when he knew she had nothing but angry forest creatures in her cupboards. But I couldn't afford this sort of distraction. I'd come to the Hollow for a purpose, not for friendships and flirtations with smoldering, half-dressed neighbors.

Just as I managed to locate a chipped mug in the spice drawer, a loud, angry screech sounded from somewhere to the left of my stove. I turned and fumbled with the locked kitchen door, yelling, "Jed!"

2

Love affairs between the human and the nonhuman rarely end well for the human.

> —*Love Spells: A Witch's Guide to Maintaining Healthy Relationships*

By the time Jed had reunited the mama possum and her young, I determined I was far too awake to go to bed. I went through the house making lists of everything I would need to survive here, things such as food, sheets, towels, and mousetraps. Big ones.

I needed to go shopping, but I didn't have a car, and I thought it would be pushing already-fragile "good neighbor" impressions by asking to borrow Jed's. And now that I was able to recall more clearly moments from Dwayne-Lee's drive to the house, I wasn't about to take the cab service. Iris Scanlon proved that my love for her was not in vain. All it took was one phone call for her to send "more discreet transport" right to my doorstep.

Miranda Puckett was a slender thing, with long dark hair and keen green eyes. What she lacked in size she made up for with the obscenely large black SUV she ma-neuvered from my driveway to the gravel road with considerably fewer bumps than Dwayne-Lee. Aside from knowing where the all-night grocers were, Miranda was also a veritable font of information about the locals. She'd grown up in the Hollow and was happy to share what she knew of local history and gossip.

For instance, Miranda's boss was not a freelance miracle worker but ran a concierge service for vampires called Beeline. The special arrangements Iris had been making for me were on behalf of my landlord, a vampire named—of all things—Dick Cheney. Miranda admitted to having a "soft spot" for Dick since he'd served as her knight in shining armor months earlier when she'd had car trouble.

"He comes off like this sketchy con artist, but underneath it all, he's a marshmallow," she told me, shifting uncomfortably in her seat. "Totally devoted to his wife, which is a good thing. Otherwise, Collin would really frown on all those book club meetings."

"Book club?" I asked, my brow furrowed. But Miranda had pulled into the car park of the local twenty-four-hour Walmart Supercenter, so I couldn't question why a vampire and a chauffeur would join the same book club. Or who the bloody hell Collin was.

The Hollow, Miranda informed me as we shopped, had become quite the vampire-friendly place since the vampires had emerged from the shadows in 1999. That was the year a Milwaukee-based vampire named Arnie Frink demanded that his employers change his work hours to lessen his chances of bursting into flames. But seeing as they were as blind as the rest of the world when it came to the existence of vampires, the human resources department insisted that Arnie keep bankers' hours. Arnie's counterproposal was a massive lawsuit, claiming that he suffered from porphyria, a painful allergy to sunlight, and the company was not accommodating him. When the allergy discrimination argument failed to impress a judge, Arnie had a hissy in open court and declared that he was a vampire, a medical condition that rendered him unable to work during the day, thereby making him subject to the Americans with Disabilities Act.

Although Arnie won his case, the first year or so afterward was a dark time indeed. For the Irish, who had always kept folk tales close to their hearts, it was no surprise to hear that one of many beasties they'd been warned against was an actuality. For the McGavocks, it was even less so. We knew witches were real, so why not vampires, werewolves, and any number of fairy folk we knew to be dancing in the hedgerows? Still, it was a shock to watch the scenes of destruction play out on TV. Here in America and across Europe, mobs of people forced vampires out into the sunlight or set about hunting them for no reason other than that they existed. More often than not, the hunters were injured in the process.

Once they had quelled their fury at being launched from the coffin, an elected contingent of ancient vampires officially notified the United Nations of their presence and asked the world's governments to recognize them as legitimate beings. The World Council for the Equal Treatment of the Undead also asked for special leniency in certain medical, legal, and tax issues that were sure to come up. Oh, and for humans to stop dragging them from their homes and turning them into kindling . . . or else.

And so humans had to adjust . . . or else. For a small town, the Hollow had adjusted rather admirably. The local Council office had taken every step to ingratiate it-self with the local human population, all the while doing the sneaky, slightly underhanded errands necessary to monitor and govern its undead citizens. A local woman had even opened the town's first vampire-oriented res-taurant recently, after winning a cooking contest spon-sored by a synthetic-blood company.

Knowing that the town was paranormally liberal did not prepare me for the grocers. While I found every-thing on my list, the products and the packaging seemed garish and bright under the sickly green fluorescents. The sheer amount of nacho-flavored food available on each aisle was staggering. And there was the spectacle of the other shoppers—some without shirts and oth-ers trying to pass off other clothing as shirts. Honestly, who leaves the house wearing an athletic bra and a pair of bicycle pants?

Somehow, through this whole excursion, Miranda managed to keep up a steady stream of chatter. She talked like my uncle Jack after a few pints. Words spilled from her lips at such a clip that one wouldn't dare try to ask questions—all this despite the distinct throbbing pain radiating from her left side. She was working hard to disguise the hitch in her gait by using the shopping cart handle for support, but the ache was obvious to someone with certain sensitivities, such as myself. So I worked around her, discreetly trying to keep her from having to lift or bend.

By the time I picked up all my essentials—specifically, a teapot, some passable Earl Grey, and some industrial-sized pest traps—I was a bit dizzy, both from the strain of Miranda's discomfort and the information she had shared. And then there was the small matter of Miranda's knocking a bottle of dish liquid off a shelf as I was bent over the cart, rendering me temporarily senseless. Given the way she managed to pick up the conversation after she picked me up from the floor, I suspected this sort of thing happened to her frequently.

"Well, this took less time than I expected," I marveled as she unlocked the car. When a grimacing Miranda lifted a bag of groceries from the carriage to load into the back of the SUV, I gently took over the task.

"God bless the cultural amalgam that is the superstore," Miranda said, keeping a hand pressed tightly to her side. "Some might object, but personally, I like being able to buy my underwear and antifreeze in the same place."

"Would you like to talk about your ribs, or are you going to continue 'playing through the pain'?" I asked.

Miranda blushed. "That obvious, is it? I thought I was doing a better job of covering."

"Oh, you were the soul of discretion," I assured her. "I'm just a bit sensitive to these things."

She chuckled, wincing as her stomach muscles tightened. "I guess you would be, being a nurse and all."

I nodded, smiling blithely. Now was definitely not the time to try to squeeze "I have an extrasensory perception that allows me to feel your pain" into the conversation.

"Would you like me to take a look?" I asked.

"Right here?"

"Why not?" I chuckled, stepping closer. "Want to tell me how this happened? And why you haven't been to see a doctor?"

"No and no," she said, shaking her head.

I held my hands over Miranda's shoulders. While the pain throbbed steadily with every breath, her lungs felt clear. There was no puncture there, but her ribs were thoroughly bruised. It felt like some sort of side impact, as if she'd been thrown into a corner or a piece of furniture.

"Miranda, did someone hurt you?" I asked, feeling a sudden urge to find this "Collin" and introduce him to an old-fashioned Kilcairy arse-whipping.

Miranda closed her eyes, her face flushing red. "No," she groaned, clapping a hand over her face. "As usual, I have no one to blame but myself. Let's just say that when one is having athletic makeup sex with her vampire boyfriend, she should hold on for dear life. Particularly when there is a pointy nightstand nearby."

"Are you telling me you fell off your undead boyfriend while having sex and landed against a nightstand, bruising your ribs?"

She shook her head. "I blew the dismount."

"I don't think I want the details of his dismount," I said, laughing. I held my hand against her ribs as she snickered in response. The bones felt sound. It would be a simple enough thing to heal, but I needed to stay under the radar. So I gave her my best serious, professional expression and told her, "Ice and ibuprofen. Deep-breathing exercises and gentle stretching if you feel up to it. Just take it easy. If the pain gets worse or it becomes difficult to breathe, go to your doctor right away."

"Yes, ma'am," she said, breathing a sigh of relief as we climbed into the car. "I was really afraid I'd done myself permanent damage this time. What do I owe you for the consult?"

"Tell Collin to be more careful with his breakable girl-friend," I told her as she blushed crimson again. "You shameless sex maniac."

As Miranda started the car and backed out of the car park, I waited for her to relaunch her verbal barrage. But in her embarrassment, she seemed to be concentrating on maneuvering the car safely, so I took advantage of the silence. I breathed deeply, trying to center my thoughts and regain the energy it had taken to check Miranda's ribs.

Being a medical empath was not an easy gift. Often, when I came across people with medical problems, I felt a "tug" of pressure in my own body reflecting the area of their body where they were ailing. And I came across a lot of people with medical problems. And sometimes, if I did nothing to heal them, or at least talk to them about how to improve their problem, the pressure would get worse, and I would get sick myself.

My gift was the reason I couldn't practice in a large hospital setting. The discomfort and "tugging" were so draining that I would keel over by the end of the day. It was easy to spend time with Stephen because he was a health nut who rarely came down with so much as a cold.

Being a hereditary witch is like inheriting frizzy hair or an unfortunate nose. I had no choice in the matter. For my family, witchcraft wasn't quite a religion. It simply *was*. It was part of our lives, the way we saw and interacted with the world. I couldn't turn it off, no matter how I tried. Believe me, I tried. I couldn't always control it. And there was nothing I could do, take, or try to make my ability easier to use. Sometimes it was particularly embarrassing, trying to broach the topic of sensitive medical problems with people who didn't want to discuss such things with complete strangers. But Miranda seemed happy with the outcome of our conversation, and I don't think I'd heard a story more embarrassing than hers.

In some cases, it would have been easier to use magic to heal my patients. But I'd learned that illness had a purpose. Bodies have to go through the pain to get to the good part, the healing. It's the payment portion of the process and shouldn't be skipped over.

My relationship with magic was complicated. At one time, I had been Nana Fee's prize student. Like most witches, I had a smattering of talent in most magical areas but excelled in a particular skill. In my case, I was a gifted healer. My instruction started at a later age than that of most of my cousins, but I had taken to it like a duck to water. The problem was that I had a little too much "oomph," an erratic excess energy. When I tried a simple exercise intended to restore a withered mint plant to its former glory, I overdid it on the roots, which grew so spectacularly that they burst the pot and peppered the walls with shattered clay and potting soil. And then there were the fires. After that, I limited myself to harmless glamours and spells that made everyday life a little easier. I was too timid to try advanced spells, because I could pose a threat to myself or others.

I tended to limit friendships to members of my family or the village, because I could never quite trust outsiders with "everything." Either they'd think I was bonkers and drop me, or they'd want to use me to their own ends—quick fixes to money problems or love spells, which frankly never worked the way people hoped. I lost more boyfriends than I cared to admit over the years, because my abilities drove them away. If I lost my temper, things tended to explode. And then there was the boyfriend who was stupid enough to contract an infection when he cheated and then got indignant at me for "spying" on him using my empathy. Not to mention that shared psychic itching was just disgusting. Even the men who had no problem with my family's history became suspicious of whether I was using spells on them. Were their feelings for me real, they wondered, or the result of a potion? Eventually, they got tired of wondering and left.

Magic always muddied the waters. There was only so much "weird" that men could take, even the ones who claimed to be open-minded. And so when I'd met Ste-

phen months before, and he turned out to be someone
I thought could be "*the* one," I'd decided against using
magic anywhere near him. I saw Stephen as my chance
at a seminormal life. He was a straight, single, employed,
functional adult who was also sweet, considerate, smart,
and funny. He had treated me with nothing but kindness
since meeting me at a nursing conference in Dublin the
previous year. (His brokerage firm was holding a summit
at the same hotel.) He remembered my birthday and sent
me a huge bouquet of roses for Saint Valentine's. Coming
from a family where sensible was in short supply, that
was incredibly attractive. We'd heard that men like him
existed, but actually laying eyes on one in person was a
once-in-a-lifetime event. He was the Sasquatch of boyfriends.

Stephen always said he knew what he wanted and how
to get it. I was just grateful that he wanted me. Stephen
said he wanted to marry me, to raise a family with me.
And the way he described our life together in a sweet
suburban house with a play set in the back garden, it
seemed to be everything I wanted.

So three months before I came to the Hollow, when
Stephen began talking about moving in together, I asked
Penny for a favor. I asked her to place a binding on me.
We tried to be clever about it. She worded the spell so
that the binding prevented me from "doing harm,"
meaning I could still heal and diagnose, but I couldn't,
say, stir the air or manipulate water or any of the sorts of
things that might do harm to my relationship.

I should have known better than to trust Penny. I

loved her dearly. She was my closest friend, the youngest daughter of Nana's youngest sibling. At thirty-six, she was a few years older than I, so it was a bit like having a cool older sister. But her magic had always been, well, spotty. Sometimes she could perform beautiful spells that made gardens flourish or wounds heal without any sign of a scar. And then there was the eviscerated sofa and the inexplicable loss of Mrs. McClaren's eyebrows.

I ended up with the magical equivalent of Mrs. McClaren's eyebrows. Penny had left me for the most part completely unaffected, but then there were seemingly random times when I had no magic whatsoever, for days at a time, and *then,* as a result of the "bottling effect" of those lulling intervals, there were terrifying moments in which every bit of power I owned poured forth in torrents of energy that shattered lightbulbs, crockery, and any nearby windows. And unfortunately for me, the most recent of these explosive moments had occurred while I was at dinner with Stephen at a rather posh Italian restaurant. Since I was the only person standing nearby, I ended up paying to replace several Murano glass light fixtures and a rather heavy antique gilt mirror.

Penny had to go in halvsies with me, the twit.

It was as if I had a state-of-the-art, wall-shaking stereo but couldn't control the volume. The only time I felt remotely in control of myself was when I felt "tugged" by the pain in people around me. Penny theorized that particular grace was only granted because I had no choice in the matter. I couldn't stop feeling those tugs any more than I could choose to stop blinking or breathing. And fortunately, I had enough nursing training to heal people through conventional means.

We couldn't seem to undo the spell, no matter how many different approaches we took—countering spells, rituals, prayers, and anointments. Nothing worked. There was no magical "control Z."

When Nana began my instruction, I'd been disappointed that I wouldn't be able to make rooms tidy themselves like Mary Poppins or fly on a broom. I'd eventually adjusted my expectations and learned to enjoy manipulating the energy of the natural world. But now I couldn't even perform the most basic of "fun" magic: no more minor glamours to cover the occasional spot, no more "quick-start" fires on the hearth, no more kitchen magic to cover for my abysmal cooking. Thanks to this colossal blunder of judgment and execution, which we were endeavoring to hide from the rest of the family to prevent panic, I learned that having magic was like having an automatic dishwasher. Once you were used to having some machine do the washing up for you, even unloading the damn thing seemed like a chore. I could see that now, having become accustomed to some other force taking care of life's little details. I had, to an embarrassing degree, stopped living my own life. So I tried to do as much as I could independently of magic, even when I did have a "witchy" solution.

Nana, who took a dim view of my timidity toward practicing the craft, had told me often that there was no such thing as a "halfway" witch, particularly given my extra ability, and that dabbling would catch up and bite me one day.

I had a feeling that day was coming soon.

I flexed my fingers and toes, feeling my body coming back into balance. I blew out a long breath and gave Miranda my best smile.

"Would you mind terribly if we drove by Paxton Avenue on the way home?" I asked as we rolled through the neon-lit streets of the Hollow's "mall district." As we moved farther and farther away from Walmart, the streets grew darker and quieter. The buildings were sort of mashed together, as if they were supposed to prop each other up. Every other restaurant seemed to serve some form of fire-roasted pig. And most of the business signs were intentionally misspelled, which seemed odd.

Miranda arched her dark brows. "Sure. Any particular reason?"

"There's a bookshop in that area I was hoping to visit after I've settled in," I said, working to keep my tone casual. "I'd just like to know how to get there."

"Specialty Books?" she said. "That's where my book club meets! You'll love it."

I blinked at her. "Your book club meets at an occult bookshop?"

Miranda gave a startled laugh. "How did you know about that? I mean, it hasn't been an occult bookshop for a few years, not since Jane took over."

I could only assume she meant Jane Jameson, who was now listed as the shop's proprietor on the updated Web site. According to what my cousin Ralph could find in county court records, Jameson had taken over the store a little more than a year before, when Mr. Wainwright left it

to her in his will. I couldn't find much information about
Ms. Jameson online. Her Facebook privacy settings were
stringent. She had no Twitter account. In 2002, she gave
a comment for a Kentucky Library Association newslet-
ter article about electronic card catalogues. At the time,
she was listed as a youth service librarian for the Half-
Moon Hollow Public Library, but the library now listed
that position as "vacant." Other than the Specialty Books
Web site and a memorial Facebook page on the Half-
Moon High School reunion group, her Google presence
was virtually nonexistent.

"The Internet," I said. "I try to find little independent
bookshops whenever I can. They usually serve great
coffee."

"Well, if Jane offers to make it for you, wait for Dick
or Andrea Cheney."

"My landlord works at this bookshop?" I asked as she
turned the SUV toward Paxton.

That seemed like a strange coincidence—the man
who owned Mr. Wainwright's former home also worked
in Mr. Wainwright's former shop? What sort of connection did Dick Cheney have to Mr. Wainwright?

"Technically, I don't think they pay him. He just
spends a lot of time there. Anyway, he and his wife, Andrea, are the only ones who can make decent coffee for
humans. Jane's coffee experiments have been known to
convulse innocent bystanders, living or otherwise. She
says it's not her fault. She couldn't cook before she was
turned, either."

Jane Jameson was a vampire?

"Oh, sure, she was turned about three years ago," Miranda said in response to the question I hadn't realized I'd asked out loud. That explained the memorial page. "Nice lady. Married to her sire, Gabriel. And she made her own vampire son earlier this year. Collin says I should call him a 'childe,' but when I call Jamie her son, it makes Gabriel's eye twitch. And that's way more fun."

She slowed the car as we approached the one well-lit building on a sad, careworn street lined with dilapidated shops. Specialty Books was like a beacon, its bright windows and security lights accentuating the recent coat of sky-blue paint on the exterior brick. The inside appeared to be painted a darker purplish blue. The walls were lined floor to ceiling with light maple bookshelves. I could make out the shapes of four people sitting at a long polished bar, laughing and chatting. This was not what I expected.

Given the neighborhood and the state of Mr. Wainwright's house, I'd expected the shop to be sort of beaten and half-finished. What had Ms. Jameson had to do to get the building into this condition? How much of the stock had she moved around?

"Are you sure you don't want to stop in now?" Miranda asked, making me jump a bit. Apparently, the anxious expression on my face was coming across as eager. "They keep vampire hours, so customers are welcome any time of night."

I shook my head, struggling to find words that wouldn't set off Miranda's bullshit sensor. Frankly, I was fighting the absurd urge to slink down in my seat so no one in the shop would see me. I wasn't ready for this. I needed to prepare for my visit to the shop. I cleared my throat and reminded Miranda about the perishables we'd loaded into the car. "I'll come back some other time, but thanks for showing me where to find it."

Miranda shrugged and sped the car down the street. The farther we got from the store, the more I was able to relax. I leaned back against the seat and mulled over this latest development. My plans would have to change. I would need to do more research on Dick Cheney. I would need to change the way I approached Jane Jameson.

The woman who owned my grandfather's shop was a vampire. That could make my life a lot more complicated.

Sleep didn't come easily that night, and not just because of my faulty internal clock or the lingering possibility of small mammals scurrying about my bedroom while I slept. It was a combination of worries, including the fact that I was sleeping under the roof my grandfather once owned. Penny called it a "beautiful coincidence" that she'd found it on a Web site listing local rentals. It made me edgy and uncomfortable, for reasons I hadn't quite pinned down yet. So I tossed and turned in my newly outfitted bed, thinking of Nana Fee and the night she died.

For a witch, Nana Fee died a shockingly normal death. Her heart was old and simply couldn't give any more. When the body is unable to carry on, there's only so much magic can do. She was tired of fighting nature and decided to let it take its course.

So on one unremarkable evening a few weeks ago, she sat propped up in her bed, the same one where she'd spent a lifetime alone, well aware that she was breathing her last. She sent everyone from her cozy little bedroom except me. My uncles, aunts, and cousins did as they were told, knowing it was likely the last time she'd boss them around, but they weren't happy about it. Death was rarely a solitary event in the McGavock family. We were practically our own Greek chorus.

Nana tried to keep a stoic face through the whole affair. Although the family had never held an official election, Nana was definitely the leader. And somehow they'd gotten it into their heads that I was inheriting the position, no matter how much I pleaded for someone else to step in. Nana insisted that we dress her in the lavender bed jacket that Uncle Jack had given her for Christmas. Her snowy-white hair was piled high on her head. The fire was burned down to embers, giving her pale-blue eyes an unearthly glow. "It's time," she said, her voice steady but weak. "I made a mistake, putting it off for this long. He's gone now."

"Who's gone?" I asked.

Moving slowly, she pointed to the foot of her bed, to the space between her mattress and box spring. I reached in and pulled out a well-worn manila envelope. She smiled, a slight lift of the corner of her mouth. "Your grandfather."

"Gilbert Wainwright?" I read the address on the envelope, listing a resident in Half-Moon Hollow, Kentucky, and looked up at Nana, a million questions burning the tip of my tongue.

"He was a good man. Smart, just like my Nola."

I emptied the envelope into my hand and found several black-and-white photos of a much younger Nana laughing into the camera, her arms slung around a slight man with light hair and dark eyes. He was grinning down at her, a look of fond admiration on his face.

"He didn't love me," she said. "But I didn't care. I was young. A little foolish."

"You got his name tattooed on your bum?" I asked, sniffing as I sorted through photos, letters, and what appeared to be Nana Fee's journal.

"Impudent chit," she muttered. "Shouldn't have expected anything less from you."

"You would worry if I was behaving any other way."

"He has them," she said, leaning back against the pillows. "Had them."

"Them?" I stared at her, not comprehending. My eyes widened. "Them? *Them* them?"

"Yes. I gave them to him for safekeeping," she said, tapping a photo in which Mr. Wainwright stood next to a packed motorcycle, giving the camera a sad little wave. "On the day he left."

"Nana, the whole family has wound themselves up over this for *decades*. How could you—*why* would you? Why in God's name would you—"

"Don't curse at an old woman on her deathbed."

"Stop calling it a deathbed!" I exclaimed.

"That's what it is, sweetheart," she said, squeezing my hand between her dry, brittle fingers. "No use pretending it's not. It's my time, you see, it's run out. And your time is just coming. I'm sorry this has fallen to you, the responsibilities, the burden. But it couldn't be helped."

"Nana, I don't want to talk about this."

"Promise me," she said. "Swear that you'll go to America to retrieve them."

"How do you even know he still had them? He could have lost them on the way back to America. What if he sold them?"

"He swore he would keep them safe. He knew how important it was. I contacted him every few years, to check on him. The last time I called, they told me he was gone."

"And what if his family has sorted through his effects and sold them off?"

"He had no family."

"He had a daughter and a granddaughter," I snapped. I was immediately sorry for my tone and pushed a stray lock of hair away from Nana's face.

"It was better this way, Nola," she assured me. "There was no reason to tell him about your mother, although I know it caused her pain. I had all of the best bits of him, right here. How could I ask him for more? I couldn't ask him to spend his life with someone he didn't love. And if he knew there was a baby, he would have come back."

"I'm sorry, Nana, I really am, but maybe it's best just to leave the past in the past. There's no reason for me to go halfway around the world and open old wounds—"

"If you don't go to America and find the Elements before they do, the whole family will be bound. No magic, no healing, no more help for our neighbors when they need it. Have you seen what happens to a village when they're suddenly without magic after generations have lived under its care and protection?"

"Let's not talk about this now," I told her.

"Oh, yes, we'll talk about it some other time." She sighed. "Let's schedule an appointment next week. It will be so much more convenient after I die."

I groaned, pressing my fingers against my eyelids. She pulled my hands away from my eyes and gave me a stern look. As weak as she was, it was still enough to make me sit up and speak plainly. "I don't know if I'm up for this, Nana. I don't know if I can do what you're asking of me."

"Magic won't tolerate a practitioner who dances around it. You use your talents as you see fit, but there's a price for it, Nola. And the price has to be paid. If you continue to live as half a witch, you'll lose your gifts. Promise me that you'll find them."

"Nana . . ."

"Promise. Me," she ground out, as if the very effort exhausted her. "Unless you want my spirit stuck on this plane with unfinished business. It won't be pleasant haunting. Lots of flies. Portents of doom. Midnight wailing."

"Fine. I promise," I said. "Just lie back and get some rest, all right? I love you."

"I love you, too, darling." Nana closed her eyes and leaned back. Her breathing evened out, and her pulse went steady. Just before she fell asleep, her eyes fluttered open. "Nola, your mother . . ."

"Shh." I leaned against the bed and whispered against her temple. "Don't worry. Get some rest."

When her breath evened out and faded into light snores, I went into the parlor to assure my family that she was resting comfortably. In other words, they should get out and let both of us rest, for pity's sake. The next morning, I woke propped against the bedside with my hand still twined in Nana's. The fire was out, and the room was cold and dark. I'd fallen asleep against the mattress, my face cradled against her journal. At some point, she'd taken off her great-grandmother's wedding ring and closed my fingers over it. It had no magical significance. It was just an old family ring, passed from mother to daughter. I was the only one in Fiona McGavock's line left to pass it along to.

And she was gone.

3

With my internal clock still all wonky, I ended up sitting in bed reading over my notes on the artifacts. The problem was, I was looking for four everyday objects: a candle, a clay plaque, a knife, and a bell. Apart from being old, they probably wouldn't catch much attention at your average yard sale. And all supernatural clues from my grandmother had stopped the moment I decided to go to the States. That was maddeningly unhelpful.

I pored over the sketches Nana had left me, trying to memorize the symbols that had been painstakingly etched into the candle to represent protection. My head drooped over the papers until the landline rang, a sharp, shrieking jangle next to my ear. I jerked awake, blinking blearily at my new alarm clock to see that the numbers on its face were indecently low. I may have muttered a few obscenities into the receiver when I pressed it to my ear.

"Well, that's a fine greeting for your favorite aunt."

I sat up in bed, wiping at my eyes. "Pen, what the hell are you doing calling me at three in the morning?"

"Ah!" Penny cried. "Sorry, love, forgot about the time difference."

"I'm going to reach through the phone and strangle you, Penelope," I growled.

Penny scoffed at the very idea, and rightly so. She had about thirty pounds and four inches on me.

"Any progress?" Penny asked.

"Well, I have food in the house but no angry marsupials. That's progress."

"I'm assuming that you're just tired and not spouting gibberish to annoy me," she retorted.

"No, no, it's going well. I've found the shop. I'm going to visit tomorrow. And I've shopped for groceries and managed to evict a minor possum infestation from my rental house."

"Have you called Stephen yet?" she asked.

"Oh, shit!" I gasped. "No. I sent him a text when I landed, but after that . . . everything's a little hazy."

"Well, you should call him. He's been calling here, asking for your contact information at the hospital in Boston. You know I can't lie for anything, Nola. Why didn't you just tell him where you were going?"

"Because Stephen would think this is insane," I grumbled, forcing myself out of bed and untangling myself from the seemingly endless amount of spiral phone cord keeping me tethered to the receiver. I hobbled across my darkened room toward the window, glancing out to the moonlit garden.

"Well, if he's going to be a part of your life, he's just going to have to accept that you're—"

"What the hell is that?" I blurted as my eyes came to focus on a strange hulking figure at the edge of my yard. It had the basic shape of a man, only bent and twisted. The stark light of the full moon showed a broad, dark back. Its movements were halting and irregular, as if its long, rangy limbs weren't working properly. It looked almost canine, like one of those werewolves from the old Universal Studios monster movies. It lumbered toward the treeline, sniffing and scratching.

"Don't change the subject," Penny admonished me.

"There's something in my back garden."

"Another marsupial?" Penny chuckled.

"It almost looks like a Yeti." I stepped toward the cheap little nightstand I'd bought to retrieve my glasses, but the movement dragged the sheet with me and knocked a heavy pile of books and notes to the floor with a loud *thunk*. The shape shifted, its "face" obscured by angled moonlight.

It stepped toward the house. I scrambled away from the window, pressing against the wall. I could hear Penny's voice from the receiver, shouting for me to answer her. I tried to remember if the doors downstairs had decent monster-proof locks, but at the moment, all I could see in my head was a series of increasingly grotesque potential Yeti/werewolf bite wounds. Should I try to warn Jed? How would I get to his part of the house without going outside?

I was snapped out of this mental runaway train by Penny calling my name. I pressed the receiver to my ear. "Yes?"

"I thought the Yeti was a Himalayan beastie," Penny said as I slipped my glasses over my nose.

"Werewolf is another possibility," I whispered, peeking from the window frame and forcing myself to look into the yard. Nothing. Whatever it was had gone. What the hell? I was sure there was something out there. This wasn't some flash out of the corner of my eye. But what was it? As far as I knew, there were no wolfmen or Yetis in this part of the world. And what were the chances of one showing up in my back garden?

There was also the small matter of my reflection, frightful rat's nest of dark hair included, which could very easily be mistaken for a furry beast.

I laughed, wiping at my eyes. "False alarm. No werewolves in sight."

"If you don't stop talking nonsense, I'm coming over there," Penny warned.

I let out a shaky laugh, my shoulders sagging as the tension in my chest eased. "It's fine, Pen, I swear. I'm just jet-lagged and a little loopy. I didn't have my glasses on, and the moonlight is playing tricks on me. It was probably a dog or a bear or something. Do they have bears in Kentucky?"

"I don't know. All the more reason for you to be

careful. I don't like the idea of you being over there by yourself. Rumor has it that several Kerrigan cousins have made plans to 'sightsee' in the States. That means they're up to something. Da wanted me to call to say we could spare Richard, James, and myself if you thought we could be of help."

"You know why it had to be this way. Nana Fee only wanted one of us tramping all over the countryside, digging up family dirt. Four strangers with funny accents in a town this small would definitely cause a stir. And your sudden disappearance from the village would attract attention *there*."

"It's too much for one person to deal with, no matter how strong you think you are."

"Well, I'm not disagreeing with you. But the word is 'badass,' not 'strong.'"

"All right, then, Miss Steven Seagal, what are you not telling me?" she demanded.

"Don't know what you mean."

"You've got that weird excited tension in your voice. And it's not because you've located the shop or managed to find your Nutella. I know you, Nola. You're crap at keeping secrets. Confess."

"My gorgeous new neighbor has an aversion to wearing shirts. And for reasons beyond my control, he may or may not have seen me wearing nothing but a towel . . . at close range. But that's all I'm going to say on the matter."

"You tramp!" Penny cackled. "You're not getting away that easy!"

"That's. All. I. Have. To. Say."

Huffing at my "mule-headedness," Penny updated me on some of our patients, and I gave notes on their treatment, and for a moment, we sounded like any other medical team in the Western world. Gifted though we were, there were limitations to what we could do. Magic was not the answer to every problem or ailment, which was where my training came in handy. Nana and the others graciously tolerated my little eccentricities when I insisted on using modern techniques and equipment. So in return, if herbal teas would resolve issues such as indigestion, irregularity, and irritability, I prescribed them happily. Treatment at the clinic was a mix of magic and medicine, and our patients had come to expect a little of both.

My relatives were bolder in their practice of magical healing. Penny, for example, was a dab hand at what she called "replenishing spells." She could spend just a few minutes talking with a patient who had been run down by a chronic illness or a bout of flu, and that person would walk away feeling as if he or she had spent two weeks at a health spa. She got incredibly offended when I suggested that the soothing, musical lilt of her voice sent the patients into a posthypnotic state that led them to believe they were relaxed and refreshed. If I teased too hard, she'd threaten to perm me again.

The clinic was what brought the family together, when none of the McGavocks were sure how to handle the scandal of my mother's birth. Nana was the strongest witch in the family, the best healer in a bloodline that had always had healers in spades. Nana had organized the renovation of an old shearing barn into a sterile facility. She'd arranged for the beds, the medicinal herb garden out back, and the donation of supplies.

Instead of waiting for a situation to become so dire that they showed up at the McGavock farm at midnight, our neighbors could come to the clinic during office hours. At any given time, there were at least three McGavocks on hand to provide care, although I was the only licensed medical professional in the bunch—a fact we didn't quite broadcast to the agencies that governed health facilities. It was rare that they approved a form containing the phrase "we heal our patients with herbs and energy manipulation."

As a nurse practitioner, I loved working with my neighbors. I liked the fussy seniors with their imagined ailments, who were in reality visiting us after confession failed to provide them with the social contact they craved. I liked solving the real problems, soothing colicky infants and arthritic hands, and, yes, wiping up plain old colds. I loved knowing I was part of something. Even if I didn't fully accept my extra gifts, I liked knowing that I was drawing from the same source that had been easing the suffering in Kilcairy for ages in exchange for pennies and, occasionally, chickens and sheep.

Plainly put, the clinic was what sent me to Half-Moon Hollow. According to family legend, if I didn't find the four artifacts Nana had left to Gilbert Wainwright by the summer solstice, we would lose our magic. Even with my medical education behind us, the family would close the clinic. For years, the McGavock healers had been doing the near-impossible. My relatives wouldn't feel right continuing to operate without meeting those high expectations. Without affordable medical care nearby, our patients would put off the ninety-minute drive to the nearest doctor's office until minor problems became emergencies. Perfectly treatable illnesses would become big problems.

I would not let this happen to my neighbors or my family. These were the people who took me in when I arrived at the village gate, parentless and wary. They didn't care that my mother had caused no end of trouble in her short tenure there years before. I was one of their own.

Hearing Penny's voice brought on a wave of homesickness so fierce it made my teeth ache. I gave a brief update of my activities so far and promised I would e-mail a follow-up as soon as I met with Jane Jameson. After swearing that I would call if I needed help, I hung up. I opened my phone to dial Stephen's number but stopped myself. "Not the right time," I muttered. "Call when you get enough sleep to stop hallucinating mythical creatures . . . and you stop talking to yourself."

I rose again, staring out the window. I was awake now, awake enough to stock my kitchen, unpack my clothes, and start my life here. And before the next sunset, I would pay Jane Jameson's shop a visit.

In the light of late afternoon, I could see that Specialty Books was indeed located in a run-down neighborhood that seemed to be bouncing back slowly toward respectability. There was a consignment shop next door to the bookstore and a medical clinic down the street. The buildings looked as if they were being gradually rehabbed out of a state of ruin. It was difficult for me to understand—having lived for years in a country where the age of buildings was measured in centuries rather than decades—how Americans let their buildings fall to crap so quickly. Then again, considering Kentucky's heat and brain-softening humidity in flipping May, maybe the buildings simply melted.

I sat across the street from the shop in my newly acquired heap of a car, purchased with Iris Scanlon's help at Bardlow's Used Cars. The twenty-year-old Nissan featured four tires and a motor. There were no other features. It was a hunk of junk, but at seven hundred dollars, I couldn't afford to pass on the deal. Poor Miranda couldn't be saddled with driving me every time I needed to go into town.

Beyond purchasing transportation, I had not had a productive day. I woke up late, remembering that I needed to call Stephen, who was not pleased to be an "afterthought" in my travel agenda. But he was back to his same sweet self in a few moments, asking how I was sleeping, if I'd taken my vitamins, if my caseload was rewarding. He was always concerned about me pushing myself too hard, and the way he cared warmed my heart as it always did. Of course, our conversation was riddled with none-too-subtle hints that I should abandon this silly fellowship, come home, and discuss his proposal to move to Dublin. I pretended I was still travel-addled to avoid the topic. He ended the conversation with "Be sure to get enough rest." Which, in terms of a loved-up phone signoff, was extremely lacking, but still, he worried about me. And that was nice of him.

I wasn't sure what to do about this ambivalence I'd felt about calling Stephen since arriving in the Hollow. And even more shocking was that I'd barely devoted any time or thought to Stephen in the last few days. There was no bone-deep, visceral ache to keep me from sleeping without him or concentrating on the task at hand. And that was disturbing. I liked that "head over heels" feeling. Losing it felt like going through emotional withdrawal.

With guilt-inducing speed, my mind flashed to Jed, who was proving to be a considerate neighbor. He'd swept off my side of the porch and placed one of his rickety rocking chairs next to my front door. Apparently, he'd been given permission to fix my back patio, too, because this morning, he began breaking up the old one with a sledgehammer just as the sun came up. And he looked like Hephaestus's well-built, better-looking brother while doing it. That was not right.

Since I was most definitely awake and alert, I took a cup of tea out to him after changing into some shorts and completing several rounds of anti-morning-breath tactics. He seemed a little chagrined to see me, his face flushing an adorable pink as I approached with my carefully balanced tea mugs. "Mornin'," I called.

"Mornin'." He cleared his throat, wiping his forehead with a red bandana. "I, uh, should probably apologize for the other night. As pleasant as it was to have my hands full of naked new neighbor, my mama wouldn't have approved of the way I behaved. My only defense is that I'm not used to ladies introducin' themselves by climbin' me like a jungle gym . . . Well, that's not true; it does happen on occasion. But that's why I stay away from bachelorette parties nowadays."

"Are you blaming this on me? You groped my ass while I was terrified."

The worry clouding his expression faded away, shifting from tense to playfully indignant.

"It was a comforting grope," he protested.

"I don't think there's any such thing as a comforting grope."

Jed's lips twitched. "Clearly, you've never met a man who did it well."

I really wished this wasn't working on me. Smiling at lines this lame was demoralizing. "You know, you're not nearly as attractive as you think you are."

He snorted. "Well, that can't possibly be true."

It was just quick, cheeky conversation over tea, after which Jed went back to work, and I went upstairs to organize my meager belongings. But it had left me confused and twitchy. I was not a cheater. I was not the sort of woman who flirted with other men while her boyfriend waited at home. I was going to have to find a way to interact with Jed that didn't involve cheekiness. Or shirtlessness.

And so I'd walked up and down this generally abandoned street all afternoon, working off excess energy and gauging what I might be able to see through the front windows of Specialty Books. (Thanks to thick metal sunproof shades, nothing.) Whether the shop could be accessed from the back door during daytime hours, when there were no vampires lurking about. (No.) And if there was a position available at the consignment shop next door. (Also, no.)

Eventually, I'd returned to my car to wait for Jane Jameson and her staff to arrive. Like clockwork, as soon as the sun set over the horizon, a large black SUV pulled into the spot directly in front of the shop. Two women piled out, one a redhead, one a brunette, chatting animatedly as the brunette unlocked the heavy front door.

I waited, watching through the front windows as they moved about inside. A half hour passed, and I ambled casually across the street as if I hadn't stalked the place for most of the day. I wiped my sweating palms across my dark jeans and straightened the casual green top I'd chosen. Why was I so nervous all of a sudden? It wasn't as if I'd done anything wrong—yet. And it wasn't as if I needed the approval of a vampire shopkeeper, even though she could prove to be a great help or hindrance in accomplishing the task at hand.

I wasn't sure what I would say to Jane Jameson when I met her. It depended on what I found in her shop and the impression I got from her. If she seemed untrustworthy, I would pretend to be selling calendars for an orphans fund and run as if the devil was chasing me. If I got a good feeling from her, well, I hadn't worked that out just yet.

"Please stop giving yourself pep talks, Nola," I grumbled to myself. "Or your next stop will be a narrow window ledge."

Taking a deep breath, I opened the door, the tinkling of a little bell overhead announcing my arrival. This was my grandfather's shop? It looked so modern and . . . well, girlie.

The view from outside hadn't done the place justice. Specialty Books' decor was playful and whimsical, not at all what you would expect from a vampire-owned shop. The walls were painted a cheerful blue, with a sprinkle of twinkling silver stars. There were comfy purple chairs and café tables arranged around the room in little conversation groups. Little pewter fairies danced on the shelves around rings of marble eggs and geodes.

A large cabinet to the left of the register displayed a huge collection of ritual candles. Although they weren't the sort of candle I needed, I picked up a pink pillar marked "Romantic Love" and sniffed the wax. Rosemary and marjoram, not your usual rose-scented mix. I could appreciate that. Candle magic was one of the more approachable arenas of magic for a "dabbler." While most people were uncomfortable with rituals and poppets, they didn't see any harm in lighting a candle. You just chose a color based on your needs—red for passion, green for monetary gain or fertility—inscribed the candles according to what you wanted, and lit them up. But you had to be careful what you asked for. Spell-based love was notoriously fickle. Casting for financial gain often resulted in quick money fixes but long-term crises. As with most areas of the Craft, I didn't bother with it.

But I liked the smell of Nana's homemade candles, made with herbs and oils from her garden, and sometimes burned them just for the pleasure of the scent.

Most witches consecrated their own candles with special oils, herbal mixes designed for their particular purpose. But if you were dealing with novices, which this shop likely would, it made sense to sell candles made of prescented wax. And the candles seemed to be of high quality, good strong scents without being overpowering. Even if Jane Jameson wasn't a practitioner, she seemed to appreciate what her customers would want and tried to give them a little more than was expected. That made me smile.

Beyond the candles, the leaded glass and maple cupboard that held the cash register displayed a collection of ritual knives. My heart seemed to stutter a bit. Ritual knives? Athames, right up front? My hands shook slightly as I looked over the display. It couldn't be that simple, could it? I couldn't just walk into my grandfather's shop and find the first two items on my little shopping list.

I looked over the neatly arranged knives and candles. I'd only seen sketches of the athame in question—silver, with a black enamel handle, inlaid in perfect silver spirals, a large cloudy blue gemstone set in the center of the handle. The candle was thick, white, and round, standing nearly a foot tall, inscribed over and over with a distinctive double version of the Celtic knot.

My buoyant little bubble of hope popped and deflated as I scanned the items in the cabinet. The shop had a fine collection, but none of them matched the descriptions I'd been given.

Sighing, I wandered a bit around the neatly arranged bookshelves, running my fingers over the spines of the books. Jane Jameson had scattered large black-and-white framed photos on the walls, smiling people, happy to be together. Was this her family? There was a wedding picture of the tall brunette and a handsome dark-haired man, though they looked to be dressed like something out of a BBC Jane Austen production. A holiday picture involving some hideous sweaters. I recognized Mr. Wainwright in a few of the shots—much older than he was in Nana's photos, wizened to the point of being rather adorable, with a fringe of frazzled white hair and bifocals perched on top of his head. His face nearly crackled with laugh lines. He looked so happy, grinning broadly at the camera, particularly in the photos with the others. In one shot, near the register, the brunette had her arm slung around Mr. Wainwright's shoulders, both laughing at something behind the camera.

I didn't know how to feel about this. I'd pictured Mr. Wainwright as this lonely little hermit, living above his shop. And somehow, that's what I wanted. He'd left my Nana Fee alone all those years. Some part of me was unsure that I wanted him to be this happy. I'd never understood why Nana Fee never married Jimmy O'Shea, a charming bachelor who lived down the lane. He had been courting Nana Fee since they were in school. But she'd refused him, so many times. His failed proposals were the stuff of legend in Kilcairy.

The single most depressing thought I had was that Nana Fee had truly loved Mr. Wainwright. And all the while, he'd moved on. Had he ever thought of her after he returned to America? My Nana Fee was a good woman. She'd deserved second thoughts.

Not to mention that Mr. Wainwright seemed to have replaced me with taller, prettier granddaughter models, which was causing no small amount of latent jealousy.

Abandonment issues aside, I was comfortable here. There was a good energy in this building, as much as I hated to admit it. The rental may have been Mr. Wainwright's house, but this was his home.

Stepping closer to one of the shelves, I noticed a title. *Miss Manners' Guide to Undead Etiquette*? Chuckling, I continued down the shelf.

From Fangs to Fairy Folk: Unusual Creatures of Midwestern North America.

Have You Ever Seen a Dream Walking: A Beginner's Guide to Otherworldly Travel.

When, What, Witch, Were, and Why? The Five W's of Safe Interactions with the Paranormal.

I picked up a trade paperback, arching an eyebrow. "*Tuesdays with Morrie*?"

From the back of the store, I could feel a little mental tickle, a nudge at the back of my brain. Holy shit! A mind-reader? I wasn't prepared to deal with a mind-reader now! I stopped in my tracks, closing my eyes and sliding down what Nana would have called my "mental shield," picturing a rather large Jell-O mold forming around my head, protecting my brain from intruders.

Yes, it sounded silly. *It's my brain, and I'll protect it however I want.*

The tickle turned into an all-out poke. The slim brunette from the photos stepped out of some nook in the back, followed by an irritated-looking redhead. The brunette gave me a warm, if perplexed, smile. She was wearing jeans and a beautiful red silk blouse. The redhead, cool and elegant and far more wrinkle-free than anyone had a right to be at this time of night, was also featured heavily in the photo display. She was more subtly attired in a candy-floss-pink blouse and gray silk slacks.

"Can I help you find anything?" the brunette asked, her eyes narrowing at me slightly. She blinked a few times and shook her head, as if she had water in her ear.

"Just looking around," I said, holding up the paperback.

"This one again?" The brunette groaned, taking *Tuesdays with Morrie* back to the section marked "Fiction" and reshelving it. "I swear to you, Andrea, this book is possessed. It's like the stories about those porcelain dolls that move around while you sleep."

Andrea, the gorgeous redhead, rolled her eyes. "I'm ninety percent sure Dick moves that book every time he comes into the store, just to mess with you." She turned to me. "Jane has issues with dolls . . . and puppets . . . and clowns. We keep a list in the back, if you're interested."

Despite myself, I found myself snickering. I cleared my throat. "You have an interesting selection here. You stock ritual items?" I nodded toward the display cupboard.

The redhead frowned a bit. "Some. We're primarily a bookshop, but the previous owner had quite a collection, and we keep the athames and candles around as sort of a tip of the hat."

Jane stared at me, blinking as if she was having trouble concentrating.

"That's very sweet," I said, ignoring her blatant perusal and pointing to the little ownership plaque by the register. "So I take it you're Jane Jameson, proprietor?"

Andrea sighed. In a lifeless, resigned tone, she said, "I will never be as smart as Jane Jameson-Nightengale."

"I'm sorry?"

"She lost a bet," Jane said, grinning evilly at her companion. "Every time she hears my full name, she has to say that. Do not try to out-trivia me, Andrea. You have no one to blame but yourself. Which reminds me, I need to have that plaque updated."

"I could have sworn Nicholas Nickleby's sister was named Sarah," Andrea muttered.

"Her name was Kate," I said, just as Jane did.

"Oh, hell, there's two of you," Andrea groaned, marching behind the counter. "I'm making myself a bloodychino."

"Bloodychino?" I asked, turning toward Jane, who was giving me a speculative look.

"Hmm? Oh, yes, Andrea has figured out how to make coffee drinks more palatable for vampires."

I lifted my brows. Andrea was fair-skinned, but she didn't strike me as the vampire type. She was so put-together and polished. It was as if someone had vampirized a Kennedy, which was a terrifying thought. Was everyone who worked in this shop a vampire?

Upon closer inspection, Jane had that quiet, sturdy sort of beauty, with flyaway hair over bright hazel eyes and a wide, mischievous smile. She also had ink smeared across her cheek and a pencil holding up a rather haphazard bun. And she looked absolutely content about it. She was staring at me, and when I made eye contact, she seemed to give herself a little shake.

"Sorry. I don't think I caught your name."

"Nola Leary," I said. "I'm new in town. I heard this was the place to go for a good book."

Jane seemed to study me, scanning me from head to toe. Whatever she found seemed to bother her, given the way she kept squinting and working her jaw, as if to pop her ears. "Well, good obscure books, anyway."

Given Jane's scanning, I decided to hold off on any pointed questions about my grandfather. I ordered a coffee, bought a werewolf romance set in Alaska, and made myself comfortable. I sat at the bar and chatted with Andrea while customers filtered in. A book club met in the little circle of chairs near the back. Jane served coffee and sinfully good chocolate biscuits while they had a spirited discussion of the Black Dagger Brotherhood series.

I spent a good deal of time just looking around the shop. What had it looked like when my grandfather was alive? How had he run the store? Did this work make him happy? For the first time since I'd learned his name, I wished so much that Gilbert Wainwright was still alive.

I wished that Nana Fee hadn't been so stubborn about contacting him. I wished that she'd chosen a slightly more convenient baby daddy to bequeath our family legacy to.

Every time I looked at Jane, she was studying me, a little line of concentration marring her smooth white forehead. After about two hours of this studying/staring cycle, I decided I'd pushed the limits of normal customer loitering and hopped off my bar stool. Jane caught up to me before I reached the door, smiling brightly at the book club as she pulled me toward the shop's office.

I resisted, I pulled, but, well, she had all that vampire strength on her side. The office was small but tidy, with pale-yellow walls and a low shelf that ran the length of the room. Instead of books, the shelf displayed framed photos, running the gamut from old black-and-white shots to color photos of Jane with the man from the wedding photo. Jane wasn't hurting me, but her grip was awfully firm as she sat me down in her desk chair. I tried to push to my feet, but she shoved me back down, then pulled a bottle of synthetic blood out of the little fridge behind her mahogany desk. She stared me down while we waited for the bottle to finish heating in the mini-microwave.

Although her habit of mental poking was somewhat annoying, it was rather nice sitting there with Jane. She had no biological functions, therefore no ailments. Other than a constant, niggling thirst that manifested as a dry, buzzing sensation in the throat, I didn't feel anything from her. I seriously doubted she had any "I fell off my boyfriend" injuries I would have to diagnose.

"OK, why don't you just go ahead and tell me what it is you're trying to do. It will save us both some time and Tasering," she said casually.

"Beg pardon?"

She sat in her chair, her expression wary. "I'll tolerate a lot, lady, but I won't put up with people who try to pull one over on me. It's been done one too many times. Now, why are you so interested in Mr. Wainwright and his former shop? I can't get much from you; all I see is rolling green hills and old pictures of Mr. Wainwright. And an old lady with an Irish accent in a purple bathrobe. And then I just get a bunch of static, which is really annoying, by the way. It's like having nonstop radio feedback in my head."

I stared at her. So that explained the mental poking. Some vampires had special talents beyond their strength and speed, such as mind-reading, finding lost objects, or just being very good at board games. She said she hadn't seen much, but how could I know that? What should I tell her? I'd hoped to fly under the radar here in the Hollow, but having Jane's input could help me track down the Elements. But could I trust her? These items were valuable, if for no other reason than that they were incredibly old. What if she started looking for them on her own and cut me out? Mr. Wainwright had trusted her, but I didn't know her. And what was with the radio feedback noise? Was that because of Penny's misfired binding spell?

"OK, whatever you're thinking about, please stop," she

said, wincing. "We just went from radio static to that ear-splitting tone the Emergency Broadcast System uses."

During this internal rant, I'd forgotten about my mental Jell-O shield. I stared at her for a long moment, picturing the Jell-O solidifying around my head. The moment I felt it snap into place, Jane's tense face relaxed.

"OK, that's better. Whatever you did, just keep that in place, would you? You might as well tell me about whatever you're looking for. I'd like to help." Leaning her elbows on her desk, she asked, "Now, how do you know Mr. Wainwright?"

"He's a distant relation."

"I've met all of Mr. Wainwright's relations," Jane said stiffly. "He was the last living person in his family line. Now, try again."

"He visited Ireland about fifty years ago. He didn't know about his daughter, my mother. He wouldn't have known about me."

I felt another little mental nudge. Apparently, Jane was double-checking my story. I gave her an exasperated frown. She started when she realized I could feel it and returned a sheepish grin. "Force of habit." She scanned a row of framed photos on a shelf behind her desk, before selecting one. "Mr. Wainwright was in Ireland research-ing a family of were-deer. Was your grandma named Bridget?"

I shook my head and explained that although he'd been seeking were-creatures, Mr. Wainwright had been just as happy to discover my grandmother, a hereditary witch who healed the leg he'd shattered in a motorcycle accident near the family farm.

Mr. Wainwright saw enough to know that Nana Fee wasn't just a particularly skilled nurse. While she cared for him, she explained about the McGavock family's magical talent for healing and how we'd used it for generations. According to the journal, they talked about magical theory and books and films until the wee hours of the morning. And at some point, I'm assuming they did things that I'd rather not picture my grandmother doing, because nine months later, long after Mr. Wainwright had packed up and moved to seek a herd of weredeer rumored to be living near the shore, my mother was born.

I pulled Nana Fee's photos from my purse and slid them across her desk. Jane's eyes widened slightly, then she looked me over. She picked up one of the snugglier shots, her eyebrows raised. "Mr. Wainwright, you dog."

"My mother was the result of their . . ."

"Let's say 'union,' for both of our sakes," Jane suggested, holding up her hands in a defensive pose.

"All right, then. Nana Fee never contacted him to let him know about the baby. They weren't in love. She didn't want to hold him back from whomever he might meet that he would love."

"What about her?"

I shook my head. "Nana Fee never revealed her lover's name until just before she died, not even when my great-grandfather and great-uncles pressed and threatened and outright begged. She moved into the empty herder's cottage on the edge of the farm proper and went about making a life for her new baby. No simple feat for an unmarried twenty-year-old. But Nana was gifted, and frankly, I think the villagers were too afraid of losing her services as a healer to shun her completely. Likewise, her family loved her too much to send her away. She never married. She had her daughter, and she was happy with her choice."

Jane stared at me for a long while. "I want to believe you. The idea of Mr. Wainwright having a child and a grandchild makes me very happy. And I don't think you have any bad intentions here. But you need to understand that we've been burned before by someone claiming a connection to Mr. Wainwright. Do you mind if I ask what brings you here now, after all these years?"

I gave an equal measure of considerate staring. "That's a really long story, and I'd like to wait until your shop is cleared out."

Nodding, Jane blew out a breath and sank back into her chair. "Well, hell, I wish Mr. Wainwright had stayed around now."

I frowned. "I wish that he'd lived, too. I would have liked to meet him."

"Yeah, that's what I meant," she muttered.

4

Never overestimate any supernatural creature's sense of humor.

—*A Guide to Traversing the Supernatural Realm*

Andrea was staring at me. Hard.

I wouldn't say that my new vampire friends "detained" me, but it was made quite clear that any attempts to leave would not be met with friendly handshakes and an exchange of e-mail addresses. With the customers cleared out, I was sitting at the coffee bar, trying to suss out exactly how much I should tell them. Since they'd kept me from dinner, Jane was nice enough to provide me with something called "lemon bars," an odd cross between a biscuit and a custard pie. And Andrea was staring at me. It wasn't an angry stare. She seemed to be looking for coded messages in my eyelashes. I started to blink in odd patterns while I chewed on lemon bars, just to see what happened.

Nothing, just more staring.

"Should we wait for Dick?" Jane asked, pulling the "Closed" sign over the front door of the shop.

Andrea gave me a quick, furtive look. "Um, Dick has a business meeting. I'm not able to reach him."

"Why do the words 'business meeting' seem to be in unspoken subtext quotation marks?" I asked.

"My husband," Andrea told me, in a tone that brooked no further discussion. "You'll meet him later."

"All right, then."

Jane moved behind the bar as if she were going to make more coffee, until Andrea hopped over the counter with vampire speed and chased her away from the large, shiny cappuccino maker. Jane pouted a bit and plopped into the seat beside me. Andrea gave me a sweeping hand gesture and said, "Floor's all yours."

I straightened in my chair, clearing my throat. "'Once upon a time' is the best way to start, yes? Well, once upon a time, there was a happy little family in the wilds of Ireland, practicing what they called magic. For years and years, they kept the locals happy by caring for the sick, taking care of ailing livestock, and keeping the crops fertile. Even through the Inquisition and the witchcraft trials, the villagers kept peace with the family, because they needed them to prosper, and vice versa. You would think the lack of pitchfork-toting townsfolk would keep the family safe, but of course, in stories like these, there are always problems.

"It boiled down to a difference of opinion on magical policy. The family had always operated under the tenet of 'do not harm.' But a small branch of the family grew tired of being 'servants' to the locals. They argued that the family should take a firmer stance, domination instead of appeasement. They seemed to think that we should be leading the people around us, instead of working with them—through force, if necessary."

"Are you telling me that there's a real Voldemort?" Jane asked, what little color she had leeching from her face. Andrea smacked Jane's arm and rolled her eyes. Jane winced and cried. "What? It's a legitimate question!"

I chuckled despite myself. "These rebellious family members said that the witch who can't harm can't heal, that there has to be a balance of both. And unfortunately, this philosophy led to a few . . . well, let's call them magical amputations. This was unacceptable to the main contingent of McGavocks, and they asked these rogue relatives to leave.

"So that branch left the village and settled halfway across the country. Several of the witches married into the Kerrigans, a local family who raised their children according to a more strident magical philosophy. While the McGavocks flourished and enjoyed plentiful harvests and peace, the Kerrigan branch got more aggressive and bitter—although as a side note, they have made a considerable amount of money in the last century or so manufacturing small arms. Anyway, the Kerrigans went out looking for problems to 'solve' with their magic. Because, in their opinion, some people just needed smiting. And eventually, that included members of the McGavock family, which started a vicious cycle of retaliation and misinterpretation."

"It's like the magical Hatfields and McCoys," Andrea marveled.

"You're not entirely wrong," I admitted. "We lost people on both sides, to violence and curses. About three hundred years ago, the two matriarchs of the families met and agreed that matters had gone far enough. They selected four objects representing each of the elements and blessed them with magic from both sides. These objects, which they called the Elements, were scattered to the winds, given to strangers, sold to tinkers, that sort of thing. The matriarchs agreed that the family that found all four objects first would be able to bind the other branch."

"Like magical Pokémon?" Andrea asked.

"If I wasn't under an enormous amount of stress, I would find that funny," I assured her. "The potential of losing our magic was a considerable risk, a risk I can only imagine was inspired by desperation. It took decades, but we rounded up the Elements first and bound the Kerrigans from doing magical harm. For the most part, they're no more powerful than the average disenfranchised teenager who has seen *The Craft* once too often. The most they're able to pull off is a stirring of air, which, honestly, could be done with a strategically placed fan, so it's not terribly impressive. But every one hundred years, on the night of the summer solstice, the binding has to be repeated by the family's strongest witch. This leaves a small window of time in which the Kerrigans have the chance to obtain the objects and undo the binding, reversing it onto my family. They tried it once in the early 1900s, and my nana Fee's great-grandmother laid down a witchcraft bitch-slapping of epic proportions. I also hear there was a mighty non-magical slap involved. And now it's my generation's turn, and by some bizarre accident of birth, the so-called strongest witch in my family happens to be sitting here in front of you."

A Cheshire cat's smile split Jane's face. Andrea held up her hand and said, "No!"

"You don't even know what I was going to ask!" Jane huffed.

"Whatever juvenile, ill-conceived test of her abilities you were about to demand could only end in tears."

I stared at both of them. These were the people Mr. Wainwright had entrusted with his shop? They were the ones who were supposed to help me track down the Elements?

I was doomed.

"Sorry, Nola, you were saying?" Andrea asked, pouring me another cup of coffee.

"Under normal circumstances, the binding wouldn't be a problem," I said. "It's just a minor incantation spoken over the artifacts. Around the time Mr. Wainwright visited all those years ago, Nana got rather worried about an increase in Kerrigan-related violence. She saw that he was trustworthy, that he was devoted to the pursuit of knowledge. So she took the objects out of the family vault and entrusted them to his care. She thought they would be safer with him."

Both women winced, the corners of their mouths

drawing back sharply. Jane said, "She probably should have rethought that. I don't want to alarm you, but when I first got here, the shop looked like an episode of *Extreme Hoarders: Book Edition*."

"I have a basic idea of what I'm looking for. There are some old sketches. Why Nana Fee didn't think to take some pictures, I have no idea. But according to my family, she was incredibly secretive about the objects. She wouldn't show them to anyone, for fear of the infamous McGavock loose lips. In other words, my aunt Margaret."

"Quick question. Why the solstice?" Jane asked.

"Solstices are considered times of beginnings, endings, new cycles, so it made sense. And I guess no one wanted to travel to meet on the winter solstice."

Nodding, Jane pushed up from her chair and paced a bit, straightening a picture frame here, shelving a book there. Andrea seemed to understand that her employer's silence meant something, so, along with her, I waited patiently for the other vampire to speak. When she finally came to a stop, she said, "So, basically, you need to rifle through my stock and my records to determine if any of those objects are still in the store. And if they're not, you need to use any information you find here to try to track down where they went?"

I nodded. "Yes. Please."

Jane shrugged her shoulders. "OK."

"That's it?"

"Yes."

"No other questions?"

"No," Jane said, shaking her head. She stepped closer,

her eyes narrowing suddenly. "Understand that we will be monitoring what you do very carefully. You will not be given free access to the shop. You will not be given a key. And if you try to tell me how I should be running things, so help me God, I will—"

"Jane!" Andrea barked.

Jane cleared her throat, seemingly forcing herself to relax. "Sorry. One day, we will get you drunk and tell you about your great-uncle Emery." Andrea shuddered violently.

I did not quite know how to respond to that, so I said, "I'll start tomorrow."

I rolled into the driveway to find Jed frantically moving some tools into his part of the house. It was cloudy, the banks of wispy fog moving over the waxing moon in patches. Given the dim lighting, I wondered how he was able to see. I would have smashed my face into the porch steps by now.

Jed practically flinched when he saw my car, such as it was, pulling to a stop on the gravel. Irritation, fueled by the gnawing tension left behind when I bared my soul to the vampires, flared in my belly. Really? He wanted to avoid me that badly? The sight of my seminudity was so unappealing that he was eyeing the open front door with desperation?

That seemed like an overreaction.

I threw open the car door. As my sight adjusted to the scant light of the porch lamp, I watched his eyes dart from me to the sky and back again. He seemed skittish, like a colt not quite sure of his master's goodwill. His sandy hair fell over his eyes, giving him the perfect excuse for not looking up. A strange energy emanated from his entire body. A sort of restlessness of his cells, as if he was going to jump out of his skin at any moment. Was he on something? He seemed so healthy, too healthy to be a drug user. And his jumpy, erratic energy was different from that of my mother, who'd made enthusiastic use of every recreational substance she could get her hands on. His head snapped up, and he pulled an angry face, as if he could feel me staring at him.

"What?" he demanded, keeping a wary eye on the moon as the clouds slipped away. He was nearly flinching, as if he expected a slap instead of silvery light.

"Jed, is everything OK?" I asked, following him up the porch steps, under the protective shelter of the porch. The closer we moved to the house, the less agitated he seemed.

Once inside his front door, he said, "I'm sorry. I'm bein' rude. I've just had a long day. Work stuff. I was just about to warm up some chicken and dumplin's. How about you take over the stove while I take a shower? And then you can help me eat some of it?"

"You invite me to dinner, and I end up cooking? What sort of swindle is this?"

"You're not cookin', you're warmin' up," he told me, eyeing the leather portfolio in my hand with some interest before turning that handsome grin on me.

"And I can't use the microwave to do this?"

I was firmly antitechnology when it came to tea, but

I didn't see the point in dirtying up a bunch of dishes if I didn't have to.

Jed unbuttoned his shirt and tossed it into a little laundry room off the kitchen. Oh, come on, now. I was starting to think he was doing this to provoke me. "Mrs. Reilly's dumplin's have been known to explode when nuked."

I thought about the warmed-over chicken and rice casserole in my fridge and the prospects of trying to piece together a meal at this time of night. "Yes, if you explain to me what a dumplin' is."

He chuckled and dropped a heavy leather toolbelt near the front door. "You have your choice; you cook, or you eat dinner with someone smellin' like he's been diggin' ditches all day."

"Cooking sounds like the lesser of two evils," I said, shuddering.

I placed the sketches in a drawer in my own kitchen, peeled my contacts out of my dust-plagued eyes, then locked my front door before rejoining Jed in his kitchen. He was setting out a large pot, French bread, and butter on the counter.

"Next week, I'll invite you over to make me dinner," I muttered, feigning indignation and trying hard to ignore the way he was stretching his massive arms over his head, making his shirttail ride up. This just wasn't fair.

"Well, it would be the polite thing to do," he said, grinning at me while he kicked off his boots, and I was thankful that he at least left the jeans on. I opened the fridge, boggling at the sheer number of labeled Tupperware containers stacked inside. "Just keep stirrin'. You don't want it to stick."

"If you don't want to discuss your harem of church-lady caterers, can we talk about your tendency to strip in front of me?" I called after him. I dumped the congealed dumplings into a pot as he jogged up the stairs.

"Don't pretend you're not lookin'!" he called back.

I rolled my eyes but stirred as instructed. The food smelled delicious, particularly after I warmed up the loaf of crusty bread in the oven. Standing at the stove gave me time to look around Jed's side of the house, which was considerably more comfortable than my own. He'd painted the walls a light, creamy beige, making the rooms airy and bright. It was a vast improvement over the dark, cavelike spaces on my side. The polished living-room floor was covered with an extra-large blue rag rug. He'd added a few sturdy, no-nonsense pieces of furniture in each room, but there were few personal touches. No pictures, no knickknacks. Several large bookshelves flanked his windows. When I got closer, I could see that they were full of language guides. *Moon Phases, A Chinese to English Dictionary, Hieroglyphics, Translating Gaelic, The Dummy's Guide to Understanding Ancient Sanskrit.* The rooms told me very little about Jed as a person, other than that he had good color sense and hated reading subtitles in foreign-language movies. Or he'd bought a bunch of coffee-table books at a garage sale.

By the time Jed trotted down the steps, smelling pleasantly of Dial soap, I had the table set and the dumplings dished. I was bending over the oven to retrieve the bread when I heard, "This is why men like to watch women cook. It has nothin' to do with bein' sexist. It's the bendin' and liftin.'"

"Which is also sexist." I turned to offer a rude response, only to find him wearing another pair of arse-cupping jeans and a T-shirt that showcased his indecently large biceps. I was standing in the presence of living, breathing arm porn.

"Oh, come on!" I cried, throwing up my hands and nearly flinging the bread across the room.

"What?" he asked, crossing to the window and closing the curtains.

"You know what," I shot back. "When you go out and buy a shirt like that, do you actually calculate the number of bicep curls you'll have to perform in order to do it justice?"

"I don't work out that much," he said as he held my chair away from the table.

I sat down, glaring up at him. "Well, then clearly, you have discovered some sort of magic testosterone tree in the back garden."

"I can take it off if it bothers you," he offered, peeling the hem away from a tanned expanse of stomach.

Please, I prayed, *don't let there be such a thing as a magic testosterone tree.*

"Stop that!" I yelped, a laugh bursting from my chest as he dropped his shirt back into place. "Why do you think all situations can be improved by the removal of clothing?"

He snickered, taking his own seat and offering me a

slice of bread. "Well, first—nah, that's too easy. Anyway, I do it because it freaks you out, and that's pretty damned adorable."

"You are an altogether bizarre personality."

"Right back atcha, honey."

I giggled. I couldn't help it. This strange, thrown-together meal was the first opportunity I'd had to relax since I'd arrived in the States. And here was a beautiful, peculiar man sitting in front of me, who didn't know anything about me or my family or what we could do. I could be normal with him, or what seemed to pass for normal between the two of us. It was lovely.

"So, I noticed the quote-unquote 'car' in the driveway."

"Hey, it's transportation," I protested. "And when I find a job, it will get me there, so I will eventually be able to pay for an upgrade."

"What brings you down to the Hollow, if you don't mind my askin'?"

"I just needed a change of scenery. Too many northern winters," I lied smoothly. "What about you? How long have you lived here?"

"A couple of months," Jed said, taking a large bite of dumplings. "I'm from a little town in Tennessee, just a few hours' drive from here. I do carpentry work and general construction, especially in older buildings where the restoration work can be delicate. Jobs in my area were dryin' up. A contractor from the Hollow put an ad in the paper, lookin' for people who could handle that sort of work, so I moved. My boss, Sam, was hired to renovate this house. I needed a place to stay, so the owner agreed to give me a break on rent while we completed the work."

"What does your family think of your moving here?" I asked, trying to avoid questions about potentially angry girlfriends who might not appreciate his constant state of shirtlessness in my presence.

"They're not happy about it," he admitted. "We're pretty close-knit, and I'm the first one to move away in a long time. But it was just somethin' I had to do. You know?"

"Oddly enough, yes, I do," I said. "And it's nice here, so far. The people seem friendly. A little strange sometimes, but I think that's expected anytime you move somewhere new. That reminds me, have you seen anything weird around the house at night? Like a big dog in the back garden?"

A flicker of surprise warped his features for just a second, before he tamped it down. "No, nothing weird. Unless you count our neighbor Paul, who's built a full-size wrestling ring in his backyard. He and his friends have 'matches' on the weekends."

Well, that did qualify, I supposed. "Do they wear the spandex and tights?" I asked, struggling to keep a straight face.

Jed nodded. "If he invites you over this Saturday, just say no."

I shuddered, and we fell into companionable silence as we ate.

"So what's your deal?" he asked suddenly.

"Beg pardon?"

"Your deal," he said again. "Married? Boyfriend? Vow of celibacy?"

"Do you always pose personal questions so abruptly?"

"You get more honest answers that way."

"Boyfriend," I told him.

He nodded. "Is he gonna be movin' here anytime soon?"

I burst out laughing, picturing Stephen attending the monster-truck rally scheduled at the McLean County fairgrounds that weekend. As much as the "woo-woo supernatural shite" irked Stephen, his apprehension around my family had a lot to do with our "earthiness." Living in the Hollow would be the equivalent of a permanent migraine for Stephen. "No, I don't see him moving here."

Jed shrugged. "I give it six months."

I choked on a bite of bread and downed a large gulp of water to clear my throat. I spluttered. "What is wrong with you?"

"Long-distance relationships don't work. And you said yourself, you're makin' a life here, and you don't see this guy movin' out to the Hollow. So you either didn't think this move through, which is doubtful because you seem the type to think everything through. Or you did it on purpose, because you knew that movin' out here would eventually kill off the relationship. You broke up with him without havin' to be the bad guy."

I stared at him, my spoon frozen halfway to my mouth. "Are you on medications I should be aware of, or is this some sort of personality disorder at work?"

"Neither. I just don't like it when ladies use the long-distance boyfriend as a human shield," he retorted. "Why are you making that face?"

"I'm trying to determine whether this dinner is good enough to put up with your nonsense or if I should abandon my bowl and storm out."

He nodded and took another bite. "Come to a decision yet?"

"Curse Carol-Anne Reilly and her devil dumplings," I grumbled into my meal. Jed laughed. "But honestly, you can't say that sort of thing to people."

"Why the hell not?"

"The bounds of common courtesy?" I proposed. "Conversational filters that most people grasp by the time they're ten?"

"Your prim Yankee voice sayin' 'common courtesy' while you look over the top of your little wire-rim glasses is doing strange things to me," he said, grinning impishly. "Do you think you could put your hair up in a bun when you say that?"

"Of course." I sighed. "You have a librarian fetish."

He shook his head, all innocent brown eyes and choirboy smiles. "Not a fetish, more like a fascination. So what do you say?"

"I really don't want to ruin our burgeoning friendship by reacting honestly to that."

"Fair enough," he said, offering me another slice of bread and none too subtly moving the knife to his side of the table. "So where do you think you'll look for work?"

And that was the end of the confrontational portion of our conversation. Jed seemed to sense how far he could push me. All discussions of Stephen were off-limits from then on. We talked about his hometown of Hazeltine and about his family, which seemed almost as large and "colorful" as my own. I got the impression that there was a lot of information he was leaving out. That was fine, since I gave him a heavily edited version of my own childhood—growing up in Boston, the only child of Anna McGavock and her physician husband, moving in with my grandmother after my father died.

Jed was a good listener, although there was a lot I couldn't tell him. I could have said that my parents had divorced but not that when my dear departed mother met Martin Leary, an American medical student touring through Dublin, she assumed she would be marrying into money. In her mind, "doctor" equaled "rich," although Dad was traveling as cheaply as possible. Dad's parents, who had died when I was a baby, had saved for years to send him overseas as a graduation present.

Getting pregnant with me as quickly as possible seemed like the best way to secure her future, or so she thought. She wasn't counting on marrying a student who was working his way through medical school while bartending. Dad said the look on her face when he brought her home to his tiny walk-up apartment over a pizza shop had been priceless.

I couldn't tell Jed about my mother's meager magical gifts, how she saw them as a natural advantage over regular people. That she would take the neighbors' wives for their pin money by offering tarot readings, telling them what they wanted to hear, even if she saw trouble in the cards. I couldn't tell him about the irresponsible fertility rites, the love spells on Dad's coworkers, just for her own amusement, or the money spells my aunts and uncles were smart enough not to try that she did two or three times a year. Her "prayers" always created a wind-fall, but then we would end up with a major car repair or a cracked foundation at our new house or some disaster that sucked up whatever money she'd gained and then some. I couldn't tell him about her abandoning us, about the years of absence and that final explosive argument before she left for good. This was definitely not appropriate getting-to-know-you banter.

Clearly, being irritated and sharing personal history were not a good combination. I hadn't thought about my mother this much in months. But now that I knew a bit more about Nana Fee, it was ironic that my mother did just as Nana had, seducing the first American tourist she came across. Mother just did it a bit more permanently.

Dinner was followed by pecan pie, prepared by yet another church lady. I helped Jed clear the table and looked up at the clock on the microwave. How could it be eleven o'clock already? Between my confessions to Jane and Andrea and trying to keep up with Jed's abrupt directness, I was exhausted.

"Thank you for dinner," I said, moving toward the door. "It was an experience."

"Anytime," he said, throwing a dishtowel over his shoulder as he followed me through the living room. "I, uh, I'm sorry if I threw you with the questions about the boyfriend."

"Were there questions?" I chuckled, opening the door wide. The moon had risen, bright and full, casting silvered light across the dark expanse of lawn. "I thought it was mostly insulting assumptions and forecasts of impending doom."

"I did feed you," he noted, eyeing the door warily. He stepped back toward the kitchen. "That has to count for something."

"It does," I assured him. "Next time, I'll make dinner, so I can demand extremely personal information from you."

"Me?" he scoffed. "I'm an open book."

An open book who seemed to have some serious issues with being outdoors after dark. He seemed absolutely incapable of stepping closer to me as long as the front door was open. What was his issue? Was he phobic? Did he owe vampires money? I opened the door a bit wider, and he immediately took another step back.

"Somehow I don't think so. Good night," I said, slipping into the moonlight and closing the door behind me.

5

Dream journeys are rare and beautiful gifts. If you are blessed with a spirit guide, it's best not to sass him.

—Have You Ever Seen a Dream Walking:
A Beginner's Guide to Otherworldly Travel

The judgmental panda bear was not amused by my rich fantasy life.

I was in the middle of one of my usual "Daniel Craig is hypothermic and needs your body heat to survive" dreams when, suddenly, Daniel morphed into Jed. And in my subconscious, a low-core-temperature Jed is a randy Jed. Sadly, my neighbor and his pouty, slightly blue lips disappeared before things could get interesting. I was left wearing some strange, quilted clothing, walking up the foothills of a densely forested mountain. But instead of trees, I was carefully picking my way through bamboo stalks two and three stories high. The air was cool and fragrant with the green scent of growth and turned earth. To my left, a fat panda sat hunched against a rock, munching on a stalk of his favorite green treat and giving me a look that said, "Like you would have a shot with Daniel Craig, you silly twit."

"I thought panda bears were supposed to be all sweet and cuddly," I muttered, stepping carefully around an outcropping of jagged rock.

"In my experience, they can be nasty little sneaks," a slightly creaky voice said. My head snapped up, and I found a thin, elderly version of Mr. Wainwright sitting before me on the outcropping. He was sitting cross-legged, wearing the same sort of quilted pajama-style jacket and trousers I'd donned. "Especially if they think you have something edible on your person. Lost a pair of pants to a panda once. Lesson learned: do not keep beef jerky in your front pocket."

My jaw dropped, and my eyes flicked toward the panda, whose baleful expression now said, "Don't look at me. I'm only here for the buffet."

"What is this?" I whispered.

"This is a dream," he said, stretching a cool, dry hand toward mine. And when I was unable to respond, he shook it gently. "And I'm your grandfather, or at least, your subconscious's idea of what your grandfather would look and sound like. Can I just say it's wonderful to meet you? I have to say I'm a little surprised it took you this long to show up. But no matter, we're here now, and we can get to know each other under the watchful eye of that gluttonous panda."

"Mr. Wainwright? Really?"

"I never thought—I never dreamed I would have this

opportunity." As he smiled broadly, his eyes disappeared. "Do you think you could call me Grandpa?"

I shook my head. "No, I don't think I can," I said, my face still frozen in an expression of shock and confusion. "Can you tell me where you stashed the Elements, so I can pick them up and can go home?"

"No, I told you, I'm not really your grandfather. I'm a figment of your subconscious. I don't have any answers or information that you don't already know."

"That's supremely unhelpful."

Mr. Wainwright frowned. "Isn't there anything you'd like to ask me that's not related to the Elements?"

I stared at this sweet-faced old man with his conical straw hat. There were a lot of questions running through my head at the moment, most of them more hostile than I'd anticipated. How could he have abandoned my grandmother, who loved him? Did he realize how different my mother's life would have been—how different she would have been—if he'd stuck around? Did he really want to know me, or was this only his way of socializing now that he was dead?

I kind of wanted to slug him, which was just confirmation that the panda was right to judge me.

"No," I told him. "I didn't come here for a family reunion. I came here because Nana left the task to me. I didn't have a choice."

Mr. Wainwright eyed me speculatively. "Well, I see Fiona passed her obstinate nature on to you. Good for you, I suppose. I guess I wouldn't want you to make this too easy for me."

"What exactly is 'this'?" I asked, gesturing at the rural Chinese landscape.

"It's whatever you want it to be," he said. "It's your dream. It's your way of processing all of the information and emotions you're absorbing. Sometimes people know the answers to their own questions, but they're either unable or unwilling to express them."

"So you're my id's bitchy spokesman?"

"I'm not comfortable with that label," he said, wincing.

"Well, it's my label, and I'm sticking with it."

Mr. Wainwright lifted a bushy gray eyebrow. "Just to annoy me?" I nodded. "Good girl. Now, since you seem single-minded in your line of conversation, I have a piece of advice for you."

"What's that?"

He grinned impishly, hopped to his feet with surprising spryness, and slung a heavy rucksack over his shoulder. "You're trusting the right people, for the most part."

I turned toward the panda, who was shaking his head at me. "What?" I cried. "How has this been helpful?"

"And Nola?" Mr. Wainwright was already yards away, but I could hear him clear as a bell—an advantage, I supposed, to dream logic. He winked at me. "We always have a choice, dear."

True to her word, the moment Jane opened the shop the next night, she welcomed me into the storeroom and helped me sort through the last of Mr. Wainwright's dirty, much-abused cardboard boxes. Jane told me of the first night she wandered into the shop after a disastrous flirtation with a career in telemarketing. The store was crowded with messy, decrepit bookshelves, one of which nearly collapsed on top of Jane. The former librarian was in physical pain at the sight of such disorder and began organizing the titles. Mr. Wainwright found her like that, surrounded by neat stacks of books, and hired her as his assistant on the spot.

"Until I was hired, the storeroom was like that village in *Brigadoon*. Wainwright would find something—a book or artifact—and shove it in here, and then a bookshelf would fall against the door, and he would lose track of it for a decade or so. I'm sorry. I wish I could remember more details of what I sorted through, but to be honest, the weeks after your grandfather's death were a blur. I could have chucked Excalibur into the recycling bin, and I wouldn't have noticed," Jane said, carefully lifting what looked like a mummified monkey's paw from its cardboard tomb. My shoulders slumped as we sifted through the remaining boxes and found nothing.

"Why did you keep these, if you don't mind my asking? There doesn't seem to be much of value here," I said.

"Something in that box over there bit Jane's hand, so she gave up and declared that she was done," Andrea said from the doorway of the storeroom.

I dropped the box I was holding.

Jane winced, grabbing at her head. "Nola! Jell-O shield! Panic makes your brain sound like a car alarm!"

"There are spiders in these boxes?"

"She didn't say spiders," Jane muttered. "Your grandfather collected a lot of bizarre artifacts. Some of them were 'interactive.'"

Jane didn't look up at me while she said this. In fact, she hadn't looked me in the eye since I'd arrived earlier in the evening. I couldn't help but notice that she and Andrea were a bit off-kilter. They kept glancing at the door and then at the clock, and they seemed to be having quiet, quick arguments whenever I was out of earshot. And every time I tried to ask them what was wrong, they asked me random questions about magic. Did I have a familiar? (No, but I did have a lovely tank full of tropical fish.) Could I really cast a love spell? (Yes, but relationships based on love potions or spells were notoriously fickle and required nearly constant contact with the subject to maintain the "thrall" of the caster.) What did witches do on Halloween? (In my case, stayed home and tried to avoid the costume party at my uncle Jack's.)

The interrogation was becoming rather annoying, a compounding factor on top of my "panda dream" tension. I didn't know what to make of my grandfather's presence in my dreams. It had been easier, I supposed, to think of Mr. Wainwright in terms of his faded photographic image. Talking to him, having him ask me to call him Grandpa, was a strange mixture of getting what I'd wanted for years—a grandfather—and confronting feelings I wasn't quite ready for.

With the storeroom search at a standstill, Jane sent me out to my car to retrieve the sketches of the Elements while she made me some tea. I was in such a tizzy to start the search that I'd left them in my passenger seat. When I returned, a tall, handsome man with dirty-blond hair was standing behind the bar, making some notes in a ledger.

"Well, hello there," the man drawled. "Dick Cheney. What can I do for you this fine evening?"

Dick Cheney, my landlord. It was odd that I hadn't seen him enter the shop, but Jane said she and the rest of the staff often used the back entrance. I didn't particularly care for Mr. Cheney's impish grin or his insinuating tone, which, now that I knew Jed, I recognized as a classic flirtatious opening. Considering that he was married to Andrea, I did not find this flattering in the least. He seemed so . . . not quite trustworthy. The tacky "Come to the Dark Side—We Have Cookies" T-shirt, the shaggy hair, the smirk.

"I'm Nola Leary. Jane's helping me with some research," I said coolly. "And if you have time, I'd like to talk to you about a not-so-small pest-control issue at the Wainwright house."

"Ah, the new tenant," Mr. Cheney said, a wide, friendly grin breaking through that smirk. He set his bottle of synthetic blood aside, took my hand in his, and pressed it between his cool ones. "A marked improvement over your predecessor. Cranky old woman with a lot of cats. Awfully fond of mothballs."

"Is that what the smell is?" I asked as Jane and Andrea emerged from the back of the shop. Both stopped in their tracks and exchanged significant glances when they saw that I was talking to Dick. What was with the two of them? Was I in danger? Was Mr. Cheney in the habit of dragging renters into dark alleys and making snacks of them?

"Um, Dick—" Andrea started, but Jane stopped her.

"Iris said you were from Ireland!" Dick exclaimed, the soul of cheerfulness. "I only detect the slightest bit of an accent, but it's there."

There was a pregnant pause. Andrea clapped a hand over her face. "He's trying to come up with a good Lucky Charms joke and/or nickname."

"Leprechauns are also an option," Jane told me.

I gave the vampire my sweetest smile. "Mr. Cheney, are you interested in a debilitating crotch injury?"

He shook his head emphatically. "No."

"Then you should probably keep those jokes to yourself."

Dick beamed at his wife. "I like her."

Andrea sighed. "Dick, sweetheart, Nola claims to be Mr. Wainwright's granddaughter."

The news seemed somehow to stun my landlord. He nodded slowly, his face sagging and blank, as if he'd just been struck by a frying pan. "Well, of course, she is." And suddenly, the vampire threw his arms around me in a spine-cracking hug and lifted me off the floor. "Oh." He sighed, giving me a long squeeze. "I am so happy to meet you."

"Can't . . . breathe," I wheezed into his shoulder, and he loosened his grip immediately.

"I can't tell you what a surprise this is," he said, a pleased smile breaking through the shell-shocked expression. "I thought Gilbert was the last, you see. But now here you are, and you're just so beautiful. Look at you!" He took my face between his hands and scrunched up my cheeks. "You—you've got Gilbert's eyes. And his nose! Look at that, Andi! She has his nose! Isn't she gorgeous?"

Jane cleared her throat. "Dick?"

Dick gave me an apologetic smile. "Crossing a line?"

I nodded, my eyes wide and alarmed, like one of those upsetting anime characters.

"Dick and Mr. Wainwright were really close," Andrea told me, carefully removing Dick's hand from my face.

Dick looked in Jane's direction and seemed to be thinking furiously at her, which was rather funny to watch. Dick would squint. Jane would make a vague gesture. Dick would squint even harder. Jane would shrug.

Meanwhile, Andrea retrieved the sleeve of sketches I'd dropped on the floor during Dick's hugging tirade. "These are beautiful, Nola. Even if they weren't of historical value, your nana had a wonderful eye for detail." She carefully shuffled through the old papers. "So each of the artifacts represents one of the four elements?" she asked, while Jane tried to give a Dick a brief summary of why I was in the Hollow and what the hell Andrea was talking about.

I took out the sketch of the object Nana had called "Sea," which was your typical silver bell, dotted with intricate Celtic designs that spiraled out like ripples on the surface of water. Nana described it as heavy and "flat," meaning it never quite rang with the delicate, resonant note it was meant to have. The next sketch showed a circular clay altar plaque, "Earth," which was vaguely shaped like an acorn. Then there was "Air," the long, thin ritual knife used to direct energy flowing through the air. Ritual knives were also associated with fire, but I suppose my ancestors wanted to be as obvious as possible by using a magically preserved candle—"Flame"—to represent fire.

Jane joined us, poring over the sketches to see if she recognized anything. When her gaze landed on the rendering of Flame, she gasped. "Oh, no!" She clapped her hands over her face and began cursing vehemently.

"What?" I cried. "Please don't tell me you threw it out, Jane."

"No, nothing like that," she promised, looking up at me with a distinct grimace. "I may have given that candle to my mama for Mother's Day last year."

Dick broke out of his near-catatonic staring-at-me state and let out a loud, barking laugh. "You regifted your mama something from the shop for Mother's Day?"

"No one ever gave it to me as a gift; therefore, it is not a regift."

"You didn't pay for it!" Andrea protested.

"Did you see the storeroom before I got here?" Jane demanded. "Trust me, I paid for it."

"Can we focus on the fact that Jane's mother may be using my family's magical heritage to decorate her guest bath? We need to get to your parents' house before she decides to light it!"

There was a long pause, followed by Jane and Andrea laughing hysterically.

"I'm glad you two find this so amusing."

"No, no." Andrea giggled, wiping at her eyes. "Jane's mama would never put something that Jane gave her as a gift in a public area of the house. Someone might *see* it!"

"Skeptical Nola is skeptical." Jane snickered. She was very good at reading human facial expressions. "Trust me, I couldn't have put it in a safer place."

When we arrived at Jane's parents' perfect little brick house, a woman with a pert brown bob practically ran out the front door to greet us. I was introduced to Sherry Jameson and immediately smothered with hugs, which were only half as intrusive as the hugs Dick had showered on me when I attempted to leave the shop. Andrea threatened to "tranq-dart" him when he insisted that he would come with us, that he didn't want to let me out of his sight just yet.

I thought she was kidding right until the moment Jane's handsome husband, Gabriel, showed up at the shop and asked why Andrea had wanted their tranq gun. Personally, I was curious as to *why* Jane and Gabriel had their own tranq gun.

Mrs. Jameson was so pleased to meet a young person she could feed that she sat me down at the table and heated up a plateful of chicken pot pie. Mr. Jameson, a quiet, academic sort of man, sequestered himself against the counter, by the stove, and shared commiserating glances with his daughter. There was something off about the way he was standing. He seemed a bit pale, as if he wasn't at his full strength.

"Is your father all right?" I whispered.

"He's had that same pinched expression on his face ever since he retired. He spends a lot of time at home." Jane sent a significant look at her mother.

"Come on, now, Nola, take a great big bite!" Mrs. Jameson chirped, sliding the plate in front me with near-maniacal glee.

"I actually had a really large lunch, Mrs. Jameson, and I don't know if I'm hungry enough to eat again—"

"Oh, shush, you need some meat on your bones," Mrs. Jameson said, nudging the plate toward me.

If you can hear me right now, Jane, I am going to smack you later, I thought while glaring at her. And despite a clear expression of discomfort on her face, she was still smirking. She could hear me.

Stop smiling like that, or I'll do the Emergency Broadcast System beep again.

Jane's lips twitched, but she said nothing. Still, it was very convenient having a mind-reader around. It was far more efficient than text-messaging.

"Would you like some sweet tea, Nola?"

I sighed in relief. "I'd love a good cup of tea, Mrs. Jameson, thank you."

Mrs. Jameson fairly flitted to the refrigerator, pulled out a tall pitcher of brownish liquid, and poured a tall glass over ice. I tamped down the small flare of disappointment. I'd forgotten that hot tea wasn't exactly the beverage of choice in Kentucky. It was no problem, really. My dad had enjoyed the odd iced tea now and then, so I accepted it graciously when Mrs. Jameson handed me the glass. I took a long sip, and a sickeningly sweet, near-syrup concoction flooded my mouth, making me choke and sputter.

Mrs. Jameson fussed and cooed, patting me on the back while I coughed.

"What is this?" I wheezed.

"Ah!" Jane said, pouring me a glass of water. "I forgot to warn you about sweet tea. It's basically liquid cotton candy, equal parts sugar and tea. You'll get used to it."

I shook my head, wiping my mouth with my napkin. "No, I don't think I will."

"I'm so sorry, honey," Mrs. Jameson fretted. "From now on, you should probably stick with unsweet."

"I think I'll stick with coffee," I muttered.

My attention was drawn to Mr. Jameson, whose shoulders seemed hunched while he stirred a pan of sauce on the stove. I could sense a painful red buzzing somewhere in the vicinity of his head. A nagging, throbbing ache. It was almost powerful enough to distract me from the burgeoning tooth decay in my own mouth.

Can we ask your mother about the candle before she feeds me something that causes violent hives or vomiting? I thought to Jane.

Jane cleared her throat and seemed to compose the question carefully in her head before speaking. "Mama, do you remember the candle I gave you for Mother's Day? It was a white candle with pretty symbols carved into the wax? Do you know where it is?"

Jane's mother blanched but managed to cover it quickly. She chuckled, waving in an offhand manner. "Oh, well, I'm sure it's around here somewhere. Why don't you give me a few days to look around, and I'll call you when I find it?"

"Actually, Mrs. Jameson, it's really important for us to find it straightaway," I said. "Would you mind if we looked for it?"

"Oh, honey, I can't imagine where it is," she protested.

"Mama, it's important."

Mr. Jameson cleared his throat. Mrs. Jameson snapped her head up to glare at him. "Sherry, you need to show them the closet," Mr. Jameson told her.

"John, no!"

"Sherry," he said in a stern, warning tone.

Mrs. Jameson sighed. "Come with me, girls." She pulled me gently from my chair and led us toward the stairs. "John, stir those peas," she called over her shoulder.

Mrs. Jameson led us upstairs, past an impeccably decorated master bedroom done in mauves and creams, into a smaller guest bedroom. Jane informed me that this had been her room until she left for college. Her mother had only removed Jane's boy-band posters and unicorn figurines the year before when Jane got married.

"Now, Jane, I don't want you to think I don't appreciate the things that you give me," her mother said, standing as a human shield between us and Jane's old closet.

"Just open the door, Mama."

Mrs. Jameson cringed as she turned the doorknob. The closet was packed floor to ceiling with various gift boxes. It was like that scene from *Raiders of the Lost Ark,* where the Ark of the Covenant was packed away with rows and rows of other priceless treasures. Jane was looking at the preserved remains of every gift-giving occasion since her elementary-school days.

And given the way her mouth was hanging open, I don't think that made her very happy.

"We just have different tastes in décor," Mrs. Jameson offered weakly.

Instead of throwing a box-pitching tantrum, as I expected, Jane burst out laughing. She bent at the waist and guffawed like a deranged hyena. "When I think of all the time I spent in Pier One!" she exclaimed. "You're on a strict diet of gift cards from now on."

Mrs. Jameson bit her lip and nodded. "I think that would be best."

"Why not just sell them at a garage sale? Or give them away?" Jane demanded.

"Well, that would be rude!" Mrs. Jameson cried.

"Bet you don't put Jenny's gifts in a closet," Jane muttered.

"Don't start that," her mother warned her.

"OK, so are these in chronological order?" Jane sighed. "If I dig deep enough, will I find the clay handprint I made for you in kindergarten?"

Since Jane seemed to find the situation funny, Mrs. Jameson had relaxed a bit and stopped trying to wedge herself between us and her trove of rejected treasures.

"No, there's no order to it. It was sort of like playing Jenga with gift boxes. I just stacked it however it would fit."

Jane shot an amused glance my way and rolled up her sleeves. "I hope you like tedious stacking games, Nola."

I bloody hated Jenga.

We'd been through nearly every box in the closet, and so far, we'd found tea towels, sets of bath products in various smells, and a frightening number of angel figurines.

"I thought you collected these!" Jane exclaimed, chucking another reject over her shoulder.

"No, your grandmother used to give them to me every year, and I didn't have the heart to tell her that I found them downright creepy," Mrs. Jameson confessed with a shudder. "And then you girls got to the age when you started buying us gifts, and you sort of latched onto the angels. And by then, it was too late."

"I need to take a break," Jane muttered. "Mama, do you still keep the—"

"Faux Type O, red label, in the vegetable crisper," Mrs. Jameson assured her. "Nola, can I get you something?"

"More water, please?" I asked, smiling despite the fact that my teeth still tingled a bit from the sucrose assault on my dental enamel.

I heard their voices fade as they descended the stairs. I flopped back onto the guest bed and closed my eyes. My head felt cloudy, and my nose itched from all the dust in the closet. How in the bloody hell did I get here? I wondered. Lying in some strangers' guest room, rifling through their unwanted knickknacks. Just a few weeks ago, I'd had a normal life with a normal job. Well, semi-normal. I was able to pretend well enough that Stephen hadn't run for the hills.

Aw, hellfire, I'd forgotten to call Stephen again.

He was going to be furious with me! And rightly so. I'd been in town for days, and I had only called him once. Even after my shirtless Neanderthal neighbor mocked our relationship, I'd just sloughed off to bed and fallen asleep. This did not bode well. It boded . . . very badly.

I was starting to realize how little Stephen really fit into my life. I tried so hard to compartmentalize our time together so it wouldn't overlap with my family life. That wasn't healthy. I could imagine Jed sitting around with my uncles at the Black Sheep, sharing horrid, manly stories. I could see him charming my aunts in a way that didn't make them feel condescended to. I shook off these thoughts, as they were neither likely nor productive. Nor were they fair to Stephen.

Squirming on the purple quilted bedspread, I dug my cell phone out of my jacket pocket and dialed Stephen's number. It was ungodly early by Dublin time, but I thought perhaps I could blame exhaustion and time difference for my lack of communication. I sat up slowly as the call went to voice mail. I yawned loudly and tried to sound addled and sleepy. It wasn't that much of a stretch.

"Hullo, darling, I'm sorry I haven't called already. I think I'm still a bit wiped out . . ." I trailed off as I caught sight of a box at the very back of the top shelf. It was about the size of a shoe box and just the right size for the candle with a swatch of Specialty Books's signature blue wrapping tissue. Realizing that this soundless voice-mail message was costing me a fortune, I hastily added, "I'll call again soon. Love you. Bye-bye!"

Unfortunately, Americans believed in building impossibly high closet shelves. Even with the help of a small stepping stool, I had to lean a bit on the shelf to brace myself up. It was at times like this I wished I was telekinetic instead of a witch. Then again, I already had the unstable mother. I didn't want to risk falling into *Carrie* territory.

No, wait, I was falling anyway.

"Yipe!" I shouted as my weight shifted forward. Yanking the shelf down with my weight, I tumbled off the stool and onto the piles of boxes, crushing several of them as I landed. Just when I thought I could sit up, the box I was reaching for slid off the tilted shelf and landed on my head. "Ow."

"Are you OK?" Jane cried, running back into the room.

"I'm so sorry," I groaned. "I believe I broke a couple of things."

"Really, it's not a problem," Mrs. Jameson told me, helping me to my feet. "It gives me an excuse to throw them out."

"Clearly," muttered Jane.

The box that had clobbered me was half open on the floor, the blue tissue spilling over the lid. I crouched over the box, removing the lid carefully. Inside was a long, creamy-white pillar candle, carved with ancient symbols for fire. I checked it over carefully. But I could tell from the pleasant, nearly electric hum I felt coming from the wax that this was the candle in question.

"I found it!" I exclaimed, beaming up at my companions.

I hugged the box to my chest as Jane and Sherry Jameson clapped and cheered for me. I felt like crying and laughing and screaming all at the same time. It was such a relief to know that I was one-quarter of the way to my goal, that the Kerrigans were that much farther away from it. And I'd done it without spending any of the buy money, leaving me that much more to work with for the other three.

Suddenly, the goal of finding all four objects didn't seem so impossible. It was a bit like fishing. You got one little taste of success and lost all perspective regarding the amount of time or frustration that had led you there. I couldn't wait to get back to the shop and look for the others.

"I'm very happy for you," Jane told me, throwing an arm around my shoulder.

"Mrs. Jameson, I'm going to have to take this candle away from you."

Jane snorted. "Mama, if you let Nola have this candle, I will forget all about the Closet of Misfit Gifts. Also, I will write the remaining thank-you notes for the wedding gifts."

Mrs. Jameson cried, "You haven't finished all the thank-you notes yet?"

"Mama." Jane's face was passive as she nodded her head toward the mountain of unappreciated presents.

Mrs. Jameson sighed. "Done." She turned on me. "Now, Nola, are you still hungry? Because I have some leftover pot pie, smothered pork chops, smoked chicken, Salisbury steak, and some other goodies in the fridge. Would you like me to fix you a plate? Or I can just make up a little leftover care package to take home!"

I shot a frantic glance Jane, thinking, *Jane, your mother seems to think I'm some sort of goose for the gorge. Could you please tell her that your dad is suffering from a serious toothache? He's trying to ignore it, but he could end up needing a root canal if he doesn't get it treated. It might distract her enough to get me out of here.*

"That's what that is?" she whispered, while her mother rattled on.

Jane frowned at me, arching an eyebrow. I added silently, *I'll explain later.*

"Actually, Mama, I was hoping to talk to Daddy," Jane said. "I noticed he was awfully pale earlier, and he wasn't eating. Has he said anything about his teeth?"

Mrs. Jameson fell on the information like a bloodhound on scent. "No, is he all right? Is this something you picked up using your . . ." Jane's mother paused and made a face that was half squinting, half constipation.

Jane studied the expression for a moment longer than necessary, I would think. It seemed "Funny Faces with Sherry Jameson" amused her. Finally, she said, "Oh, yes, the mind-reading thing. That's right. That's how I picked it up. And he's trying to hide it from you, hoping it will go away on its own."

"That man." Mrs. Jameson sighed. "I swear, you'd think

he would be more mature about something like going to the dentist. I had two babies, including Jane and her big ol' pumpkin head, without drugs, and you didn't hear me complaining." She took a deep breath and called, "John, I need to talk to you!"

"You complain about that all the time!" Jane exclaimed as she followed her down the stairs. "Otherwise, you wouldn't have already come up with the phrase 'Jane and her big ol' pumpkin head.'"

While Mrs. Jameson started in on poor Mr. Jameson and his dental phobias, Jane turned on me. "I hope we just threw my dad under the bus for a good reason."

"I think your mother not smothering me with Southern cuisine is an excellent reason for your dad to get the dental attention he needs."

"You're going to explain that later," she insisted. "All I could hear him thinking was that his drink was 'too damn cold' but if he said anything, my mom would fuss at him. You owe information, witch."

"Oh, yes, 'cause psychic powers are clearly something you're uncomfortable with, mind-reader."

"Leprechaun," she shot back.

"Cow."

6

When you are invited to partake in the rituals of supernatural creatures, it's best to follow the lead of the closest human—if that human seems sane and somewhat likeable.

—Miss Manners' Guide to Undead Etiquette

Using Jane's computer, I sent a short e-mail to Penny reporting on my progress: "Fire's lit. Update soon."

The problem was that now that I had one of the Elements, I didn't have a place to store it safely. My uncle Jack had built a canny little storage cabinet to keep the items "clean" once they'd been found and purified. The cabinet had arrived in Seamus's shipment earlier that afternoon, along with what Penny called an "emergency witch kit": an athame, incense burners, candles in various colors, tiny vials of herbal oils, a silver altar pentacle, and a carved wooden box (also Jack's handiwork) that doubled as an altar.

But I didn't have a safe location to store said cabinet. Considering its vulnerabilities to local angry wildlife, I didn't think I could trust the house.

Jane's shop had an old-fashioned heavy-duty safe.

After I completed my "dance of joy" in her mother's guest room, she offered to let me store my things there. Although I'd only known her a few days, I trusted Jane. She didn't have to tell me her mother had the candle. She seemed content helping me complete a task that was important to me, because I would have been important to Mr. Wainwright.

Penny had highlighted purification rituals in *Witchcraft for Total Morons* for me, which I would have found insulting if not for the fact that it had so many helpful illustrations. After enclosing the candle in its compartment full of sea salt and securing the cabinet in Jane's safe—along with Nana's sketches—I went back to the Wainwright house and collapsed.

Jed's windows were dark, and for that I was grateful. The man was an unpredictable, sexy storm cloud. I never knew if he was going to make pretty shapes or rain all over my parade.

I climbed into my bed and slept soundly for the first time in weeks, without benefit of herbal tea or soothing pharmaceuticals. I slept deep and dreamless for about an hour before my mobile rang. Grumbling murderous threats against humanity at large, I slapped my hand around on my nightstand until I closed my fingers around my phone.

"Jane, if this is you, I am not responsible for your father's dental bills. I merely pointed out a problem. I never told your mother to take him to an all-night dentist," I growled into the phone.

"Darling, how are you? Why are you threatening random callers? Is it that awful and primitive there?"

I bolted upright. "Stephen?"

"Don't sound so surprised. I have left messages."

"You have no idea how good it is to hear your voice." I sighed. "I'm sorry I haven't called, Stephen. I just didn't expect the travel to be so hard on me," I said, allowing a yawn to escape through and emphasize my "delicate" constitution. "Delicate" was a far more desirable quality in a girlfriend than "deceitful *and* forgets to call."

"Well, you are a bit of a homebody," he said. "So how are things there in the wilds of America? Do you need me to send you anything? Soap? Magazines? Cigarettes?"

"Stephen, I'm overseas, not in prison! And Boston is one of the largest cities in the country," I reminded him. Of course, I wasn't actually staying in Boston, but that was beside the point. "And it's very pleasant, actually. Warm, nice people, interesting tea."

"Interesting as in strangely prepared, or interesting as in that time your aunt Maisie gave me tea that made me see butterflies fluttering out of my own arse?"

I suppressed a giggle. Aunt Maisie had never warmed to Stephen, but she did love creative herbalism.

"The first one," I said, remembering that Bostonians had probably never heard of sweet tea. "They steep it right in the cups, can you imagine?"

"Well?" he said expectantly.

"Well?"

"Don't you miss me?"

"Of course I do," I protested. "I've just been busy. That's all. New apartment, new job, remembering to drive on the right side of the road."

Again, I judiciously edited, because I didn't think Stephen would be impressed by my finding long-lost vampire relatives or making friends with mercurial construction workers.

"Well, I miss you terribly," he said. "Nothing is fun without you. There's no one to put her ice-cold feet on the backs of my legs while I'm sleeping. No one keeps up a steady stream of trivia and interesting facts while I'm watching films. I actually had to resort to watching a DVD with the director's commentary. It was demoralizing. And the bread! I'm wasting the heels of my bread loaves shamelessly without you around to toast them."

A pleased, sweet warmth flooded my chest. Stephen was always noticing little things like that, which gave him considerable skill when it came to date planning. He knew exactly how far to push the gooshy romantic factor before it became too saccharine to tolerate.

"The heels make the best toast," I told him, my tone soft and amused. "The outside crust forms a protective layer to hold more jam."

"When are you coming home?" he asked.

"Soon," I promised him. "It's just a few months; it will be up before you know it."

"It's not fair to put our lives on hold for that long, Nola. I'm holding off on this move for you, you know."

"I didn't ask you to do that," I reminded him. "You

could pick a flat, move in, and get settled. I'll meet you there when I'm done."

"I don't want to make those decisions without you there. What if I pick the wrong place? I don't know why this fellowship was necessary." He sniffed. "You could have earned the same credentials here at home if you'd only looked. Every time we get close to moving in together, you find some way to sabotage it. Or your family does. I'm starting to think you're happy living in that backward little town."

"Well, it's not without its charms," I insisted. "Once you get past the driving issue and the strange tea. I told you, the people are quite nice here."

"I was talking about Kilcairy."

"Well, why wouldn't I want to live there? My whole family is there."

"Yes, *your family*," he said in a tone he might have used if he were saying, "Yes, *toe fungus*." It was difficult for Stephen to understand how large families worked. He saw his own parents for holidays and the occasional fly-by dinners, and that was the extent of their relationship. He had no siblings, no uncles or aunts or cousins, and his grandparents died when he was in primary school. It was easy to understand why my family overwhelmed him. Although it didn't hurt my feelings any less.

"Stephen, I need to get off the phone. It's late here, and I need to get some sleep. I have work tomorrow."

"Fine," he said with a sigh. "Fine. I'll call you in a few days. I love you."

"Me, too." I rolled over, tucking my pillow over my

chin, feeling vaguely sick to my stomach. How had the conversation gone from sweet to sour so quickly? How could Stephen seem to know me so well one minute and then not at all the next? How was I going to fix this? I couldn't go running back home, abandoning a sacred duty because my boyfriend was peeved.

Stephen was just going to have to deal with it.

I awoke to the sounds of pounding and hammering on the walls outside my bedroom. I started awake, rolled out of bed, and landed on my face. "Oh, what in the—" After stumbling to my feet, I shoved the window sash up and shoved my head outside. Men on ladders seemed to be ripping off the wooden siding in places, while others were climbing on the roof and tossing damaged shingles into the yard, where yet another man scooped them up and threw them onto an open-top wagon. At the edge of the yard, I could see a woman (who I later learned was the much-beloved Iris Scanlon) directing the delivery of several hydrangeas and rosebushes.

Jed was on the ladder just a few feet from my window, yanking a rotten shingle away from its moorings. And, of course, he was shirtless, his tanned skin glistening as he moved under the morning sun.

So far, this was a mixed bag in terms of a wake-up call.

"What in bleeding hell is going on?" I called to him.

He grinned brightly . . . or perhaps he was amused by my bed hair. "Mornin'! I don't know what you said to Mr. Cheney, but he had Sam hire four new daytime guys to come out and put a rush job on the renovations.

He said, and I quote, 'Fix everythin' up. Make it nice for her. No detail is too small. And don't skimp on the flowers in the front flower beds.' Also, there's an exterminator coming out this afternoon. And if you don't mind, I'm gonna come in tomorrow and paint the downstairs rooms. Dick said you can stay with him for a few days if the fumes bother you."

"Huh." It was a brilliant, eloquent response, I know. Dick had explained the night before that Mr. Wainwright had sold his family home sometime in the 1970s and, for convenience's sake, moved into the apartment above his shop. The new owners had divided it into apartments and neglected the house terribly before selling out to Dick the year before. Because of what Dick would only call "Jane problems," he hadn't had time to fix it up before now. Why the sudden rush after meeting me? And what did he mean, I could stay with him and Andrea if the paint fumes were too much? I barely knew these people. Why would I impose on them in that way?

If I'd had the energy, I would have whacked my head against the window frame.

"You know he's married, right?" Jed said.

"No—I mean, yes. I've met his wife. I just guess I've made a good impression on him, is all," I said, frowning while I recalled his inappropriately friendly greeting at the shop.

First, the hugs and face squeezing, and now this? What was with Dick Cheney? Had I developed my very own vampire stalker? I wondered if it was a good idea to stay in this house. Dick had keys. As my landlord, he had to give me notice before he entered, but I doubted fair rental laws would do much to protect me from an obsessive vampire. I would have to talk to Jane about this.

And if I ever woke up to find him watching me sleep, like that creepy Edward What's-his-name, I would not be responsible for my actions.

"Did you meet him wearing just a towel, too?" Jed asked sourly, yanking me out of my reverie. When I shot him a filthy look, he appeared vaguely contrite and added, "Well, you got me job security for the next few months, so thanks for that. You go on back inside; we'll be done with the loudest work by the end of tomorrow."

Mumbling indignantly, I backed into my room, searching for my robe. There was a scraping noise against the outside wall and a series of metallic clangs. Suddenly, a disembodied tanned hand slipped through the open window and dropped a small sprig with a fist-sized cluster of hydrangea blossoms onto the sill, then disappeared. I laughed, retrieved the offering from the sunny sill, and pressed my face into the velvety blue petals.

Construction time estimates being what they were, the job went on for weeks. I would wake up in the early morning to the sounds of men scraping off the outer layer of the house. Before leaving for Jane's shop, I'd make breakfast and coffee, which I magnanimously offered the work crew, since they were decent enough not to look into my windows while I was in the house. Then again, Jed did imply that Dick had threatened the crew within an inch of their "miserable mortal lives" if they were anything less than courtly.

After a week or so, I established a sort of schedule. Each day, I would spend the afternoon searching through Jane's shop and sales records, looking for any sign of the Elements, under the watchful eye of Zeb Lavelle, Jane's best friend since childhood. Jane made this concession after a few nights of my research being interrupted by customers who thought I worked at the shop. Using the store's off hours allowed me to concentrate on my task, and I didn't mind Zeb serving as my babysitter. He was a kindergarten teacher, after all, and seemed fit for the task. When he wasn't reading comics or sorting through school-supply catalogues, he offered me random, sometimes sensible tips on how to survive interactions with supernatural forces. His first and foremost tip: walk softly and carry an econo-sized can of vampire pepper spray.

Whether that pepper spray was used against loved ones and acquaintances was a matter of discretion, he told me.

Strangely enough, Jane happened to have a large rolling whiteboard, like the sort used on *Law & Order,* in the stockroom. I used to it record any potentially germane receipts, addresses, or notations I found in Gilbert Wainwright's records. Well, officially, I didn't find any of those things, but Iris was impressed with the way I divided the board into four sections and created a graph for cross-referencing. Iris was a girl who appreciated the obsessive need for order.

By turns, Dick, Andrea, Jane, and sometimes Jane's husband, Gabriel, or Zeb's wife, Jolene, would rotate into the shop to inquire about my day's progress. Zeb was sunny and adorable, like a man-sized Labrador puppy. Jolene, on the other hand, was intensely beautiful and seemed surrounded by this odd crackling energy, as if she was always on the verge of becoming something else. When I turned my powers to that mystery, all I could discern in her was an all-consuming, gnawing hunger.

They were an odd and motley crew of humans, vampires, and whatever Jolene was, but all very nice people. And they didn't seem fazed by the odd and urgent circumstances of my situation. Apparently, they had considerable experience with the odd and urgent. They simply divided the store by sections, rolled up their sleeves, and helped me sort through the stock.

I discovered an unexpected joy in spending time with Jane and Andrea. It was a bit like spending time with Penny, only they had less tact and restraint, if that was possible. They had an unnatural obsession with seeing me do magic and wouldn't accept my "wonky powers" excuse or the fact that I didn't want to do damage to the shop. I was considering pulling a rabbit out of a hat just to get them off of my back.

Both women were slightly left of center, looking at the world from a skewed but extremely funny perspective. They didn't fall into hysterics when there were obstacles or emergencies. They cracked a joke, made a plan, and moved on. And after Jane dropped by my house to deliver a casserole from her mother—ogling Jed shamelessly, I might add—teasing me about my comely shirtless neighbor became a regular source of humor for them.

They loved fiercely, from their spouses to their friends, and yes, even Jamie, the irritatingly beautiful teenage boy Jane had been forced to turn the previous year. Once you were accepted into the "pack," you were in for life, and woe betide the fool who crossed you. Zeb told me it was a bit like the Mafia, only with snarky insults instead of cement shoes.

Now that I'd found one of the Elements, a bit of the pressure I was under eased. I was far more aware of my surroundings, the sultry heat of late afternoons, the sunshine. Clothes that I had previously worn once, on holiday in Spain—tank tops, sundresses, light sweaters, and sandals—were now the main staple of my wardrobe. My skin, previously an insistent milky white, was now lightly tanned. I made sure to get some out-of-doors time each day to recharge my internal batteries with vitamin D. But I missed the wind. While I enjoyed the novelty of the heat, I missed the constant stirring of air, the whisper of the sea.

Still, I felt at home. Most people were friendly, if slightly baffled by my accent. I found myself having to repeat things, not because they didn't understand me but because they wanted to hear me say certain phrases with my inability to properly pronounce Rs. And the more time I spent around vampires, the more I could focus on fine-tuning which parts of my brain interacted with living tissue in other people. With Dick or Jane, I could feel parts of my mind reaching out to their energetic bodies, seeking out injuries and illness. When I felt my mind "pinging" off empty space, I found I was able to turn off the reaching. It made going to Walmart on crowded Saturday mornings a lot less painful.

Jed was an unabashed morning person, singing off-key country songs and letting the sunlight soak into his skin as he worked. He continued his cheerful, ladder-bound flirtations at my bedroom window each morning, usually teasing me about my "epic" case of bedhead or asking me about my agenda for the day. I would have taken offense, if not for the sprigs of hydrangea that found their way onto my windowsill, wrapped in a damp napkin and foil and tied with a white ribbon. I kept the bouquets on my nightstand, in a sweet blue pressed-glass bud vase I'd found in a thrift store down the street from Specialty Books. By the third bouquet, I was beginning to worry for our poor hydrangea bushes and their impending baldness. But they were still lush with blooms. I did notice that our neighbors' bushes were looking a little patchy.

It's the thought that counts.

Late nights were blissful experiments in prolonged sleep. I was so used to being on call, just in case some medical emergency came up, I hadn't realized I was down to four or five hours of sleep per night. Here, I outfitted my bed in thin summer-weight quilts and lush cotton sheets. I built myself a veritable fort out of pillows, fluffing them into the most comfortable configuration possible before entering a semicomatose state.

It was odd, living for myself for the first time. For years, I'd taken care of Nana and run the clinic. I never realized how much energy I expended diagnosing people—intentionally or otherwise—and the additional stress of keeping the clinic running. In her e-mails, Penny kept me updated on patients and assured me that everyone was fine, the clinic was running smoothly, and it was her turn to take care of things for a while. Still, it pricked my conscience not to be there helping her.

At this point, who knew when I'd be returning? After another week of searching, I'd found nary a clue to the other three Elements. I'd composed a list of pawn shops and noted which were closest to the bookstore. I'd contacted the list of buyers Jane described as Gilbert Wainwright's "whales," but they seemed interested primarily in books. We hadn't managed to find the ledgers that listed any specific items sold, although it seemed unlikely that Mr. Wainwright would not have kept a record of such sales. The early success of finding the candle had made me cocky, I suppose. Now my lack of progress was a bit unsettling.

Dick's strange attentions were another sore point. I'd tried to talk to Jane about the renovations to my house and whether Dick's intentions were honorable. But she only assured me that I was perfectly safe, but she'd promised Dick that she'd let him talk to me himself. I found this to be cryptic and unhelpful.

If I were home, I would have taken a walk down to the cliffs to clear my head with cold sea air and blessed quiet. In the Hollow, I had only the somewhat decrepit area surrounding the shop. So I wandered the streets in the late-afternoon sun, worrying over my problems like a surreal jigsaw puzzle.

What was I doing wrong? Did the magical world smell the stink of desperation on me? Generations before me had found the Elements. But they'd searched as pilgrims, with open, curious hearts. Was I so slow to progress because I was too businesslike in the approach? Or should I be even less sentimental? Approach the issue like one of those crime procedural programs with spreadsheets and forensics and such?

Early one evening, after I cleared the block, I turned right and slowed my pace. The light was warm and pleasant. And the fresh, book-dust-free outdoors was a definite plus. I couldn't say I was comfortable with the neighborhood, all darkened storefronts and abandoned streets, but I was wearing sturdy shoes and jeans. I could outrun a bloody cheetah if startled properly.

It was interesting to see how the dividing line of commercial success ended at Paxton Avenue. On the opposite side of the intersection, I could see a prosperous town square, with restaurants and quaint little shops. But in this area, there was little bustling besides Jane's shop. The consignment shop on Prescott was flanked by a defunct comic-book store and an empty barber shop. The one business with lights blazing was a corner store that looked as if it had once been an eyewear shop. It now displayed a sign advertising "Half-Moon Hollow Community Walk-In Clinic. Services Free."

I walked closer to the door, where a small yellowed

sign read, "Help Wanted," in bold red letters. I pushed the door open to find . . . complete feckin' chaos. I was bombarded by the sensations of nausea and chills rolling off of the crowded waiting room. There were women lined up five deep at the registration desk, with no nurse to check them in. Children sat slumped against chairs lining the walls, listless and pale, scratching halfheartedly at reddish spots on their arms and legs. One boy had stuffed his head into the wastebasket and was puking for all he was worth. It took me a minute of deep breathing to keep myself from rushing to the wastebasket and tossing my own breakfast.

It was after eight P.M. Every single child in this room had chicken pox. Everybody was talking at once, demanding answers, demanding that someone come out and help them. And no one seemed to be in charge.

Finally, a situation I was prepared for.

"Right." I rolled up my sleeves and slipped in past the door marked "Staff Only."

Down the hall, I could hear an older man's voice as he told a Mrs. Loomis to keep Tyler hydrated and covered in calamine lotion and to give him a cool bath if his fever spiked. I assumed this was the doctor, so at least we had that going for us. I rummaged through the mess of papers until I found a sign-in sheet. At the sight of someone who seemed to know what was happening, the would-be patients and their mothers surged forward, surrounding me like something out of an itchy zombie movie.

"Excuse me," I called over the din of questions and complaints. "Excuse me, if everybody would please just—" No one was listening to me. They were too busy attempting to storm the registration desk. Finally, I yelled, "Oy!" over the noise. "Oy! If everybody would just shut it for a moment and line up like good boys and girls, we will be able to get everybody signed up to see the doctor as quickly as possible. Now, if you haven't filled out an intake form, I suggest you do so right now."

For a moment, everybody just stared at me as if I were speaking Greek.

And then one mother handed her son off to a woman I assumed was his grandmother, marched over to a desk behind me, and found some clipboards. Two more mothers searched through their enormous purses until they found ink pens and distributed them to the others. Eventually, a single-file line was formed, and I managed to determine which kids were worst off. Every time a patient emerged from the doctor's office, I sent another kid down the hall.

This was a different, more frustrating experience than working in my clinic. Despite cousin Ralph's illegal efforts, I wasn't licensed in the state of Kentucky and couldn't practice there. I wasn't covered by the clinic's malpractice insurance. So I could not ethically make any sort of judgment calls regarding patients. I couldn't so much as slap a Band-Aid on a boo-boo. I could, however, place my hands over some of the lesser cases' foreheads when their parents registered them, and if their fevers happened to drop before they went back to the exam room, what a wonderful coincidence that would be.

Eventually, the waiting-room crowd dwindled to a

half-dozen children. A frazzled-looking elderly man in a white coat wandered behind the registration desk. Well, his coat was white once upon a time. There was a distinct orangey splash across the breast pocket, almost obscuring the swirly embroidery that read, "R. Hackett, MD."

The good doctor was what Penny would have called a silver fox, or he would have been, if he'd had a full head of hair. He had a perfectly trimmed salt-and-pepper Van Dyke and a head as bald as an egg. He was wrinkled and wizened but cute as a button, with steely-gray eyes and a tanned face with distinct laugh lines.

Dr. Hackett's eyes narrowed when he saw me sitting behind the desk, sorting the various reports into piles. "Who the hell are you?"

Maybe those weren't laugh lines.

"Nola," I said, reaching out to shake his hand. "Leary. I am a nurse practitioner, and I run a small family clinic in my hometown. I'm here on an extended visit. But I know how to move people through a waiting room. You were drowning. I threw you a lifeline. You're welcome."

Dr. Hackett cast a glance around the desk and scowled. "Did you move things?"

"Yes," I said, looking around at the neat stacks of files and papers. "Lots of them."

He frowned at me. "Are you mentally unstable, a drug user, a gossip, or looking for a senior-citizen sugar daddy to keep you in spray tanning and designer purses?"

"No, to all of those," I said, shaking my head.

"We haven't been open this late in ten years, but one

of the local day cares had a chicken-pox outbreak like a biblical plague. I've been on my feet for sixteen hours, and I'm too damn old for that, let me tell you. We normally open at eight A.M. and close at five P.M. Does that work for you?"

"Uh, sure."

"I'll pay you. It won't be much. We're funded through donations from different civic groups, but the budget does provide a small stipend for clerical support. In the future, try not to move things without asking first," he griped, and called for his next patient.

Did he just hire me? Did I even want to work here? Would I treat patients, or would I stick to administrative work? What would my hours be? Would it interfere with my search for the Elements? Exactly how much was not much in terms of payment?

"Don't you want to see some references?" I asked as he moved down the hall. "Some identification? Anything?"

"We'll get to it later," he said, waving me off.

I sat back in the half-padded office chair, which was apparently mine now.

"First, Jane falls into her job at the bookshop, and now, this," I muttered. "Doesn't *anyone* do job interviews in this town?"

7

No happy story has ever included the words "Ouija board."

—*A Guide to Traversing the Supernatural Realm*

Although I was sweaty, disheveled, and drained, I was serenely happy as Miranda's car rolled up the driveway to the Victorian just before one A.M. I'd stayed at the clinic long after the last patient had been released, clearing off the front desk and putting the waiting room back to rights. Dr. Hackett had given me keys after I filled out my employment paperwork. After informing me that everything valuable or prescribable had been locked up tight and that this was a test of my character, he marched out the front door at midnight.

And then, because I'd left my car keys on the counter in the bookshop and was embarrassed to admit such a blunder to an exhausted Dr. Hackett, I'd called Miranda. To my surprise, my favorite chauffeur to the undead was already awake. She'd done the "lost keys/embarrassing emergency walk of shame" enough times that she was happy to help out another damsel in frequent distress.

"You're just lucky I keep vampire hours," she told me.

"And that Collin is in the middle of a History Channel marathon on the War of 1812 on his TiVo. I love him dearly, but I will use any excuse to get out of watching that."

"I am ever so grateful to serve as that excuse," I told her, closing my eyes and resting my head against the seat rest.

My bones ached. My feet were screaming. There were substances I preferred not to think about on my clothes. And I was dozing off in the front seat of Miranda's SUV. All I wanted to do was shower and crawl into bed.

"Wow," I heard Miranda say from the driver seat. I opened my eyes and saw her staring through the windshield, her expression one of delighted awe.

My own mouth fell open in astonishment. It was the first time I'd seen the house in its fully refurbished state. My home looked like something out of a fairy tale. The siding had been replaced and painted a fresh, vibrant yellow that shone in the weak light of the fingernail moon. The roof had been reshingled. The porch had been painted to match the trim. Dick's work crews had added flower boxes to the railing, bursting with a profusion of pansies in yellow, purple, and white.

I knew about the changes to the interior. My rooms had been painted a cheerful pale pink. The dark wood and gothic wall sconces had been replaced with what Andrea called comfy farmhouse chic. The huge bank of cabinets in the kitchen was gone, and in its place was an old-fashioned tin-front pie safe. The appliances were new, and the tub upstairs no longer threatened to fall through the ceiling. The remaining cabinets had been painted white and artistically distressed. I'd drawn the line at Dick buying me new bedroom furniture. I was truly frightened by the prospect of what he would choose.

I climbed out of the car, marveling at the changes Jed's crew had made. "Thanks, Miranda!"

"No problem, babe," she called. "There's a whole series of specials on the Spanish American War next week. Call anytime."

I waved at her as she backed out of the driveway, then returned to staring at the house in the moonlight.

"You know, you keep your mouth open like that, you're gonna catch mosquitoes."

My jaw snapped shut. I turned to find Jed, wearing an actual shirt *with sleeves,* standing in his front door.

"I thought that was flies."

He smirked. "Not around here."

"You do beautiful work," I told him. "It's just gorgeous altogether."

"Thanks," he said, his smile boyish and pleased as we circled each other. "We're finished here and movin' on to Dick's house. Andrea saw some of the things Sam did here and wants them for their house, too. It's roofin' tomorrow, which means an early start before the hottest part of the day. It's a shame. I liked being able to take my coffee breaks in my own kitchen. So what have you been up to? I haven't seen you in a few days."

"I accidentally started a new job tonight."

He frowned. "Accidentally?"

"It was totally unintentional. I fell right into it."

"Oh, honey, you didn't answer one of those ads on Craigslist, did you?" he said, his eyes wide and intentionally shocked.

"Hey, the nice man in the unmarked panel van said the nudity will be tasteful!" I exclaimed, making him laugh.

"Well, congratulations on your new Internet porn job," he said. "Do you want to come over for dinner tomorrow night to celebrate?"

"I have plans tomorrow night."

I really did have plans. I had to retrieve my car keys and make up for lost research time. But he didn't need to know that.

"Plans." He frowned. "Like a date? So the very serious boyfriend crashed and burned already?"

I had to bite my lip to keep from smiling. Why would he be worrying over whether I was dating? Unless . . . "You like me!"

"Me? Like you?" He shook his head. "Can't prove it."

"You *like* like me," I singsonged.

"Now you're just being ridiculous," he said, scowling as he stepped forward, trapping me between his body and the wall. I could smell that forest-and-field scent rolling off of him, and the heat of his skin made me feel as if his hands were rubbing against my arms. He bent his face toward mine, and warm, minty breath feathered over my cheeks. "If I *like* liked you, trust me, you would know it."

My eyes locked with his, light meeting dark, and

I couldn't move. This was completely unfair. He was a human thought scrambler, sent to make me lose all semblance of dignity. His lips were just a few heartbeats away from mine.

"I don't have a date. I'm working," I told him softly. Sorting through the contents of an occult shop to find magical knickknacks could be considered working, right?

The crescent moon rose slowly over his shoulder, giving him a faint halo around his shadow-cast face. I shivered. He looked down at me for a long, silent moment. I could feel his breath moving against my cheek like a caress. I honestly thought he was going to kiss me. And then he gave me one of those warm molasses smiles. "Well, good luck to you."

He stepped away and sauntered back to his door. He knew what he was doing, walking like that. It was patently unfair to leave a girl high and not quite dry and then walk away with his buns twitching under skintight denim. I called after him. "Thanks."

He waved his hand over his shoulder without even looking back at me.

Completely. Unfair.

Over the next week or so, I fell into a routine. I worked at the clinic each day until five and then researched at the shop until just before sunset to avoid uncomfortable interactions with certain vampire landlords. Then I hightailed it home, leaving Jane detailed notes on what I'd searched through that day and any materials I'd taken home for the night. Occasionally, Jolene would drag me out of the shop to Southern Comforts, the vampire-friendly restaurant she managed with her friend, chef Tess Maitland. Jolene was apparently worried that I wasn't getting enough smoked pork in my diet. I'd discovered that this was a grave concern for Kentuckians.

I enjoyed working at the clinic. I'd tamed the chaos of the front desk and organized the patient records into a more user-friendly configuration. I wore scrubs for the first time since nursing school, as Dr. Hackett didn't believe jeans were a professional look for a medical setting. I had to pass a background check, which was disturbingly easy considering that I hadn't lived in the country for more than ten years.

I explained my dilemma to Dr. Hackett, and he helped me apply for the paperwork I would need in order to help people rather than just run the office. Until my papers came through, I would not be responsible for patient care. It was just too risky. In the meantime, he was happy to listen to my "instincts" about a patient's condition based on my observations and the intake questionnaires. After hearing him referring to some of his contemporaries as hippies, I decided not to bring up my diagnostic abilities. But if I noticed something about a patient, say, black radiating pain flaring out from his stomach, I would advise Dr. Hackett that the patient was most likely suffering an ulcer.

It was a little bit of a relief, not being entirely responsible for treatment. And I found I had a talent for the administrative duties that I wasn't allowed to do back home.

After hearing so many "free clinic" jokes over the years, I expected to see nothing but patients with questionable rashes. But each day was much like the first: sick kids and overwhelmed adults. There were a lot of young mothers with children who didn't have health insurance. And seniors who couldn't afford to see doctors without the free services Dr. Hackett provided. Like any other doctor, he had "regular" patients he saw frequently, and their files were kept in a special filing cabinet separate from those of the walk-in patients. It was a sad commentary on the state of the health-care system, but I was glad that the patients were getting the help they needed.

The job was tiring, and Dr. Hackett was right when he'd told me he wouldn't be able to pay me much. But it was rewarding, and it was nice to take my mind off of the Elements for a few hours each day.

I arrived home around the same time Jed did nearly every evening. Sometimes he was waiting on the porch with a beer for each of us. (I didn't have the heart to tell him that we would call that stuff water back home.) Other times, we just had some brief conversation about the house or work before retiring to separate corners. He was always flirty and mildly inappropriate, but he never took it past that level. He moved in close but didn't touch beyond the occasional casual brush of the arm. He spent half of our conversations staring at my mouth but never so much as kissed me on the cheek.

And it was driving me bloody insane.

Jed was an enigma. He was a prime specimen, but he never dated. He was clearly intelligent, although he tried to play it down with Southern-fried, aw-shucks-ma'am charm. He was friendly and warm, and then, when he decided our conversation was over, he ran. What sort of man flirted like that and then managed to turn it off completely and walk away? Was there something wrong with me? Was I too much of a Yankee? The wrong size? The wrong gender? Was he doing this on purpose? And if he was, was he aware that he was the biggest tease in the world? Was he trying to drive me round the twist?

I knew this wasn't really my problem. I had more pressing matters to worry about. It was a waste of time to spend my nights wondering what the hell was going on inside Jed's head. His dense, beautiful head.

One not-so-special evening, I was searching through Jane's sales records from two years ago and found a thread of old ritual items sold to a collector in upstate New York that looked promising. Gabriel was hanging another photo on the wall, a shot of a Halloween party in which Jane and Tess Maitland were dressed as Elvira and Wonder Woman, respectively. The Mistress of the Dark herself sat discussing new titles at the coffee counter with Andrea. Dick was absent. The girls claimed he was on another business trip, but given the way Jane's mouth quivered when she said it, it seemed a little suspicious.

Neither Jane nor Andrea was thrilled with the news about my hiring at the clinic. The idea of my working seemed to make Jane feel guilty. She twisted a tea towel between her hands and shot Gabriel distressed looks as I described my evening at the clinic. "You've got too much on your plate already, Nola. What if I gave you an allowance from your fair share of the shop?"

"I can't take money from you, Jane."

Jane scoffed. "Why not? This is money I wouldn't have had without Mr. Wainwright leaving me the shop. And if he'd known about you, I'm sure he would have wanted you to have a stake in the store. I thought about it when your great-uncle Emery came to town, but he was a gigantic douchebag."

"You mentioned him before," I said as Andrea's lips peeled back from her teeth in a growl. And after hearing Jane's succinct explanation of my great-uncle's time in the Hollow, I couldn't blame her. The moment Emery had rolled into town, he'd started sifting through the stock, stalking Andrea, and generally annoying the hell out of Jane. They'd found later that he was a mole sent by another vampire trying to steal an important book from Jane's collection. This vampire had turned him in exchange for his service, and he had kidnapped Andrea and turned her against her will. Jane had taken great pleasure in turning Emery over to the Council for punishment.

"Hell, if that was the precedent set, I'm surprised you let me through the shop door."

Jane gave a sincere shudder, her mouth crimped into an expression of distaste. "The point is, you're here doing something I'm sure Mr. Wainwright would have wanted you to do. There's no way I'm going to let you spend valuable time waiting tables when you could be looking for these artifact thingies."

"I'm working at a medical clinic. I'm hardly slinging drinks," I protested.

Jane gave me an expression she called the "stink-eye." I returned it with the bitch-brow. And we sat back and let the two expressions battle it out.

"What do we do now?" Andrea whispered to Gabriel.

"Stay still and try not to attract their attention?" Gabriel whispered back.

Eventually, Jane won the staring contest, because I'm pretty sure she never had to blink. I hated to admit it, but Jane had a point. I wouldn't be making much at the clinic. In fact, I *would* make more money waiting tables, but it made me feel better to know that I was doing something I was (sort of) qualified for, and I was helping people. Also, it gave me something to think about besides the search. It couldn't be healthy for me to obsess over it every minute of the day.

But I knew I would probably have to get another part-time job, in addition to the clinic, to make ends meet. It would be terribly convenient to spend those working hours here in Jane's shop. I blew out a breath and thought about what Nana Fee would say. McGavocks had their pride. But if she thought that my pride was keeping me from fulfilling my purpose, she would probably whack me one with her walking stick and tell me to stop behaving like the back end of a mule.

I growled in defeat, holding up one hand and giving her a stern glare. "Agreed, but I'm keeping my job at the clinic and you're not *giving* me anything. I'm *earning* a wage. I don't know what I'll do for you, but it will be an honest day's work."

"OK, I hereby appoint you director of magical artifact location." Jane shook my hand, her tone prim.

She gave me a "job" doing exactly what I was doing anyway. "You're a smart-ass, Jane Jameson."

I barely noticed Andrea's grumbled "I will never be as smart as Jane Jameson-Nightengale" from the end of the bar.

"See, you're adjusting to the corporate culture already," Gabriel said brightly, tossing me a midnight-blue Specialty Books T-shirt.

"I'm glad we have that settled." I sighed, leaning back in my chair. Jane gave my shoulder a little squeeze and handed me a cup of chamomile tea. "But it doesn't get me any closer to finding the other Elements. And I'm running out of places in the shop to look."

"Well, I've been meaning to talk to you about that," Jane said. "I thought we might try asking Mr. Wainwright."

"The deceased Mr. Wainwright?" I asked while Jane cringed and nodded. "I swear to all that's holy, you lot, if I find out that Mr. Wainwright is a vampire, or in the witness-protection program, or any condition other than dead, I will throw a hissy and destroy that very expensive display of crystal figurines over there."

"See what happens when you hire people without a background check?" Andrea asked Jane.

"Shut it, you," I retorted.

Jane was back to twisting the tea towel between her hands. "Look, I wasn't quite sure how to tell you this, but your grandfather only moved onto the next plane a few months ago."

"Next plane?"

Jane nodded, clearly trying to choose her words carefully. "He died here at the shop. I found his body a few hours later. His spirit was already haunting the shop. He said that he was far too interested in what was happening here on earth to move on just yet. Of course, I didn't know at the time that part of 'what was happening' was his dating my aunt Jettie, who was also a ghost."

I wouldn't quibble with a vampire about the existence of ghosts. It seemed like a doomed argument. And Nana Fee had all but told me she would come back to haunt me if I didn't accept her task. I sincerely hoped that she'd run out of postmortem steam with her otherworldly reminders and had moved on to the next plane.

"Wait, ghosts can date?"

"Apparently," Jane said. "The pair of them stuck around for almost a year. Until they both decided that it was time for them to move on. They couldn't define it, and I don't want to try to explain it, but wherever that is, we aren't supposed to be able to contact them."

"So why are you telling me this?"

"We aren't 'supposed' to be able to contact them, but that doesn't mean we can't. I haven't tried yet because I wanted to respect their wishes. But I figured between a vampire mind-reader and a witch, we might have enough mojo to make a connection for an emergency call."

I grimaced, thinking of my surreal chat with Mr. Wainwright in the panda dream. If that was the sort of conversation I could expect, I wasn't sure I wanted to make that call. Of course, it might be different, since, ostensibly, we would be speaking to Mr. Wainwright and not my imagination's version of him. I hoped it would be different. I didn't think my imagination was being very kind to him.

Then again, Ouija boards weren't something my family toyed with. We respected the life cycle. While it was often devastating, death was as much of the process as life, so it didn't make sense to bother a spirit after the person had moved on. For Nana Fee's sake, I hoped she'd moved on. I didn't like the thought of her hovering around semirural Kentucky just in case I needed her. "So, what, we're going to break out a Ouija board and leave him a voice mail?"

Jane shook her head vehemently. "No, no Ouija boards. The channel is too wide open. You don't know whom you're inviting into your emotional space. Plus, every scary story that ever started with a Ouija board ended in bloody, grisly death. Or getting in touch with Jim Morrison."

"Does this conversation seem circular to you?" I asked Andrea. She shushed me.

"I think we need this." Jane held up an oddly shaped hunk of red plastic.

Andrea tilted her head. "Is that a—"

"A twenty-sided die from my parents' Scattergories game, yes," Jane said. "I figured we would ask questions while we roll the dice. We would have just as good a chance of getting a message spelled out this way, maybe without the spooky ironic death messages."

"How is this different from a Ouija board?" I asked.

"Well, we're not going to keep our hands in constant, sustained contact with this. Less chance of the wrong spirits getting a connection."

"You just pulled that explanation out of your bum, didn't you?"

"It's a total rationalization," she admitted. "But it's all I can think of."

"I'm leaving before one of us gets possessed by the spirit of an evil prom queen," Andrea said, turning on her heel toward the door. Jane and I caught her through the elbows and dragged her back. Jane flipped the sign on the door to "Closed," which made sense. I would hate to walk into a bookstore and find the staff trying to commune with the dead.

As we sat around one of the coffee tables, prepping the "board," Jane turned off the lights and lit a few candles for the right ambience. Gabriel shared a commiserating look with me. "I'm only here because Jane thought it would be strange to leave a seat open at a four-person séance table. Which only goes to show that some of the etiquette lessons her grandma tried to hammer into her skull took root."

"Bite your tongue," Jane warned him.

"And I would like to go on record as saying this is a stupid idea and will only lead to trouble," Andrea said.

"Noted," Jane said, handing her a notebook. "Now,

you take down the messages. You have the neatest hand-writing."

Andrea grumbled, "Yes, because penmanship is going to make a huge difference when we accidentally contact that demon from *The Exorcist*."

Jane ignored her. "OK, Nola, have you ever done any meditation or visualization exercises?"

"No."

"Oh, good." She sighed. "They're for hippies. What we're going to do is close our eyes and clear our minds."

Andrea rolled her eyes but complied with Jane's in-structions. I exhaled slowly through my nose. I tried to picture myself standing in a bright, white room, empty of people, colors, and sound. But I kept thinking about Jed, about my grandmother, about the Elements.

Jane cleared her throat. "Clear your head, Nola."

"I am," I whispered.

"No, you're not. I can tell, remember?"

I harrumphed, which made Andrea snicker.

"I want you to picture Mr. Wainwright. His gray hair is all frizzy and standing off of his head like he's been struck by lightning. He's smiling, because he thought he'd lost his glasses again, but they were just stuck on top of his head. Can you see him?"

I nodded.

"So talk to him."

"I feel silly," I whispered.

"Mr. Wainwright has seen us do far stupider things than this," Andrea muttered. "Someday we'll show you all the pictures from the Halloween party."

"Gilbert Wainwright," I called. "This is your grand-daughter. I need your help. Please, wherever you are, please come closer to this place, where you used to spend so much time, and speak to your friends."

I sighed and rolled the dice several times. The letters spelled absolute nonsense. Sheepishly, I told Jane, "I feel ridiculous."

"G.R.F.K.B.," Jane said. "Maybe it's a Klingon ghost?"

Andrea buried her face in her hands and dropped her forehead onto the table. I giggled and took the die. "Please," I whispered, completely sincere. "I really need help. I don't know what I'm doing. Anything I've managed to accomplish is the result of blind stinking luck. I could really use a clue or a hint or something."

"K.J.O.W.P.L.," Jane said as I rolled the die.

"Come on!" I cried. "My grandmother made a glowing moon appear against my ceiling. You can't play a silly word game with me?"

"S.O.R.R.Y.," Jane read, grinning widely and jostling Andrea's arm while she bounced up and down in her seat. "Mr. Wainwright? Thanks for talking to us. We miss you. Is Aunt Jettie OK?"

"L.O.V.E."

"Aw, that's nice," Jane said. "Tell her I love her, too."

"Very sweet," I agreed. "It's nice to, uh, meet you. Mr. Wainwright, I'm sorry to cut to the chase, but I'm afraid we could lose this connection any second. I need to find the objects Nan—Fiona gave you."

"N.O.T. G.I.L.B.E.R.T."

Gabriel's eyebrows shot up, his hand gripping Jane's even more tightly. "*Not* Gilbert?"

"I told you!" Andrea hissed. "This way leads to pea-soup vomiting and madness."

"Who are you?" Gabriel asked.

"N.A.N.A."

"Nana Fee?" I shouted.

I couldn't seem to find words or air. I'd missed my grandmother so much, and here she was, talking to me through a silly party game. Even though I'd had time to prepare for her death, there were still so many things I wanted to say to her. I felt the tears trail down my cheeks. Jane slipped her arm around my shoulder and squeezed me against her side.

Jane rolled the die again. "M.O.T.H.E.R."

"My mother's dead," I whispered to Jane.

"Maybe it's mother as in my mama?" Jane said.

"Well, your mother had the candle. Maybe she's refer-ring to that," I said. "Yes, Nana, we know Jane's mother's had the candle. Do you know where we might find the other three?"

"M.O.T.H.E.R.," I said after we rolled the dice and it spelled the same word.

"G." Jane said. "A.G.A. Was your nana a Lady Gaga fan?"

Glaring, I took the die and rolled. "D.E.S.K."

"Mother Gaga desk?" I said. "That doesn't make any sense."

"L.O.V.E.," Andrea said, after rolling the die. "Aw, that's nice."

"Love you, too," I told her. "And please, don't stick around this plane for me. I need to know that you've moved on to a better place. And that you're happy."

Gabriel rolled nothing but As over the next few minutes.

"It would seem your grandma took your advice," Andrea said, nudging it with her pen.

We tried rolling the die again but ended up with more nonsense Klingon words.

"I think that's all we're going to get out of her. I'm sorry I put you through all this, Nola. I don't think we got a lot of usable information," Jane said, pushing up from the table.

Andrea grabbed her wrist and dragged her back into her chair. "Sit down!" Andrea yelped. "You don't leave the table without closing the circle, the portal, the connection, or whatever. Otherwise, the spirit can attach itself to you like a parasite and hitch a ride to your house."

"What movies have you been watching?" I asked.

"You are on a strict regimen of the Oprah network after this," Jane told her. "No more *Celebrity Ghost Stories* for you."

"Please?" Andrea pleaded.

"Fine," Jane sighed, then called, "OK, spirit world, we are hereby hanging up, closing the channel. Don't call us. We'll call you."

I asked, "Don't you own a whole section of books on appropriate ritual language? And it's not true, what you said earlier. We did learn quite a bit tonight. We learned that Nana was a closet Gaga fan."

"What do you think she meant? Love. Mother. Gaga. Desk. Those words don't make any sense," Andrea complained.

"Maybe I need to look through your desk again, Jane," I said, returning some of the candles to the display shelf.

"You looked through my desk?"

"We refinished Jane's desk before we moved it into her office. There were no papers or anything left in the drawers," Andrea said, squinting when I turned the lights back on.

"Are you sure your mother hasn't taken any other objects out of the shop?" I asked, my voice trailing off as I noticed one of Jane's photos hanging over the shelf where the candles were displayed. It showed Jane's mother, wearing a black T-shirt with two white triangles on the chest and a logo that read, "FFOTU." Was this more Klingon nonsense? She was standing next to the cash register with this thunderstruck expression on her face. Jane's mama was a funny little thing. It seemed odd that Nana would mention her twice, when we'd already located the candle. What did Nana want us to know about Jane's mother?

I looked at the picture more closely. "Hey, Jane, what's that?"

"It's a picture of our first meeting of the Friends and Family of the Undead. It was the first time my mother saw the shop, and Andrea wanted to capture my mother's stunned expression when she saw how nice everything was."

"That's horrible," I told Andrea.

Jane shook her head. "No, it's fair. The moment she stepped inside, she said Andrea must have worked very hard to organize and decorate everything." Andrea snickered when my face drooped in disbelief. Jane added, "Mama and I used to have a pretty rocky relationship."

I poked at the photo, my hands shaking. "And that little brown blob by the cash register? The one vaguely shaped like an acorn? The one I'm pretty sure is the altar plaque representing Earth?"

"Our take-a-penny dish?" Jane asked, peering around the maple and glass counter, as if she were looking for it.

"Take a penny?"

"You know, when you get pennies back as change, you leave them in the take-a-penny dish, so when other customers are trying to give exact change, they don't have to dig around for them," Andrea said. "Pennies are basically the redheaded stepchildren of the currency world."

"You were using my family's centuries-old altar plate as a change dish?"

"Have you noticed the Irish accent gets a lot stronger when she's angry?" Jane asked her husband.

"We didn't know that's what it was. I found it lying loose in Mr. Wainwright's storage room!" Andrea exclaimed. "It looked a lot more acorn-like in your sketch, by the way. In reality, it's just blobby with a stem hanging off of it." I glowered at her. She threw up her hands. "OK, you're right. Not the appropriate time to criticize your family's prowess at arts and crafts."

I looked toward the register, but the spot to the left

of it was being used to display copies of a book called *The Guide for the Newly Undead.* "Where is the dish now?"

"It was right here," Jane said, looking under the counter and behind the promotional supplies, just in case the plaque had fallen.

Andrea's expression was a mix of confusion and guilt. "Jane, when I think about it, I don't think I've seen that thing for months. I thought you'd moved it."

"When was the last time you remember seeing it?"

Andrea chewed her lip. "A month or two ago. The day Mama Ginger came in."

"Mama Ginger?" I said. "Another *mother*? Starting with a G?"

"Mama Ginger is Zeb's mother. She and Jane have a checkered history," Gabriel told me quietly.

"Don't you remember, Jane?" Andrea asked. "She 'dropped by' before opening hours to give you your extremely late wedding present . . . and you kicked her out of the store . . . and banned her for life?"

"Why did you do that?" I asked.

"Well, kicking her out was part of my New Year's resolutions," Jane said. "The lifetime ban was because I caught her swiping some of our fairy figurines and shoving them into her purse. She was standing right by the register, like I was too dumb to see . . . oh, hell. The plaque was right here next to the register. She must have taken it."

"We can't prove that."

"It's Mama Ginger," Jane said with some emphasis,

as if Andrea was missing some important and obvious
point.

"OK, but we can't just go into someone's house accusing them of theft."

"It's Mama Ginger," Jane said again. "That happens to
her at least once a week."

8

Vampires are expert travelers. Because of the many perils that traveling poses for the undead, they prepare for all contingencies.

—A Guide to Traversing the Supernatural Realm

Mama Ginger was a bizarre, bulbous woman with bright bottled-red hair and an unfiltered cigarette permanently attached to her bottom lip. She did not welcome us into her house, and not just because it was after midnight and we'd awoken her from her "beauty rest." There was apparently some ugly history between Jane and Mama Ginger, something about Mama Ginger's attempts to sabotage Zeb's wedding to Jolene and subsequent attempts to make Jane's life more difficult after she realized that Jane (a) would never be her daughter-in-law and (b) was a vampire. It took Jane using something she called the persuasion voice for her even to let us through the entryway.

"Jesus, Mary, and Jerome!" I cried, backing away from a side parlor entirely populated by Precious Moments figurines. No matter where I went, their sinister over-sized eyes followed me. I desperately wanted to turn my back, but I knew the moment I did, one of them would attack me from behind with a tiny porcelain machete.

Mama Ginger had a multitude of health problems that set off my alarm bells. Her heart was under stress, and her lungs were damaged from what I imagined was years of steady smoking. The conditions combined were enough to make me lean against the wall, Precious Moments be damned, so I could construct a shield between Mama Ginger's energy and mine.

By the time I was able to focus on the conversation around me, Jane was questioning Mama Ginger in earnest.

"How could you just walk into my shop and take something from me?"

Mama Ginger sniffed. "Well, if you hadn't been so rude, I might not have taken it."

"So your criminal behavior is my fault?" Jane asked frostily.

"Don't you take on airs with me, Jane Jameson. I knew you when you were still in pigtails."

"I've known you for a while, too, Mama Ginger. You need to remember that."

"This is getting nowhere," I shouted over their shouts of "Don't you threaten me, missy!" and "Calm down, you thieving whackaloon!" "Look, I don't care that you took it, Mrs. Lavelle. I just want it back. Could you please tell me what you did with it after you took it from the shop? If your information leads to my finding the plaque, I am willing to make it worth your while."

Jane protested rewarding Mama Ginger's larceny—

loudly—but I shushed her. Suddenly, Mama Ginger's wounded dove persona melted away. Her eyes narrowed, her expression calculating. "How much?"

"I won't discuss specifics until you either produce the plaque or share your info."

"Why would I show my hand early? How do I know you'll pay up?"

"I'm a woman of my word, Mrs. Lavelle. I'll give you what you're owed."

"Not much of an enticement." Jane snorted. "She knows what she's owed."

"Jane!" I hissed, shaking my head vehemently. I turned pleading puppy-dog eyes on Mama Ginger. "Please, Mrs. Lavelle."

"It's nice to know some young people still have pretty manners." She sniffed. "My Zeb should have married a nice girl like you. Not that redheaded hussy . . ."

Jane growled. "Watch it, Mama Ginger. You're already on thin ice. Now, what happened to the blobby acorn thing?"

Mama Ginger made a study of her talon-like fire-engine-red nails. "I may have mailed it . . . to Georgia . . . as a wedding present to my cousin Hubert."

"You used a shoplifted item as a wedding gift?" Jane exclaimed.

I didn't think Jane had much room to judge, regifting-wise, but I also didn't think this was the appropriate time to point that out. And suddenly, I realized. "Georgia," I said. "As in the abbreviation GA? Georgia." But Jane was too busy staring holes in Mama Ginger's head to note my amusement. "Well, *I'm* happy to know my nana wasn't a Gaga fan. Life makes sense again. Sort of."

"Hubert loves squirrels!" Mama Ginger exclaimed. "His wife, Mindy, wrote the sweetest thank-you note. Well, it was e-mailed. But they loved it, you could tell!"

"You are double-banned!" Jane exclaimed.

I persuaded Mama Ginger to give me Cousin Hubert's phone number for a small fee and on the condition that Jane had to leave her house while I conducted my business with Hubert's wife. Mindy was sweet as peaches and clotted cream about the "misunderstanding" with her wedding gift, until we started discussing a price for its safe return. Let's just say that any buy money I saved locating the candle for free had been spent. But I was grateful that Mindy had simply chucked the gift box containing the plaque into a closet and forgotten about it, instead of disposing of it or regifting it, as seemed to be the secret custom around here. Jane, by the way, called through the window that I should demand that Mindy text-message a digital picture of the plaque and a dated newspaper to my phone, to prove that she still had it, before I promised any money. Mindy huffily complied and then informed me that I had until five P.M. the next day to come pick it up before the price doubled.

Before Jane could object, I handed Mama Ginger the cash I'd promised her and lit out for Jane's car. "I can't say I'm pleased that you gave the thieving she-troll money, but at least you'll have another Element in your hands by tomorrow," Jane said as I buckled my seatbelt.

"The only problem is that my car is held together with duct tape and prayer," I told her. "It would never make the drive to Georgia and back. Do you think Miranda would be willing to take me? I could pay her."

"Miranda is out of town on an assignment," Jane said. "She's driving some Council member to California. I would loan you my car, but it's with one of Dick's people, getting fitted with fireproof seats. I'm relying on Gabriel's car for transportation."

"So this is what shit creek feels like, and me without my paddle."

"It's not that bad."

I scoffed. "It's, what, one A.M., now? I'm completely knackered. The drive to Georgia will take at least seven hours, so if I want to make Mindy's deadline, I'm going to have to find a car within the next nine hours and make the drive. The only good thing I can say about this situation is that at least it's Saturday and the clinic is closed, so I won't have to call in 'flaky and unavailable.'"

Jane patted my hair, but I believe it was to keep me from whacking my head against the seat. "Look, this isn't a big deal. Dick and I will find a solution. You need some rest before you leave tomorrow. I'll drop you at home, and by the time you wake up, we'll have worked something out for you."

"By the way, are you ever going to tell me what the hell is going on with Dick?" I asked.

Jane shook her head. "It's not my place. All I can tell you is that Dick is absolutely mortified that you think he's an obsessive pervert, which is why he is trying to 'give you space' right now. Well, to be fair, he is a bit of an obsessive pervert, but not when it comes to you."

"I'm not sure this is making me feel *better*."

"I will say that when he tells you, you're going to laugh," she said. I snorted derisively, closed my eyes, and tilted my head against the seat. Jane reached across and clicked my seatbelt into place. "Come on, let's get you home and tucked into bed."

"I would protest that I am an adult and capable of doing this myself, but as I mentioned, I am exhausted," I muttered. "And I just don't have the energy for false displays of independence."

"If anyone asks, I'll swear you put up a mighty protest," Jane promised.

I opened one eye, giving her a sideways glance. "By the way, fireproof seats?"

Jane rolled her eyes. "I have a teenage vampire living in my house. It's best not to ask questions."

An hour later, I had showered and felt vaguely human as I scrambled to pack a bag for the mini-break to Georgia. It was late, and I was desperate to get enough sleep that I wasn't entirely addled for the drive. But then I looked at my mobile and saw that Stephen had called twice while I was at Mama Ginger's. I dialed his number, hoping I could keep the conversation quick and get to bed. That was the appropriate attitude when calling one's lover from a long distance, right?

Stephen's tone when he picked up did not bode well

for the quick, light interchange I'd hoped for. "Oh, so you finally decided to call me, eh?"

"I'm so sorry, Stephen, I've just been so busy. I was really thrown into the trenches on my own today, and I'm exhausted. I wish I could tell you all about it, but I'm on my way out of town. I have to leave first thing in the morning."

"Out of town? For what? Are you telling me you can't be bothered to call, but you've had time to book a holiday?"

The flinty tone to his voice had my stomach rolling. The weight of fatigue and frustration pressed against my chest, and I just wanted to lie across the bed and curl into a ball. I hadn't meant to say anything about the trip, but I had no filter when I was tired. If he pressed too much more, I would tell Stephen all about the trip to Kentucky, the Elements, and the shirtless neighbor I may or may not have flirty butterfly feelings for.

"No, no, nothing like that," I said. "It's for . . . work. I can't tell you much about it. Just boring old clinical stuff, really."

"If it's just boring old clinical stuff, why can't you tell me about it?"

I was sincerely regretting that I'd backed myself into a corner with this line of lying, because he had a good point. "Look, let's just talk about something else, OK?"

"What are you up to over there that you're not telling me about, Nola?" he demanded.

"What are you implying?" I shot back.

"I mean, this sudden offer of a mysterious job you'd

never mentioned before, the urgency of leaving right away, the fact that this hospital you claim to work for doesn't have you listed among its nursing fellows. I want to know what you're really doing over there and who you're spending your time with!" His voice rose to an angry shout. That shocked the hell out of me, because at that time of day, he was at the office, where he rarely ever showed emotion, much less lost control of it.

"You've been checking up on me?"

"You gave me no choice!"

"You did have a choice. You could have believed me." I should have dialed down my righteous indignation, the logical part of my brain knew that. But somehow the fatigue and the fact that he was accusing me of something I had successfully resisted so far—cheating on him with Jed—fueled the irrational portion of my brain and its control over my verbal faculties. *Ignore the fact that he's right not to believe you, Nola,* it told me, *and that you were quite tempted to kiss Jed the other night. You have every right to be virtuously indignant! Virtuously!*

"I can't talk to you when you're like this," I told him. "If you don't trust me, that's your problem. I haven't done anything wrong."

"I'm tired of coming last in your life, Nola. You need to make our life together more of a priority."

"We don't have a life together, Stephen. We have your life and my life, and occasionally they intersect."

"And whose fault is that?" he demanded. "I've done everything I can to lure you away from that circus you call a family. And you fight me at every turn! I'm only doing what's best for you."

The use of that phrase and his superior tone, as if I were a naughty child he had to steer, struck a long-buried nerve deep within me. A hot, angry bubble burst forth from my throat in the form of "I don't have time for this. I'm going to sleep now, because I am exhausted. You would know that if you asked me one single question that had to do with my day or my work or even how I am. All you ever ask is why I had to come here in the first place and when I'm coming home. I'm sick of it. Don't call me anymore. If I decide that I want to talk to you again, I might call you."

On the other end of the line, he gasped. "You don't mean that."

"The hell I don't." And then I hung up.

I clapped my hands over my mouth, shocked at the words that had just spilled from my lips. Their tone, the sound of my voice, had sounded so much like *hers* that it frightened me to my soul. The wretched, angry altered state of it, as if I was barely hanging on to the faculties that kept me from strangling the nearest bystander. I let out a stifled little sob and swiped my hands across my eyes. The memory of that voice sent waves of panic and distress through my belly, to the point that I bent at the knees and worked sincerely at not running to the bathroom and throwing up.

I focused on breathing in through my nose and out of my mouth. I pictured that spare white room that hadn't been so successful with Jane's Ouija die experiment and willed a feeling of peace and calm to spread from my chest to my arms and legs, to steady my hands. I exhaled loudly, forcing my fingers to scoop up the neatly stacked pile of clothes and stuff them into my overnight bag. Then I added toiletries and a Dakota Cassidy paperback I'd picked up at the shop.

Satisfied that I'd completed the task, I stripped and slid into bed without bothering to shower. My stomach was still roiling. I pressed my face into the pillow and prayed for it to settle. The dark room and exhaustion finally led me to an uneasy sleep, with thoughts of my mother creeping into my head.

I was twelve. I was running home from school, my "grown-up" plain Jansport backpack bouncing against my spine as I kept my face tilted to the late-afternoon sun. Pretty, popular Katie Jordan had asked me to her big sleepover birthday party at school that day, and I desperately wanted to go. I was already coming up with a logical, well-constructed argument for why Dad should allow this, even though he didn't know Katie or her parents very well and was pretty strict about that sort of thing. My ace in the hole was that my best friend, Allie Noonan, was going, and Dad often caved to parental peer pressure when it came to Allie's privileges.

Just thinking about that afternoon, I could feel the warm rays of light on my face. I could feel the weight of the backpack against my shoulders and the way the sun caught my long dark hair, much longer than it was now.

I was so happy, giddy at the possibility of being Katie Jordan's friend, of climbing the social ladder a bit and escaping the dreaded curse of "middle-school nobody," that my chest ached with it.

I nearly tripped coming up the steps to our house, which was a frequent occurrence, what with my coltish limbs and oversized feet. I called out to my dad before I even got the door open, but the moment I walked in, I could sense a chill in the house, a weight to the air that made it harder to breathe. My good mood deflated immediately. My mother was back.

A silly, babyish part of me wanted to drop my backpack and run for Allie's house. My mother had been bouncing in and out of our lives for years, coming back every once in a while when she ran out of money or just forgot how little use she had for Dad and me.

For a few weeks, everything would be roses. She was "centered" now, she'd promise, and she had gotten her priorities straight. But after a few weeks, that desperate edge would come back to her voice, the wild look in her eyes, and she would disappear again. Usually with whatever pawnable objects we had lying around the house. After three years of losing it, I learned to stuff all of my birthday money into a sock in my laundry hamper. She never looked there.

Having recently graduated from my school's DARE program, I thought my mother was a drug addict, but Dad swore she'd never had *that* problem. He just said Mom was restless and confused and didn't know what she was missing, not being able to watch me grow up. Even then, I knew he didn't believe it, either.

As I came in, I stumbled over the little pink rolling suitcase by the front door. It was my suitcase, the one I used when Dad and I took summer trips to Cape Cod. For a terrifying moment, I thought Dad had decided to give me over to her, and I considered grabbing the bag and running for Allie's house after all. Then I heard my dad yelling. I'd never heard Dad raise his voice to my mother before, even when she pawned his mother's brooch. But now he was giving her what for.

"You think I'm going to let you walk out the door with *my* daughter?" he shouted. "Not this time, Anna. I've put up with your bullshit for years, hoping you'd come back and be a decent mother to our child—that sweet, smart little girl, who still loves you despite the fact that you checked out as soon as she could walk. No more, do you hear me? I won't let you drag her down with you."

I couldn't help but feel a little sorry for my father. Dad hadn't seemed to catch on to the fact that any remaining daughterly adoration I had for my mother had faded several "returns" ago. My dad was my whole family. He was the one who sewed the patches on my Brownie uniform. He made sure my lunches were packed and learned to French-braid my hair. He suffered the indignity of shopping for my first training bra. I'd figured out my mother's limitations a long time before that.

To my surprise, my mother's voice was even, calm. I'd never heard her so casual and cool before, and that scared the hell out of me. Her being sure of her "rights" in any situation was not a good thing. "You have no say in this matter. This is her birthright. She may be your daughter, but she's a McGavock first. Really, Martin, you can't keep her from me."

What was she talking about? I didn't know much about my mom's family. All Dad would tell me was that they lived in Ireland and they believed in things that not everybody believed in. He'd liked the McGavocks when he'd met them, he said, but Mom didn't want to have anything to do with them when she moved to the States to be married. And now my mother seemed to want to haul me away to some sort of McGavock indoctrination camp?

"Don't act like I shut her off from your family!" Dad exclaimed. "I was all for traveling to see them, making sure that Nola at least got to meet her grandmother. But you haven't exactly fostered an open relationship with them. Don't blame me that she's been cut off from her heritage."

"Daddy?" I said, stepping into the kitchen.

"Hi, honey," he said, schooling his features into a loving, untroubled expression. "How was school?"

My parents were so different, it seemed impossible that they had been married. Dad was tall and trim, with thick dark-blond hair and warm blue eyes. He was wearing his work clothes for Boston Medical Center, a crisp white shirt with the red-and-blue checked tie I'd given him for Father's Day. My mother looked as if she was ready to head out to a club, in too-tight jeans and a clingy, silky red shirt that was cut low in the front. Silver bangles clanked against both wrists. Her eye makeup was heavy and dark, making her already large brown eyes appear even bigger. Her mouth was painted a bold bloodred.

"What are you doing here?" I asked.

She frowned, that lovely motherly energy fading like mist. "I haven't seen you in almost a year, and that's the hello I get?"

I ratcheted up my voice to a level of cheer only my father would recognize as my "dealing with an annoying babysitter" voice. "Hello! What are you doing here?"

"Can't a mother come see her daughter without a special reason?"

I looked to my dad, who was glaring at my mother as if he could make her explode with the power of his mind. I returned my own gaze to her face. Underneath the makeup, I could see the signs of aging. Her lipstick was feathering into the network of tiny wrinkles around her mouth. Permanent dark circles had begun to form under her eyes. Those eyes were sharp and calculating as she looked me over.

"So tell me all about school," she said, her lyrical voice ingratiating and saccharine sweet. "Are your grades still good? Are you still playing soccer?"

I stared at her, long and hard, without saying a word.

"Oh, fine, I do have a reason for coming to see you. I just thought it was time for you to come live with me!" Mom said, smiling brightly. "I've been staying at this beautiful place in Florida. We're right on the beach, and it's so lovely and warm. And there's enough room for you. I mean, I know you've never liked Boston, Nola. Your dad told me you don't have any real friends."

"I never said anything of the sort!" Dad protested.

Mom rolled her eyes and shared this weird little wink with me, as if we were conspirators. "Don't you want to spend some time with me? You've been living with your dad for so long. Don't you think I deserve some time, too? A girl needs her mother, Nola. You need me."

Pointing out that she didn't get any time with me because she'd left us to go "find herself" would have been pointless, so I just said, "I'm not moving to Florida."

"But, Nola, there's nothing to keep you here." Mom sniffed. "Now, I already packed your bag while your father was at work. He'll post the rest of your things to Florida."

"Anna, this is ridiculous. No matter how you try to strong-arm me, I won't allow you to take her."

"Be quiet, Martin," she said, without even looking at him.

"I'm not moving to Florida," I said again, my voice louder this time, begging my mother to hear me just this once.

"Oh, sweetie," Mom said, giving her patronizing little sneer as she pushed me toward the foyer. "Stop being silly and get in the car."

I planted my feet, and for the first time, I defied my mother. "No."

My mother leaned in close, her dark, glassy eyes threatening to draw me in as she hissed, "Now, you listen to me. I've put up with your spoiled little arse for years, and now it's time for me to collect my due. Get out to the car right quick, before I give you something to fuss over. You'd think I was trying to bloody kidnap you, the way you're carrying on. I'm only doing what's best for you. Now move it." And with that, she grabbed me by the shoulders and shoved me toward the door, hard.

"No. No. NO. NO. NO!" I screamed, so loudly I felt something in my throat tear. An enormous pressure squeezed my temples, and all I could think was that I wanted that pressure *out* of my head. I felt a snap between my eyebrows. The lightbulbs in the fixtures above my mom's head flickered and burst, pelting her with shards of glass.

Mom's face went paper-white, and she scrambled back away from me, against the wall. I stared back at her—she looked like a little mouse cowering in front of a snake—wondering if I could make that pressure build back up somehow. And then an angry red flush crept up my mother's neck. She grabbed at me, nearly closing her grasping, clawlike fingers around my wrists before my dad swept me behind him.

"Get away," he growled. "Don't touch her. Leave, and don't ever come back. I'm not going to let you do this to us anymore, do you hear me, Anna? Don't come back again."

Mom snarled at us both, her face twisted and ugly like some awful Halloween mask, and shoved past him to the front door. She slammed it behind her, and both of us let loose breaths we hadn't realized we were holding. With my mother gone, my brain could finally process the bits of broken glass scattered around our feet, the faint smell of ozone, the small cut on my father's cheek, presumably from the bulbs exploding over his head.

"I'm so sorry, Daddy."

"You don't have anything to be sorry about."

"But what about the lights? And your face?" I sniffled. "How did that happen?"

"It's all right, honey," he said, putting his arm around my shoulders. "It's all right."

I never made it to Allie's sleepover. We moved to a different neighborhood a few weeks later. My mother wasn't able to find our home address, and it was years before I saw her again.

That summer, Dad made more of an effort to contact my mother's family. We flew to Ireland to meet them just before my fourteenth birthday, and I formed a special bond with Nana Fee. We flew home, and two months later, my dad was dead, the victim of a heart attack at forty-four. Nana Fee took me in and raised me, which was fortunate, considering that the number of bizarre lightbulb explosions only increased, what with teen hormonal changes and my damaged emotional state.

I was grateful to be completely immersed in the McGavocks' loud, loving madness. I'd wanted so badly just to disappear into the family, to blend in, so no one would see me as the Yank cousin brought home to foster. It seemed easier to forget that I had a life before Kilcairy. But Nana Fee had insisted on saving a few of my father's things when she and Aunt Penny had flown over to help me settle his affairs. It hurt so much to see his Red Sox cap, the bottle of his aftershave, and his wallet. Nana Fee had hidden these things away for me in her hope chest, for when I was ready. I'd only found them after she died.

Nana did her best to teach me to control what I could do. And I loved her for it, but I wanted no part of it. I shut myself up in logic, what I could see and control. I only accepted my natural ability because I had no choice. After seeing what my mother had become after years of practicing witchcraft, desperate and bitter, greedy for what she couldn't have—from money to youth to power—I could live without magic.

9

Negotiation is a very important process to some supernatural creatures, such as gnomes, trolls, fairies, and brownies. The intricacies of this process are likely beyond the capabilities of the average human and should not be attempted. Yes, this means you.

—*From Fangs to Fairy Folk:*
Unusual Creatures of Midwestern North America

I woke up with stiff, sticky eyes, which was fairly typical after nights spent thinking of dear old Mum. I walked into the bathroom and splashed cold water on my face. I looked like hell, with dark circles under the aforementioned eyes and an unhappy slant to my mouth. It was a disturbingly familiar arrangement of features that I blotted out with some blush and wide "buying these after binge drinking seemed like a good idea" sunglasses.

My magic was bottled up and restless. Considering the timing—so close to a dream of my own blessed mother—I was beginning to suspect that the binding was less a result of Penny's actions and increasingly because of my own emotional instability. I could feel the magic itching below the surface like a phantom limb. I was completely drained of energy, listless, practically hungover from the lack of magical spark. I couldn't so much as stir the air at the moment. And I had no idea what sort of situation I was heading into and how long this magical constipation would last.

What a wonderful time for a road trip.

I pulled my dark hair into a sloppy twist. I threw on jeans and a red tank top with some cute sandals. I grabbed my mobile and overnight bag and trudged down the stairs. I had about two hours before I had to leave town, and I was extremely curious to know how Jane and Dick planned to get my depressive arse down to Georgia.

Just as I'd reached the landing, there was a loud pounding on my door. I opened it to find Jed, wearing faded jeans, a short-sleeved button-down plaid shirt, and a contrite expression, while holding out a travel cup of coffee as if it was a shield.

"I was told keeping you caffeinated would be an important part of my survival," he said, pressing the cup into my hand and stepping away quickly. I knew I shouldn't have told Jane that story about punching Uncle Seamus in the throat when he tried to wake me during a fire drill at the clinic.

"What are you doing here?" I asked, sipping the coffee and willing the caffeine to flood my brain with sense and energy.

"Andrea Cheney called me late last night and said you needed someone to drive to Georgia with you. And unlike your car, my truck has a good chance of makin' it past the town limits without the engine fallin' out."

"Why would you agree to this?" I asked. "Don't you have better things to do with your Saturday?

Jed shrugged. "Why not? I like to drive. I think Andrea liked the idea of you having someone around to keep Zeb's family in line if things got rough. And when my landlord asks a favor of me, I hop to."

"How rough could his family be?" I scoffed.

"I saw the video from the Lavelle twins' christening. Don't even joke about it."

I was fairly average in height, and it still took a boost from Jed to crawl into the cab of his truck. There were moving vans in Ireland that weren't this large. When had American vehicles become such an . . . overcompensation? Still, the interior smelled pleasantly of pine air freshener and the woodsy aftershave Jed used. The seats had been recently vacuumed, and the dashboard shone. Had he gone out and cleaned the truck because he knew I would be riding in it all day . . . or because Dick had threatened him when he made his "request" and told him to treat me with kid gloves? I wasn't sure which was the preferable, less invasive alternative.

I slid my sunglasses up on my nose, sipped my coffee, and rested my head against the seat, willing the vague headache located just above my eyebrows to go away. Jed seemed to sense that I needed quiet, so he remained silent as we coasted smoothly out of town, over the Tennessee River, and into central Kentucky. He eventually switched on a country-western station playing old Loretta Lynn songs. He asked about working in Boston, and I had to scramble for an answer. From what I remembered, my dad worked a lot of night shifts, and the morning commutes were a bear.

I repeated stories Dad had told me about working in the hospital where he practiced emergency medicine. Unfortunately, most of these stories had been edited for younger audiences, so they weren't terribly interesting. But the more I talked, the more I was able to focus on the world rolling past the truck windows. We rolled through towns that were barely towns at all, just a few buildings cobbled together on a street, usually situated around railroad tracks. And then we drove through Nashville, bustling and alive with traffic and noise. And as soon as you adjusted to the urban landscape, boom, back in farm country.

The landscape was so different from the hills and seascape surrounding Kilcairy. Instead of the relentless emerald I was used to, there were dozens of shades of textured green. Instead of rolling, gentle hills that eventually rose into peaks, mountains seemed to spring up from nowhere. There were sections of road that took my breath away, random patches of bright-red poppies growing between the lanes, rushing creeks, and the occasional random monument in the middle of a cow pasture. Throughout this landscape were little neighborhoods of house trailers, long metal boxes with windows.

"Haven't you ever seen them before?" Jed asked as I stared at another configuration of trailers on a hill.

"On television, maybe, but never up close. They look so small from here."

"It's not so bad. I grew up in one."

"What was that like?"

"Crowded," he admitted. "I have this huge family: three brothers, a sister, and myself. We played outside just so we could breathe our own air."

"Did you all get along?"

"For the most part. I'm closest with my oldest brother, Jim. Sometimes the extended family was a different story. We argue over the usual stuff, you know, who borrowed whose lawnmower, who pinched whose wife's ass at Christmas."

"Actually, I don't believe ass pinching comes up in normal family discourse."

"Well, you're a Yankee. Who knows what y'all talk about," he said. "We moved from Louisiana to Tennessee about three generations ago, and my grandpa never quite got over it. He's still pissed about it, to be honest with you, says he misses the bayou. It's funny, 'cause he was a baby when the family moved away. He never really lived on the bayou. We're the only family in Hazeltine with semi-Cajun accents. Anyway, we all settled on this farm in the 1920s. There was a main house, where my great-grandparents lived, and then we built a sort of complex of trailers around it."

"I can sympathize," I told him. "My family lives close together, too. Do you miss them?"

"Sometimes," he admitted. "But there are other times when I appreciate having all those rooms to myself in the Hollow. Not being able to see the inside of my house from one end to the other is a good thing."

"Gets a little lonely, though," I mused. "Do you have a young possum enthusiast waiting for you back home? I have noticed the distinct lack of Hollow girls doing the walk of shame from your front door."

"Why don't you just ask if I'm seeing someone?"

"Get better answers this way," I said, smirking at him.

"No, I haven't dated anyone seriously in years. I haven't had a real girlfriend since high school."

"Why not?"

"No reason," he said, his lips pressed together in a frown. "Why are you asking me all of these questions?"

"Since I've arrived, I've been subjected to nothing but questions. Now it's your turn. So why no girlfriend?"

"Just never found someone I thought could handle all of this," he said, making a broad gesture down to his toes.

"Defensive and secretive, the Southern male deflects the personal question with posturing and a sexual reference intending to make the inquisitor uncomfortable," I said in my best nature documentary narrator's voice.

"OK, fine. My family is sort of nuts, right? There are a lot of traits I don't want to pass along to kids. And most women, if they're the nice, marrying sort of girl you want to date seriously, are going to want kids. I have learned from experience that if you leave that little detail out in the first couple of dates, it only ends in tears and thrown drinks."

"That is a refreshingly honest answer," I told him. "See what happens when you're forced to keep your shirt on?"

"Smart-ass."

We stopped somewhere in northern Georgia so we could eat a late lunch of fried bologna sandwiches at a Huck's convenience store. I had never before experienced the delicacy of fried bologna, but I can't say it was anything worse than what Penny came up with for some holiday meals.

After answering several questions about defensive driving and basic auto maintenance, I was "allowed" to take over driving to give Jed a chance to rest. I filled the gas tank, since it was my errand we were running. While I was pumping the gas, he emerged from the convenience store with a bag filled with beef jerky, Corn Nuts, Twizzlers, and other culinary delights.

"We just ate," I reminded him, although I hated to do anything to jeopardize the broad white grin on his face.

"If you're going to have an American road-trip experience, you should have all the trimmin's."

"So you promised Andrea I would receive the full-service package?" I asked, climbing into the driver's seat.

He buckled his seatbelt, clearly less comfortable sitting in the passenger seat. "How can you say things like that and not expect me to turn them into a filthy joke?"

"I fully expect you to turn them into a filthy joke. Sno-Balls!" I cried, snatching the pink package from the bag and diving into coconut-covered goodness. "I haven't had these since I was a kid!"

"Can't have a road trip without them," he said solemnly as I pulled the truck into traffic. He winced as I carefully changed lanes and pulled to a stop at a yellow light. Men were such babies when it came to their vehicles.

But it wasn't a baseless concern, as it turned out. The farther south we drove, the heavier traffic got. I noticed there seemed to be more lanes, transitioning from two to three to six. The road department seemed to be doing random experiments in how to frustrate drivers, because I could see no rhyme or reason in the way they chose to repair the roads. My fellow drivers and I would move at a reasonable rate until I came screeching up to a car parked in the middle of the bloody lane. I would switch lanes, sometimes looking over my shoulder beforehand. And on occasion, Jed's head would end up smacking against the window.

"You know, you can pull over anytime," he said. "I'm good to drive again."

"We're in Atlanta city limits. Every exit I've seen is either closed for construction or blocked by idiots."

A semi-truck swept past us, changing lanes and nearly clipping us. I was so worried about that I barely noticed that the car right in front of us had slowed to a near stop. I yelped, whipping the wheel to the left and pulling past, only to have another car slide into the lane ahead of us, honking like mad and zipping around a bus full of schoolchildren.

"I am not prepared for all this traffic!"

"It's fine," he promised. "It's always like this."

"It's not fine. I am on the verge of a nervous breakdown! Which is a problem, because we are moving at eighty bloody miles an hour!"

"Just breathe, baby. Just breathe, and try to focus on one thing at a time, make one decision at a time."

"Don't talk to me like I'm a mentally challenged toddler. And this is not because I'm a woman driver. This is because I am used to living in a place where traffic jams are caused by truant sheep!"

He frowned. "Are there a lot of sheep in Boston?"

Just then, the rather large tanker truck marked "explosive" stopped to avoid stalled traffic ahead of us. I saw an opening between two cars and switched lanes, then switched again and made a sudden turn into the last before screeching to a halt on the shoulder of the road. I was shaking so badly it felt like shivering. Jed had to put the car in park, because my fingers were clamped around the steering wheel in a death grip. His fingers gently pried mine from the wheel, and my hands wound their way around his neck. Once again, I was clinging to him like a frantic primate.

"It's OK." He chuckled, rubbing my back.

"No, these people are crazy, and they are trying to kill us," I said, sniffing. He laughed, threading his fingers through my hair and pressing my face against his neck. How could someone who spent so much time sweating in the sun smell so good and clean? He was a one-man fabric-softener commercial.

Jed kissed my temple, my cheekbone, an innocent gesture. I tilted my face toward his and let his breath wash over my skin. A strange, giddy excitement fluttered through my chest, making me grip his shirt even tighter. My nose nudged against his, and I could feel the tips of his eyelashes against my brows.

I surged forward, pressing my lips against his. He made a shocked murmuring sound before sliding his hands against my back and pressing me closer. He pulled my bottom lip into his mouth and nibbled at it. I tried to move closer, but my seatbelt yanked me back against the seat. Grunting, he fumbled for the belt release, cupped my face between his hands, and hauled me to him. I was this close to crawling into his lap when a truck passed by and blared its horn.

I jumped, backing away and leaning against the window. My lips were tingling. Why were my lips tingling? I'd never had tingly lips before. I touched my fingertips to them, tasting the salt of Jed's skin and my own peach-flavored lip gloss. Jed relaxed back into his seat.

"What just happened?" he asked, looking straight ahead at the lanes of traffic whipping by us.

"I don't know. I got all confused by the multiple lanes. I still haven't figured out the whole driving-on-the-wrong-side-of-the-road thing."

"No, I mean the kissin'. What happened to 'I'm seeing someone, I'm not available'? Not that I'm complainin.'"

My hand whipped up to smack the side of his head.

"Ow! Hey, you kissed me. Why am I gettin' hit?"

"Sorry, sorry. Instinct. I will keep my lips and my hands to myself."

"Well, let's not go crazy. Anytime you want to make out with me in a panic, feel fr—Ow! Stop hittin' me!"

I did not make out with him again that afternoon. We made it to our destination a few hours later, and I was still sorting out whether I'd officially broken things off with Stephen the night before, or if I had been at all ambiguous. But it was very difficult to concentrate on driving and relationship status when my lips were still tingling with the memory of Jed's.

I simply did not do things like kiss men in a panic on the side of a crowded roadway. Well, there was that one time with Neal Dunnigan after our graduation dance, but that was an aberration. A delicious aberration. What the hell was Jed doing to me? I was a mature, educated woman with the livelihoods and health of a whole village on my shoulders. And yet every time he got near me, I behaved like an addled, horny teenager. I had to nip this in the bud. I had to gain control of the situation.

I just didn't think this was the place to do it.

Helton, Georgia, turned out to be a tiny village. There were no major retailers or restaurants. All of the homes and businesses were on one long stretch of street intersecting with a railway, with a box-shaped white church nearby. The houses ran the gamut from sturdy brick bungalows to dilapidated shacks.

Of course, we were heading for one of the shacks.

Jed had been told that I was reclaiming a valuable piece of merchandise that had been "misdirected" from

Jane's shop, but I hadn't given him specifics. As we got closer to the address, I could feel the waves of concern rolling off of him, as if we were walking into a bad situation. Frankly, given the number of NRA bumper stickers on the early-model truck parked in the driveway, I was getting a little nervous myself.

"I think you should stay in the car," he said, looking the house over.

I scoffed. "What?"

He gave me a look I can only describe as "focused" and said, "Do as you're told."

My jaw dropped. No one had ever talked to me like that before and walked away without a limp. Jed had never shown signs of this sort of command. He'd always struck me as the funny, goofy sort. But here he was giving me orders, and I wanted to do exactly what he told me to do. The tone of his voice and the smoldering expression on his face made me want to give him whatever he wanted.

Of course, I couldn't tell him that. Instead, I exclaimed, "I beg your pardon! Like I'm supposed to fall to my knees at the sight of your freakishly large muscles? Who the hell do you think you're talking to?"

Jed seemed to snap out of whatever bizarre alphamale haze had prompted such a speech. "Right, sorry."

I shoved the truck door open and slammed it in his face, or at least near his face.

"OK, so that was the wrong way to go about it," Jed admitted. "I'm just—I don't like the look of this."

"Get over it," I told him.

"Fine," he huffed. "But at least let me do this." Jed hooked an arm through my elbow and led me forward. "I'm about to devolve into some pretty serious Bubba-ness. Don't judge me based on what I am about to say or do. And no offense meant, but it would be best if you didn't say anythin' over the next few minutes. And try not to make those faces, OK?"

"Faces?" I asked.

"The 'I am an alien explorer in a strange world, and I don't like what I see' faces."

"I don't—" I protested, but cut myself off when he gave me that grave, serious look. I grumbled, "I don't see how that's not supposed to offend me," just as the door opened.

Hubert Lavelle towered over even Jed's tall frame. He had some sort of handlebar mustache and was dressed in camouflage from head to toe. He was the most ter-rifying person I'd ever met. And I had several cousins who would head-butt complete strangers over a soccer match.

"Hi there! We're lookin' for a Mr. Lavelle," Jed said, his accent far more pronounced than I'd ever heard it. "My girl here talked to your wife on the phone last night."

"Who sentcha?" Hubert asked.

"Your aunt Ginger," Jed said.

Hubert's eyes narrowed. "She say anything about the credit cards? 'Cause it's not our fault she left that ap-plication on the counter. Anybody could have picked it up."

"No, just the wedding present," Jed assured him.

After establishing that we were not door-to-door evangelists or salesmen, Hubert ushered us through the front door and pushed us onto the green velour couch. The key design element of the living room seemed to be the deer's head mounted on the wall, with some sort of cheap garter around its nose. The garter had a little tag that read, "Helton High School Prom, 1992." This seemed disrespectful both to deer and to cheaply made underwear.

Hubert's wife, Mindy, was a tiny powerhouse of a woman with a halo of wild blond hair and eye makeup so complex it took me a while to locate her pupils. She was clearly the brains of the operation, such as it was. And I was distinctly uncomfortable with the way she was eyeing Jed. But I was starting to think her threats to sell the plaque on eBay were a bluff, because they didn't appear to have a computer. And given the length of Mindy's nails, I doubted she spent much time typing sales information.

"Can I get y'all anything?" she drawled, her voice smooth and silky as custard.

"I'd appreciate a sweet tea, ma'am," Jed said, plucking at the hat in his hands. Mindy turned to me, expectant.

"Oh, please don't go to any trouble," I said, trying like mad to keep the grimace from crinkling my face at the thought of liquid diabetes.

"No trouble at all, shug," she said, teetering toward the kitchen on see-through plastic wedge heels. Hubert gave us an awkward smile, settling back into his Barcalounger.

"What did she call me?" I muttered out of the side of my mouth.

"Shug," he said. "It's short for 'sugar'; it means she likes you. Or, at least, she likes the money you're about to pay her. If she called you by your first name, she'd be indifferent. If she called you Miss Leary, she'd have already written you off."

"Good to know."

Mindy came toddling back into the living room with two hot-pink plastic tumblers of iced tea. She put a little extra wiggle in her step when she served Jed's. He offered her a bland smile and took a long drag from his glass. How was he able to do that without gagging? But I was ever so grateful that her attention was directed otherwise, because it meant no one noticed when I poured my tea into her potted plant. Which turned out to be plastic.

Mindy shot a sultry look over her shoulder as she disappeared into the back of the house.

"Well, we're real grateful to you for being so understanding about Mama Ginger's wedding gift," Jed said carefully as Mindy carried a gift bag with a cabbage rose pattern into the living room.

"You're lucky you called when you did, 'cause we were going to use this as a backup ashtray when Mindy's mama comes to visit," Hubert said, his tone magnanimous.

I nodded. "I appreciate your restraint."

"Course, I couldn't just hand it over," Mindy said pointedly. "Not without some sort of fair trade. After all, it *was* a wedding present. There's sentimental value."

"Right, sorry," I said, digging into my purse. I handed her the envelope of cash I'd prepared to save myself the awkwardness of counting it out. I pressed the envelope into her hand. Meanwhile, Jed started a conversation with Hubert about "the Dawgs" and their chances in the playoffs. I didn't know what sport they were referring to, but Hubert lit up at the chance to discuss his beloved Dawgs and engaged in a spirited debate. Mindy's attention could not be swayed.

"Of course, with you payin' us, that would only mean we broke even. Still leaves us without a wedding gift."

"You want me to buy you a blender?" I asked. I was grateful to get the plaque back, but these people were getting on my last nerve.

"No, at this point, we've got the whole house set up," Mindy said. "It would be nice to have a little extra cash, in case we wanted to splurge a little."

"Would a hundred be enough?" I asked flatly as I plucked a bill from my wallet.

"Well, we are pretty close to Aunt Ginger," Hubert hedged. "She'd probably want to give us at least two hundred."

I slapped the two extra bills into Mindy's hand with a humorless smile and took the bag from her hand. The plaque tumbled into my hands, wrapped in a wad of pink tissue paper. I had a hard time containing my giggle. I didn't want Mindy to decide I was too happy with my purchase and owed her another hundred.

The cool weight of the plaque was wondrously solid against my palm. Jane was right; it was rather blobby.

The acorn-cap pattern barely stood out under the patina of aged clay. But even if it smelled of old pennies, it was unchipped and intact. That was all I cared about. I whispered, "Thank you."

"Happy to help." Mindy smiled, tucking the cash into her bra. "Y'all are welcome to stay for supper, if you'd like."

I frowned at the display of cleavage and the implications of staying for "supper." Oh, I could only imagine the extravaganza of hospitality that would await us, right down to Mindy changing into something "more comfortable."

"That's mighty kind of you, ma'am. But we have to drive home yet tonight," Jed said. "Work, you know?"

"Maybe the next time you're in the neighborhood, then." She simpered, batting her eyelashes for all they were worth.

Having wrapped up the "happy to meet yous," Jed and I booked it out to the truck before Mindy decided she wanted a matching dinette set, too. My blood thrilled in my veins as we climbed into our seats.

"I can't believe I have it." I sighed, pressing the tissue-covered bundle to my chest. "Two down, two to go."

"What do you mean by that?" he asked, starting the engine.

"Oh, it's just a project I'm working on with Jane. Personal interest."

He gave me a long speculative look. "Well, I am too tired to drive any farther," he said. "There was a motel just outside of town. Does that work for you?"

"I have proven myself to be untrustworthy driving on the right side of the road, so yes," I said, clicking my belt into place as we roared onto the main street. "You really went full-on Bubba, didn't you?"

"I warned you."

"Nothing could have prepared me." I chuckled, shaking my head. "That poor deer."

I was not familiar with motel tourism. When I'd lived with my dad, we were strictly Holiday Inn or Ramada travelers. The few times I'd traveled overseas, I'd stayed in smallish historic hotels with "character." (Read: water damage and manky carpet.) And still, the damp-flooring issues were preferable to the comforts of the Sleep-Tight Inn. This was beyond the Bates Motel. It was a brick block building with rusty stains dripping down under the window air-conditioning units. There was a pool . . . and it was full of sludgy green water and leaves.

But the Sleep-Tight was the only motel for the next fifty miles, neither of us had another hour of driving in us, and after paying Mindy off, it fit my cash-on-hand budget. That was the only positive thing I could say about the Sleep-Tight. Jed insisted on being the one to go into the office to rent the rooms. I was concerned that he might have ulterior motives and would come back claiming that there was only one single-bed room available for the night. But it turned out he was concerned that the motel clerk might see a woman alone and "get the wrong ideas."

It was a manly, almost cavemanly, gesture, but I could see the value in it. Nana Fee would have told me to stand up straight, make direct eye contact, and demand respect. And as healthy as that was, in this environment, demanding respect would have probably resulted in the clerk slapping the "bitch" label on me and doing something weird to the truck. I appreciated the direct caveman approach if it meant circumventing all that.

I dragged our overnight bags out of the back of the truck as he returned with the room keys. "If I am stabbed to death in the shower, I will come back and haunt you," I told him.

"Fine." He sighed. "I will come and watch over you while you are in the shower."

"You completely misinterpreted that."

My room was connected to Jed's through an adjoining door. It was spare and outdated, but at least I didn't see anything crawling across the threadbare orange carpet. Of course, the first thing I did was pull the comforter off of the bed, because there was no way I was going to sleep under that. I pulled out my travel sleeping bag and spread it over the sheets, with a prick of regret for Stephen and his practical gift-giving habits.

I'd showered (without being stabbed) and was seriously considering just going to bed, when Jed knocked on the adjoining door. He yelled through the door, "How do you feel about barbecue?"

"You mean hamburgers?" I yelled back. "I have no particular philosophy about hamburgers."

There was a long pause. "I'm going to pretend you didn't just say that."

10

There is no such thing as magical glue. Any witch
who tries to sell you magical glue is a lying hag.
                    —*A Witch's Compendium of Curses*

We went to a restaurant called High on the Hog. It
was careworn but well populated. The green pleather
booths were sprung and peeling. The napkin dispensers
consisted of paper-towel racks mounted against the oak
paneling. Pictures of people holding up large fish and
neon beer signs decorated the walls. I could barely see
the kitchen through the smoke, but I could make out a
huge brick pit in the middle of the space.

It was a bit like a pub, with the same happy, boisterous
crowd, people drinking more they were supposed to and
most likely flirting with people they weren't supposed to.
Loud country music blared from an old jukebox in the
corner. The smell should have been revolting, nothing
but smoke and grease and beer. But my mouth was wa-
tering to the point where I felt like wiping at it with my
sleeve.

Jed ordered for me, because after the hamburger
comment, I couldn't be trusted to do it myself. While

the meat was smoky and delicious, it was the side dishes I gorged on. There were things I remembered from my childhood. Corn on the cob and macaroni and cheese. But then there were hash brown casserole, collard greens, and hush puppies, which I had never tried.

"Wow, you are just throwing yourself into that plate, aren't you?" Jed marveled.

"I know, it's probably revolting. You've probably spent your adult life dating women who eat the cucumber from their salad and proclaim they're just too full to go on, but I am starving. And this is really good."

"Naw, hell, I was going to offer you my black-eyed peas if it means you'll keep makin' those little sounds in your throat."

"I'm making little sounds?"

He nodded. "If you stop, I'll cry. A lot."

I drank the watery-but-no-one-knew-any-better beer, and I ate my fill. And when a stocky man in a Georgia State T-shirt asked me to two-step, I politely declined. He almost argued, but Jed gave him sort of a no-doubt-terrifying-to-the-male-of-the-species territorial glare, and Mr. Georgia State scampered away.

Two more, I thought. Two more, and I could go home. With the plaque locked up tight in Jed's truck, I was well and truly relaxed for the first time in days. It was the same relief and euphoria I'd felt after finding the candle. I was getting a little bit addicted to that feeling, and it was leading to some dangerous thoughts.

Those thoughts focused on Jed's lips and how they'd felt against mine earlier that day. And how relatively easy it was to sit here in this crowded bar and talk about nothing at all with him. I didn't feel that constant nagging pressure to say the right thing or use the right fork. Because Jed had seen me having a possum-fueled panic attack wearing nothing but a towel. After that, there was nowhere to go but up.

After a bit too much Hank Williams, Sr., and far too much good food, Jed drove us back to the motel. The car park was dark, the night moonless under a cloudy sky.

"I had a really nice time," I told him as we walked to the doors.

"Try not to sound so surprised," he chided gently.

"I'm not surprised! All right, I'm a little surprised. Thank you for driving me down here and helping me. Thanks." I leaned forward and meant to kiss his cheek, but he turned his head at the last minute, and I managed to catch his mouth instead. I gave an exasperated little huff. "Really, again?"

"You kissed me!"

"It was an accident!" I cried.

"There's no such thing as accidents, only things you mean to do and put off until a moment of panic."

"That's awfully philosophical," I mused.

"No, I'm not talkin' about all mankind, just you in particular."

I stared at him, long and hard. I watched as the smug little grin faded from his expression. And he was just a man, looking at a woman, as if he wanted her desperately. I don't think anyone had ever looked at me that way.

I was not drunk. The beer we'd had was barely enough

to give me a pleasant buzz. I *was* making a decision without thinking, for the first time in a very long time. It felt really good, but in the morning, I was probably going to regret it. At the moment, I did not care. I wish I could blame it on the drink or being tired or homesick or under the influence of some bizarre magical ritual. But I just wanted him. His skin was warm and smooth under mine. He was solid and strong, and he was looking at me as if I hung the moon and stars. I wanted to feel his skin against mine, to have him drag that stubble across my collarbone and bite at my throat.

"Oh, hell." I sighed, shoving him against the door and attacking his mouth. I didn't even care when our teeth clacked together. His tongue slipped past my lips, tangled with mine. Hands that had hesitated with uncertainty at my sides now curled around my back.

I hitched my leg over his hip, rising against him. Once again, his hands found purchase under my rear as he lifted me. He pushed into my room and whipped me around, pushing me against the door. He yanked my shirt over my head. I pushed him back onto the bed and unbuttoned his shirt, grinding down on the growing bulge of his lap. He moaned.

"Are you sure about this?" he asked, lightly pulling at the ends of my hair. "You're not drunk, are you?"

I laughed. "No! On that beer? Don't be silly!" I kissed him again. "No, I'm not sure about it. But I'm going to do it anyway. It's a new thing for me."

He chuckled. "Well, thank you for experimentin' on me."

"You're so pretty!" I exclaimed as I pulled his shirt

away. "It's just not fair. I mean, really. You're just . . . so damned pretty! Do you get that a lot?"

"Not nearly enough," he said, shaking his head. He pushed my hair from my face and grinned up at me. "And you're pretty, too." He kissed the tip of my chin, nuzzling my neck. "The first time I saw you, I couldn't look away from your face."

I slipped my fingertips up the length of his spine, twisting them into his hair and pulling his head back, so we were eye-to-eye. "You mean, when I was naked?"

He grinned wickedly. I jiggled my hand slightly, forcing him to nod. "Yes."

I bit my lip, keeping my head tilted even as he turned and lowered me to the mattress. "I don't know whether it's a compliment that you could only look at my face when I was naked."

"I will stare at your breasts right now if it will make you happy."

I considered it for a long moment. "I think it would."

He helped me unclasp my bra and threw it over his shoulder. He sat back on his heels, pursing his lips and squinting as if he was considering my nipples very carefully. After a few moments of this, I became uncomfortable and tried to cross my arms. He caught my wrists, shaking his head. He dipped his head to mine as he pressed my wrists to the mattress.

"I still like your face," he muttered, making me laugh as he nuzzled my cheek.

"Can I ask you something?"

"I don't think I could stop you if I tried."

"You're right. I'm sorry," I said, kissing him again. "I'm not going to talk myself out of this. I am going to have sex with you. Like the dirty, nasty, make-the-priest-drop-his-Bible-during-confession sort of sex. I am very bendy. You wouldn't know it to look at me, but . . . *very* bendy. And if I start talking again, I will talk until you lose interest or I start snoring. And if I start snoring, you definitely won't have sex with me."

"You snore?"

"Rumor has it."

He unzipped my jeans and tugged them down my hips. "I like snoring." Suddenly, he was back at face level and drawing his cheek along the width of my collarbone as my panties seemed to disappear into thin air. "Love it." I wrapped my legs around his hips, and he planted a kiss on the hollow of my throat. "Think it's the sexiest thing ever."

As I was laughing, he closed his lips around mine and slowly, but surely, slid between my thighs. I could feel him smiling against my mouth as he rolled his hips. I giggled shamelessly, nuzzling against his neck until he ducked away.

"Ticklish," he murmured.

Every nerve, every cell in my body seemed to sizzle to life. I could feel everything—skin, lips, hands, warmth, comfort, home. This was right where I should be. I could feel it in my bones, the magic working its way loose from my marrow and warming me down to my toes. It wound around the two of us, like a golden ribbon only I could see.

That was new.

Our legs wound together under the rough sheets as we moved. An aurora of sunny light drifted around the bed while I was trying to concentrate on the slow, steady pace Jed was setting. It was a bit of a distraction, taking on a life of its own, flashing and moving as we did, sharing Jed's playful energy as he nibbled at my jawline. But somehow we managed to slide along until Jed's chest was heaving and my skin felt too hot and tight.

Every part of me pulsed, and the light pulsed with me. Jed moaned over me, tilting his head against mine. Just before I closed my eyes, Jed's skin changed in my light, rippling into scales, golden oval scales like you'd see in medieval illustrations of dragons. I blinked rapidly, eyes wide, running my hand down his shoulder. And with that, it was his normal, smooth skin again.

Jed chuckled and rolled to his side, dragging me with him. The golden ribbon faded from sight as I slumped against his ribs, slightly boggled.

Clearly, mind-blowing sex combined with hash brown casserole had hallucinogenic properties.

We lay there in the dark, wrapped around each other, Jed's chin resting on my shoulder. I was so relaxed and content that I was drifting on that line between sleep and waking. And Jed suddenly nudged my cheek with his nose and said, "What were you going to ask me?"

I yawned. "Before you so rudely interrupted me with sex?"

"Yep."

I turned over to face him, balancing on my elbows as my hair fell back over my shoulders. "Why are you so weird around me?"

He frowned and paused midnuzzle. "What do you mean?"

"You're nice one minute, and then the next, you're running into your house like your arse is on fire to avoid me. When we do talk, you're funny and charming and sweet, but then I haven't been able to talk to you that often over the last few weeks, because you hide out in your side of the house."

"I thought you were going to ask me if they looked real," he said, nodding toward my chest. "Which they do."

"And when I ask you anything the least bit personal, you deflect with a dirty joke."

"Force of habit."

"Well, cut it out."

"I'm used to having my family living on all sides. I've never had a hot neighbor before. I don't know how to act when I like someone and she's living so close. I figured if I was always at your door, asking you over for dinner, I would come across like a crazy stalker." His face was suddenly so serious, little worry lines forming around his mouth in an expression like regret. "I like you, so much more than I expected, and it's made things more difficult than they should be."

"So you like me *too* much?" I asked, skeptical.

"I think so," he said, his tone surprised, as if he hadn't thought about this until now.

Well, it was a reason. It wasn't a good reason, but I would accept it.

He shifted on the mattress, running a hand down the length of my side to curve over my hip. He ran the tips of his fingers over the small of my back, stroking the base of my spine. "Now I have a question for you."

"Is it about my snoring?" I asked.

"No."

"Then go ahead."

"Why the hell are you here?" he asked. "Why would a girl move from the big city to Middle-of-Nowhere, Kentucky? And don't tell me change of scenery. Because no scenery could be that bad that you'd move to the Hollow."

I'm a witch on the hunt for magical artifacts that will guarantee our continued magical domination over an evil former branch of our family.

Well, I should probably phrase it some other way.

I looked up at him, tracing the contours of his cheekbones with my fingertips. I'd omitted or outright lied to him about so many things. Lying to Jed weighed on me more than I'd expected. I wanted to tell him the truth for once, about this one little thing. I didn't have to tell him about witchcraft or where I was really from, but I could give him this tiny bit of truth.

"I have family in the Hollow," I said, carefully lacing my fingers through his. "I only found out about them a few months ago. My mother never knew her dad. It was always this big family secret we were never even supposed to ask about. My grandmother died recently, and right before she passed, she shared his name with me. Have you heard of Gilbert Wainwright, the man who owned the house before Dick?"

Jed's eyebrows rose. "Really?"

I nodded. "It turns out my grandfather died a while ago but left behind other relatives. Aunts and uncles and cousins," I said, thinking of my vampire friends and the more trustworthy branch of the Lavelle clan. "And I wanted to get to know that side of my family."

"So you never knew this whole section of your family existed, and bam, instant aunts and uncles?" he asked, propping his head against a pillow. "What's that like?"

"Bizarre," I admitted with a sniffle. He was quiet for a long moment, staring at me and running his fingertips down the length of my cheek.

"Family can be that way. Bizarre, I mean. Have I ever told you about the time my brother Jim threw a dart at my head and put me in an eye patch for two months?" he asked, rolling me onto my side and pulling my back against his chest.

"How would you have possibly told me about that?" I chuckled.

"Don't laugh. I made that eye patch look good," he grumbled, jostling me. "Had to wear the damn thing on school picture day. So this is the story of how Jed learned when Jim says, 'Duck,' to take him seriously."

"Are you telling me an absurd, painful story about your childhood to make me feel less awkward about this postcoital confessional?" I sniffed.

"Yes."

"All right, then," I said, turning and nestling my forehead against his collarbone.

I didn't remember falling asleep. I remembered Jed telling his eye patch story (I found out later this was one of several incidents involving his brother that ended in Jed wearing an eye patch), and then I was walking along a fern-choked trail in a jungle with a figure in front of me, chopping through vegetation with a machete. The air was sticky and hot, smelling of rotting plants. And in the distance, I could hear church bells over the din of a thousand squawking tropical birds.

"Hi there," Mr. Wainwright called over his khaki-clad shoulder.

"Aw, hell, again?" I sighed. "Do you know how off-putting it is to fall asleep in the arms of a naked man and wake up on a field trip with your grandfather?"

"Oh, come on, dear," he admonished, leaning against a tree for a breather. "Where's your sense of adventure?"

"I'm staying at the Sleep-Tight Inn, aren't I?" I muttered. "That's adventure enough for me." Glancing up the trail, I saw a decrepit whitewashed church in the distance. Its bell clanged loudly, although there was no one to yank the pull.

"Where are we?" I asked as he adjusted his dark-blue neckerchief.

"South America?" he guessed. "I hate to belabor the point, but it's your dream."

I hissed as a banana leaf snapped back and thwacked me across the face. "So what nonhelpful advice do you have to offer me this time?"

"Never trust a man with the middle name Wayne," he said.

"What?"

He grunted, hacking his way through a clump of banana leaves. "You never said the advice had to be related to the Elements."

"Why am I even bothering?" I sighed, following him. "You know, I managed to find two of the Elements on my own. I don't need your help."

"Of course you don't," he said as a large yellow butterfly fluttered past his shoulder. "But you're the one who keeps bringing me back here."

"Mr. Wainwright," I growled.

"You're still not going to call me Grandpa, are you?" he said sadly.

"Not for a while," I told him. "I don't know you that well yet."

"I hoped that spending time at the shop would help you get to know me."

"I thought you were a figment of my imagination. Do figments hope?"

He snickered. "Touché. You know, this might go a bit

faster if you used a little . . ." He waggled his fingers as if casting a Las Vegas magician's spell.

"Really?" I scoffed. "You want me to use magic because you're having trouble with some landscaping?"

"No, I want you to use magic because it can be fun," he said, gesturing to building-scale trees towering over our heads. "Maybe just peel all the greenery back like curtains. Or make the trees dance around like those 'Sorcerer's Apprentice' mops in *Fantasia*. I just want to see what you can do. It's not like I ever got to watch you perform in a ballet recital."

"I never took ballet. And didn't Nana tell you anything about our magic?" I asked.

"She said your family's talents were a gift, not that you were only allowed to put them toward practical purposes," he said. "Just think of how boring life would be if you received gloves and car-detailing kits every Christmas."

I thought back to my grandmother's many, many lectures on magic. She had never told me that magic wasn't supposed to be fun. In fact, I remembered several lessons in which she taught me to create shapes in colored smoke through concentration. Or to make fire dance. But the fire-dancing lesson had ended in tears and damaged drapes. So we'd stuck to the area in which I excelled, which happened to be healing. There aren't a lot of laughs to be had in curing rashes and boils.

Come to think of it, in addition to the motel sleeping bag, Stephen had also given me gloves and a car-detailing kit for Christmas.

"I think you're being too hard on yourself," Mr. Wainwright said. "I think the search for your Elements is a bit like keeping a grip on that altar plaque. If you try too hard to hold on to it, you'll break it."

"So I need to relax." I snorted. "In the face of an impossible task and a looming deadline, I'm supposed to relax and have fun."

"It couldn't hurt."

"I'll try. Thanks, Mr. Wainwright."

"Still not budging on that 'Grandpa' issue, are you?"

I shook my head but grinned at him and squeezed his hand. "No."

Mr. Wainwright squeezed my hand tightly, then turned on his heel and commenced chopping through the jungle plants again.

"Nola?" he called as he pushed into the brush. "Take it easy on Dick. He means well."

Muttering to myself about unhelpful figments, I woke up with my head propped on my arm and the bare expanse of Jed's back turned toward me. He was up on one elbow, holding something, shifting it back and forth in his hands.

"Are you all right?" I asked. Startled, he turned, and there was a strange, unfamiliar expression on his face. Sadness, regret, a touch of anger. I'd never seen those emotions on Jed's sunny, open face. He looked down at me, a quick grin spreading across his features, chasing the sad expression away. "Yeah, just fine."

"So this is incredibly awkward," I said. I sat up, with the sheets pressed to my chest. I looked over Jed's shoulder to find that he was holding the altar plaque in his hands, turning it over and over. "What are you doing?"

"I just didn't get a very good look at it last night," he said, turning onto his back and pulling me with him so I was splayed across his chest as he toyed with the plaque. "It's just a chunk of clay. I was tryin' to figure out what was so special about this that Jane Jameson would send us all the way down here for it."

I carefully retrieved the plaque from his hands and wrapped it in the unbleached cloth I'd packed for just such a purpose. "I think it was the principle of the thing. Jane got really pissed at the idea that Mama Ginger had not only stolen from her but had also used ill-gotten goods to get out of shopping for a present. Reclaiming the gift would embarrass Mama Ginger, so the effort was worth it."

"But why send you?"

"I've spent a lot of time at the shop lately, and I haven't stolen anything from her yet. It fostered a sense of trust."

"Not for me," he said. "I plan on pattin' you down after you get out of my truck."

"Well, I was also one of the few people she knew who could make the trip down here," I said. There was a pause, not awkward, just pleasant. I pressed a finger into the little divot in his chin, making him dip his head and bite down on my fingertip. I laughed and drew it away, but not before his rasping tongue on the ridges of my skin sparked some rather pleasant tingles between my thighs. "So last night . . ."

". . . Was not a one-time occasion," he informed me.

"That was new for me. The whole talkin' and actually tellin' you what I think, instead of what I think you want to hear—I don't do that with everybody. In fact, I don't think I've ever done that before. This is a beginning, not a brush-off, understood?"

I nodded. "Still, it is incredibly awkward."

"Did you have a good time?" He leaned across the sheets and pushed my hair back from my face. I nodded. "Do you think I'm easy?"

I burst out laughing. "No."

"Good. I don't think you're easy, either. I think you're sexy and fun and bendy in all the right places."

"I told you, 'bendy' is a selling point."

"Honey, I saw all kind of potential in you last night."

The drive back was pleasant enough. I ended up sleeping for a good portion of it, which made Jed snicker about having worn me out. I snarked back that I was just trying to avoid further trauma from Atlanta traffic. We only made a few stops for coffee and Sno-Balls, and by midafternoon, we were rolling back into town.

I liked that despite the fact that we'd seen each other naked, nothing seemed to change. He still made inappropriate jokes. I made vague threats to his manhood. It was lovely, relaxed. But I felt strange that I didn't feel worse. I'd fought with Stephen, but I wasn't sure if I'd broken it off with him officially. He'd left me ten voice-mail messages, most of which I'd ignored. As far I knew, he was ordering bloody apology flowers and sending them my way. If so, I was a terrible girlfriend. But what bothered me the most was that I didn't actually feel bad. Physically, I felt good—balanced, limber, and untroubled. The last time I felt this loose was after getting a massage at one of those day spas when Penny got married and insisted on a girls' do.

I was a morality-free zone.

Still, it was hard to feel bad, knowing that the plaque was resting comfortably in my overnight bag. Jed pulled the truck into the driveway and slowed to a stop. "So, frankly, I'm sick of the sight of you," he told me with a distressingly straight face. "Get out of my truck, and definitely do not come to my side of the house for dinner."

"You are truly a bizarre man," I told him.

"Is pizza OK?" he asked, grinning.

"Fine, pizza, with a potential side order of repeat sex."

He climbed out of the truck and craned his head back through the door. "If I place the order that way at Pete's Pies, the lady who answers their phones will pass out."

"But she will remember the order."

"I'll get the bags," he called from the truck's tailgate. "Can you grab my mail?"

"Sure!"

I was halfway to the door-mounted mailbox when I heard Jed yelp, "Shit!" and then a crunch. When I rounded the truck, I saw him standing over my suitcase, which was lying on its side in the gravel.

"What happened?" I asked, fumbling with the zipper. I'd placed the plaque inside a zippered pocket on the outside of the bag. I could only hope that Jed hadn't dropped the bag on that side.

Jed's expression was stricken. "It just slipped out of my hand."

I scrambled through my overnight bag to find the cloth bag I'd wrapped around the plaque. My heart sank as the bag tinkled and crunched in my shaking hands. The clay was shattered. There were three or four pieces the size of my thumb, but everything else was practically dust. It wasn't surprising, I supposed, considering how old the clay was. I took deep breaths and tried to keep myself centered. I couldn't risk having a meltdown and blowing up Jed's porch lights.

"I'm so sorry," he said, his face ashen. "How bad is it?"

"Bad," I told him, holding up the clay shards. I took a deep breath and forced my voice to stay steady. "Accidents happen, Jed. It's not your fault."

Jed bent to examine the bits in my hand. The outsides of the larger pieces were distressed and old, but the interiors were just as bright and fresh as a new penny. Maybe the hum of magic that had cloaked the plaque all those years had formed some sort of stasis?

"How angry is Jane going to be?" he asked, taking one piece and turning it over in my palm. "I can tell her it was my fault."

"Jane won't be angry at all," I told him honestly. I tried to manage a smile for him, so he wouldn't beat himself up over this. "It's just an ashtray."

Later that evening, I tried to piece the plaque back together like a jigsaw puzzle. I managed a flat, vaguely round shape, but that was it. I even tried to use the plaque's own magic to get the pieces to call out to one another, to re-form to its original state, but it didn't respond the way I thought a magically infused item would. They were just bits of clay. Instead of contaminating those bits with the fumes of Super Glue, I decided I would take them to the shop, put them in an unbleached cotton bag, and close the lot up in a drawer full of good Kilcairy soil. That was the extent of what I could do.

I heard Jed walk out his front door and listened for the sound of his truck, but I got distracted when the phone rang. My dear Penny didn't have an opinion about whether the plaque would "work" when it was broken. It was possible it wouldn't work, but at the same time, I felt sort of free. The Kerrigans couldn't get all four items. They couldn't bind us, which would ease my family's anxiety and keep the clinic running smoothly. Of course, we couldn't bind them, but that was another problem entirely. Still, I'd failed to protect centuries of family history. And I was depressed beyond the telling of it, and Jed was embarrassed. The evening I'd hoped would be spent having the aforementioned bendy-straw sex was spent in separate quarters. I sat in the kitchen, staring down at the dust, trying to figure out what to do.

Penny did, however, think it was rather hilarious that of all the people in the family, I'd been the one who inadvertently destroyed our heirloom.

"You are hereby the worst witch in the family!" she hooted. "I mean, clearly, it's a tragedy, but the fact that you did it, and not me—"

"Too soon, Penny."

"Stephen came by the clinic," she said, in a quick change of subject. "It was rather shocking, him just showing up out of the blue. I know he avoids coming here unless it's absolutely necessary. Anyway, he seems to think you've lost your mind. Did you really break it off with him?"

"I'm not sure. The conversation didn't end with kissy noises, that's for certain."

"Well, if you did, I, for one, am glad. I was getting tired of talking to him. And I didn't even have to sleep with him."

"So, other than casting doubts about my mental capacity, what did Stephen have to say?"

"Nothing memorable; it was a conversation with Stephen. You know I only pay attention half the time he's speaking. But do us a favor, and call him to settle things, so he stops pestering us? Uncle Seamus's hexing hand is getting itchy."

"I'll call him and clear things up," I promised. "Just not today."

"And who, may I ask, is the person you are choosing to spend time with instead of our *dear* Stephen?" As I made an indignant squawking noise, she added, "And don't try to deny it, I can hear that 'I just did naked things' quality in your voice."

"I didn't do naked things," I said primly. "We were only seminude."

It was true. Jed had left his socks on.

Penny gasped noisily. "Seminude as in shirtless?" she cried. "As in your shirt-hating neighbor? You got seminude with the gorgeous, shirt-hating neighbor?"

"I will neither confirm nor deny."

"Well, it's about time you started making stupid decisions. It was getting lonely out here on the 'screw-up' limb of the family tree."

"And who told you that getting your boyfriend's name tattooed on your ankle was a good idea? You were limited to men named Dave until you saved up enough to have it removed. Now, if all you're going to do is mock my not-so-youthful indiscretions, I'm hanging up."

"No, wait!" she cried. "Just tell me one thing."

"What?"

"The last time you saw him, was he wearing ripped jeans and a muscle shirt?"

"No!" I exclaimed, before adding, "Not today . . . Did you know they call them 'wifebeaters' here?"

"Well, that's off-putting."

"Tell me about it."

"No." She pressed me. "*You* tell *me* about it. What's this Jed like?"

"He's just a nice man who lives next door."

"And he's good-lookin'?"

"Ridiculously so." I sighed. "But nothing serious is going to happen, because that's not why I'm here."

"Right, the whole family expects you to shut yourself off from the waist down."

"No, but I'm pretty sure Stephen would want me to," I muttered.

"Well, that would be the only way I would survive sleeping with Stephen."

"Shut up, Penelope."

After several very expensive minutes' worth of harassment from Penny, I hung up on her. But she did ask whether I would qualify Jed's arse as "squeezable." The woman had it coming.

Eager to shake off the images of Penny sexually harassing my neighbor, I went to the sink to start tea. There was a squarish window over the sink, with a pretty blue flower box outside overflowing with white impatiens, thanks to the work crews. I was loath to admit it, but I was afraid to look out the window into the back garden. The clouds had cleared, and even the half-moon was bright. And I was convinced that the moment I looked up, I would see a Chupacabra pressed against the window like a suction-cup Garfield doll. But damned if I didn't accidentally look up anyway.

I shouldn't have.

Near my brand-new arbor, I could see something moving. The hair on the back of my neck stood up. It stood on two feet and seemed human. The shape seemed thinner than last time, larger, but I was viewing it from another angle. It crept past the arbor toward the house. Gasping, I dashed toward my kitchen door and flipped the lock. I fumbled for the light switch, and the room plunged into darkness. The outlines of the trees stood in sharp relief without the interference of the kitchen light. The shape stilled, swinging its head toward the house. I backed away from the door, wondering if it was smarter to run upstairs or out the front door. Of course, this had to happen on one of my "powerless" days, so I couldn't even work up the juice to neutralize whatever it was if it broke into the house.

A voice sounded behind me. "What are you doing?"

Shrieking, I pivoted on my heel and swung my fist as hard as I could.

"Ow!" Jane cried, dropping to her knees and clutching her chest. She glared up at me and wheezed, "Why did you punch me in the boob?"

Jane and Jolene were standing in my kitchen. Well, technically, Jolene had collapsed to her knees, cackling with laughter. And Jane was crumpled on the floor, hit by friendly fire. I looked toward the back garden, but the shape had disappeared.

"You startled me!" I exclaimed.

"How does 'startled' end with me getting punched in the boob?" she griped as I helped her to her feet. "If this is about Jed driving you, that was Andrea's idea, not mine. Personally, I don't really like the guy. His thoughts are all cloudy. Makes me uncomfortable."

"You have vampire strength and speed. How could I hit you in the first place?" I countered while Jolene continued to hee-haw.

"I don't use my vampire speed when I'm around human friends, whom I expect *not* to punch me in the boob. And how is superstrength supposed to make this hurt less?"

"How did you even get in here?" I demanded.

"Your front door was unlocked," Jane said, wincing as she settled into a kitchen chair. "We came by to see how your little dip in Mama Ginger's freaky gene pool went and to give you hell over spending twenty-four hours in a truck with your hot neighbor. Andrea would have come by, but I think she was afraid you'd be mad at her for setting you up. We knocked. We called for you, but I guess you were so busy staring out your back window that you didn't hear us. What are you staring at, anyway?"

"I think I'm going crazy," I groaned, pouring a cup of tea for Jolene.

"Why would you think that?" Jolene asked.

"I think I saw someone in my back garden," I told her. "I've seen it before. I think it's a Yeti or a werewolf or something."

Jolene cleared her throat. "Yeah, that would be . . . nuts."

"I keep seeing this weird shape outside in the yard," I said. "It seems to be watching the house but never comes close enough for me to get a good look at it."

"It's probably just an animal," Jane assured me. "We get all sorts of weird critters around here. And some animals, like deer, don't think twice about coming close to a house. Hell, if you're not careful, they can end up in your house. Just ask my cousin Junie."

"It was on two legs. It looked human. Just dark and hairy."

"OK, then." Jolene squared her shoulders and pushed the back door open.

"No, Jolene, wait!" I hissed as she stepped onto the back porch. Jane put a hand on my shoulder and shook her head. I heard Jolene take a deep breath through her nose and hold it. She looked back at Jane and shook her head.

What in the hell was going on?

Jane turned to me. "The Kerrigans. Those people you were talking about before. They wouldn't know to look for you here, right?"

"I don't think so. I mean, they have more resources than we do, financially. I suppose it wouldn't take much to track me through customs, though it wouldn't explain how they would know I'm renting this place."

"Well, no more jaunts out of town without vampire escort. And no jaunts into the backyard after dark. Basically, you will do no jaunting of any kind. And we'll talk to Dick about putting some extra security lights back here."

I groaned. "Must we?"

"Yes," Jane insisted. "And you two are going to have a long, clarifying chat. He's let you stew about this too long. He's wasting precious time being afraid of freaking you out."

I frowned. "Beg pardon?"

"The other bruised boob owes you an explanation," Jane deadpanned.

11

If you stumble upon a family ritual involving vampires, move along. They're too odd and twisted to get involved with safely.

—*Miss Manners' Guide to Undead Etiquette*

The next night, I secured the plaque dust in Jane's shop safe. I opened the drawers in Uncle Jack's cabinet, as if I could make the other two Elements appear by force of will. Two left. It had taken me nearly a month, but I'd managed to find two. I knew this was a minor miracle, and that I should have been thrilled. But the fact that Earth was broken into bits was more than a little disheartening. It had certainly taken the shine off being halfway to my goal.

I had another month. I didn't know where to begin looking for the other two Elements. I didn't know whether I could try contacting Nana through the die again. There had been ridiculously few clues in Jane's sales records. So far, I'd skated by on chance. And I didn't know how to kick-start chance.

"Nola!" Jane called. My favorite vampire's head suddenly appeared in the doorway to her office. Her lips were twitching a little. I was so glad she could find amusement in my abject discomfort. "Can you come up front?"

Oh, right, the heart-to-heart with Dick.

That sounded wrong, even in my head.

"I would really rather not."

Jane laughed lightly. "Look, I know what you're thinking. Literally. And I promise you, this situation is absolutely nothing like the disturbing worst-case scenario that's going on in your head. Could you please just come and talk to Dick?"

I peered up at her over my reading glasses, skeptical.

"I promise you, if you're propositioned in any way, I will serve as your getaway driver," she said, holding up her hand in a mockery of the Girl Scout promise.

"Fine," I grumbled, following her to the coffee bar.

Dick was a vampire the worse for wear. In the weeks since I'd seen him, he'd developed little worry lines where the undead weren't supposed to get lines. He looked tired and pale, like a man who'd been beating himself up night after night, only to stay up half the day to do it some more.

This was about as comfortable as one of those intervention shows, when the clueless alcoholic walks into a hotel room to find a circle of friends with tear-jerking letters. When I stopped, Jane prodded me to keep walking. I walked around the bar and stood at the point farthest away from Dick, which Andrea seemed to find really amusing for some reason.

Dick was making a study of the ceiling and would not look at me. Jane cleared her throat. Dick shifted his eyes to the track lighting.

"Dick!" Jane exclaimed. "Out with it."

Dick cleared his throat. "Um, Nola, Jane tells me you seem to have some misconceptions about my intentions toward you. I just wanted to apologize for any occasions on which I made you feel uncomfortable or objectified in any way."

"Did someone write that speech for you before you came?" I asked flatly.

"I think he cobbled together portions of those 'leaving to spend more time with my family' speeches given by disgraced politicians," Andrea said, sipping fresh blood and coffee.

Jane snickered.

"You both suck," Dick told them. "OK, look, Nola, I didn't want to just throw this out at you when you first showed up. I wanted you to get to know me better so it wouldn't come as a shock. But I guess I got a little over-enthusiastic, and instead of being friendly to you, I came across like a . . ."

"Creepy stalker?" Jane suggested cheerfully.

"Sex predator?" Andrea added. "Which made me an accessory to said predator."

Dick pointed a finger in their direction. "That." He cleared his throat and reached toward my hand. Thinking better of it, he awkwardly changed directions and wiped his hand on his jeans. "Gilbert Wainwright, he was my great-great-, well, a couple of times great-grandson," Dick said. "Which would make me your great-great-, several more times great-grandpa."

My jaw dropped. The room seemed to list like a ship's deck under my feet. I studied his face closely. I could see the slope of my mother's nose on his face, the irregular bow to his lips. "Holy shit!"

Behind me, Andrea slapped Jane's shoulder and hissed, "I told you so!"

Jane yelped and said, "I thought she would find Dick being a relative a preferable alternative to him wanting to sleep with her. Damn it, Andrea, get a cold rag. I think Nola's going to faint."

"Nope. Panic attack," I wheezed. "My whole life is one long series of barely averted panic attacks. I'm going to sit down."

My knees buckled as I leaned onto the bar stools. My face seemed so cold all of a sudden, and my stomach roiled. Jane exclaimed something about wanting the news to be "a surprise, not a bad talk-show reunion!"

"Are you OK?" Dick asked as my head swam.

Dick was my ancestor? Mr. Wainwright may have been a little disheveled, but he seemed respectable. But Dick? Sometimes I had to fight the instinct to clutch my purse to my chest to keep him from snatching it.

I couldn't keep taking shocks like this. I'd lived for years believing that my life was arranged in a specific, if slightly bizarre, way. And now these little bombs of revelation kept dropping on my head and changing the way I saw myself, my family, my whole damned life. Part of me wanted to throw that stupid bottle of synthetic blood at his head and tell him not to speak to me again.

And yet there was the curve of my cheek and the odd long line of my mother's nose in this man's face. And I felt the loss of my nana all over again. She would know exactly what to say in this situation, and here I was as stunned as a half-dead fish. Whatever momentum I'd built toward the stool shifted, and I knew I was on a collision course with the floor. A pair of cool, strong hands caught my elbows and held me upright. And the next thing I knew, my face was pressed against the worn, clean cotton of Dick's T-shirt.

Andrea appeared at his side with a bottle of water and pressed the cool plastic into my hand. Dick apologized over and over as he helped my bum locate the seat.

"If it makes you feel any better, for weeks, Dick has been running himself ragged, fussing over stuff like 'Is that chair safe enough for Nola to sit in?' and whether he should baby-proof his house," Jane mused. Dick glared at her. "What, it's not my fault that you're a wide-open channel when you receive emotionally charged news."

I stared at Dick. "Baby-proofing?"

"I've never been able to spend much time around my kin while they were living," he said, shrugging. "And you look so fragile."

"And so fixing up the house I'm living in now . . ."

"Is a much-needed business investment," he assured me. "Which just happens to ensure your safety and comfort. While we're talking about the house, you can take your rent checks back. There's no way I'm going to charge my own granddaughter to put a roof over her head."

"I want to pay my own way . . . what do I call you now? It seems wrong to call you Dick."

"Grampy?" Jane suggested with a wry grin. Andrea threw a coffee filter at her head.

"I don't know," Dick said, and if I wasn't mistaken, the slightest bit of pink-tinged moisture was gathering at the corners of his eyes. "You could call me Grandpa if you want. Or Papa. Whatever makes you happy."

"I don't know if I'm comfortable with any of them."

"It's going to take some time for everyone to adjust," Andrea said. "Don't worry. We'll figure it all out. But if you call me Granny, I will smack you so hard your eyes will cross."

"You actually sound quite a bit like my granny," I mused, ducking when Andrea tossed another filter my way. "Though I think if anybody has to the right to smack anybody, it's me. I can't believe you two kept this from me! I thought—well, Jane knows what I thought. How could you?"

"It wasn't our place," Jane said. "Andrea wanted to let Dick find his own way to tell you, which was clearly a mistake. And I'm not related to you, and no good has ever come of me blabbing secrets that don't belong to me."

"Also, it wouldn't have been nearly as funny," Andrea said.

"Shut it, Granny," I said as Andrea made rude and unladylike gestures. "And while I appreciate the fact that you're fixing up the house, none of this is necessary."

Andrea snorted and gave me a wink. "You haven't even seen the Christmas presents."

"If I go out back and find out you've bought me a pony, I don't know what I'll do, Dick."

Ruffling my hair, Dick gave me an even better gift. He handed me a family tree he'd diagrammed on graph paper, including birth and death dates, marriages, and children. It showed that Gilbert Wainwright's father, Gordon Wainwright, was the son of Albert Wainwright, son of Eugenia Wainwright, a laundry woman who had worked on the Cheney family farm when Dick was human. She had Albert in 1879 but died a short time later.

"When Eugenia had the baby, I was young and mortal . . . and stupid. I let my parents talk me out of claiming him, even when his mama died," he told me, a sheepish, forlorn expression wrinkling his handsome face. Andrea rubbed his back and nudged him a little, encouraging him to continue. "Albert grew up, and I was able to watch him from a distance. He married, had a son. His son married, had a son. And I watched over them, all of them, watched them live their lives, enjoy their successes, make their mistakes. I never made contact with them," he said. "Not until Gilbert."

"How did you make contact?"

"When his father died and his mother was having troubles making ends meet, I came forward. I didn't tell his mama who I was, exactly, just a distant cousin who was interested in making sure the family was well taken care of. I made sure Gilbert and his sister had new clothes, enough to eat, money for college and books, and whatever else they needed."

"Why? What was so special about my grandfather?"

"He was the first in our family who looked like he might amount to something. He was such a *good* boy, and he was so interested in learning more about, hell, everything. He turned everything he did into an opportunity to understand more about the world. He was the first man in our family to start college, much less finish it." Dick smiled proudly. "And then there's you. Look at you. You went to college. You're a nurse. You help people. You're just like him. And you're a girl. Our family hardly ever gets girls."

"That explains the pink roses you planted outside my door." I chuckled.

"I know you're part of a pretty long line, over there in the old country. But the line you have here? It's just as long. Maybe not as distinguished, but we're colorful. Please believe me, if Gilbert had known about your mama, about you, you have no idea what it would have meant to him. He was fond of Jane, but knowing that you were out there would have made him so happy. Hell, I'm happy to know you. Now, sit down and tell me all about yourself."

So we talked. The more he talked about his love for his descendants, the more I felt sick and guilty for assuming that Dick was a polyamorous lecher. It was sweet that he was trying so hard, even if some of his gestures made me extremely uncomfortable. And he seemed to be operating under the assumption that I was both a preadolescent and an innocent flower. He was not happy that his wife had arranged for me to go on an overnight trip with "a man composed entirely of testosterone and aftershave." I felt that was unfair.

When I'd first moved overseas, my uncles had tried to make up for the loss of my father when I was growing up, making sure that I had someone to escort me on the school's awards days, to teach me to drive and where to strike first if my date got fresh. But they had their own children to attend to. Even if Dick was . . . unconventional, he was doing his best to show me how glad he was that I existed. And really, that's all any kid hopes for.

Stephen called. A lot. He begged me to reconsider ending things between us, which helped settled the debate about whether I'd broken up with him. I called him back once to tell him to stop calling, but all I got was his voice mail. Unfortunately, that seemed to encourage him to double his calls. I was considering buying a new phone, but that would mean reprogramming my entire address book. I had a lot of cousins.

In less conclusive dating news, my pizza date with Jed was postponed by several nights. Jed had to work overtime on a vampire's home theater, and then I ended up getting caught in the middle of a stomach-flu epidemic at the clinic. I came home from the clinic the following Friday smelling strongly of Lysol but determined to spend some prearranged time with him.

I did bathe first.

For some reason, discussing various aspects of witch-craft with me had inspired Jane to stock more "Crafty" items, including incense and bath oils. I was experiment-ing with said oils tonight—neroli, a citrus extract that was supposed to, er, stimulate one's partner, and sun-flower for creative thinking. I'd never bothered before, but it couldn't hurt and smelled downright delicious. I sank in the warm, frothy water up to my chin. Now that I knew that Dick was trying to do something nice for me as his descendant and not draw me into a creepy love web, I could enjoy the tub.

As much as I'd come to appreciate Dick's improve-ments to the house, it had made the place feel different. When I came home from work, the house felt off. Shoes that I thought I'd left in front of the closet showed up by my dresser. The furniture I'd purchased from different thrift stores around town seemed to have moved a few inches. A carnelian necklace that belonged to Nana Fee disappeared from my bathroom drawer. The house even smelled different, a strange musky note over the soft green and floral scents I preferred.

I wondered whether it could be a ghost. Jane had mentioned that my grandfather remained on the earthly plane for more than a year after he died. And this house had belonged to several generations of Wainwrights before him. But Jane insisted that Mr. Wainwright had moved on. And Nana Fee wouldn't waste her time mov-ing my shoes and retrieving her costume jewelry.

The examples were so minor I felt silly bringing them

up to anyone. But it was making me edgy. Between my house possibly being haunted by a furniture-moving ghost and my ex-boyfriend issues, if anyone needed a bubble bath at the moment, it was me.

I closed my eyes, tipped my head back, and let my arms float to the surface. I hadn't made any progress in my search for the two items left, the athame and the bell. The bell represented water and was usually rung to mark the beginning and end of rituals. It made sense, on a certain level. The ripples of sound waves weren't that different from the undulating surface of water. And although some Wiccan groups disagreed over whether air was best represented by a wand or an athame, McGavocks had always favored blades to direct energy.

I always found it amusing that sweet little old Nana Fee had so many knives around the house: ritual knives, small blades for taking cuttings from her garden, and, of course, kitchen knives. This also explained why no one broke into our house. Ever.

The warm water lapping over my skin had my mind drifting from image to image. The athame sliding through the air, pulling energy from one edge of the circle to the other like thick ropes of viscous blue taffy. The ropes thinned and curled, becoming ocean waves flowing past the shores near my village. I blew out a long breath, taking in the sweet scented air. I imagined the waves rolling and ebbing, creating a continuous glowing white line over my head. The line looped into circles, pulsing and growing in strength. I flexed my hands under the water, moving them like a conductor leading a symphony. I pulled that glowing line in my mind with a turn of my wrist, strumming it against my fingertips.

I heard footsteps coming up the stairs. My eyes popped open with a start. The small funnel stream of water that had formed on the surface of the bath, a tiny hurricane I'd created during this impromptu meditation exercise, collapsed on itself with a splash. I blinked rapidly.

That was new.

And suddenly, the spout exploded toward the ceiling, taking most of the bathwater with it as it grew. Panic had my ears buzzing as the footsteps grew closer and the water covering my body dropped to nothing. What if whoever it was saw this unnatural bathtub weather phenomenon? Worse, what if the the person saw me naked?

Another footfall sounded in the hallway. My head whipped toward the sound, and the water spout collapsed on itself, dumping buckets of water over my head and splashing all over the floor.

Bollocks.

But I had more pressing problems than a flooded bathroom. I knew I'd locked the front door. The only person who had a copy of the key was Jed, in case of emergencies. But what if it wasn't Jed? I eyed the heavy pewter candlestick I'd placed near the sink. As the steps came closer to my bedroom, I slid down the length of the tub and picked up the candlestick.

Moving quietly, I rose to my knees. I wondered if I could jump out of the tub and get to my robe before whoever it was got to my door. The noise stopped just outside my door. My arm froze over the edge of the tub, tensed for a swing.

Suddenly, Jed's head appeared in my bathroom doorway.

"Well, this is a picture," he said, grinning down at me. "You know, conventional wisdom says you should keep the water *inside* the tub."

I chuckled, relief flooding my chest as I set the candlestick aside. "I was just making room for you."

Jed grabbed some towels, got on his hands and knees, and mopped up the water I'd spilled. I groaned, and not just because his delicious jean-clad bum was in view. "That is the hottest thing I have ever seen. A man cleaning up after me."

"You're such a sexist." Grinning wickedly, he slipped out of his boots and rolled up the legs of his jeans, sliding behind me, balancing his bum on the lip of the tub while he settled his feet on either side of me. He settled my temple against his thigh and carefully massaged my neck as I refilled the tub with warm water.

"So you're the one who got the master bed and bath." He sighed. "I'm jealous. I think my part of the house was the servants' quarters. And just so you know, the tub in this room is twenty percent longer than the standard tub. Apparently, Mrs. Wainwright was a large woman."

It would have hurt my feelings that he just called my great-grandmother fat, but he was doing an awfully nice job with the neck rub. It pricked at my conscience that I still hadn't told Jed why I was in the Hollow. I mean, the man had seen me naked, but I wasn't willing to tell him about my family's unorthodox history? I ached to tell him about the recent development with Dick, but it would have involved an excessive amount of explaining, when all I wanted to do was sit quietly with someone who knew nothing about magic or centuries-old magical yard-sale finds. (And had abdominals you could use for laundry.)

With recently ended relationships, cultural differences, and as-yet-undisclosed vampire relatives, we were dealing with enough issues without adding magic into the mix.

"Rough day?" he asked.

"I learned a lot," I said as he brushed the wet hair out of my face. Like the fact that I could create tiny storm systems with my mind. That was a life lesson if there ever was one. "Why don't you take off those clothes and join me in this big old tub?"

"Because if you're all wet and slippery and I'm all wet and slippery, one of us might get hurt when I do this." He leaned down and kissed me softly on the lips. I rose to my knees, plucking at the buttons of his shirt with my wet fingers. I threw it onto the floor, and before I could get to his jeans, he pulled me against him. He was right, it was slippery. My skin slid against his, and he nearly dropped me as he dragged me out of the tub and wrapped a towel around me, although he didn't give me time to dry off as we fumbled toward the bed.

I looped my ankle around his, pushing him back onto the bed so I could yank the jeans and boxers away. He chuckled. "Well, this is an exciting new side to you."

Grinning wildly, I climbed up on the bed, hovering over him, and settled my hips over his. I tucked my feet under his calves and stretched down the length of his body.

"Soooo bendy," he murmured, threading his hands through my hair and pressing his lips to mine.

"Really, Jed—"

"Nola, there's something I've been wantin' to tell you for a while now," he murmured against my lips.

"Hmm?"

He gently pinched my lips shut with his fingertips. "Shh."

I rolled my eyes as he smirked. His hips surged forward with a snap, and my whole body sang.

12

Never trust a werewolf when life is on the line.
— *When, What, Witch, Were, and Why?*
The Five W's of Safe Interactions with the Paranormal

Dr. Hackett took a week off to go trout fishing in Arkansas, leaving me with time to throw myself into searching Specialty Books. The solstice deadline was looming in three weeks. I tried to use the die to contact Nana Fee (without Andrea's help), but all I managed to do was make contact with one of Jane's former step-grandfathers. He just wanted to say hello and tell her that "Grandma Ruthie is still secured," whatever that meant.

As I had officially scoured every inch of the shop space, including searching for the athame in the utensil drawer of the coffee bar, I called or e-mailed Mr. Wainwright's contacts in the artifact market, anyone who might have supplied him with items for the shop, on the off chance that Mr. Wainwright had traded the athame for stock. Giving them a sob story about my grandmother accidentally selling a family heirloom to Mr. Wainwright, I asked if they would mind sending me a picture of any athames they'd bartered through the shop. If it was the item I was looking for, I offered to buy it back for fifty percent more than they'd paid for it.

A buyer in California told me to mind my own damn business and hung up on me. A buyer in Canada was only too happy to help, but the handle of his athame was blue enamel with a dark onyx stone. And the buyer in Spain . . .

"I know my Spanish is rusty, but I'm pretty sure *cuadros desnudos* means 'naked pictures,'" Andrea said, handing me a printout as we sprawled around my living room, sorting through these e-mails. Jed, who had been spending more and more time in my half of the duplex, was perched on a ladder in the middle of the room, replacing the old globe light fixture with a ceiling fan. Because I still wasn't ready for the whole witchcraft confession, we'd told him we were searching for some antiques to complete a collection for one of Jane's customers.

"If you want to see what he has, he wants to see what you have. It's your classic tit-for-athame scenario."

"You are enjoying this far too much," I told her.

"Yes, I am," she said, nodding. Behind her, Jane gave me a wicked grin.

"I am not comfortable with this line of conversation," Dick muttered, walking away. "If I see you with a camera, young lady, you're grounded."

Jed, who seemed wary of my protective vampire great-great-great-grandpa, raised his hand. "I'm with Mr. Cheney."

"Yes, sir." I sighed, tossing the e-mail in the trash.

"You don't have to call him Mr. Cheney," Andrea assured Jed as he made the last adjustment to the ceiling fan.

"Yes, I do," Jed responded.

Dick nodded as Jed climbed down the ladder. "Yes, he does."

I snorted, making a paper ball from the other e-mails and tossing them, too. Jane watched me closely as Jed climbed down the ladder.

"You're taking this far too well," Jane observed as Dick and Jed carried the old fixture and the ladder out of the room. "You've been really relaxed the past few days, despite the fact that you've struck out with those buyers."

"Well, with the Earth plaque broken, it feels like the pressure is off a little bit," I said, shrugging. "I'm going to keep looking, because it's the right thing to do, but I don't know if the binding will work, even if I do find all four."

"No, that's not it," Jane said, her eyes narrowing. "You've had sex. With Jed."

"Shh!" I hissed at her. "Dick will hear you. We haven't actually told him that Jed and I are involved, for Jed's sake. And we haven't told Jed that I'm related to Dick, because explaining my whole twisted family backstory is not something I'm ready for."

"So why is Jed all nervous and twitchy?" Jane asked, glancing out to the backyard shed, where the menfolk were putting away tools.

"Because Dick keeps glaring at him and muttering

under his breath," I told her. "And don't poke around in my head; we've talked about that."

"She doesn't have to poke around in your head," Andrea protested. "It's written all over your face. You might as well get 'recently banged' tattooed on your forehead."

"I don't know if I can be friends with someone who sleeps with a 'Jed,'" Jane pondered, pointing at her friend. "Andrea, you set them up on that drive to Georgia; I blame you for this. Nola was such a nice girl."

"So Stephen is no more?" Andrea asked, slapping Jane's accusing finger away from her face.

"Well, I didn't murder him," I said. "I just stopped taking his calls."

"So what's going to happen when you have to go back home?" Andrea asked. "Are you going to try to keep seeing him?"

"It's not like we've made any big commitment to each other," I said. "I like Jed. And he clearly likes me, or, at least, parts of me. He's a very nice man. He's sweet and funny and smart. And he doesn't ask a lot of questions about the amount of time I spend with vampires in an occult bookshop."

"And he looks good naked," Jane added.

I sighed. "Sooo good. But there are so many things I can't tell him. As much as I like him, how could I have a real relationship with someone I have to lie to and omit huge portions of my life? How could that ever work?"

And that was what had been missing in my relationship with Stephen, I realized. I couldn't share my life with him, because there was so much he couldn't accept.

He never directly asked me to give it up, but the message had been subtly clear. If I wanted Stephen, I would have to give up the connection with my family. I felt like an idiot now for not having seen that. He wouldn't have made demands. He wouldn't have forced me. He just wouldn't have been happy otherwise. He wasn't a bad man, just a "normal" one. And normal was something I was never going to be, no matter how hard I tried.

But where did that leave me with Jed?

I'd told myself I was keeping things from Stephen to keep the peace and to protect him. But that was based on that fact that I'd known he couldn't accept the witchcraft or the weirdness. I thought perhaps Jed was just quirky enough that he could. At the very least, I could tell him about Dick. Or warn him about Dick.

"So you haven't told him about the witchy stuff or the Elements or anything?" Andrea asked.

"It's kind of hard to fit into a conversation," I told her. "How did you tell people that you were a vampire?"

"I didn't tell people, really, until I told my parents," Jane offered.

"How'd that go?"

Jane frowned. "My mother asked me if I could *try not* to be a vampire anymore."

"My parents disowned me way before I was turned," Andrea said. "But they did get really indignant when I didn't invite them to our wedding."

"That's remarkably unhelpful," I said, covering my face with my hands. I was going to have to talk to Jed about some of these things. And the small matter of my returning to Ireland in a few weeks' time. Otherwise, we were doomed to end up just like Stephen and me. And that wasn't fair. If anything, I should let my personality and emotional baggage doom the relationship.

"You want to go back to talking about sending that Spanish guy the naked pictures?" Jane asked, nudging me with her elbow.

"No."

It took a while to pry my vampire friends out of my living room. Jed had given up hours before, finding some excuse to retreat back to safe quarters on his side of the duplex. Jane and Andrea finally persuaded Dick to leave before he could try to replace other fixtures by reminding him of a *Dukes of Hazzard* marathon starting at midnight. I waited until I saw the taillights clear the driveway before sprinting across the porch. Before I could knock, Jed opened his door, yanked me into his foyer, and pinned me against the wall. Without saying a word, he pressed his lips against mine in a searing kiss. I moaned, twisting my fingers in the light cotton material of his long-sleeved workshirt as his hands slipped around my waist. Breathless and dizzy, I pulled away from him.

"Your family scares me," he said.

I arched an eyebrow. "Family?"

"Well, you're obviously not blood-related, what with the opposing accents and pulse differences, but I know family when I see it. Those people love you. They're happy to spend time with you. And Dick spends most of his time glaring at me and making crotch-specific threats when you're not around. That's family."

I frowned. Were they my family? Was I ready for any sort of family beyond the McGavocks? The clan and the clinic had been the focus of my life for so long. Did I have room for anything more in my head or my heart? I liked them all so much—Dick, Andrea, Jane, the whole company. They'd made me feel welcome and warm when I had no clue how to go about my search. They'd done all they could to help me, sometimes crossing the line of what was appropriate or sensible. I wasn't a leader. I wasn't expected to know what to do every moment of every day. I made an absolute fool of myself when necessary, and nobody panicked. It was lovely. If I could somehow blend the two groups—the overwhelming love of my living family with the unquestionable acceptance of my undead relatives—I might turn out to be a somewhat normal person.

Probably not.

I kissed Jed again—Jed, the man who'd done nothing but help me without demanding details or even questioning whether driving me across three states was a waste of time. And I felt a prick of guilt for keeping so much from him. How could he really like me when he only knew such a small part of me? No magic, no mission, no crazy vampire family. Maybe he would find those "quirks" charming and attractive.

Probably not.

"There's something I need to tell you," I said, kissing him one last time. "Several things, actually."

He nodded, the flirty, sweet energy draining from his face. "There are some things I need to tell you, too." He kissed me again, and there was a strange air of finality to it. As if he was bracing himself for bad news. Did he know something was "off" about me? Was he more comfortable wondering than not knowing? A buzzing noise sounded from the kitchen, making me break off the kiss.

"What's that?" I asked.

"Dinner," he said. "I noticed you don't eat much around the vampires, so I warmed up a chicken pot pie. We'll eat, and then we'll talk, all right?"

We gorged ourselves on pot pie and watched some silly Chuck Norris film Jed had insisted on, after I told him that I'd never seen *The Delta Force*. Apparently, this was a felony in some states.

We cleaned up the dishes, then settled in for discussion, coffee, and the most feared beard in the universe. And for about twenty minutes, I was content and relaxed. Of course, it was all downhill from there.

"Hey, could you take this into the living room for me?" he asked, handing me a bowl of rocky road ice cream. "I'm having a fistfight with the coffeemaker."

"Why does everyone in this town have an adversarial relationship with coffeepots?" I muttered as I carried the ice cream into the living room, carefully balancing the bowl to keep it from sliding off onto the floor. Penny never had forgiven me for the "Christmas trifle" incident.

But the television blaring Chuck Norris's all-around badassery was too much of a distraction, and I wasn't watching where I was stepping. Just as I passed the farthest edge of Jed's blue rag rug, my shoe caught on the fringe, dragging it back. I grumbled about my own clumsiness as I settled the bowl on the coffee table. I knelt to straighten the rug and noticed that one of the floorboards was loose, set slightly higher than the rest. I shot a guilty look toward the kitchen, where Jed was humming tunelessly. I hadn't damaged the floor, had I? I didn't remember dragging anything but the rug. I pushed on the board, trying to slide it back into place, but it listed and slid down into empty space.

"Shit!" I whispered, tilting forward as my weight shifted. I grabbed at the board, and my hand brushed against a cloth-wrapped bundle tucked away in the space underneath. "What's this?"

There was a stack of photos under the bundle . . . and one of the buildings in the corner of the photo looked awfully familiar. I pulled on the bundle, but it wouldn't come up without pulling up more boards. I popped another board out of place and pulled the cloth up, bringing the stack of photos with it. They showed long-range shots of me, walking away from the clinic in Kilcairy. There was another one of me out to dinner with Stephen in Dublin. And another, with Penny, just before I'd left for Kentucky.

"What?" The cloth slid out of my hand and to the floor with a dull *clunk*. My hands shook as I pulled the cloth loose to find the plaque—the acorn-shaped plaque I'd believed was smashed and stored in pieces in Jane's shop.

Jed had taken it. He must have switched the bundles when he took my bag out of my truck and then "accidentally" dropped my bag to make me think the plaque was broken. I was so stupid. I knew something was off with the age of those clay bits, but I'd wanted so badly to believe that I held two of the Elements, that I could trust Jed, that I shut down any doubts I should have listened to.

"I lost the fight with the coffeemaker," Jed said, carrying two mugs into the living room. "Just think of the loose grounds as 'sprinkles.'" He saw me on my knees, with the plaque in my hand. He dropped the mugs to the floor with a clash of broken pottery. "Nola, please."

"Don't," I ground out. "There's no trying to convince me that 'this isn't what it looks like.' Just explain to me, why the hell do you have this? Why would you make me think it had been destroyed? Why would you even want it?"

Jed blanched, and his gaze immediately shifted downward. "I'm so sorry."

"I didn't ask for an apology, I want a goddamn explanation!" I shouted. "You know why I'm here. You had pictures of me in your hidey-hole. You knew who I was as soon as you met me, didn't you? You knew I was a McGavock, about the witchcraft, the Elements, all of it. And you've been pretending all this time to be this clueless, sexy, himbo neighbor man. Why? Who the hell are you, Jed? Is Jed even your real name, or did you pick it out of the *Redneck Alias Handbook*?"

"Nola."

"Every word you've ever said to me was a lie." I seethed. "Here I was feeling guilty for keeping things from you—my family, the vampires, my boyfriend—and you were outright lying!"

"Not every word," he said, shaking his head. I shoved him away, cradling the bundle against my chest. "Please, Nola, you have to understand. There's a good reason for this."

"Fine, what's your reason?" I growled.

"I can't tell you right now," he said, wincing. "There are things you need to understand first."

"Bullshit."

His voice was soft as a breeze as he said, "I never meant to hurt you."

"Bullshit!" I yelled, pushing past him toward the door, the plaque pressed to my chest.

"Nola, please." He grabbed my arm. At first, I thought he would grab for the plaque, but he was only trying to keep me from leaving. "The Kerrigans—"

Before he could finish his sentence, a rage I could only describe as volcanic bubbled up from my belly and surged through my arm to my hand. He knew the Kerrigans? Was he working for the Kerrigans?

And suddenly, Jed's arm was on fire.

He yelped, waving his flaming sleeve back and forth, feeding the fire oxygen and making a small situation much worse.

"Stop moving!" I exclaimed, I shoved him into the kitchen and pushed his sleeve into the sink. I picked up the sprayer and shot an arc of water toward him. After briefly dousing Jed's face, I aimed the stream at his arm and put the sleeve fire out. His face was pale and dripping wet as we stripped him out of his sodden shirt. While the flames hadn't left a mark on his flesh, the outline of my hand was clear, as if my palm had given him a contact burn. I jerked my hand away, unable to see anything but the blistered, bright-red handprint I'd left on his arm.

Backing away, unable to take my eyes from the mark of violence I'd left on his skin, I told him, "Don't come near me again."

I marched out of Jed's apartment and drove directly to the shop.

How could I have been so stupid? How was it possible that Jed was some sort of witchcraft spy? Who was Jed, really? Was he working for the Kerrigans, or was there some new third party involved in the feud? How would the Kerrigans know someone from Tennessee? Was Jed really from Tennessee? Was the accent fake, too?

Oh, good night, I'd let that man see me naked.

I'd been had. I was the dumb henchman in the Bond movies who was distracted by female sidekicks with overtly sexual names who eventually strangled the hench-man with their thighs. I'd been used. He'd never liked me. He'd never found me "adorable" or "sweet" or any of the little endearments he'd tossed about so casually. And I think that was what hurt so much. I'd really believed he liked me just for me. Not because of what I could do, be-cause I was Nana's heir, or because I fit conveniently into his life as his lovely normal girlfriend. For me.

I do not remember anything about the drive, other than that I skipped going to the store in favor of pulling over in the Half-Moon Hollow Baptist Church car park to scream and beat on my steering wheel. And at the BP station. And the Bait-n-Beer.

It was a long drive.

Maybe, on some level, I'd known. Maybe that was the root of whatever had kept me from telling the truth about why I was here, about the search. Some part of me must have known he wasn't trustworthy, too good to be true.

No, that was a rationalization. I'd been completely taken in. I was a moron, a moron who would be taking a voluntary moratorium on dating for the foreseeable future.

Wherever Jed was, I hoped that burn mark on his arm really stung.

Yes, I was committed to doing no harm first, but screw it, Jed had taken advantage of me. He'd known exactly what he was doing. If anybody had some magical blistering coming, it was him. If that meant I was sending bad energy out into the universe, so be it.

I worked. I sulked. I searched. After I finally cooled off, I spilled my sorry tale of floor busting and betrayal to my vampire friends. While Jane stroked my head, Gabriel practically had to climb onto Dick's shoulders to hold him back from marching out of the shop and "whipping that boy's ass!" It is really difficult to explain to your vampire ancestor why it's not OK to smash your sort-of-boyfriend's lying face in for betraying you to another magical family. It's even more difficult to explain that it is not a legal reason to evict someone from the house he's renting from you.

Dick settled for showing up later at my side of the house with a copy of *The Notebook,* a pint of Ben and Jerry's Phish Food, and a bottle of wine, dropping them off on my doorstep, patting me on the head, and departing without another word. I was really starting to love that man.

Jed's proximity didn't seem to be much of an issue, as I hadn't seen him since the "handprint incident," as Jane had dubbed it. His windows remained dark and the driveway empty, other than my car. The house felt empty, too, as if I could sense the absence of his energy from the other side of the walls. I tamped down the sense of loss and longing I felt. It didn't make any sense to miss someone I barely knew, someone who had only been sent to track me. With the Kerrigans clearly close on my trail, I needed to focus on my efforts to find the athame and the bell—not tracking down my erstwhile neighbor and shaking answers out of him.

The one person who seemed thrilled with this situation was Penny, who answered the news that I'd recovered the intact Earth plaque with a whooping cry that woke up her husband, Seamus. She even took back her previous mockery. She was concerned to hear about Jed's part in it, however, and insisted on sending some reinforcements to the Hollow.

"No, I've got all of the help I need here," I told her

as I parked my car in front of the house. "Indestructible vampire help that won't end up being used against me as some sort of bargaining chip." Over Penny's protests, I added, "Just keep an eye on the Kerrigans still in country, let me know if they start traveling in large groups or stockpiling spell supplies. Speaking of which, how go the preparations for the binding?"

"We have everything we need except for the Elements," she said. "Everyone here is very proud of you, Nola. I know it's difficult, spending all of your time searching for something that you don't believe makes a difference, but it means a lot to us that you're trying so hard."

I made a noncommittal noise as I walked across the yard. Could I deny the validity of the Elements or the magic my relatives practiced, now that I was creating mini–water spouts and setting sleeve fires with my mind? Something inside my head, the logical, resistant way I looked at the world, was shifting. And I wasn't entirely sure I was comfortable with that.

"And look how far you've come!" Penny exclaimed. "Two down already. We know you'll be able to find the next two before the deadline. You just need to stay focused, keep your eye on the ball, stay on target, follow through the swing."

"That's enough of a pep talk, Pen."

"Oh, thank goodness. I was running out of cheerful sports metaphors."

I bid Penny good-bye as I approached the front porch. As was usual lately, my side of the house was lit, but Jed's half was dark. I was actually a bit nervous about walking across the darkened steps. But I made it to the front door unscathed and was in the process of unlocking the *new* new locks when a sleepy voice mumbled, "Nola?" from the porch swing.

I cried out at the familiar voice, turning toward the porch swing, hands raised. "Stephen? What the bloody hell are you doing here?"

13

Never sneak up on an irritated witch, sorceress, or conjurer.

—A Witch's Compendium of Curses

At least I avoided punching anyone's breasts. I did, however, blow up the glass globe on the porch light. This time, it was not my fault. People really had to stop sneaking up on me.

Stephen was sitting on my porch swing with his raincoat folded over his suitcase and flowers clutched in one hand.

"I just had to come see you, darling," he said, his voice sleepy and hoarse from the strain of his long flight. "I know we left things in an awkward place. I wanted to apologize in person." He pressed the flowers into my hands, a pretty but generic arrangement of roses, the sort of thing you could buy in one of those airport vending machines by the arrival gates. "Aren't you happy to see me, at all?"

I offered him a stilted smile, accepting the flowers. "I just wasn't expecting you."

That was the feckin' understatement of the century. I

felt guilty. I'd expected to feel annoyed and embarrassed if I saw him again. But the interesting thing was that I wasn't embarrassed at the thought of Stephen meeting my friends and judging them. I didn't want them to meet *him*. He no longer fit into my life, which had expanded and changed and become so much more complex since the last time I'd seen him.

It would have been so easy to relent, to apologize for having been harsh with him, to go back to him and re-claim some sense of normalcy. Clearly, things weren't going to work out with Jed, and I didn't have a talent for being alone. But I couldn't do that to Stephen. I was still angry at him, on some level, but he was a good man. I didn't want to make him a consolation prize. At one point, I'd seen our future together, bright and clear, but I couldn't look at him that way anymore. We were just too different. I'd spent so much of my time working to make him happy so he would stay with me and give me the kind of love I wanted so badly. I didn't think about whether that made me happy or not.

Now I sincerely doubted it would.

"Penny told me all about you discovering your grand-father and your family here. I'm sorry you felt like you had to lie to me about it. I suppose that I deserved it, though, after the things I said."

I arched an eyebrow. Why didn't Penny tell me she'd told Stephen where I was? It wasn't like her to share in-formation with him at all. I stared him right in the eye as I said, "Yes, you did. But I am sorry for the things I said. If I had been thinking clearly, I would have hung up and called back the next morning." I opened the door and ushered him into the living room. "Tea?"

He nodded. "Please, and then I'd like you to explain a few things to me."

"I will; I just need something to do with my hands."

I put the kettle on to boil and pulled out the bags of oolong, which he preferred. As my hands moved, I tried to figure out exactly what I wanted to tell Stephen. My chronically unhelpful brain was coming up blank. So I went with the "let it all just tumble out of your mouth" method.

"I didn't tell you about coming here to meet relatives because I didn't want you to have one more thing to hold against my family. I could almost hear you in my head. 'Here we go, another dramatic debacle, courtesy of the McGavocks.' You say those things so often I don't think you even realize you're doing it."

"But even you make jokes at your family's expense," he protested.

"Yes, but I'm not serious when I do it," I said, trying to think of a way to explain the principle of "it's OK when I pick on my family, but no one else should try" to someone whose parents used an intercom to communicate dinner plans. "You know there are large portions of my life that I hold back from you—hell, I hold them back from myself—because I am afraid that you can't handle them. And it's not fair to either of us. I've only given you a partial, watered-down version of myself, and you shouldn't want that. *I* want better than that for you, better than a half-relationship with a half-person. I just don't think what we have works anymore."

"Wait, I thought you were just angry on the phone. Are you really breaking it off with me?"

"I'm sorry, Stephen," I said, rethinking the wisdom of handing him a cup of boiling-hot tea.

"Haven't you wondered why I haven't introduced you to my parents?" he sputtered. "I kept waiting for the weird shit I had to put up with to bottom out. I wanted to know how bad it could get. But it just kept getting worse! You want to know why I wanted to move with you to Dublin? Because I wanted to know whether you were someone I could consider proposing to. But you just kept putting me off! It doesn't have to be this way," he insisted. "If you could just draw some boundaries with that band of loonies, then—"

"Do you realize you're actively making my point for me?" I asked.

"All right, all right," he said. "I'm sorry, darling, I'm just upset. I don't want to lose you. I will learn to watch my tongue, but you have to make some changes, too. We can make this work. Don't you see how easily we could fit into each other's lives?"

"Maybe it's not about fitting into each other's lives but making one life together. I shouldn't have to feel like I should hide things from you. I can't keep compartmentalizing and tucking away the bits of my life I'm afraid will upset you."

"But I came all this way to see you."

"I didn't ask you to. And I'm sorry. I didn't mean to hurt you."

And round and round we went, until I lost track of the time and our tea grew cold. We hashed through every angle of our relationship, my inability to separate from the family, his unwillingness to take my job seriously or meet my family halfway. Stephen got more and more upset as the conversation went along and I didn't budge on splitting.

"I refuse to accept this," he spat. "We love each other. If we're not going to be together, it won't be caused by something so silly. Lots of people don't get along with their in-laws."

I nodded to his cold tea. "Would you like me to warm that up for you?"

"Why do you keep worrying about tea at a time like this?" he asked, exasperated.

I cupped my hands around the mug, closed my eyes, and thought of what I'd thought and felt right before burning Jed. I dredged up that hurt, the red-hot singe of anger, and pictured the energy flowing from my heart down to my hands. I imagined heat traveling from my skin, through the mug, and into the liquid, moving the water molecules around at such a pace that the water boiled. I could see the surface rippling, steam rising from the cup. I could feel the energy building, gathering, pushing through my flesh and bone to do my will.

I opened my eyes and saw Stephen, mouth agape, horror-struck, as he watched his tea bubble and boil. It popped and hissed merrily even after I moved my hands away, the steam curling up toward us like misty fingers. I jerked my hands away from the ceramic before it split or exploded.

"This is what I am; this is what I can do," I told him. "To pretend to be anything else would be wrong."

"I didn't know," he whispered. "I knew your family claimed that they had mystical whatnot, but I never imagined. Have you always been able to do that? All this time?"

"Yes. Do you still want me, Stephen? Do you? Because I've been twisting myself into knots trying to keep this from you, but I can't anymore. The people I've met here, they've shown me that you can't shut yourself up and pretend to be something that you're not. I've acted shamefully toward my own family because I was afraid of disappointing you or scaring you. You believe in facts and figures, and that's fine. I don't disagree that algebra exists. But you're missing a whole big world out there. You're blind to it because you're afraid of what you might see."

"I'm sorry," he said, softly, stepping back out of range. "I can't deal with this."

"I know," I told him. "It's all right. I can barely deal with it. I'm sorry I lied to you."

He stepped back to the kitchen table, slumping against it. "No, no, I should have guessed, I suppose. Your family took this far too seriously to be faking it," he said, staring off into space.

A long, heavy silence hung in the air between us.

"So . . ." he started. "As far as breakup stories go, this

will be different from my friends' tales of sad-face text messages and requests that we 'still be friends.'"

"Do you still want to be friends?" I asked.

He shook his head. "No."

"All right, then."

Stephen had questions, lots of them. I answered as many as I could without telling him about the Elements or the Kerrigans. I had the feeling that might make his head explode. By the time we finished talking, it was two A.M., and I felt guilty asking him to leave. He was calm and collected. He was Stephen, Lord of Rational Thought. So I made up the couch for him to sleep on.

The next morning, I heard him up before I rose. He left without saying good-bye. Not that I could blame him. This was an awkward way to end a relationship. I will say that he was classy until the end. He folded up the blankets and placed them at the foot of the couch. Nothing in the house was disturbed. We were over.

At least, that's what I thought.

Without the distraction of Jed and with no leads at the shop, I threw myself into working at the clinic. I learned all of the patients' names, their family histories, how they fit into the puzzle that was the Hollow community. It was nice interacting with normal people in a normal way, no magic, no intrigue. Dr. Hackett was no friendlier than he'd ever been, but he seemed to respect my skills.

Jed didn't return to the house for nearly a week. He didn't call. I didn't see his truck parked outside. One might think this would be a good thing, that his absence would help me forgive and forget. But the less I saw him, the angrier I got. And then, of course, he did come home (to find a less-than-legal eviction notice on his door), and he was careful to avoid me. But every morning, I would find on my doorstep beautiful spherical bunches of little blue flowers—hydrangea—with a note that said, "I'm sorry."

I took an inhuman amount of glee in practicing my mental firestarter powers on the flowers and leaving the wreckage on his doorstep. Efforts to confront him directly were met with silence and darkened windows. The man was far sneakier than I gave him credit for.

Unfortunately, my floral abuse resulted in overexerting myself, and I ended up draining myself completely for a few days. I was out of balance in so many ways, and it was definitely affecting the reliability of my powers. Some days, I nearly set the porch aflame with Jed's floral offering, and others, I could barely warm a mug of water.

I redirected my anger into cleaning rather than pyromania, so the shop and the clinic were spotless. Well, the lobby and the reception area were spotless. Dr. Hackett didn't need me to clean his office. Why he could keep that room perfectly organized but not the rest of building, I had no idea.

My energy continued to alternate between bottoming out and spiking at inopportune moments, like water sloshing over a dam. No lightbulb, ceramic cup, or window was safe around me. Jane informed me that destroying one shop window in a fit of witchy temper was written into my employment contract, but I would have to pay for the next one. This was odd, considering that I didn't remember signing an employment contract. In hopes of finding some way to rid myself of Penny's binding, I started reading more books from Jane's shop on magic and psychic senses, faith healing, and holistic medicine. I read about magical bindings and how to undo them, noting how important psychology was to the process. I found several location spells, but they involved darker magic than I was willing to attempt. Whoever first looked at baby teeth and thought, "You know what, these could have magical applications," was a sick, sick person.

I decided to try something counterintuitive. I stopped actively searching for the Elements. So far, Fire and Earth had fallen into my lap through bizarre coincidence, the latter accompanied by a sort of life lesson. (Never trust attractive, shirtless men in pickup trucks.) So instead of trying to force the issue, I was going to go with the flow.

For three days. And then I would go right back to my obsessive ways.

I had two weeks left. Two weeks, and I could go home. I missed my family with an ache so acute it sometimes stopped my breath. I would never take them for granted again. I would never again wish for Uncle Seamus to be struck dumb during football season. Or for Penny to stop trying to charm me into a happy love life. I wouldn't wish for silence or solitude, because I'd had plenty of both since I'd arrived in the Hollow. They weren't all they were cracked up to be. And I wouldn't wish to be normal, because that was something I would never be. I was a witch. And as soon as I accepted that, my life would get easier—or whatever qualified as easier for a girl with magical powers and vampire relatives.

Of course, in keeping with the rules governing lost car keys and remote controls, the moment I stopped looking so desperately for the Elements, one of them fell right into my lap.

It had been a long day at the clinic, involving everything from stitches to psoriasis to a six-year-old who had managed to lodge a tiny Lego component in his ear. I locked the front doors to the lobby, shut down my computer, and shuffled my way back to Dr. Hackett's office on tired, aching feet. Still, there was a smile on my face. I was happiest when I was working with patients, and I'd worked with a multitude that day.

Tugging a pen from my loosely twisted hair, I knocked on the door and poked my head into his office. "Dr. Hackett, I have those supply forms ready for your signature. By the way, some of the things you were trying to order are no longer manufactured. We've come a long way since leeches and quinine."

"Smart-ass," he muttered as I handed over the files.

"And the mail," I added, placing the scant stack of letters on the lovely green leather blotter. Dr. Hackett was definitely old-school in terms of desk accessories. On one side of the blotter, he had arranged an aged Montblanc pen and a large glass globe paperweight. On the other, he had an antique silver picture frame, holding a picture of four young men sitting around a card table.

He reached into his drawer and pulled out a letter opener.

A letter opener with a long silver blade, a black enamel handle, and a milky blue stone set in the hilt.

"Sonofabitch!" I cried, staring at the athame as it flashed in the light.

Dr. Hackett jumped at my oath, dropping the blade onto his desk.

"I've been working down the hall from it all these weeks?" I exclaimed.

Dr. Hackett raised an eyebrow. "Beg pardon?"

I cleared my throat. "Dr. Hackett, where did you get that letter opener?"

Dr. Hackett glanced down at the athame, and his papery cheeks flushed. I glanced at the photo and realized that I recognized one of the figures in the photograph. "Dr. Hackett, did you know Gilbert Wainwright?"

Dr. Hackett grinned sheepishly. "Yes, we were classmates at Half-Moon Hollow High. We played cards every week with our buddies, Jimmy Mayhew and Bob Puckett." He nodded toward the framed photo. "I found the letter opener at Gilbert's shop, mixed in with some antiques, right after he died," he said. "Miss Jane was clearing out the storeroom at the time, and there were boxes all over the store. It seemed like something that someone should hold on to, that it was special to Gilbert, or should have been. So I offered Jane a good price for it. I don't think she wanted to sell it to me. She wasn't finished with her inventory, and she wasn't sure where the knife had come from. And I may have played the 'old friend' card a little bit. To be honest, I haven't felt right about taking it since the moment I walked out the door, but I thought returning it would seem silly. I hardly ever take it out of the desk."

She said she'd never seen it before! I was going to kill Jane Jameson-Nightengale.

"Would you mind if I took it back to the shop? It's part of a personal collection, and we've been looking for it for some time. I can reimburse you whatever you paid for it," I said.

He pursed his lips into a frown. "Why would you want it?"

"Personal reasons."

He stared at me for a long time, studying my face. "Consider it a thank-you gift," he said, pressing the hilt into my hand. "You have been a great help to me here in the clinic. And now I don't have to get you flowers when you leave."

I threw my arms around him in a fierce hug.

"You must really like knives," he said, patting my back hesitantly. "Go on, have a good night."

I raced to my desk, pulled an unbleached cloth out of my purse, and wrapped it around the blade. Three down. I'd found three Elements. Maybe if I wandered through random car parks in the Hollow, I would eventually trip over the bell.

"Thank you, Dr. Hackett!" I called.

"Good night, Nola," he responded, sticking his head out of his office doorway. "And Nola?"

I paused on my dash to the front door.

Dr. Hackett grinned at me. "You have his eyes."

* * *

"Jane! You'll never believe it!" I called, racing into the shop. The door was unlocked, but I couldn't see anyone on the sales floor, which was unusual. It was only 10:20. Someone had turned off all of the lights, with the exception of the track lights over the coffee bar. "Hey? What's with the lights? If you close up shop, it's a good idea to lock the door, you know!"

No response. I glanced down at the security-system panel over the light switch. It was scorched black, as if someone had zapped it with a cattle prod. In the darkened shop interior, the brass fixtures of the coffee machine dully reflected the street lamps. I reached for the light switch, and the hair on my arms rose. Before my fingers could make contact with the switchplate, I was nearly doubled over at the sudden throbbing pain in my head. It felt as if someone had kicked me across the temple with a steel-toed boot. Dizzy and sick, I swayed into the shop, bracing myself against the surface of a coffee table.

I heard a soft, wet moan from behind the coffee bar. I struggled to move my feet forward. There was someone here, someone in pain. I mentally shielded myself to keep from being incapacitated by the person's pain.

"Jane?" I whispered, dropping the athame on the bar.

I turned the corner to find a slim male form with sandy hair.

"Zeb!" I shouted, dropping to my knees next to his crumpled body. He lay on his side, curled inward. His face was battered and bloody. His knuckles were bruised and swollen, as if he'd managed to fight back. I placed gentle hands on his shoulders, and suddenly, he was coughing and heaving, blood dribbling from his lips.

"Shh." I pressed my hands gently against his ribs, trying to discern cracks or breaks. The blood appeared to be from a smashed lip and not any rupture to his lungs. "Try not to move too much."

"Somebody hit me from behind," he wheezed. "But I got a few swings in. One. I got one swing in."

"Someone hit you over the head? How many times?" I asked. I crouched over him, examining him thoroughly.

"Don't know," he said.

I closed my eyes and concentrated on his body, bones, heart, lungs. He was bruised and battered, but nothing seemed torn. Still, I wanted him to be checked over. I could be missing something. I pulled out my cell phone and dialed 911, barking out the address and a brief description of Zeb's injuries.

I placed my hand over his head and tried to picture his brain, the tiny networks of nerves and veins, the bones of his skull. I pictured smooth, solid bone and healthy tissue, but I couldn't seem to settle long enough to send any energy his way. I could feel the heat gathering underneath my skin, but I couldn't direct it outward. I shook my hands, as if they were faulty cigarette lighters, and tried again. But the magical signature was even weaker.

"This would be so much easier if you were a vampire," I told him. "I could feed you some blood, and everything would just fix itself."

"Jane says that all the time," he mumbled as I tried to focus.

A bell tinkled toward the front of the shop. We both cowered against the sudden intrusion of light in the room. I sprang to my feet and grabbed the athame from the counter, brandishing it at whoever had just walked through the door.

I squinted against the light, but I could see now that the shop had been ransacked. Books were scattered on the floor, their pages ripped. The glass of the display cabinets had been smashed, and anything of value had been taken.

"Zeb? Nola!" Jane called as she came in, with Gabriel close at her heels, his face filled with concern. "What's going on? Why does your brain sound like a car alarm, Nola? And when did we decide to electrocute the security system?"

"Jane!" I yelled. "Back here!"

Jane found me crouched over Zeb, trying to stabilize his head and prevent further injuries. Whatever color remained in Jane's face drained away, and she seemed frozen to her spot on the floor, staring down at her friend's battered body.

"What happened?" she cried, dropping to her knees next to Zeb and pulling out her cell phone.

"He said he was attacked," I told her.

"Well, fix him!" she commanded me.

"I tried. It's not working," I told her, my voice cracking. "I don't know what's wrong with me. I checked him over, and his injuries seem minor. But I want a doctor to look at him. The trick now is keeping him awake and still. Why was he here alone?"

"Jane's childe, Jamie, had a meeting with his parents, trying to mend fences," Gabriel said.

Jane's face went even paler as she surveyed Zeb's injuries. "We went for moral support. Then we were supposed to meet Zeb here to talk about some plans he had for his and Jolene's anniversary." She glared up at me. "Did you see anything strange when you came in?"

"I don't know. I came in and found him like this."

"What about sounds, a weird smell, a car parked out front, anything?" she demanded.

"Look in my head if you want, Jane. The shop was dark and unlocked, and the security system was toast. But I didn't see anyone there."

"Jane, calm down," Gabriel told her. "This isn't Nola's doing."

"I'm sorry." Jane grunted. "It just feels too much like before, with Mr. Wainwright and Andrea and . . . Gabriel, please call Jolene. She's going to want to meet him at the hospital. Tell her Jamie will watch the kids if she wants to leave them at our place."

Gabriel nodded and turned away to dial his phone. Jane was edgy and protective, hovering over Zeb, waiting for the ambulance to arrive. She asked him silly questions about his mother to keep him agitated enough to stay awake. I took the opportunity to look around the shop. The framed pictures were moved but intact. The register had been pried open, the cash taken out. Every single athame had been swiped from the display case. Most of the ritual candles had been knocked around.

Jane insisted on riding in the ambulance with Zeb, threatening dire consequences for the paramedics if they tried to stop her. As the ambulance pulled away from the shop, I marched to Jane's office and checked the safe. Her desk was overturned, the papers and bits of glass tossed about on the floor. The safe door had been gouged and scratched, but it was closed. I spun the lock to the combination and yanked it open. The little wooden case was still inside, with the plaque and the candle intact. I breathed a sigh of relief.

I opened the drawer packed with white cloth and wrapped the knife, saying a quick and dirty version of the purification ritual. I didn't have the time or the energy to do anything else. I secured the safe door and walked back to the coffee bar, surveying the damage with hot, wet eyes. Gabriel had said we had to stay so I could give my statement to the police.

All I wanted to do was go home and hit something. The shop had been torn apart with a purpose. The athames, the candles, the safe—all connected to the Elements. Had Jed done this? Was he so desperate to help the Kerrigans that he'd hurt someone I knew and liked? He'd been next door to me all of this time; why would he suddenly become aggressive?

Should I tell the police about him? What would I say? *I believe my neighbor may have broken into this shop to steal ancient magical artifacts, but he assaulted my friend instead*? I would end up answering a lot of uncomfortable questions, and I didn't know if I could lie to the police. And what would I tell the others? If I told Jane or Dick about my suspicions, Jane would probably separate Jed's head from his shoulders before she asked him any questions. I didn't want to know what sort of creative revenge Dick would come up with, given even more ammunition against Jed.

I needed to handle this on my own. I didn't want anyone else to be in harm's way. Vampires or no, my friends were still vulnerable. I wasn't going to let anyone else get hurt on my behalf. I leaned my head against the coffee bar. Zeb could have been hurt, badly. He had a wife and two beautiful little kids. Was it worth this? Was the power my family used worth the risk? The hurt?

What was I preserving, really? This stupid feud? Maybe my family deserved to lose its magical heritage if this was the cost. Maybe I needed to locate the bell just so I could burn the whole deal.

The arrival of Half-Moon Hollow Police Sergeant Russell Lane interrupted this self-pitying train of thought. He flipped open his notepad, ready to take a lackadaisical stab at recording my version of events. Gabriel stood at my side, giving Sergeant Lane the evil eye every time he questioned my motivation or ability to relate the story honestly.

"And you didn't see anything?" Sergeant Lane asked. "Nothing? Not even someone walking out of the shop right before you walked in?"

"I've already told you I didn't. Three times," I told him.

Sergeant Lane closed his notebook with a snap. "Look,

ma'am, I make quite a few calls at this shop, and the case files rarely get closed. That reflects against my productivity. And that makes me cranky."

"Well, I'm so sorry to inconvenience you," I deadpanned.

"I'm just saying, if you have information, you need to share it. Now, let's go over it one more time."

I sighed, prompting Gabriel to nudge my arm. Long pauses while Sergeant Lane scribbled down my answers left me plenty of time to think. I knew I was overreacting, thinking of destroying the Elements. I was shocked and hurt and felt guilty, and it was clouding my thinking. I'd come too far to give up now. The problem was that I'd resorted to lazy tactics to find the Elements. I would be much more proactive in finding the bell. Once I left town, no one here would be at risk.

Right. I shoved my sleeves to my elbows and crossed the room to the magic section. Jane had an interesting stock on darker magic, written from a purely academic perspective. Stuff that I'd never seen before, because, frankly, no one in my family would dare try some of the rituals involved. There had to be some sort of magic LoJack spell here somewhere. I didn't care if I had to sacrifice a small goat or a car or something, I was going to find that bell. I was through with this bizarre journey through other people's problems and past deeds. I flipped through the pages of *Most Potente Magick,* looking for keywords such as "location" and "lost object."

Nothing.

I dropped the book to the floor. And another, when

it didn't give me the answers I wanted. And another. I tossed books over my shoulder, one after the other. Sergeant Lane was ignoring this erratic behavior while staring at a painting of a naked wood nymph.

Gabriel quietly stepped to my side. "What are you doing?"

"Nothing!" I snapped, tossing another book aside. "Because I can't actually *do* anything. I can't keep people from dying. I can't keep them from being hurt. I can't keep them happy or safe. I'm this walking time bomb of potential disaster."

"Stop!" he ground out, grabbing my wrists. "Nola, just stop."

I whispered, "I'm so tired of this, Gabriel. I really am."

"This isn't your fault," Gabriel assured me as Sergeant Lane wandered out of the shop without bidding us good-bye. "This sort of thing happens a lot around here. One of us is always being sprayed with silver or shot with arrows. You know, when I turned Jane into a vampire, it was because a local drunk mistook her for a deer and shot her. Jamie had to be turned when he was run over by a car right in front of the shop. Our little family is a magnet for trouble. The remarkably underwhelming attentions of Sergeant Lane are the result of his repeat visits here at the shop. And Jane's come a bit unglued because Zeb's never been hurt before. He's her oldest and dearest friend. She's not angry with you, understand that. If anything, as soon as Zeb is recovering, she's going to throw herself into the search for the final Element."

"Right," I said, nodding as I grabbed my purse from behind the bar. "I'm heading home."

"Let me drive you," Gabriel offered.

I shook my head. "You go on to the hospital, be with Jane and Zeb. I'll be fine."

"I'm calling Dick!" he shouted after me as I walked toward the door.

"I know!" I called back, entering the darkness on full steam, almost wanting something to attack me just so I could strike back at it.

14

When all else fails in polite conversation with any supernatural creature, just smile and nod.
—*Miss Manners' Guide to Undead Etiquette*

I came home to find that whoever had broken into the bookstore and attacked Zeb had made a night of it. My living room had been thoroughly trashed. My kitchen windows had been smashed with my own tea kettle. Upstairs, my bed was torn to hell, my soft sheets and quilts ripped to ribbons. My books were burned and torn.

"Right," I growled, walking out the back door. I threw open the storage shed, the light of the full moon shining over my shoulder and bathing the complement of gardening tools in silver. I grabbed the first shovel I saw. Jed's windows were dark, but I didn't care at the moment. I got a cricket grip on the shovel handle and smashed the glass in Jed's kitchen door. Gingerly, I put a hand through, but without cutting my arm to ribbons, I couldn't reach low enough to get at the lock. I took a step back and swung the shovel at the doorknob, hoping to disengage the lock by brute force.

The shovel blade struck the metal knob with a deafening *clang*. I grunted, swinging again, the blade only glancing off the doorknob. "I really need to start going to the gym."

As I once more raised the shovel over my shoulder like a bat, I heard a shuffling noise behind me and turned to find a hulking, dark shape looming in the darkness. A huge monster towered over me, with the legs of a man, a gray leathery torso, and a long, curved, and tapering snout. In the light of the full moon, I could see small, bright eyes and wide paw-like hands with razor-sharp claws. I screamed and swung the shovel wide, whacking the creature in the face with the broad side of the blade.

"Ow!"

Ow? Did the evil, drooling creature before me just yelp, "Ow?" I didn't expect that.

Was this the strange shape I'd seen lurking in my back garden all this time? A creature that seemed to be covered in gray leathery skin and . . . was that an armadillo's head? I'd watched a nature special on armadillos once with Nana. She called them "the sport-utility animal," because nothing that ugly could go without purpose. The shovel's handle slipped through my hands, the blunt blade edging my palms. I turned and swung for the fences, bringing the wood down across the creature's thighs.

The thing dropped to its knees. "Ow!"

I whacked it again like a big monster piñata.

"Stop hitting me!" it yelled. "That hurts!"

Wait, I knew that smooth, honeyed-whiskey voice. "Jed?" I cried.

The creature struggled to its knees, glaring at me with glassy black eyes. I raised the shovel again. It held up its paws. "Truce! Truce!" it yelled.

With the doorknob smashed, the Jed monster simply nudged the back door open and limped into the kitchen. Mouth hanging open, I choked up on the shovel handle and followed. The moment the creature lumbered across the threshold, out of the moonlight, the shape morphed back into human Jed. His face bore a purpling bruise where I'd whacked him, along with a sheepish expression.

"Hi."

It took several moments of shocked silence for me to process what had just happened before my very eyes. And I once saw my Aunt Lizzie set fire to her own eyebrows with a curling iron. After the sheer spectacle of Jed's shape-shifting passed, I found my voice. And my voice was pissed off.

"You arsehole!" I shouted.

"Drop the shovel!" he yelped as I advanced.

"You stupid, no-good arsehole!" I yelled, smacking him repeatedly with my shovel-free hand. "What is wrong with you? You lie to me. You lead me on. You trick me into giving you information. And now you're an armadillo monster?"

"Stop!" Jed grunted as I struck out at him. He smacked the shovel out of my hand, knocking it to the floor with a clatter. He caught one wrist, but I managed to poke him in the eye with the other hand. He cornered me against the counter, pressing his hips against mine and catching both of my wrists. I wriggled an arm loose and popped him on the chin.

"Ow!" He hissed, cradling his injured face. "What is wrong with *you*? Were you raised by freaking ninjas?"

"I have protective uncles," I growled. "Lots of them. But I'm sure you knew that already, didn't you? Didn't you get that information in your Kerrigan spy orientation packet?"

"I'm sorry about that." He groaned as I dug a knuckle into the sensitive hollow between his armpit and his ribs.

"What the hell are you?" I demanded as he finally released my arms.

"I'm cursed," he said, and when I didn't respond, he added, "I'll make some coffee."

Jed stepped away from me, and his eyes widened at the sight of blood on my shirt. Apparently, he hadn't been able to see it in the dark. He pulled my arms away from my sides, looking for damage. "What happened?"

Oh, right. I suspected him of assaulting Zeb.

"Let me see your hands," I demanded. Frowning, Jed showed me his unmarked palms. "Over."

His knuckles were unmarred. There were no gouge marks or defensive wounds on his arms, although it was clear that Zeb had done damage to somebody. And Jed's ability to change form didn't seem to promote speedy healing, because the hand-shaped burn I'd left on his arm was still there, and that shovel smack to the side of his face was bruising nicely. So Jed wasn't the one who beat Zeb.

That was something, at least.

"Someone came into Jane Jameson's shop earlier to-night and hurt Zeb Lavelle. I found him on the floor, all bloody and battered. They had to take him to the hospital. This is probably a rude way to approach this, but it's been a long night, and I'm all out of patience. I was pretty sure you did it. And I was trying to figure out a way to report it to the police without them hauling me away to the loony bin. I couldn't."

He rubbed his hand along the back of his neck. "Well, that was mighty decent of you."

"I didn't do it for you. You have some explaining to do." I pulled a chair away from the kitchen table and watching while he made coffee.

"I told you before. My family is Cajun, really, really Cajun. At least, we were before the move to Tennessee. Stilt shacks, deep-fried alligator, zydeco music . . ."

"I get it," I snapped.

"There was a local voodoo woman. And my great-great-great-grandfather pissed her off somethin' awful, left her at the altar and ran off with some other woman. She declared that he'd been a two-faced cheater the whole time they'd been together. And that if he wanted to have two faces, she'd give him a thousand. He wrote it off as the ravings of a crazy woman, until the full moon a month later. Family legend is that he turned into some sort of two-legged gator creature. Scared the hell out of his wife. And from that moment on, every time he stepped out into the light of the full moon, he turned into something. Nearly every adult in the bloodline has been cursed, too."

"What, like a werewolf?"

"I wish." He sighed, putting a coffee cup in front of me and sliding into the opposite chair. "That would mean just one form. We can become anything. Scales, fins, fur, gills, bat wings. Every time it happens, it's something different. We can't control it. It just happens.

"For my family, this curse controls everything we do. It controls where we go, how we work, who we get close to. My dad had a big family, but I have relatives who refuse to get married because they don't want to pass this along to their children. Do you know what that's like, to see people you love choose to live alone for their whole lives?"

"As a matter of fact, I do," I told him.

"Well, I couldn't stand it. I couldn't stand having my father apologize to my brothers and sisters every time the moon rose because he was so wrapped up in guilt. I couldn't stand the look on my mother's face every time I changed into some new monster. So I started doin' some research. I joined some Internet forums where people discussed myths and legends as if they were real. And I learned a lot about the different were-creature mythologies and curses. But no one could explain how it happened or what could be done to stop it. Until I stumbled into this chat room for witches, that is. I started askin' some questions, makin' contacts, and then next I know, some guy named Kerrigan is private-messagin' me, tellin' me he can solve my problem for me, lift the curse from my whole family. All I had to do was find some stuff for him, track down some valuables."

"Why would he ask you in particular?"

He shrugged. "My user name is redneckcreature95. He said he needed some things from a Southern town, and after talking to me on the phone a few times, he guessed I could fit into the area better than he could. All he gave me was an address for this house. It seemed too good to be true when I showed up and it was for rent. And then, a few weeks later, he sent me a description of the objects and those pictures of you. He told me to keep an eye out for you."

"So you moved here with nothing but a couple of clues and pictures?"

"I was desperate for help," he said. "After a few weeks, I started thinkin' I'd been bunked. I wasn't makin' any headway with Jane, who doesn't seem to like me much. I couldn't break into the shop to look around. Have you seen the security system on that place? What kind of bookstore has laser sensors on the doors, windows, and ceilin'? And then there you were, running out of the house in nothing but a towel."

He smiled at me, and it seemed so sincere it made my chest ache. I had to bite back the urge to smack him. I would not be manipulated by pearly whites and puppy eyes.

"I tried telling myself that spending time with you, distracting you, was only helping myself, giving myself time to beat you to the Elements. And then you were just so damn sweet. Well, not sweet, exactly, but funny as hell, with generally good intentions. I wasn't lyin', that night at the motel, when I said I liked you more than I expected to and that it made things difficult for me. I sent Kerrigan a bunch of e-mails, callin' him an asshole and tellin' him to get some other monkey to dance for him. That didn't go over well, let me tell you."

Suddenly, Zeb's attack at the store made more sense. The Kerrigans had received Jed's kiss-off e-mails, if he indeed sent them, and they had come looking for the Elements at the shop. Zeb had the bad fortune of being in the wrong place at the wrong time.

"But how could you just keep lying to me?" I asked. "You knew me. I thought you were—well, I don't know what I thought you were, but at least a friend. And you just kept lying. Our whole friendship is a palace of lies! And keeping the plaque? How am I supposed to trust you?"

"That mornin' in Helton, I sat on the bed, and you were lyin' there all sleepy and beautiful. And I just panicked. I wanted to be the kind of man who could go out with a girl like you any night he wanted, with no strings, no concerns. And I was willin' to do anything to make that happen. I'm not proud of myself."

"Did they tell you what would happen when you gave them the Elements?" I asked.

"Kerrigan told me that they were just a collection of old magical artifacts, that the value was sentimental, but that your family was looking for them, too, because you have a shared ancestor. He promised me that he could remove the curse if I helped him find the items before your family did."

"Why didn't you tell me about this?" I demanded.

"How? How could I possibly bring this up in conversation? 'Hello, darlin', how was your day? By the way, every once in a while, I turn into some monster from Scooby-Doo. Oh, and that mission that your family sent you on? I am doin' everything I can to undermine it and find the Elements first.'"

I conceded, "That would be a date ender."

"And don't forget that you didn't exactly give me the whole story. You didn't tell me you were Wainwright's granddaughter, or a witch, or anythin'. You gave me that bullshit story about coming from Boston."

"Technically, that's true. And really, you're going to criticize the white lies I told to protect me from you?"

"Not when you put it that way," he said. "After I took it from you, I wanted to give that stupid plaque back to you so badly, but then I would think of my parents and all of my younger cousins who are just now going through the changes. I'm sorry, I had to put them first. What would you do, to help your family?"

"Damn it," I groused. "If you hadn't said that, I probably would have been able to stay pissed at you—which I still am, by the way, and will be for a while yet."

I lifted his wrist, inspecting the burn mark on his forearm.

"It still hurts as bad as it did the day you gave it to me," he said, wincing. "Not that I didn't deserve it."

"You really did," I told him.

I was tempted to leave his arm in that state. I hadn't been able to heal Zeb earlier in the evening, after all, and it felt as if Zeb deserved my help more than Jed did. But hearing Jed's explanation seemed to shift the energy within me. I felt I was back in balance and might be able to make my energy follow my intentions in ways that would help him.

I curved my hand around the burn mark and closed my eyes. However irritated I might be with Jed, that mark was my fault. I needed to fix it. Nana had told me to think of the healing magic as if my cells were reaching out to the other person's and fixing all imperfections. I put my hand over the burned skin and pictured it bright and pink and new as a baby's. I saw cool, soothing waves of energy flowing over the burned tissue and taking away the sting. And when I opened my eyes, I was relieved and grateful to see that his skin indeed was pink and healthy.

I would visit Zeb's hospital room as soon as I could.

"Thanks," he said, twisting his hands and admiring his newly repaired flesh.

"That thing I can do, healing you with my hands? If the Kerrigans get the Elements, that goes away. My whole family's magic goes away."

"I'm sorry. I didn't know."

"Not good enough," I said, toying with my coffee cup. "So you're a giant armadillo monster."

"I kinda wish you would stop putting it that way."

"Not going to stop me from saying it," I shot back. "I don't understand why your status as a supernatural creature should change my plans to keep you as far away from the Elements as possible."

"Because I can help you find what you're looking for."

He dragged an old-fashioned trunk into the kitchen and opened it. It was filled with small leather-bound notebooks, covered in dust. I gaped at the sheer number of volumes. "What?"

"They're travel journals," he said. "Mr. Wainwright seemed to travel a lot. I found this trunk while we were fixing some pipes in the basement."

"So in addition to lying to me, you stole family heirlooms. You are just a charmer, aren't you?"

"No!" he exclaimed. "OK, yeah, but I would have returned them to you eventually."

"That's a comfort," I muttered. "Jane said Mr. Wainwright spent a lot of time looking for were-creatures and vampires, after he came back from World War II. She said he actually knows Sasquatch, who is Canadian, by the way."

"That makes sense."

I opened the first one I touched. The paper was dry and brittle, and tiny grains of sand actually shook out of the pages as I moved them. Here and there, pictures of a young Gilbert Wainwright in a pith helmet were tacked onto the pages. And the entries were carefully, meticulously written in—

"Are these hieroglyphics?" I asked, lifting an eyebrow.

"Your grandpa seemed to take learnin' the local languages pretty damn seriously when he traveled." He handed me journals, pointing out the language used in each. "Sanskrit, Chinese, Greek, and what I think is Old Norse. Other than looking at the photos and making a guess, I can't tell where he was or what he wrote. He switches languages a few times in each journal. I've been through a dozen of them with different language guides, and I can't make heads or tails of them."

"Are you showing me these for a particular reason or just to give me fresh reasons not to trust you? Why didn't you just turn these over to the Kerrigans?" I asked.

"If I just gave them the information, I couldn't trust them to keep their word. I figured if I found the items first, I had a better shot."

"Really nice people you're dealing with," I told him.

"What part of 'desperate cursed man' are you not getting? But I think you're more likely to meet the terms of our agreement. And I want to help you, to show you how sorry I am about how things have worked out. I'm sorry, Nola," he said. "I'm sorry I betrayed your trust. And I'm so sorry that I hurt you."

"So what do you want from me now?"

"I don't know, really. I just wanted to tell you how sorry I am. I don't know if you can help me. I don't even know if it's right to ask, considering what I've done."

"You really hurt me," I whispered. "I don't trust people very easily. And I thought you liked me."

"I did. I do!" he exclaimed. "I didn't expect you to be so sweet or so funny. I thought you'd be a crazy, wild-haired old chick with a million cats and a black muumuu. And you show up, and you're no-nonsense and terrified of small mammals."

"Marsupials."

"Whatever."

"I don't know if I can ever trust you again."

"I have no reason to lie now. You know everything," he said. "And I have something to make you feel better."

"What's that?"

He opened the fridge and took out a large green mixing bowl, displaying it with a flourish. "Banana puddin'."

"You think a little pudding is going to make me feel better?"

"You haven't lived until you've had real homemade banana puddin'."

"Church-lady harem again?"

He pursed his full lips and gave me the puppy-dog eyes again. "There's something I need to tell you about that."

I gave him an exasperated look. "Oh, come on."

"I made all of the food," he said, cringing.

"Palace of lies!" I exclaimed. "Why—why would you lie about that?"

"I didn't know what you liked in a man, and I didn't want to come across all domestic and feminine. I happen to be a very good cook. My mama insisted that all of the boys learn to take care of the house, so when we found nice girls to marry, we would stay married."

"I never saw you bring home groceries or smelled cooking from your side of the house."

"You have a pretty regimented schedule," he said, shrugging. "It was easy to work around you."

"Is your name really Jed, or is that a lie, too? Are you really Gary Horowitz from Hoboken, New Jersey?"

"You still don't trust me, huh?"

"I've said so, several times. I feel I've been very honest about it."

"What's it going to take to change your mind?"

15

Vampires are slow to trust and quick to attack. Do your best not to piss them off. And if you've already done so, run.

—A Smart Girl's Guide to Living with the Undead

It turned out it took a lot for me to trust him again. But it took even more for my friends to be willing to give him license to breathe in their presence.

"Ow!" he yelped as Jane attached her hands to either side of his head, yanking out a bit of hair.

"Hey, if your brain wasn't so patchy, I wouldn't have to get so close," Jane admonished. "You're lucky we're not calling Sophie the lie detector."

"Who?" he asked, wincing as she dug her fingers against his scalp.

Even with his—frankly, delicious, but I would never tell him so now—banana pudding, I held Jed at arm's length until we could hold what Zeb called a "family meeting" at Specialty Books as soon as he was released from the hospital. Zeb was bruised and battered, his arm in a sling. I offered to take care of it for him, but he declined. He said it was good for him, to feel human, to remind him to pay better attention when he was in the shop alone. Jolene, who was now left to care for their twins while Zeb was on the injured list, objected to this strongly. But when Jane offered to take care of the hospital bills since the injury had occurred on her property, she seemed mollified.

It was strange spending time with Jed again with this new perspective. I'd missed him. It seemed strange to admit that. I missed the version of Jed I thought I knew. I didn't know if that Jed really existed. He did his best to make it up to me. He helped me restore order to my ransacked living room and replaced my windows. The problem was that if it wasn't Jed, who had broken into the shop? Who had gone through my things at the house? Had the Kerrigans sent another operative into our area?

Gabriel and Dick asked those questions and many more after I insisted that Jed confess his part in the Kerrigans' plot. The vampires made it clear that they did not like or trust Jed. Zeb was confused about exactly who Jed was. But once he realized that he was once considered a suspect in his ass-whupping, he chilled considerably. Jolene was careful to stand between them at all times and appeared to be baring her teeth. Jane picked Jed's brain over with a mental fine-tooth comb. She couldn't detect any dishonesty, but she added that didn't mean anything if Jed was good at covering up.

Dick also "offered" to let Jed stay in one of the other properties in town. Well, actually, Dick waited until Jane had Jed by the hair and leaned in close, growling like a jungle cat. "Just so you understand, that little girl over there is very important to me. If you hurt her again—I mean, if she's the least bit unhappy, if she returns from any outing with you with so much as a hangnail—I will fix it so if people ever find your body, they won't be able to tell if you're human or a raccoon that got caught in a mulcher."

"Dick!" I shouted. "I'm not a little girl!"

"Well, compared to Dick," Andrea began.

I pointed a finger in her face. "Quiet, you!"

"Hey, I didn't get to do this when you were younger, so I'm making up for it now," Dick said.

"I had lots of uncles who did this when I was younger, and I hated it then, too."

"He is being a little overprotective, but that's sort of a thing with him and Gabriel," Jane told me.

"Thank you."

Jane turned to Jed and gave him a grim smile. "You do realize, of course, that none of us trusts you, and we reserve the right to whack you over the head with various blunt objects if the mood strikes us?"

Jed nodded after a moment's consideration. "Understood."

"How is that better?" I demanded. Jane shrugged.

"Before the head bashing begins, could I make a peace offering?" Jed asked before disappearing out the front door. He returned, hefting the heavy trunk full of journals under one arm. Suddenly, his ability to haul around paving stones made more sense. Did shapeshifters have above-average strength? Seeing Mr. Wainwright's name stamped on the trunk, Jane was immediately intrigued.

She knelt before the collection of old books and stroked the covers reverently.

"You're still on probation," she reminded Jed, who smirked at her.

She opened one and sighed. "It's . . . in gibberish."

"Jane," Andrea admonished her. "I'm surprised at you. This isn't gibberish. OK, who here speaks Mandarin?" Gabriel grinned broadly and raised his hand. Andrea handed him a journal. "And . . . Latin?" Dick raised his hand and accepted another. "I happen to read some Old Norse, thanks to a horrible ex-boyfriend whom we will not mention because it makes Dick pull his angry face. Which leaves us with old Gaelic, Sanskrit, and hiero-glyphics."

"I can take the Gaelic portions, or at least muddle through them," I said. "And if you have some books on Sanskrit and hieroglyphics or, even better, Mr. Wain-wright's guides to those languages, we can get to work on them. Maybe we can find something in the journals that will give us some clue about the bell."

"Oh, good." Zeb sighed, shifting his arm uncomfort-ably while he and Jolene settled into the comfy purple chairs with their assignments. "Homework."

It was a relief to have something to do, something we could all focus on for the week before the deadline. Although I found nothing to do with Mr. Wainwright's trip to Ireland, the journals were pleasant and interesting reading. I did learn that I should consider the possibility that every animal I saw was actually a middle-aged man named Wally. Nana had told me that Mr. Wainwright was looking for were-deer, but it was still a bit shocking to find out that there were people out there who turned into skunks and weasels. Think of the dry-cleaning involved.

Using the journal dates, we constructed a timeline of where he had traveled when. To give our eyes a rest from Mr. Wainwright's small script, we took turns contacting his favorite buyers, asking about bells, just in case. We visited every pawn shop in the surrounding two counties, but bells didn't seem to be frequently pawned items. I continued working at the clinic, but each afternoon, I left earlier than my previously established routine, something that Dr. Hackett frowned on. He knew, though, that I'd be leaving soon and he would have to adjust to running the clinic without me.

I sent scans of the Gaelic portions to Penny, a swipe to my pride, considering how often she'd told me to study the language more faithfully, as I would need it someday. Her translations were interesting but ultimately unhelpful. Eventually, we were able to determine which journals were the volumes written just before and about two years after the Ireland trip, but we couldn't seem to find the Ireland volume. The only bright spot, Gabriel observed, was that Mr. Wainwright never referred to selling or giving away the Elements in subsequent journals. We were sitting around the shop again, going over the journals, when Dick suddenly dropped to his knees in front of the trunk and knocked on the interior of the lid. Jane watched him warily, but as he tested the lid, she seemed to pick up on his line of thinking.

She laughed. "Mr. Wainwright, you crazy, adorable old bastard."

Andrea raised an eyebrow. "And the award for abrupt and inappropriate statements goes to . . ."

Grinning at me, Dick peeled away the fabric inside the lid. A sort of shell popped out of the lid, and two books fell out into his hands.

"A false top?" I laughed as he handed me the two journals. "I haven't heard that one before."

"Clearly, you've never met my cousin Junie." Jane snorted.

"Gilbert was a good boy, but he wasn't stupid," Dick said proudly.

The first thing I saw when I opened one volume was a sketch of each of the Elements. The writing surrounding the sketches was a mix of Gaelic and Old English. I could pick up words my family used regularly: "magic," "fire," "tradition," and "mother." But everything else was nonsense. "I'll send this to Penny, too, which means I will have to put up with more of her 'I told you sos.' Fortunately, we won't be on video chat, so I'll miss out on the accompanying dance."

Tucked inside the journal, I found pictures of Nana and Mr. Wainwright. It was nice to see them from his perspective. In his pictures, he was smiling down at Nana, pulling her close to his side. She was grinning widely at him, a look of complete adoration on her face.

Andrea picked up one of the pictures. "Hey, the inscription on this one is in English!"

I plucked it from her hands and read aloud. "'Fiona is a beautiful, intelligent woman who shares my open view of the world. I could easily see myself spending every day happily with her. But I don't think she will ever be ready to leave Kilcairy. And I would never be ready to stay. She is needed here, and I would not make her choose between myself and the people she cares for. But I cherish our time together and hope that our paths may cross again.'"

"I thought that would make you feel better," Jane said. "But you look like you're ready to burst into tears."

"It's sad," I said. "Nana loved him. And if he'd asked, she might have followed him home to America. My mother would have grown up with a father. She would have had an entirely different life. It sounds like they were held back by bad communication skills and fear. Mostly fear."

Jane ran her hand over my shoulder. "I'm sorry, Nola."

Gabriel carefully thumbed through the other journal. He grinned broadly at me. "I don't think you'll need to contact Penny. This is the last journal, Mr. Wainwright's daily journal from seven years ago, which he tucked into the lid along with the Ireland volume 'to protect Fiona.'" This section is in Latin, which I speak just as well as Dick, thank you very much. And he says he entrusted the bell to a friend. He says he couldn't bear looking at the bell because it reminded him too much of what he left behind."

"Aw, that's sweet," I said.

Gabriel grimaced. "He apparently meant someone named Bridget, whose father was a silversmith."

"That's less sweet," I grumbled.

"Your grandfather was a bit of a man-whore," Andrea informed me.

"Yes, thank you, I blame genetics," I said, eyeing Dick.

"Those are your genes, too," Dick reminded me sternly.

Gabriel cleared his throat. "Would you two like to know who he gave the bell to, or will this uncomfortable family moment continue for the rest of us to enjoy?"

My palms were sweating as Jed and I waited outside the outdated offices of James H. Mayhew, Esquire. It was late in the afternoon. The reception area had certainly seen better days, with its worn leather chairs and battered tile floors. The secretary's desk had long been abandoned, so we were left to wait while Mr. Mayhew finished up a phone call. Jed was amusing himself by sorting through six-year-old copies of *Ladies' Home Journal* and *Newsweek.*

This was what a last resort felt like. I had no idea what our next move would be if this didn't pan out. And the depressing thing was, I was sure it wouldn't. Jed tried keeping a more optimistic perspective . . . until I threatened to smack him with a rolled-up magazine.

Jimmy Mayhew was exactly what I expected in a small-town lawyer. Elderly, with a full shock of pure white hair and out-of-control matching eyebrows. His suit was a dapper if unfashionable blue silk, with a tie that set off his clear cornflower-blue eyes.

"So, you're the appointment Miss Jane referred to me?" he said, flashing some very respectable dentures at me.

Having long since tired of subterfuge, I introduced myself as Mr. Wainwright's granddaughter. Mr. Mayhew's white eyebrows shot up to his hairline. He sat back heavily in his club chair while I gave him a brief summary of the events that had brought me to his door. A parade of conflicting emotions crossed his handsome face as I told my story, ending with shocked resignation as I concluded with, "So, we were hoping, Mr. Mayhew, that you might still have that bell he gave you all those years ago and, if so, that you would be willing to part with it."

"He really had a daughter?" he asked.

I nodded. "You can ask Dick Cheney," I said. "He'll vouch for my story."

"Why would Jane's shifty friend know anything about it?"

I offered him an easy smile. "Never mind."

"Well, you do favor him. And if Miss Jane believes you, that's enough for me . . . Gilbert having descendants would have drastically changed his will, you know," he said, frowning. "Are you here to challenge it? Because he was very fond of Miss Jane, and I wouldn't be comfortable—"

"Oh, no," I assured him. "I think the shop is in very good hands. I was just curious about the bell."

Mr. Mayhew blew out a long breath. "I haven't got it."

My heart dropped somewhere near the location of my feet. Jed gave my hand a squeeze, but at the moment, I couldn't find it in me to look up at him.

"Gilbert did give me a bell, about twenty years ago," Mr. Mayhew said. "He asked me to put it in my safe, something about not feeling right about keeping them all together. And then, five years ago, right before Miss Jane started working there, he took it back. Said it was time and that he was going to hide it in plain sight."

"He didn't tell you where that might be?" Jed asked.

Mr. Mayhew shook his head.

"And what about your friend Bob Puckett? He was one of your card circle. Would Mr. Wainwright have given it to him?"

"Bobby Puckett died ten years ago," Mr. Mayhew said, shaking his head. "I'm sorry, Miss, but if Gilbert said he was going to hide it in plain sight, then you should look in the most obvious place first."

"We kind of covered those," Jed told him.

"I'm sorry I can't be more help," Mr. Mayhew said, shaking his head.

I stood, my knees shaking, and took his hand.

"After all this time," Mr. Mayhew said. "Gilbert has a grandkid. He would have gotten such a kick out of you, young lady."

"Thank you."

"You know, I have something for you," he said, crossing to his bookshelf. "We started playing poker together about fifty years ago. And one night a few years back, your grandpa ran out of cash. He had a lot of confidence in his hand, so he threw this into the pot." He took an old linen-bound edition from the shelf and handed it to me. "It was one of his prized possessions."

I ran my fingers over the cover, stamped in gold: *A Guide to Traversing the Supernatural Realm.* Mr. Mayhew grinned sheepishly. "It's a first edition. He read that book I don't know how many times when we were kids. An uncle gave it to him when he was home sick once with a cold, and it sparked his interest in the paranormal. From that moment on, all he could talk about was traveling the world to look for werewolves and vampires. I didn't really want to take it. He had four of a kind, but I had a straight flush. He never could spot a tell."

"Family failing, apparently," I muttered, turning the book carefully in my hands.

"I held on to it," he said, guilt tingeing his voice. "To teach him a lesson about bringing enough cash to the games. I always meant to give it back . . . I'm sorry. I think he would want you to have it."

I smiled up at him. "Thank you, Mr. Mayhew."

I leaned my head back against the car's seat, clutching Mr. Wainwright's book to my chest.

"Hey, hey." Jed slid across the seat and tried to put his arm around me. Instinctively, I pressed my hand against his chest to push him away, but my arm went limp. I let him wrap an arm around my shoulders and pull me close. "It's OK. We knew it was a long shot."

"I don't know what to do now," I said. "I don't know

where to look. And I looked closer at those locator spells. You're right. That is definitely some Dark Lord, point-of-no-return sort of stuff."

"You tried one of them, didn't you?"

I held up my thumb and forefinger, measuring a tiny amount of evil. "Just a little one."

"And since we just harassed a perfectly nice old lawyer, I'm assuming it didn't work?"

I shook my head and buried my face in his shoulder. He stroked my hair away from my face to press a kiss against my forehead. "You're exhausted. Let's get you home, honey."

I closed my eyes and stayed quiet for most of the ride home. What the hell would I do now? I had used up all of my luck, all of my happy coincidences and convenient clover patches.

What had I missed? Although I'd already done it a dozen times, I reviewed each find in my head and the steps that led up to it. Could anything be repeated? Mined for more information?

And I was back to blind luck again.

I must have dozed off, because I woke to Jed carrying me up the porch steps and using my keys to unlock my door. I should probably have objected to this. He was still the guy who had lied to me for months and stolen priceless artifacts from me. But he also smelled like the forest and fresh laundry, and every time his chin brushed my forehead, a little thrill zipped up my spine.

I let him stretch me across my bed, opening my eyes long enough to catch his hand and drag him down next to me. Jed scooted in behind me, pulling my back against his chest, and laid his face against my hair.

"If you keep all that sad to yourself, it's going to leave a bruise," he murmured against my neck.

"I don't think there's such a thing as emotional contusions," I whispered back, wrapping his arm around my waist as I rolled onto my back, facing him.

"I meant here," he said, drawing a finger over my heart.

I stared intently at the ceiling, willing away the anxious despair that seemed to have a choke hold on my throat. "What was Nana Fee thinking, leaving this task to me? I never showed any interest in being the family's leader. No one ever asked me if I was ready or even wanted the job. It was just shoved in my lap because I happened to be a good nurse. And I am drowning here. Why didn't Nana send Penny or Uncle Jack or someone who actually embraces their abilities and might have gotten through this with some dignity?"

"Maybe she knew you needed it more," he suggested gently, playing with a lock of my hair. "You needed to come here so you could get to know your grandfather."

"If she was that concerned, she could have sent me here before Mr. Wainwright died. She could have told me about him, let him know me," I shot back, my tone more than a little bitter. "She could have let my mother know him. Then maybe she wouldn't have turned out to be such a . . ."

Jed propped himself on his elbows. "What?"

"Anna McGavock wasn't a good mother. She wasn't

even a good person." I smiled to cover the odd little sob that escaped through my nose. "Everything she touched was tainted by her bottomless need for whatever she thought she deserved but wasn't getting. Nothing was ever enough. Maybe if she'd known her father, she wouldn't have felt like she had some missing piece she had to make up for. Or maybe she was always meant to turn out to be a cancer on the backside of humanity. Who knows?"

"The Kerrigans told me she died a while ago," he said quietly, and the mention of his former employers didn't exactly calm the little storm of nerves brewing between my temples.

I took several deep breaths, nodding and concentrating on slowing my heart rate. The last thing I needed was some magical spike that took out the bedroom windows. "I got a call from the Florida State Police about three years ago. They said that her remains had been found in some burnt-out fleabag motel in Sarasota. It's a wonder they were able to contact me. We hadn't spoken in more than ten years."

Jed tilted his forehead against mine, tucking my body against the curve of his hip. "I'm so sorry."

"I'm not," I admitted, in a voice so soft it was a wonder that he heard me. "It was a relief." And now the tears were slipping down my cheeks in earnest, gathering in the hollow of my throat. "It was a relief to know that she wasn't coming back, that she couldn't hurt us anymore. She had a particular talent for hurting Nana, who always seemed to think she could just *love* Mom out of being bat-shit crazy. Every time she hurt us, it only proved that I was right not to trust her. For Nana's sake, I pretended I was just as shocked as she was when Mom was arrested in Jacksonville for soliciting or that time she took Nana's money for rehab, only to spend it on a three-day bender in Atlantic City. But I'd come to expect it. I feel guilty for not loving my own mother, but I feel even worse for letting Nana believe that I did."

I sniffed. "I feel like so much of my relationship with Nana was a lie now. I don't know what to believe anymore. I've known all my life that my grandmother didn't want to discuss my grandfather. And I thought I understood it. I'd been angry at my grandfather for years, imagining him as some sort of cad who fathered my mother and ran. But I realize now the part Nana played in all this, and I didn't realize how angry I was at Nana Fee until I came here and saw what I had missed, not knowing him. She sent me on this wild-goose chase to the middle of nowhere, after giving supposedly sacred objects to a man who was some sort of book hoarder. What if Jane wanted nothing to do with me? What if his shop had burned down? What was she *thinking*?" That last bit was muffled by a hiccuping sob, which was mortifying.

"You're not used to bein' angry with her, huh?"

I shook my head, wiping at my cheeks. "I'm also not used to crying in front of some man while lying in bed with him."

"I'm not just some man." His tone was indignant. I chuckled, but he cupped my face in his hand and forced me to look at him. "Look, you know my secrets. You know things I've never told a soul outside of my family. And I gather you've never told anyone about your mother or your grandmother. That means something, Nola. I don't take it lightly."

I nodded and tucked my face into the crook of his neck. "I know."

I settled my weight against Jed's side and breathed in his spicy woods scent. I closed my eyes and let that scent soak into my skin. I knew Jed didn't take this sort of admission lightly. This was an intimacy he was sharing with me, an emotional bond one didn't forge with a convenient fling. The question was, how was *I* supposed to take it? How was I going to walk away from someone who knew so much about me? Did I really want to?

Hours later, the room was dark, and the windows were open. I turned over toward Jed. Bright beams of moonlight poured through the window, highlighting the smooth planes of his face. Jed's completely normal, human face. I sat up, my fingers pressing against his cheeks.

He inhaled sharply, sitting up. The moment his eyes opened and he caught sight of the windows, his face shifted. His skin was blue and smooth. Inky black markings highlighted the sharp cheekbones and arched brows over a leonine nose. He had fangs, long, shiny, and white. His eyes were wide and round and an electric, unearthly green.

I reached out to touch the strange blue flesh but felt

only Jed's warm, smooth skin. I traced my fingertips along his long nose, over the ridges of his cheekbones. He purred, the vibrations of the rumbling sound traveling down my arms to my heart. It was an illusion. He was still Jed underneath. I could feel his eyebrows under my fingertips. I leaned forward and kissed the blue, feline nose.

Jed flinched, drawing back from me as if I'd slapped him. The only thing I felt against my lips was Jed's plain old human nose. I chuckled, making the blackened eyebrows crease. I leaned forward, taking one of the soft lips between my own. He jerked away. I sighed, pushing up to my elbows so I could thread my hands in the inky black hair and pull him down to me. I claimed his mouth. This was my mouth. No matter what form it came in, it was mine.

Outside the windows, a cloud passed over the crescent moon, and the room was dark again. Under my fingertips, Jed's skin became his regular golden peach. His features shifted back to human. I laughed aloud, kissing him again. He dove for me, attacking my mouth with a zeal that made me glad he didn't have real fangs. He threw my leg over his hip and thrust forward, grinding his hard length against flesh that was already warm and wet for him. I cried out, the first tense pulse of pleasure seizing through me as he tugged my jeans away. He growled, nipping and biting down the length of my throat as he tore the material at my hips and threw it over his shoulder.

My nails bit into his shoulders, welting the skin, and I

was rewarded with a pleased rumble. He knelt over me, and I moaned at the broken contact. He trailed his hand between us, sliding it over my breastbone, down the line of my stomach, and between my legs. I shrieked when his thumb stroked over that little hard nub. He chuckled, so I reached up and tweaked his nipple in retaliation. He yelped and grinned down at me, redoubling his efforts.

When he finally plunged between my thighs, I was already coming. I pulsed and rolled underneath him, my breath too short to scream his name properly. All I could manage was a series of exhausted whimpers. I closed my eyes and tilted my head back, trusting him with my body as I had before, and let myself float away.

We stretched across the couch, Jed's legs sprawled across mine. My hand trailed down a back that was still a pleasant human tone. Jed was breathing, deep and even at my side, while we both enjoyed a long, comfortable moment of silence. Of course, I couldn't leave things alone.

"Am I crazy, or did you just shift into one of those things from *Avatar* earlier?" I asked.

"A Na'vi?"

"You were blue, and you had this weird tail and a cat lip."

"Huh."

"When was the last time you saw that movie?"

He shrugged. "I was flipping past HBO earlier this morning and stopped on it."

"Tree of souls scene?"

He nodded.

"Bloody pervert. So you see a sex scene between two otherworldly creatures, and then we're all snuggled up together, and . . ."

"So you think I turned into a Na'vi because I watched *Avatar*?"

"Yes, I do. And the first thing we're going to do is remove *Aliens*, *Predator*, and all zombie movies from your DVD collection, because I am not prepared to deal with that. I don't think you're cursed, Jed. I think you're some sort of were-creature. Only you're not limited to one form. You can have any form you choose. But because you never learned to control it, the form is determined by whatever is happening in your subconscious."

"So how do you explain the moonlight factor?"

"I honestly don't think it applies. For one thing, that wasn't the full moon. And second, the moon was shining on you earlier while you were asleep, and you didn't shift until you woke up and saw that the curtains were open. I think it's psychosomatic. If the witch all those years ago was some sort of sensitive, she might have been able to tell when your ancestor was getting ready to shift for the first time. She may have been able to use that, saying she was cursing him with 'a thousand faces.' When he shifted into some animal form for the first time, he was convinced it was a result of the witch's curse. I would imagine he did it under the light of the full moon, making that connection in his mind. The next time a family member shifted, he blamed the curse, and the next, and the next. You were going to shift no matter what, but the witch just used the power of suggestion against your ancestor to a devastating effect."

"You're going to explain what that means, right? In much smaller words?"

"Think about it this way," I said, sitting up. "If you've been told all of your life that you're allergic to peanuts, that everybody in your family is allergic to peanuts, you're probably going to believe you're allergic to peanuts. Especially if you frequently see your relatives having allergic reactions to peanuts. So when you're exposed to peanuts, even if you're not really allergic, you're probably going to at least hive out a little bit. Which would reinforce your belief that you're allergic, and that will start the cycle all over again. Does that make sense?"

"No, and now I really want a Nutty Buddy."

"Your brain has tricked you into thinking you're allergic to moonlight. You can probably shift anytime you want, into anything you want. Frankly, I'm amazed that no one in your family has accidentally shifted during the day or fallen asleep outside before."

"Well, this isn't something we talk about a lot."

"Really?"

"Do you run around your village telling everybody about your witchy stuff?"

I nodded. "Among my family members, yes. We talk about it all the time. Soccer and magic, those are the main topics of dinner conversation. Sometimes both together, which would be my aunt Penny making comments about David Beckham that make the rest of us uncomfortable."

"Well, we don't talk about it. On full-moon nights, we shut ourselves inside our houses and pretend it's because we want to watch TV or play cards."

"Fine, you're poorly adjusted, I get it. Try shifting now."

He frowned. "I can't just change."

"Why not?"

"Just think about whatever form you'd like to assume, and change. Feel the energy flowing up from the ground, into your legs, and spreading up through your body. Picture that energy filling in all the places between your cells and changing your shape into whatever you wish."

Jed rolled his eyes. "Hippie." He squinched up his face, as if he was concentrating, but then his features relaxed. Nothing. He squinted again, seeming to try harder. But nothing.

I patted his hand. "Don't worry, I hear this happens to a lot of guys."

He whacked me over the head with a pillow. "Shut it, you!"

For the next three days, the hours in which I wasn't retracing every step I'd taken since I'd arrived in the Hollow were filled by working with Jed on his shifting. And by that I mean I called out random animals and monsters to see if he could change on the fly. It took some concentration, overcoming decades of belief in how the shifting worked, but eventually, he was able to see it as a biological function and not something that happened to him.

Jane, of course, saw this as an opportunity to research. She looked into shape-shifting from every culture. She brought over books by the barrow load. Jed was overwhelmed. After watching the process a few times, we came to the conclusion that Jed's ability worked like a hologram. He never actually changed shape. The cells realigned to project an image, a defense mechanism against predators, like a chameleon, only in Jed's case on a much larger scale. He could change size and shape entirely, but beneath the image, he was the same adorable redneck.

Jed was faster and stronger than the average person, which was helpful. While his physical form didn't change, there were limits to what Jed could do. As long as the size and shape were close to his own and humanoid, he could master them. But he couldn't become an actual animal or another person. The image of the other person's face flickered back and forth over his own until it made bystanders vaguely ill, like an unsteady picture on TV.

Jed spent a lot of time on the phone with his parents, asking questions, informing them of our discoveries. It took him a few days to grasp that there was no cure for his "condition," because he wasn't actually cursed. He was a genetic anomaly, like were-creatures or people who could curl their tongues. Understanding that potentially he could eventually control it, he seemed to be more accepting of it.

I was sure there was an object lesson in there somewhere, but I chose to ignore it.

* * *

At this point, it shouldn't have surprised me when I found myself with Mr. Wainwright, floating down a canal in Venice in one of those old-fashioned gondolas. A man in a ridiculous straw hat and a red-and-white-striped shirt was guiding the boat along, singing a throaty song of lost love and heartbreak. The canal water smelled rusty and pungent, certainly not somewhere you'd want to swim. But it provided a beautiful backdrop for the tidy rows of aged, fading-pastel houses.

"Hi, Grandpa." I sighed, easing against his side as the water lapped lazily at the hull of our boat. He patted my shoulder in a sort of half-hug made awkward by the fluffy red-and-yellow cushions of the gondola seat.

"We're finally comfortable with calling me Grandpa?"

"Seems rude not to," I said, shrugging.

"So it has nothing to do with any sort of fondness you may feel for me?" he asked.

"Nah," I said, shaking my head while my lips twitched.

"So how goes the search?"

"Still no luck," I told him. "I'm sorry."

"You haven't anything to be sorry for," he admonished me, tapping a finger against the tip of my nose. "Unless you've given up. Have you given up?"

"No," I muttered. "I am nothing if not obnoxiously persistent."

"You get that from my side," he said. "Along with a healthy dose of bravado. Now, tell me, how are you feeling, really?"

"Like I'm running out of time and ideas and places to

look," I told him. "Oh, and I've some inconvenient feelings for a man who can transform himself into various
sorts of wildlife."

"Feelings can't be inconvenient," he said. "They're just
feelings."

"For someone I'm not entirely sure I should trust," I
added grumpily as the gondola bobbed in the currents
of the canal.

"You don't entirely trust him," he said. "Give him a
chance to prove you right or wrong. At least you'll know
you're making an informed decision."

"I can't believe I'm taking dating advice from my dead
grandfather."

"Smart-ass," he scoffed, elbowing my ribs. "You spend
a lot of time trying to make things come to you, Nola.
Maybe it would best to sit back and relax and *let* something come of its own accord."

"Because it's the opposite of everything I hold dear?'"
I asked.

"When you tried to force finding the Elements, did it
work?" he asked.

"No," I admitted. "Are you sure you couldn't just drop
me a hint or two about where you left the bell?"

"I could, but where's the fun in that?"

"Even the subconscious versions of my relatives mock
me." I sighed, resting my head back on the fluffy pillows.

"Keep your eyes up and open, Nola. You never know
what you might find."

16

Magic is a living, breathing cycle. In other words, everything you do will come back to bite you in the end.

—A Guide to Traversing the Supernatural Realm

Despite Mr. Wainwright's assurances, in the wee hours of June 21, I'd lost nearly all hope. The shop was a mess. We'd overturned nearly every shelf and sorted through every box, just in case we'd missed something. Jane and Andrea and I were sprawled across the few chairs not covered in boxes and books. Dick and Jed had gone out to visit one of Dick's less-than-reputable contacts.

"I can't believe I actually fooled myself into believing I would find it." I thumped my head against the chair. "I actually thought I'd be able to track down all four. How insane is that? I mean, how arrogant could I be?"

"Honey, you got three out of four," Jed said, patting my arm.

"That's a majority," Jane added. "And hey, even if you can't bind the evil ice skaters, at least they can't bind you."

"But the Kerrigans are going to have their powers returned to them for the first time in two hundred years. That's like giving an angry toddler an espresso and a box full of matches. You don't know exactly how it's going to turn out, but it's probably going to end in flames and tears."

"Also, I think Tonya Harding would be considered the evil ice skater," Andrea said. "Nancy Kerrigan, no relation, was the victim."

"I never liked her," Jane said. "She reminded me a little of my sister. Big teeth, bigger ego." She shrugged when Jed frowned at her. "Sorry, back to the point."

"My family can't leave Kilcairy." I sighed. "The whole point of my coming here was to make sure we kept everyone safe so we could continue serving our neighbors. The McGavocks would never want to leave the farm, anyway. We're going to have to get tougher, I guess, more aggressive."

"You can have my Taser," Jane offered. "And I'll bet Iris knows where you can get them at a bulk discount. You could get one for every man, woman, and child in your village."

"That might do it," I said, chuckling. "Thank you both for all your help."

"No problem," Jane said. "But if you don't mind, Andrea and I are going to retire for the morning."

Andrea pushed to her feet and hugged me with a tenderness that had my eyes misting a bit. "We're sorry to leave you, but if we stay out much longer, the sun will come up, and we'll, you know, burst into flames. Which most people find very upsetting."

"I'll help her clean everything up," Jed assured them. "You'll be ready to open this evening."

"Do you mind if I spend a little more time looking around?" I asked Jane. "If nothing else, I can pick up some of this mess. I don't think I'm going to be sleeping anytime soon."

"Sure," Jane said, sifting through her purse and handing me her key ring. "Lock up when you're done."

"You're giving me a key?" I laughed.

Jane's lips twitched. "I think we've established that I can trust you. I'm sorry to run off on you, but again, spontaneous combustion."

"Don't be," I told her. "You're right. I'm just moping. If nothing else, I know the Kerrigans haven't found the bell, either. Maybe I should just set fire to the other three and end this stupid feud."

"Fire has been mentioned way too often in this conversation," Andrea said, shoving Jane toward the door. "I'm switching you both to decaf."

"Good night!" I called after them. I sighed and let Jed wind his arms around my waist.

"I don't suppose you know of any magical tricks that would clean this room for us, huh?" he murmured into my neck.

I shook my head. "Does knowing the number for the Magic Maid Service count?"

"Probably not." He sighed.

Jed and I slowly, but surely, set Jane's shop back to rights. I put the knickknacks back in their little cubbies. I put the boxes of random stock back in the stockroom. Eventually, it began to look like the respectable establishment it was, and not a supernatural yard sale. I grabbed a bottle of juice from the fridge and plopped into a chair, propping my feet up on a table.

"Big. Fat. Failure."

"Aw, baby, I still love you anyway," Jed said, pushing my hair out of my face. "Or I can see myself in that particular predicament pretty soon."

My eyes popped open. "Love me? Really?"

"Well, it's not the confession I had in mind for this moment, but yeah, I do. You pulled me in with your wily, witchy ways. I don't see any other woman kissin' me after seein' me turn into a giant alien Smurf."

"You're not the first man I've brought down." I laughed, closing my eyes as he stroked a hand down my face.

"You just sit here a minute, OK? I'm gonna take these out to the garbage." He hefted up two large bags of debris we'd cleaned out of the store. He winked at me and transformed into a sort of man-raccoon hybrid. "Just adjustin' to my environment. Raccoons love garbage cans."

"Showoff," I muttered as I sat back in the chair.

A giant raccoon-man loved me. How many girls could say that?

Jane hadn't bothered to close the sunproof shades before she left. Orange-gold sunlight flooded through the windows and the glass transom, giving the shop a cozy glow. I picked up Mr. Wainwright's copy of *A Guide to Traversing the Supernatural Realm,* running my fingers over the embossed gold title. I opened the book and was surprised to find that the title page was signed by the author: "The point of any quest is not the prize but the lessons learned along the way. Keep your eyes up and open. You never know what you might find.—Warm regards, Jacques LeMoir."

"And ambiguous messages prove unhelpful once again." I sighed, remembering the last thing Mr. Wainwright said to me just the other night. "So the lesson is that failure is OK as long as I come out of it feeling like I've learned something. That's a little condescending."

I closed my eyes and yawned.

"I tried, Grandpa, Nana," I whispered to the empty room. "I'm so sorry I couldn't figure it out."

I sat there a long time, trying to figure out what would be the best course of action from here. If I asked very nicely, I wondered if the flight attendant would let me drop the Elements out of some sort of hatch while flying over the ocean. It would be safer than leaving them out in the world where the Kerrigans could get hold of them and make trouble.

I pressed the heels of my hands into my eyelids, wishing I could make time go back so I could relive this whole journey over again without making any silly mistakes. I would have confronted Jed earlier and pulled him over to our side. I wouldn't have reacted so badly when Dick paid attention to me and spent more time getting to know him. I might have brought Penny with me.

Keep your eyes up and open. A soft, warm voice whispered over my ear like a spring breeze. I jumped. *You never know what you might find.*

I blinked blearily around the room. The sun shifted through the window, bouncing off of a mirror on the wall and reflecting in a bright silver circle over the door. I wiped at my tired eyes and blinked a few times. That wasn't a silver circle. It was a bell, the old Indian cowbell Jane said had been hanging there since before she worked at the store.

I pushed to my feet, studying the battered silver shape.

It couldn't be that simple.

I grabbed a footstool and dragged it over to the door to get a better look. The designs I'd assumed were Indian were tiny rows of Celtic knots.

It was that feckin' simple.

This was the bell. This was the Sea bell. I'd been searching this stupid shop all this time, and the bell had been hanging over the door the whole time.

"If there is a Goddess out there, you have a really mean sense of humor," I griped.

I'd found it. Just in time. I'd found it. I could do the binding and go home.

Home to my family, but far away from Jed. I blew out a long breath. I would miss him so much. We were so new, so tentative, that we'd never even broached the subject of what would happen when I went home. We hadn't made promises to each other, and now . . .

"In the grand Southern tradition, I won't think about that right now," I said. "I'll think about it tomorrow." I unhooked the bell from its mount and dashed for the back office. I jerked the safe open and eased out the little carrying case.

Behind me, a footstep sounded at the entrance to the office. I turned to find a familiar figure standing just behind me.

"S-Stephen?" I stammered, confused about why someone who was supposed to be in Ireland would be three feet away, holding what looked like a rather large handgun. What was happening? Why would Stephen come here at all, much less armed? He wasn't even looking at me; his eyes were focused on the little wooden cabinet. Gooseflesh rose on my arms as I stood.

Heart hammering, I nudged the heavy safe door shut with my leg.

"Ah, ah, ah," Stephen said, smiling blandly as he stopped the door with his arm. He edged me away from the safe, trapping me between him and the bookshelf behind me. He gave me a sly, condescending grin as he surveyed the contents of Uncle Jack's cabinet. "She knew you would find them. You are such a clever girl, Nola. You know that, don't you? Far too clever to shut yourself away in that stupid little village for that godforsaken clinic. I meant that. I want you to know that not everything I told you was a lie."

Realization, cold and heavy, settled against my heart. "Sonofabitch! Did you sleep with me just so you could find the Elements?"

"Well, the lovely sex wasn't about the Elements," he said. "That was a special side benefit." I raised my hand to slap him, but he shoved the gun toward my face, making me cower back. "Let's just keep those fire-starting hands to ourselves, shall we?"

"You ransacked the shop, didn't you? You hurt Zeb."

"And the meathead out by the Dumpster." He chuckled as I made a strangled gasping noise. "And I strolled into your house anytime I felt like it. Old houses are never quite as secure as you think they are. There's always a window or door that can be jimmied. It doesn't take much to slink around this town unnoticed. All it takes is a T-shirt with an inappropriate slogan and a John Deere baseball cap. I've been here for weeks, watching you, keeping track of your progress. She wanted to intervene, but why do the work when you're doing it for us?"

"Why are you doing this? And who is 'she'?"

There was that wintry smile again. "I wish I could say I was special, like you, that I was trying to restore balance to a family that's been denied its magic for too long," he said, his lips twisted into a mocking smile. "But I'll be honest. It's the money. The Kerrigans are going to pay handsomely for the contents of this cabinet. I couldn't have gotten a mint for just one or two of the Elements, but all four together, in a handy carrying case? I'll be set for life."

"And how long do you think that life will be," I asked, "once my family hears about this? Hell, when I tell Jane it was you who hurt Zeb, your life won't be worth living. You're going to spend the rest of your days looking over your shoulder for an entire family of pissed-off vampires, not to mention angry witches. I'd almost feel sorry for you, if you weren't such a prick."

"Well, I guess we're just going to have to make sure you don't tell anyone, aren't we?" Stephen's hand tensed around the gun, raising it to my eye level. Panic constricted my throat, but my hands flew up, at the ready. I have no idea what they were ready to do, but it startled Stephen enough to flinch. I snatched up a heavy amethyst geode from Jane's desk and smashed it against his temple. He yelped, slumping against the wall, swinging the gun toward me. I darted to the side and beat his wrist against the shelves, over and over, until he dropped the gun to the floor. He growled, shoving me back against the desk so my head thunked against Jane's laptop. The pain of my back colliding with the sharp edge of the desk had me howling. I swung my booted foot up in a vicious arc, connecting with his chin and knocking him back into the shelf, which collapsed, dumping heavy leatherbound books on his head. He sank to the floor, limp and unconscious.

Slowly, I sat up, turning my aching head side-to-side. Stephen was working for the Kerrigans all this time? I felt so completely stupid. How had I fallen for this twice? From now on, I would have to ask Penny to prescreen all of my dates. I cradled my face in my hands, praying for the throbbing to stop. I had to get up. I had to go check on Jed, get him help if he needed it. I just had to make my head stop spinning long enough to stand.

Somewhere in the distance, I heard the floor creak. My head snapped up, making me wince. A woman stepped into view, tall and willowy, with dark hair. For a moment, I wondered if it was a ghost.

"Mom?" I whispered.

"Hello, darling," she said, smiling sweetly . . . right before she smashed a statue of Bast against my temple. I collapsed to my knees and fell on my face.

Ouch.

17

Some relationships cannot be fixed, no matter what you do.

—Love Spells: A Witch's Guide to Maintaining Healthy Relationships

I woke up with my hands tied behind my back. I was outdoors, in a forest clearing, tied to a tree near a campfire. The full, pregnant moon hung overhead. I could see Uncle Jack's little cabinet propped against a tree near my head, the drawers spread wide in dramatic "display" fashion. My mother was standing close by, examining the athame in the light of the moon.

"All this fuss over such a little thing," she mused, holding the athame in her hand.

The years had not been kind to Anna McGavock. The once delicate beauty had a face like a road map, lined and craggy. She tried to hide the damage with heavy makeup, but the eyeliner had smeared and bled into her crow's feet. Deep, unhappy lines bracketed her mouth, giving her a permanent expression of disdain. Her skin was sallow and had a cheesy sort of sheen. I immediately suppressed any instinct to diagnose what was wrong with her. I didn't want to know.

"Oh, good, you're awake." She tittered, tucking the athame back into the cabinet and draping the box in a white sheet. She wiped her hands on too-tight jeans that exposed everything between her belly button and her bony, protruding hips. She'd paired those with a thin black tank top and a lacy red bra. Her hair fell in a dark tangle down to her waist.

"You're supposed to be dead."

"I ran into a little trouble in Florida. I needed to disappear, and there are plenty of disposable people when you know where to look. My business associates stopped looking for me when the body turned up, and no one was the wiser."

"You let your own mother think you were dead. She mourned you. She thought about you every day."

"Oh, spare me. I came to your stupid little dirt patch a few weeks before the old lady died," Mom spat. "I was going to confront her, once and for all, to demand answers. But she wasn't there. So I looked around. I figured everything in that dinky little cottage should have been mine, anyway, so what was the point in leaving it there to rot?"

And suddenly, the silver that had come up missing shortly before Nana's death made so much more sense. "She saw you?"

"Well, she didn't exactly serve me tea. She saw me coming out of the house. I was in my car and down the road before she put two and two together."

I thought back to the night just before Nana died, how she'd urgently whispered, "Your mother," before drifting off to sleep. And then, when Nana was speaking through the Ouija die, she'd said, "Mother." She was trying to tell me my mother was alive.

When this was all over, I was going to contact Nana through the Ouija die, and we would discuss her cryptic and unhelpful postmortem transmissions.

"Why would you come to the house but not see me? Did you consider for one second that I might like to know that you were still alive?"

Wait, this was my mother I was talking to. Normal maternal, or even human, standards didn't apply.

She smirked at me. "I dropped by to look through the papers she kept buried under that mattress. I found the address for the Wainwright house. And I was able to make a deal with the Kerrigans. I bring them all four Elements, I get paid. Handsomely. I am finally going to get my due, after putting up with so much bullshit over the years. Wainwright didn't give me anything in life, not even his name. Now he owes me the Elements."

"They weren't his to give!"

"Why shouldn't I have them?" Mom demanded. "Why shouldn't I decide what to do with them? They're mine, by blood and by right. I'm my mother's only child. I'm the heir, the rightful matriarch of our family."

"You were never Nana's heir. And you couldn't get the family to follow you out of a burning building. "

"And whose fault is that?" She sneered. "Always the favorite, always kissing up to my mother. You think I didn't know what you were up to? You wanted everything for yourself; you wanted to shut me out, starting with your father. I got tired of being second best, second fiddle, so I got out, but oh, it was like I was some sort of demon for leaving you. My own mother never forgave me for it, did you realize?"

"Never forgave you? Why do you think she gave you money every time you asked? Never reported it to the police when you robbed her blind? She loved you!"

"But not like she loved you!"

"Because I loved her in return!" I shouted back. "You wouldn't know what that is. You've never loved anyone as much as you love yourself. Nothing was ever as important as what you wanted, what was best for you. How could you do this? Do you know what's going to happen to your family if you do this? To the village?"

"You think I owe loyalty to that bunch of lunatics?" she asked. "They're no more my family than your father was."

"Well, who the hell *is* your family?" I demanded. "I would really like to know. Dad wasn't enough. I wasn't enough. Nana, the aunts and uncles. Is there anybody in this world you care more about than you?"

"Not really," she said, placidly examining her manicure. She stopped suddenly, giving me a satisfied smirk. "Do you want to know what I find funny in all of this? It was your boyfriend Stephen who was so helpful. I told him all about you, you see. I arranged for the two of you to meet. I even provided him with a little liquid love po-tion to slip into your tea when you didn't respond the way a normal woman would."

I stared at her for a long moment. Love potion. That explained the ambiguous distaste I'd felt for "ideal boy-friend Stephen" since I moved to the States. He wasn't around to refresh the potion or maintain the thrall. It explained why I couldn't seem to remember all of the things we had in common or the reasons he was so bloody perfect. I wasn't a bad girlfriend. I just had a feck-ing terrible mother.

Who was still monologuing, it seemed. "He's been here all this time, didn't you realize? He followed you just a few days after you arrived. We've been inside your house, rifled through your sad clothes and your sensible shoes. The only time he's been in Ireland in the last few weeks was to pump your idiot cousin for information. Thanks to some herbal additions I put in a box of chocolates, your darling Penny spilled every secret she's ever held in that empty head of hers. And I helped him ensure that she would never remember talking about you."

I deeply regretted not whacking Stephen harder with that geode. Suddenly, my spontaneous nude snuggling with Jed didn't seem so bad by comparison.

"Stephen was a tool," she said. "A useful tool but a tool all the same."

"I won't argue with you there," I muttered.

"You don't think I know you, but I do. You want *nor-*

mal. You want to pretend you're just like everyone else. It's a criminal waste of talent. You didn't think twice about meeting some nice little broker at a business meeting. You wanted that so badly you didn't even question it. I would pity you if it wasn't so damn pathetic."

"I'm pathetic?" I started laughing. "Well, at least I'm smart enough to recognize that you're about to be screwed. The Kerrigans didn't trust you enough to leave the job to you. They hired someone else to look for the Elements. Your dear friends the Kerrigans are trying to cut you out."

Her hand was just as lightning quick as I remembered it, striking me across the cheek with a flick of her wrist. "Don't be smart."

"I'm smart enough to know that the Kerrigans don't think of you as anything but a slaggy pawn. If you think you're going to waltz away from this as lady of the manor, you're even more deluded than I thought."

In the distance, we heard a sharp *crack*, as if someone had just stepped on a limb. My mother began fussing with her hair and straightening her clothes. And then reached into her bra cups and pulled her breasts into proper alignment. Classy.

"Mom. You need to understand that if you continue with this, if you make this choice, you will be dead to me," I warned her. "Truly dead. There's no coming back from this. I'm not a little old woman you can twist and manipulate. I know exactly what you are. This is your last chance."

"Do shut up and let the grown-ups talk, sweetie," she cooed, pinching my cheek with a bit more force than necessary.

"You better have the goods this time, Anna," a voice growled from the trees. Three shapes emerged from the treeline, materializing in front of my mother. A tall, gaunt man in dark posh clothes, with a teenage boy and a woman at his side. There was a lean and hungry look about them, as if they hadn't had a proper meal in the last few years. They were well heeled and sleek but looked tired and unsatisfied. I supposed living without magic when you were genetically conditioned for it would make you feel that way.

I recognized John Kerrigan, the head of the family, which would make the other two his wife, Melinda, and his son, Cameron. McGavock children whispered about the Kerrigans as if they were bogeymen, the baby-eating ogres who made us check under our beds. But up close, they didn't seem so threatening. They were just like me, with an essential part of them bound up and unhappy about it.

"No more tricks," John grumbled. "No more false hope."

"Oh, trust me, John," my mother purred. "I'm about to make you very happy."

"So this is the famous Nola," Melinda said, sniffing and running her dark, empty eyes over me. "I don't see what's so impressive."

"I'm tied to a tree," I pointed out. "You try looking your best when you're tied to a tree."

"You have them here?" John asked, ignoring me.

My mother smirked and unveiled the Elements with a flourish. It was like the prize showcase on a witchcraft game show. John stepped forward, his hand hovering over the case reverently. My mother cleared her throat. "If you'll recall, we set a price of two hundred fifty thousand dollars."

"A fair price, to be sure," John Kerrigan said, while his wife's mouth twisted into an unhappy line.

"Well, that was before my expenses and the unfortunate emotional trauma of having to strike and truss up my own offspring. So the price has doubled."

"Doubled?" Melinda spat.

"We'll pay it," John said absentmindedly as he pored over the detailing on the bell. My mother made sure to stand in John's immediate line of sight. Melinda Kerrigan hissed indignantly while my mother preened. The reality of what I was witnessing hit me full-force. I'd lost the Elements. Centuries of heritage and tradition were at that moment slipping right through my fingers. Because I sucked at scavenger hunts. My family had only a few minutes more as viable witches. I would lose my magic. Permanently this time. That strange, occasionally annoying energy that I'd taken for granted for so many years would be gone. I would be able to adjust, but what about the others? Penny, Seamus, the cousins who hadn't come into their talents yet—they would lose everything. Silent tears began to slip down my cheeks, soaking my collar.

"Why did you bring me here, Mom?" I asked as John Kerrigan closely examined the candle. His son looked mildly bored, and when I questioned the necessity of my being present, he shot a commiserating look my way. "You could have just left me at the shop."

"I didn't want you to miss this," she said, sneering. "And neither did the Kerrigans. They wanted to do the binding right away. They need you here for that. You are, after all, the McGavocks' representative."

"You realize that they'll bind you, too," I told her.

"When you have money, you don't need magic," she said.

"You never knew how to use it in the first place," I muttered, before getting another taste of my mother's backhand. Frankly, I was lucky she hadn't used the hand that was holding the athame. My lip split under the blow, and the hot, coppery taste of my own blood filled my mouth. The tears stopped. And misery made way for the cleaner burn of anger.

How *dare* my mother do this? How dare she put me through this, have me thinking she was dead for so many years because she was too selfish and too lazy to be a decent human being? She'd terrorized me, belittled me, stolen from me, for most of my life. Why was I letting her get away with it again? Why was I just sitting there like a lump?

From the eastern edge of the clearing, something was tickling my brain. I shook my head, wondering if I was imagining it. The nudging turned into all-out poking. Impatient and persistent. Jane. My friends—the supernatural cavalry—were here.

I opened my mind fully, letting Jane see everything

that I was seeing—the number of people, their placement, a special admonition not to hurt the boy, and my suspicion that there could be more Kerrigans hiding in the woods. I would apologize for the headache this gave Jane later. The nudging retreated, and I looked up at my mother, looking so smug and sure of herself while she sold out her family.

I felt Jane's mental nudging again, closer this time. The head poking was more urgent now. What would she want? Would she want me to shut up? To stop provoking my mother? Unlikely. If anything, she would probably want me to cause distraction. She and the others would want the Kerrigans and my mother distracted so they could sneak up on them.

Magic had to work for me this time. Forget the binding. Forget inconsistency and random explosions. I was more powerful than Penny's binding. I was no longer ambivalent about my own talents. It simply *had* to work. There was no other option.

I focused on the energy around me, the light and heat coming off the campfire. I drew that into my mind, focusing on the nerves and muscles of my hands. I pictured a spark growing between them, the heat traveling along my fingertips and feeding that spark until I could feel the flame glowing pleasantly against my skin.

"Mom!" I called out while she flirted shamelessly with John in front of his wife and child. I called louder. "Mom!"

She turned her attention to me, exasperated. "What?"

"There's something I've wanted to say to you for a long time," I told her.

She simpered, as if this was some warm Hallmark moment between mother and daughter. "And what's that, darling?"

"You were never a proper mother. Despite having the best example in the world, you never managed to learn about loving someone or caring for someone more than you cared for yourself. You're selfish, cruel, and unable to see anything past your own wants and needs. You were never a mother to me. And you were never the daughter Nana Fee deserved. You want to know why you were never Nana's heir? It's because you're weak. Your soul is weak, your spine is weak, and your magic is weak. You feel so little emotion, so little real energy for anything except for what you think you're missing out on, that you're barely human enough to qualify as a witch. I think that's why the magic seems to have passed you by. It's a living, breathing thing, Mom, and you can't be trusted to care for a goldfish."

"Shut up, you little bitch!" she hissed, her grip tightening around the blade in her hand.

"You forgot about me." I chuckled, squirming against the tree in an attempt to stand, to no avail. "All those years when I thought you were out there trying to fix your problems so you could come home to us. You'd just conveniently forget about the fact that I existed, until you needed money, of course, or something from Nana Fee. You forgot that I needed you, that I loved you, that I would have forgiven you anything if you'd only asked."

"Cue the violins," Melinda Kerrigan huffed. "We're on a schedule here, John."

"Really, madam, we don't have time for this," John insisted, although I wasn't sure if he was talking to me or my mother.

"What have I ever done to need your forgiveness?" my mother demanded, ignoring them. The athame glinted in her hand as she gestured wildly, the blade coming closer and closer to my face. "You ruined my life, not the other way around. Always needy. Always noisy. And when I needed you, when I came to see you, all you did was scream and turn to Daddy."

At the mention of my father, my anger spiked, from a minor blaze to volcanic in the space of a second. Instead of trying to fight it off, I embraced it. I could feel the last of Penny's restraints fall away and the spark of proper energy flowing through my body. I took a deep breath, feeding that spark, picturing it growing into a flame, larger and hotter, until it caught the ropes binding my wrists. It wasn't burning me; it was as harmless and welcome as sunlight. I was in control. I was a McGavock. This was who I was. And no one was going to take this from me. Not even another McGavock.

I leaned away from the tree as the rope smoldered and smoked. "Never mind the fact that you tried to snatch me out of Dad's hands and kidnap me. Another thing you've conveniently allowed yourself to forget," I scoffed as the ropes' hold on my wrist weakened.

Just beyond the ring of trees, I could hear movement. Fallen leaves crackling and branches moving as something large made its way through the trees. John's and Melinda's heads turned toward the noise, while my mother's overbright eyes stayed focused on me.

"What's that?" John demanded.

"Probably just a deer," my mother assured him without even looking up. "They're thick as rats around here."

But the crackling sounds grew louder, closer. I could hear distinct footsteps now, lumbering, heavy footfalls that had John standing in front of his wife and child in a protective stance. And still, my mother was entirely focused on sneering down at me, the point of her blade hovering carelessly close to my eyes. I had no doubt she would use it, if just to intimidate me into shutting up. She was too far gone. And I was embarrassing her, which was something Anna McGavock could never abide.

Still, I continued. "I guess that's how you survive, right?"

I could hear beastly, laboring grunts as the branches just beyond our circle bucked and swayed. My mother's attention wavered as she glanced toward the trees.

"You forgot about me. You forgot about my dad."

An enormous hairy shape emerged, with long furry arms and a twisted, apelike face. I couldn't help but grin at Jed's choice of creature projection. He'd made himself a Yeti for me. My mother gasped and stumbled back from the approaching Sasquatch, closer to me. The athame fell from her hand.

"Mom, there's one more thing you've forgotten."

Her head whipped toward me, a menacing snarl half-formed on her lips.

I yanked hard and freed my wrists. I grinned at her and wiggled my free hands. "I'm a witch."

I sprang to my feet, tossing the burning remnants of rope at the Kerrigans, who instinctively ducked away into Jed's path. I pressed my palm against my mother's chest, and a strange, enormous energy surged through my arm and sent her flying back against a tree. I stared down at my hand, stunned.

John moved toward us, but Jed picked him up by the shoulders and tossed him into the trees like a rag doll.

Melinda Kerrigan shrieked and lunged for me. I cranked my fist back and swung for her face, just as Dick had instructed. My knuckles connected with her jaw. She yelped, flailing back toward the fire.

I heard a loud whooping at the edge of the clearing, and dark shapes emerged from the trees. Suddenly, the clearing was filled with vampires. Jane and Gabriel, Andrea and Dick, even Jamie. But there were others, more dark-clad Kerrigans, waiting to get their licks in on a McGavock. Jane was engaged in a hair-pulling contest with Melinda. Andrea and Gabriel were chasing the nameless Kerrigan men into the trees. Jamie and Cameron were slugging it out. Jed had shifted into what looked like a Minotaur and was charging a Kerrigan henchman alongside Dick. And from nowhere, a weight crashed against my ribs, throwing me to the ground.

"You little bitch!" my mother howled, her face white and skeletal, hovering over mine as she clawed at me.

"You think you can use magic against *me*? I made you! You're nothing without me. You're *nothing*!"

I yanked my hand loose and swung at her chin. She shouted, covering her face with her hands. I swung again, letting the heel of my hand collide with her sternum. I took both hands and popped them against her ears. She howled, falling to her side. I shoved her off of me, jumping to my feet and kicking her in the ribs.

With my mother on her knees, wheezing, the woods seemed incredibly quiet. I turned to see that the Kerrigans were subdued, their hands secured behind their backs with zip ties that Andrea had pulled from her purse. Suddenly, Jed appeared at the edge of the clearing, tossing two more strange men into the firelit circle.

My mother used this moment of distraction to punch me in the face. I stumbled back and punched her in the stomach.

"Keep your guard up!" Dick yelled.

"Let her do it on her own," Gabriel admonished. "She's never going to learn if you're hovering all the time."

My mother and I grappled, wrestling back and forth, her hands wrapped around my wrists. My muscles were starting to burn from the extended use of magic and the effort of fighting her. She had to be getting tired. I shoved her against the large oak, Uncle Jack's cabinet bumping against my shins. I felt sparks at her fingertips. She was actually trying to use magic against me. She barely had enough power to sting me. Even with her study of dark spells, she was weak. She was a weak woman, a weaker witch, and a shameful mother. I'd spent years being afraid of this woman, and she couldn't even sting me.

Ouch. She had a hell of a right hook, though.

Rather than stumbling, I threw my momentum forward, knocking her to the ground. Gasping for air, wiping at the blood dripping from her mouth, she glared up at me. "You think I'm afraid of you? Little Miss Perfect? The Half-Assed Witch?"

"You should be. I'm done letting you walk all over me. I'm done with your games. I'm done with forgiving you and giving in to you because you're the only mother I've got. Give me that cabinet, and get the hell out of my face." I nodded toward Jane, giving her a mental picture of what was about to happen. I placed my hands on my mother's shoulders and used every bit of the authority I had to say, "I bind you, Anna. I bind you in the name of your mother, in the name of our ancestors. I bind you from doing harm, from doing magic. You spent every day of your life abusing the magic in your blood. You will live the rest of your life without it."

I felt it leave her body before I spoke the last syllable. The spark of my mother's energy fizzled out like a doused candle. She was dead space, cold and empty—which wasn't much of a change, really.

My mother stared at her hands as if she were suddenly missing a few fingertips. She flicked them as if trying to spark a lighter. Nothing.

"No," she spat. "No!"

Jane gasped, but before she could move, my mother had grabbed the athame from the ground. She lurched to her feet, swinging the blade directly at my stomach. A force from my left knocked me out of the way like a wrecking ball, throwing me into the ground so hard that I left a trench in the dirt. I removed my face from the forest floor, looking up to see a giant armadillo creature standing over me, a black enamel handle sticking out of its chest.

"NO!" I howled.

She'd stabbed Jed in the heart. His life was over. I couldn't even feel his pain. Jed was going to die, and it was my fault. We would never have the chance to figure out the weird relationship between the two of us. I would lose the only man who had ever loved the real me. I would lose Jed.

As Jed stumbled back, I pushed to my feet, roaring, and head-butted my mother in the face, soccer-hooligan-style. My forehead collided with the bridge of her nose with a sickening crunch. She shrieked, her head slamming back against the trunk. She dropped like a stone at my feet, unconscious. And if the throbbing pain in my face was any indication, her nose was broken in several places.

Despite my mother's unconscious state, Andrea swooped in to zip-tie her hands together. Dick was helping Armadillo Jed sit up, attempting to draw the blade out.

"No, wait, if it's lodged in his heart, we'll want to leave it until he can get to surgery." I dropped to my knees in front of Jed, feeling his pulse at his wrist, his fast but incredibly steady pulse. I pressed my ear to the leathery gray flesh of his chest; his breathing was quick but untroubled. I peeled the shirt away from his chest and frowned. There wasn't nearly enough blood flowing for a chest wound. "What the?"

Jed's armadillo features squinched up as he concentrated on his form. The gray body armor faded away, and he slowly transformed back into human. And fortunately, what appeared to be the chest of an armadillo creature was only the shoulder of a shirtless man. The wound would hurt like hell, but he would live.

"You idiot!" I yelled, smacking his good arm. "You wonderful, stupid idiot!"

"Ow!" he yelped, protecting his injured shoulder. "I'm a wounded man, here!"

He cried out again as, together, Dick and I drew the knife from his shoulder. I placed my hands over the wound and concentrated hard. I visualized the tissue knitting itself back together into healthy muscle and skin. I could feel the warmth of the healing energy emanating from my palm. Dick grinned widely as Jed's shoulder repaired itself.

"Impressive," John Kerrigan murmured, before a stern Melinda elbowed him.

"You don't get the actual form, remember? Just the appearance of it," I said. "You do not, in fact, have natural body armor."

"I forgot about that part. I just thought of the biggest, toughest shield possible, and there I was."

"Aw, you picked a form, and you got it!" I said, smiling. "I'm so proud."

"Yeah, well, I had to contribute somehow," he grumbled, flexing his arm.

"I'm sorry my family is nuts," I whispered. "My aunts and uncles are actually really nice people."

"They're not so bad. Wait until you meet my family. At Thanksgiving, we kill everything we can find, put it into a pot, and call it 'holiday gumbo.'" He grinned down at me and kissed my forehead.

A bored but sullen voice called, "Pardon me, as fascinating as I find your vulgar backwoods canoodling, I would like to be untied."

We broke apart, turning to see an irritated John Kerrigan staring us down. In fact, all of the Kerrigans were both irritated and staring us down. I had several Kerrigans under my control. What the hell was I going to do with them? I could hold them hostage for enough money to put a new roof on the clinic and restock our dispensary until doomsday. I could bind them for another hundred years and continue the family tradition. Or . . .

I squeezed Jed's hand and knelt down in front of John and his wife.

"I give up," I told him.

John clearly expected something else, because he frowned at me as if he'd heard wrong and said, "Beg pardon?"

"Aren't you tired of this?" I asked. "This started as a policy debate who knows how long ago, and it's still biting us on the collective arse. I think we can all agree that the 'do no harm' debate is settled. It's a bad thing to remove parts of people using the power of your mind. If nothing else, it leaves behind a big mess to explain to the authorities. Let's just split the objects. Two for you, two for us. That way, there's a balance."

"Do you think that's fair?" Melinda demanded. "We've lived without our birthright for centuries, and you want us to just forget what you McGavocks did to us?"

"No," I told her. "*You've* lived without your magic for *forty* years. And I am very sorry that happened to you as a result of our families' troubles. But it didn't start with us. We can't let the decisions of people who lived centuries ago continue to control us. In a hundred years, your son's great-grandchildren would be the ones in charge of protecting the objects. Is this what you want for them? Years of worrying about magical war and protecting your family from mine? Or would you rather they live out their years exploring the gifts that your family is blessed with?"

Melinda cast a sidelong look at her son, her lip trembling. "She makes a point," she murmured to her husband.

"Our ancestors agreed years ago to the binding," I said. "Now we can agree to abandon it. It doesn't work anymore. Forcing you to give up your magic was wrong. And I am sorry."

John and Melinda whispered in hushed tones, their exchange growing heated, until John seemed to relent. Finally, Melinda gave him a curt nod, and they both turned to me.

"We would have to discuss this at length," John said sternly.

A relieved smile broke out over my face. "Agreed."

John eyed Jed carefully. "You seem fairly accepting of the fact that we lied to you."

"Well, there's no cure for what I am," Jed said. "It's not a disease or a curse. I can't change it. That doesn't mean you're not an asshole."

"I am sorry," John told him, sounding very nearly sincere. "But in our defense, you did betray us and help our rivals locate the items first."

"What are you going to do about your mother?" Melinda asked me. "A number of us have matters to discuss with her."

I looked down at my mother. I had no idea what the Kerrigans had planned for her. I did know that whatever it was, she probably deserved it. Anna hurt, stole, or defiled almost everything she touched. She'd all but admitted to murdering some unfortunate because she needed a body to throw her "associates" off her scent. I was finished with her.

"I don't know who that woman is," I told them blithely. "She's not bound to me or mine through magic or blood."

Melinda's eyes widened at my wording as she recognized its significance. I understood her surprise. Binding was one thing, but she'd probably never heard someone magically disown her own mother before, abjuring her from family and coven. From that moment on, Anna really would be dead to us, even if she showed up on our doorsteps. We wouldn't see her or hear her or even smell her. It was one of the coldest, cruelest things a witch could do to her own kin. And I'd done it to my own mother.

In terms of negotiating tactics, it was a heck of a way to establish one's position.

"That's settled, then. We'll take her home with us. You'll not hear from her again. And I'd like the use of my hands, if you please," John added, a little prim. "This is demoralizing."

I nodded to Dick, who snapped the plastic tie on John's hands.

"And Melinda's?" John asked, rubbing his purpling wrists.

"No, just you," I insisted. "I said I was open to negotiations, not that I was stupid."

Melinda's face was thunderous, but John conceded. "It's a wise decision."

Several hours later, after outlining a basic but fairly historic interclan treaty, the Kerrigans were left somewhat mollified with my offer of Flame and Air, while I kept Sea and Earth. Of course, they also had to take my mother with them, so they may have considered the whole experience a wash. We agreed to hold a full meeting at home to iron out the details. But for now, we'd split the elements, and by dawn the next morning, the Kerrigans' magic would be restored. That would be the true test of whether they took this peace seriously or not.

I figured I should probably leave town as soon as possible.

Jed stroked his hand down the length of my hair and gave me a blithe grin. "So how was your day?"

"Typical." I sighed. "My dead mother conked me

over the head with an Egyptian idol. I made fire with my mind, confronted some upsetting lingering parental issues. And I negotiated a peace treaty in a centuries-old witch war."

"Somebody's getting milk and cookies when we get home," Andrea said sweetly, patting my head.

I smiled nastily. "Thanks, Granny."

The patting turned into a light slap.

"So how did you know how to find me?" I asked.

"Well, earlier tonight, we did find your ex-boyfriend locked in my office, next to some damaged equipment and a smashed, extremely rare geode," Dick said, lifting his eyebrow. "All we had to do was shake him a couple of times, and he sang like the proverbial canary. He gave up your mom, the meeting location, everything."

"Prick," I muttered.

"Oh, don't worry, Gabriel messed with his memory," Jane chirped. "Stephen won't remember anything from your time together, other than that you were the best thing that ever happened to him, but he let you get away through his own sheer stupidity."

"Aw, Gabriel, I didn't know you cared," I said, nudging his elbow.

If vampires could blush, Gabriel's face would have been rosy pink. He cleared his throat. "From now on, every time Stephen hears the word 'tea,' he will soil himself."

I marveled. "I'm glad you're on my side."

Gabriel mussed my hair while Jed jostled my shoulder. "Always."

18

Just remember, there is no adventure without risk, no magic without payment, and no such thing as a boring journey with the right partner.
—*A Witch's Handbook of Kisses and Curses*

Packing away my Half-Moon Hollow life into little boxes was more difficult than I ever imagined. I couldn't pack up Jane or Dick or Andrea. I couldn't pack up the clinic or the shop. I couldn't pack up what was left of my furniture, books, and clothes . . . well, I could, but they took up a lot of space, and the shipping prices would kill me.

"Are you sure about this, honey?" Dick asked as he helped me tape over the last of my luggage. Gramps was not adjusting well to the looming separation. "You could stay. I talked to your uncle Seamus earlier. He said everything's running as smooth as silk over there. They can survive a few more months without you."

"My uncle Seamus would never use the expression 'smooth as silk,' and it's more likely that he told you to tell me to get my bony arse back where I belong."

"He did say that," Dick admitted. "And then I told him to watch his mouth in front of his elders."

I snorted. It was an interesting time for the McGavocks. Distant vampire relatives, my mother coming back
from the dead, unexpected declarations of peace. My
family had not been pleased when I explained the new
treaty with the Kerrigans. I believe Uncle Seamus's exact
words were, "Have you lost your feckin' mind, girl?" It
would take time for them to adjust to the idea that we
no longer had mortal enemies. But so far, the Kerrigans
had held true to their word. They had their powers back,
and they hadn't attempted to harm anyone in Kilcairy.
Most of their efforts seemed to involve nurturing rose
specimens into prize-winning blooms for village fêtes. I
took this as a good sign.

I hadn't heard back from Jed. After our ordeal in the
woods, we were so happy to escape unscathed that we
hadn't made any plans or promises—and that hurt more
than it should. He healed overnight and by the next
morning was halfway to Tennessee. He needed to talk to
his family about why he'd basically run away for months
and about my theories regarding their shifting. I'd been
putting off leaving for days, hoping that he might come
back so we could talk. But I had to get back home.

I would have a bit of a mess on my hands when I returned to Kilcairy. The McGavocks were going to have
to learn new ways to live, to get over old prejudices. And
I was going to have to stop messing about and actually
study the Craft in earnest. I would need the help of my
family to do so. And I was going to be taking some serious guff from each and every one of them for changing
my tune. There would be groveling. A lot of groveling.

"I need to get back to the McGavocks," I told Dick. "There are things that need to be said, explained."

"I only just found you." Dick groaned, wrapping his arms around my shoulders. "And I just convinced you that I'm not a creepy stalker."

"You're not losing me," I promised. "I'm just going where I'm needed right now. I'll be back to visit. You can't get rid of me that easily. And the plane routes work both ways, you know. You'll see me before you know it. You could come to visit over Christmas."

"We're going to have to do that," he agreed. "Andrea and I never did take a proper honeymoon. We just need to make sure we fly separately from Jane and Gabriel, though. They travel like something out of a *Mad Max* movie."

Dick did another one of his loving face squishings. "You're the last and best of our line, you know that? Gilbert was something, but you? You're more than I ever could have hoped for. I love you, very much. And I don't take the words lightly."

"I know. I love you, too." I hugged him. "Grampy."

"Not budging on the nickname, huh?" he asked without moving away.

I shook my head. "Nope."

I would miss them all so much, my little vampire family. I had not had any more dream vacations with my grandfather, but I expected any night to wake up in Machu Picchu or on top of the Tower of London. And I was looking forward to it.

But life would be very different for me when I got

home. In Half-Moon Hollow, I'd gotten used to being myself instead of what was expected, to saying what I felt rather than what was best for the feelings of all involved. I wasn't eager to take on the mantle of leadership when it had been so lovely just to be a link in a chain of trust and love. I would miss Jane's sarcastic intelligence and Andrea's unexpected and inappropriate humor. I would miss Zeb and Jolene's sunny enthusiasm and Gabriel's bemusement with us all. I would miss my ancestor, Dick Cheney, and the unquestionable, unshaking love he'd given me, even when I didn't want it.

I was also sorry to leave Dr. Hackett. But I'd found him an eager volunteer in Jane's father, who was more than willing to spend a few hours out of the house every day. Mr. Jameson didn't have my hand at healing, but he was organized and knew how to help people without making them feel beholden. And that was a skill set all its own. He would be taking over my shifts starting next week.

The real problem was Jed "I Am Incapable of Returning My Voice-Mail Messages" Trudeau. I didn't want to leave him. We'd only just figured each other out, or the closest we would ever get to it. I'd been well on the way to genuine feelings for the man even before he saved my life and my family and my magic by throwing himself on a sword. Well, a knife, but it still bloody counted.

I loved Jed. I didn't like that he'd deceived me, but I'd come to understand it. I'd done worse—to my own mother—in defense of my family. After a few days apart, I forgot about the lies and the hurt, only remem-

"Are they OK?" I asked.

"Well, the news that they could shift into anything they want, anytime they want, has led to some . . . security issues. All of my uncles are turning themselves into werewolves and giant turtles and frost giants. In broad daylight. Sometimes in the Little Debbie aisle at the Piggly Wiggly. They're like little kids. My dad is spending a lot of time trying to keep them in line so they don't blow our cover. Normally, that's the sort of thing I would help him with, but I told him I had urgent business to get to up here. He said I've earned a little time off."

I arched an eyebrow, a smile playing on my lips. "And what do you plan on doing with that time?"

"Well, I was thinking, and I'm just throwing this out there, that you've learned pretty much all you can, and should, about our culture. But I know absolutely nothing about Ireland other than Lucky Charms and Saint Patrick's Day. And I don't think that thing about leprechauns is for real."

"You want to come to Ireland?"

"The Kerrigans helped fast-track my passport application process by way of a goodwill gesture," he said. "Don't worry. They used bribery, not magic."

I gasped, bouncing a little in his hold. "You'll love it there. If we try hard enough, we might find someone who knows about shifters. And you could meet my family, which isn't so much a selling point as a disclaimer."

They would love him, I was sure, because he loved

me. And he wasn't Stephen, which would be enough for Penny.

"It would be nice if we had a more normal 'meeting' story to tell them, though. I mean, even when we did meet without all of the paranormal claptrap, there was a possum involved, so that can't be typical. I'm going to catch hell from my aunts for the possum bit; they'll laugh for months."

"You want something normal?"

"I would love a little normal," I confessed.

He grinned, set me on my feet, and kissed the tip of my nose. "I'll be right back."

A few minutes later, he came to the door in a pressed plaid work shirt. He bobbled a foil-wrapped pan and a much bigger spray of hydrangeas while he knocked on the screen.

"Jed, what are you doing?"

"You don't know me," he insisted. "We've never met before. I'm your new neighbor, and I'm comin' by to introduce myself."

"Oh," I said, a naughty grin spreading across my lips. "Hello, handsome stranger."

"This isn't a porn."

I frowned. "Hello, annoying person I may not want to meet after all."

"Hello, new neighbor. I'm Jed Trudeau. I live next door, and I wanted to welcome you to the neighborhood with lasagna and flowers."

"That's very sweet of you, Mr. Trudeau. I'm Nola

Leary. I just moved here to the Hollow with absolutely no agenda whatsoever."

"Really, well, I happen to have no agenda myself. But I do have some issues with body image."

"Meaning your body's image changes at a moment's notice?"

"Yep," he said brightly. "So do you have anythin' planned for this afternoon?"

"Oh, the usual, a little cleaning, maybe some laundry, stripping my new neighbor down to nothing and demonstrating various positions I found in some of Jane's more obscure antique marital guides."

His eyes popped in surprise, but he quickly schooled his features back into blithe indifference. "Sounds very normal."

I nodded. "A new guy just moved in two houses down. Good-looking, really flexible. I think he's into yoga."

His face fell into a dark expression. "That's not funny."

"It's a little funny."

"Well, you're going to have to cancel on the yoga guy, because you're going to be busy. We have just enough time for that naked demonstration thing before I have to pack."

"Pack?"

"I just got an invitation to Ireland."

"So you're coming with me?" I squeaked, throwing my arms around his neck.

He nodded. "Someone has to keep an eye on me while I figure out how to control my skin. Havin' my own personal nurse seems like a good idea. You know, for watchin' my vital signs . . . and sponge baths." I bit his ear again, making him hiss. "I'm going to pay for the sponge-bath thing later in some small way, huh?"

"Not in a small way, no." I shook my head before kissing him deeply. "Let's get you packed."

Turn the page

for a sneak peek

of the next hilarious romp by

MOLLY HARPER

How to Run with a Naked Werewolf

Coming soon from Pocket Books!

All The Pretty Pintos

If Gordie Fugate didn't hurry the hell up and pick out a cereal, I was going to bludgeon him with a canned ham.

I didn't mind working at Emerson's Dry Goods, but I was wrapping a sixteen-hour shift. My back ached. My stiff green canvas apron was chafing my neck. And one of the Glisson twins had dropped a gallon-sized jar of mayo on my big toe earlier. I hadn't been this exhausted since doing an emergency rotation during my medical residency. The only nice thing I could say about working at Emerson's was that the owner hadn't asked for photo identification when I applied, eliminating an awful lot of worry for my undocumented self. Also, in comparison to the hospital, I dealt with less blood.

Unless, of course, I did bludgeon Gordie with the ham. That would result in a serious amount of cleanup in aisle five.

I only had a few more weeks of checkout duty before

I would be moving on, winding my way toward Anchorage. It was just easier that way. Now that I was living in what I called "gray time," I knew there was a maximum amount of time people could spend around you before they resented unanswered personal questions. Of course, I'd also learned a few other things, like how to recognize a guy who planned on following me to my car, or how to lift the odd wallet for quick cash. And now, I was trying to learn the secret Zen art of not bashing an indecisive cornflake lover over the head with preserved pork products.

I turned to glance back at Gordie, who was now considering his oatmeal options.

I swore loudly enough to attract the attention of my peroxide-blond fellow retail service engineer Belinda. Middle-aged, pear-shaped, and possessing a smoker's voice that put that *Exorcist* kid to shame, Belinda was the assistant manager at Emerson's, the closest thing to a retail mecca in McClusky, a tiny ditchwater town on the easternmost border of Alaska. Because I was still a probationary employee, I wasn't allowed to close up on my own. But Belinda was friendly and seemed eager to make me a "lifer" like herself at Emerson's. I suspected she wasn't allowed to retire until she found a replacement.

"I've known Gordie for almost forty years. He can make a simple decision feel like the end of *Sophie's Choice*. Painful and drawn-out," she said, putting a companionable arm around me as I slumped back against my counter. It was an accomplishment that I was able to give her a little squeeze in return. It had taken me months not to flinch when someone new got inside my personal-space bubble, not to shut down and pull away. This was a particularly useful skill, considering I'd spent the last three years in the company of some very "demonstrative" people. Shrieking and shoving at someone when they patted you on the back tended to draw attention.

"You're thinking about throwing one of those canned hams at him, aren't you?"

I sighed. "I guess I've made that threat before, huh?"

Belinda snickered at my irritated tone. I glared at her. She assured me, "I'm laughing for you, Anna, not at you."

I offered her a weak, but genuine, smile. "Feels the same either way."

"Why don't you go on home, hon?" Belinda suggested. "I know you worked a double when that twit Haley called in sick. For the third time this week, I might add. I'll close up. You go get some food in you. You're looking all pale and sickly again."

I sighed, smiling at her. When I'd first arrived at Emerson's, Belinda had taken one look at my waxy cheeks and insisted on sending me home with a "signing bonus" box of high-calorie, high-protein foods. I was sucking down protein shakes and Velveeta for a week. Every time I put a pound on my short, thin frame, she considered it a personal victory. I didn't have the heart to tell her that my pallor wasn't from malnutrition, but from stress and sleep deprivation. I gave her another squeeze. "I haven't been sleeping well, that's all. Thanks. I owe you."

"Yeah, you do," she said as I whipped my green Emerson's apron over my head. While making my way to the employee locker room, I heard her yell, "Damn it, Gordie, it's just Cream of Wheat. It's not like you're pulling somebody's plug!"

Chuckling, I slipped out the back to the employee exit, shrugging into my coat, and waited for the slap of frigid September air to steal my breath. I snuggled deeper into my thick winter jacket, grateful for its insulating warmth. Years before, when I'd first arrived in Alaska, I'd only brought the barest essentials. I spent most of my cross-state drive shivering so hard I could barely steer. Eager to help me acclimate, my new neighbors had taken great pains to help me select the most sensible jacket, the most reasonably priced all-weather boots. I missed those neighbors with a bone-deep ache that I couldn't blame on the cold. I missed the people who had become my family. I missed the valley I'd made home. The thought of trying to make that place for myself all over again tipped my exhaustion into full-on despair.

Fumbling with the keys to my powder-blue-and-rust-colored Pinto, I heard someone say, "Just tell Jake I'll get him the money in a week."

Another gruffer, calmer voice, answered, "Marty, relax. Jake didn't send me. I'm not here for you."

I closed my eyes, hoping to block out the shadowy forms in the far corner of the employee lot that Emerson's shared with the Wishy-Washy Laundromat and Flapjack's Saloon. I didn't want to see any of this. I didn't want the liability of witnessing some sort of criminal transaction. I just wanted to go home to my motel room and stand in the shower until I no longer felt the pain of sixteen hours on my mayonnaise-injured feet. I turned my back to the voices, struggling to work the sticky lock on my driver's-side door.

"Don't feed me that bullshit," a reedier, slightly whiny voice countered. "He sent you after me when I owed him ten. You don't think he's going to do it again now that I owe him seventeen?"

"I'm telling you, I'm not here for you. But if you don't put that goddamn gun away, I might change my mind."

Gun? Did Gruff Sexy Voice say "gun"?

Who the hell has a gunfight in the parking lot behind a Laundromat?

I focused on keeping my hands from shaking as I jiggled the key in the lock. Stupid 1980s tumbler technology! I gave myself another five seconds to open the door before I just ran for the grocery's employee entrance and hid inside.

That was my plan, up until the point I heard the gunshot . . . and the tires screech . . . and the roar of an engine coming way too close. I turned just in time to see the back end of a shiny black SUV barreling toward me and my car. I took three steps before throwing myself into the bed of a nearby pickup truck. Even before I peered over the lip of the bed, I knew the loud, tortured metallic squeal was the SUV pulverizing my Pinto.

"Seriously?" I cried, watching my car disintegrate in front of my very eyes.

The SUV struggled to disengage its back end from the wreckage of my now-inoperable car. As the driver gunned the engine, I followed the beams of the headlights across the lot to a man curled in the fetal position on the ground.

My eyes darted back and forth between the injured man and the growling black vehicle. This was none of my business. I didn't know this guy. I didn't know what he'd done to make Mr. SUV want to run him down like a dog. And despite the fact that every instinct told me to stay put, stay down until Gruff Sexy Voice was a little man-pancake, I launched myself out of the truck bed and ran across the lot. I dashed toward the hunched form on the ground, sliding on the gravel when I bent to help him. I tamped down my instincts to assess the damage, assuring myself that any wounds he was suffering would definitely prove fatal if he was run over by a large vehicle. "Get up!" I shouted as the SUV finally wrenched free of my erstwhile transportation and lurched toward us.

Gruff Sexy Voice struggled to his knees. I tucked my arms under his sleeves and pulled, my arms burning with the effort to lift him off the ground.

"Get your butt off the concrete, mister." I grunted, heaving him out of the path of the SUV. I felt a set of car keys dangling out of his jacket pocket. I clicked the fob button until I heard a beep and turned toward the noise.

Just as I got him on his feet, the headlights of the SUV flared. We stumbled forward, falling between the truck that had just beeped and Belinda's hatchback. The hatchback shuddered with a tortured metallic shriek as the SUV sideswiped it. I jerked the passenger door open, slid across the seat, and dragged Gruff Sexy Voice inside.

When I pulled it back, my hand was red and slick with blood. He groaned as he tried to fold his long legs into the passenger seat. I reached over him to slam the door.

"Not smart," I mumbled, slipping the key into the ignition. "This is the 'and she was never heard from again' kind of not smart."

I watched as the SUV careened off the far corner of the lot, into the grass. The ground there was soupy and particularly fragrant, thanks to a septic tank leak. The owner of Flapjack's had warned us not to park anywhere near it, or we'd end up stuck to our axles in substances best not imagined, which is what was happening to the SUV the more it spun its wheels. I glanced between my demolished car and the guy who seemed so hell-bent on killing my passenger. At this point, I didn't know which was more distressing. Mr. SUV stepped out, slipping and sliding in the muck that had sucked him in to the ankles. There was a flash of metal in his hand as he strode toward the truck. A gun. He was pointing a gun at us.

Fortunately for me and the Barely Conscious Hulk, Mr. SUV wandered a little too close to my Pinto. And my rusted-out baby, being the most temperamentally explosive of all makes and models, had not taken kindly to being squished by the big mean off-roader. My notoriously delicate gas tank was leaking fuel all over the parking lot, dangerously close to the lard bucket Flapjack's set out back to catch employees' cigarette butts. And because the saloon was staffed by likeable, though lazy, people, there were always a few smoldering butts lying around on the gravel.

WHOOOSH.

The fuel ignited, sending my car up like a badly up-holstered Roman candle. Mr. SUV was thrown to the ground as a little mushroom cloud exploded over us.

Good. Explosions drew a lot of attention. People would come running out to see what happened and Mr. SUV couldn't afford that many witnesses. Gruff Sexy Voice would get the (fully-equipped) medical attention he needed . . . and I would end up answering questions for a lot of cops.

Not good.

I hadn't realized I'd even punched the gas until I felt the gravel give way under the tires and the truck lurch toward the open road.

Gruff Sexy Voice slumped against the window as I careened out of the parking lot, onto the highway. The closest medical facility was in Bernard, about seventy miles up the road. As we neared the town limits I passed the Lucky Traveler Motel, wishing we had time to stop and pick up my clothes and medical bag. But nearly everyone in the bar knew where I lived. The SUV driver would just have to ask a few people in the crowd that gathered to roast marshmallows around my immolated car and he'd find me in about ten minutes. He could, for that matter, have been following us at that moment. Somehow, that made my spare contact lens case and stethoscope seem less significant.

"Mister?" I said, shaking his shoulder, wincing as I noticed the blood seeping through his shirt. Lower quadrant gunshot wounds to the abdomen usually meant perforated major organs and damaged blood vessels. His blood loss was minimal. I held out hope, but I knew that that wasn't necessarily a good sign. There could be some complication or an exit wound I wasn't aware of. He groaned, opening his burnt-chocolate eyes and blinking at me, as if he was trying to focus on my face but couldn't quite manage it.

"You," he said, squinting at me.

I swallowed, focusing on the situation at hand, instead of the instinctual panic those words sent skittering up my spine. "No, I'd remember you. I'm sure. Just hold on, OK? I'm going to get you to the clinic in Bernard. Do you think you could stay awake for me?"

He shook his head. "No doctors."

I supposed this would be a bad time to tell him I *was* a doctor.

"Not that bad. No doctors," he ground out, glaring at me. I scowled right back. His face split into a loopy smirk. "I know you."

His head thunked back against the seat rest, which I supposed signaled the end of our facial expression standoff.

Gruff Sexy Voice was, well, gruff and sexy. Shaggy black hair, eyes so intensely brown they were almost black, and cheekbones carved from granite. His lips were wide and generous and probably pretty tempting when they weren't curled back over his teeth in pain like that.

"Please," he moaned, batting his hand against my shoulder, weakly flexing his fingers around it.

Well, damn, I'd always been a sucker for a man who kept pretty manners intact while bleeding.

"Fine," I shot back. "Where do you want to go?"

But he'd already passed out.

"And she was never heard from again," I muttered.

A few miles later, Gruff Sexy Voice stopped bleeding, which could mean that he'd started to clot . . . or that he'd gone into shock and died. My optimism had reached its limit for the evening.

Keeping an eye on the road, I pressed my fingers over his carotid and detected a slow but steady pulse. I took a deep breath and tried to focus. I'd been through so much worse. It didn't make sense to panic now. How had I gotten myself into this? I'd worked so hard to avoid this kind of trouble. I'd kept my head down, stayed low profile. And here I was driving around in a possibly stolen truck with a possibly dead body slumped over in the passenger seat. If I'd had one operating brain cell in my head, I would have run screaming into the bar the minute I'd heard the men arguing in the parking lot. But, no, I had to help the injured stray, because living with the less-than-civic-minded side of humanity over the last few years had apparently taught me nothing.

I saw a sign ahead for Sharpton. Since he didn't want to go to the clinic, I'd turned off the main highway and stuck to the older, less traveled state routes. I tapped the brakes, afraid I would miss some vital piece of information hidden between the words "Sharpton" and "20 Miles." As the truck slowed, the Big Guy slumped forward and snorted as his head smacked against the dashboard.

Good. Dead people do not snort. That was my qualified medical opinion.

"Hey, Big Guy?" I said loudly, shaking his shoulder. "Mister?"

He snorted again, but did not wake up. I laughed, practically crying with relief. I gently shook my . . . passenger? Patient? Hostage? What was I going to do with him? He didn't want a doctor, he said. But as much as I needed a vehicle, I didn't have it in me to just leave him on the side of the road somewhere and drive off.

Just over the next rise in the road, I saw a sign for the Last Chance Motel, which seemed both ominous and appropriate. I took a deep breath through my nose and let it slowly expand my lungs. By the time I exhaled, I'd already formed my plan. At the faded pink motel sign, I turned into the lot and parked in front of the squatty dilapidated building. There were two cars in the lot, including the one in front of the office, which seemed to double as the manager's quarters.

I reached toward the passenger seat and gently shook the Big Guy's shoulder. His breathing was deep, even. As carefully as I could, I raised the hem of his bloodied shirt and gasped. The bullet wound, just under his ribs on his left side, seemed too small for such a recent injury. The edges of the wound were a healthy pink. And the bullet seemed to be lodged there in his skin.

I pulled away, scooting across the bench seat. That . . . wasn't normal.

Calm down, I ordered myself. There's no reason to panic. This was good news.

Maybe some weird act of physics kept the bullet from penetrating deeply in the first place, I reasoned. I hadn't gotten a good look at the wound while I was playing action hero in a dark parking lot of the bar. In my panic, it must have looked much worse than it was. Either way, the wound looked almost manageable now.

"Just hold on tight," I told him, placing my hand on his shoulder again. He leaned against my touch, trying to nuzzle his cheek against my fingers. "Uh, I'll be right back."

It would appear that I was footing the bill for this little slice of heaven. I couldn't reach his wallet, as it was in his pocket, firmly situated under his butt. I had just enough cash in my wallet (a twenty and a few lonely singles) to cover one night. After that, I was dead in the water. The rest of my cash had been stashed behind a dresser in my motel room near Emerson's.

I jumped out of the truck and tried to look calm and normal as I walked into the motel's dingy little office and saw its creepy-as-hell occupant. There must be an Internet ad somewhere that read, "Do you give off a sex-predator vibe? Do you have lax standards regarding personal hygiene? Well, the field of out-of-the-way motel management is the career opportunity for you!"

And this guy fit the bill perfectly. It took no less than three refusals of a "room tour" from Night Manager Larry to be permitted to trade a portion of my precious cash supply for a little plastic tag attached to the oldest freaking room key I had ever seen.

"Two beds, right?" I asked, taking the key.

He shook his head, leering at me. "Single rooms only. We like to stay cozy here in the Great North."

"What if a family of four needs a room for the night?"

"It's never come up."

"Is there a pharmacy anywhere around here?" I asked.

"In town, about four miles down the road. Opens in the morning, around eight," he said. "But if you're feeling poorly, I have something in my room that might perk you up."

I gave him my patented "dead face," turned on my heel, and made a mental note to prop a chair against the outside door once I got to the room.

I opened the passenger-side door and saw that the Big Guy had managed to sit up and had his head resting on the seat back. He was snoring steadily. I spotted a bulky duffel bag in the backseat of the cab and threw it over my shoulder. I unlocked the room door, tossed the bag inside, and steeled myself for the task of hauling his unconscious ass into the room. Careful to keep his bloodied side away from the manager's window, I hoisted his arm over my shoulder in a sort of ill-advised fireman's carry and took slow, deliberate steps toward the open door. The movement seemed to reopen the wound; I could feel blood seeping through my shirt. We made it through the door. I heard a distinct *thud*. I looked down and saw that the bullet had rolled across the filthy carpet into the wall.

I meant to set him gently on the bed, but ended up flopping him across the threadbare bedspread. The rickety bed squealed in protest as he bounced, but he didn't bat an eyelash. I huffed, leaning against the yellowed floral wallpaper to catch my breath. "Sorry. You're heavier than you look."

I locked the door and wedged the desk chair against the knob. The room was without amenities, but too dirty to be considered Spartan, too outdated to be considered retro. The carpet may have been a sort of maroon at some point, but it was now more of a knotty brownish gray. The bedspread was the same paper-thin synthetic fiber used in all cheap motels. Not thick enough to keep you warm, but just enough material to catch a wealth of germs and bodily fluids.

I shook off the flashbacks to Norman Bates's establishment in *Psycho* and told myself it was just like any of the other crappy, indigent motels I'd stayed at in any number of cities, and I hadn't been stabbed in the shower yet. There was that one time a crazy lady kicked down my door and accused me of sleeping with her husband, but it turned out she meant to break into the room across the hall.

I turned back to the sleeping giant on the bed. The flannel shirt was a total loss. The fabric made an unpleasant ripping noise as I peeled it away, the dried blood adhering the stiff flannel to his skin. The wound seemed even smaller now, the area around it a perfectly normal, healthy color. I pushed back from him, away from the bed, staring at the minuscule hole in his flesh.

This couldn't be right.

Taking a step back, I knocked over his duffel and saw

a bottle of Bactine spray sticking out of the partially opened zipper. I arched an eyebrow and pulled the bag open. "What the . . . ?"

Never mind having to run to a pharmacy. The bag was filled to the brim with well-used first-aid supplies. And beef jerky. But not much in the way of clothes.

I glanced from the shrinking bullet hole to the enormous bag of meat treats with its distinct lack of clothes . . . and back to the bullet hole.

Oh, holy hell, this guy was a werewolf.

Love with BITE...

Bestselling Paranormal Romance
from Pocket Books!

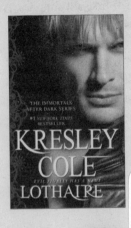

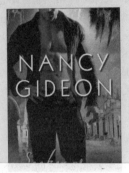